Mr. Murder

DEAN KOONTZ

Mr. Murder

G. P. Putnam's Sons
New York

This is a work of fiction. The events described are
imaginary. The setting and characters are fictitious and not
intended to represent specific places or persons.

G. P. Putnam's Sons
Publishers Since 1838
200 Madison Avenue
New York, NY 10016

Book design by H. Roberts

ISBN 0-399-13899-4

Printed in the United States of America

To Phil Parks,
for what is often within,
and to Don Brautigam,
for what is often without.
And for having all that talent
without any noticeable,
annoying neuroses.
Well, *hardly* any.

Santa Claus and His Evil Twin

Winter that year was strange and gray.
The damp wind smelled of Apocalypse,
and morning skies had a peculiar way
of slipping cat-quick into midnight.

—*The Book of Counted Sorrows*

Life is an unrelenting comedy. Therein lies the tragedy of it.

—*One Dead Bishop*, Martin Stillwater

ONE

1.

"I need . . ."

Leaning back in his comfortable leather office chair, rocking gently, holding a compact cassette recorder in his right hand and dictating a letter to his editor in New York, Martin Stillwater suddenly realized he was repeating the same two words in a dreamy whisper.

". . . I need . . . I need . . . I need . . ."

Frowning, Marty clicked off the recorder.

His train of thought had clattered down a siding and chugged to a stop. He could not recall what he had been about to say.

Needed what?

The big house was not merely quiet but eerily still. Paige had taken the kids to lunch and a Saturday matinee movie.

But this childless silence was more than just a condition. It had substance. The air felt heavy with it.

He put one hand to the nape of his neck. His palm was cool and moist. He shivered.

Outside, the autumn day was as hushed as the house, as if all of southern California had been vacated. At the only window of his second-floor study, the wide louvers of the plantation shutters were ajar. Sunlight slanted between angled slats, imprinting the sofa and carpet with narrow red-gold stripes as lustrous as fox fur; the nearest luminous ribbon wrapped one corner of the U-shaped desk.

I need . . .

Instinct told him that something important had happened only a moment ago, just out of his sight, perceived subliminally.

He swiveled his chair and surveyed the room behind him. Other than the fasciae of coppery sunshine interleaved with louver shadows, the only light came from a small desk lamp with a stained-glass shade. Even in that gloom, however, he could see he was alone with his books, research files, and computer.

Perhaps the silence seemed unnaturally deep only because the house had been filled with noise and bustle since Wednesday, when the schools had closed for the Thanksgiving holiday. He missed the kids. He should have gone to the movie with them.

I need . . .

The words had been spoken with peculiar tension—and longing.

Now an ominous feeling overcame him, a keen sense of impending danger. It was the premonitory dread which characters sometimes felt in his novels, and which he always struggled to describe without resorting to clichés.

He had not actually experienced anything like it in years, not since Charlotte had been seriously ill when she was four and the doctor had prepared them for the possibility of cancer. All day in the hospital, as his little girl had been wheeled from one lab to another for tests, all that sleepless night, and during the long days that followed before the physicians ventured a diagnosis, Marty felt haunted by a malevolent spirit whose presence thickened the air, making it difficult to breathe, to move, to hope. As it turned out, his daughter had been threatened neither by supernatural malevolence nor malignancy. The problem was a treatable blood disorder. Within three months Charlotte recovered.

But he remembered that oppressive dread too well.

He was in its icy grip again, though for no discernible reason. Charlotte and Emily were healthy, well-adjusted kids. He and Paige were happy together—absurdly happy, considering how many thirty-something couples of their acquaintance were divorced, separated, or cheating on each other. Financially, they were more secure than they had ever expected to be.

Nevertheless, Marty *knew* something was wrong.

He put down the tape recorder, went to the window, and opened the shutters all the way. A leafless sycamore cast stark, elongated shadows across the small side yard. Beyond those gnarled branches, the pale-yellow stucco walls of the house next door appeared to have soaked up the sunshine; gold and russet reflections painted the windows; the place was silent, seemingly serene.

To the right, he could see a section of the street. The houses on the other side of the block were also Mediterranean in style, stucco with clay-tile roofs, gilded by late-afternoon sun, filigreed by overhanging queen-palm fronds. Quiet, well landscaped, planned to the square inch, their neighborhood—and indeed the entire town of Mission Viejo—seemed to be a haven from the chaos that ruled so much of the rest of the world these days.

He closed the shutters, entirely blocking the sun.

Apparently the only danger was in his mind, a figment of the same active imagination that had made him, at last, a reasonably successful mystery novelist.

Yet his heart was beating faster than ever.

Marty walked out of his office into the second-floor hall, as far as the head of the stairs. He stood as still as the newel post on which he rested one hand.

He wasn't certain what he expected to hear. The soft creak of a door, stealthy footsteps? The furtive rustles and clicks and muffled thumps of an intruder slowly making his way through the house?

Gradually, as he heard nothing suspicious and as his racing heart grew calmer, his sense of impending disaster faded. Anxiety became mere uneasiness.

"Who's there?" he asked, just to break the silence.

The sound of his voice, full of puzzlement, dispelled the portentous mood. Now the hush was only that of an empty house, devoid of menace.

He returned to his office at the end of the hall and settled in the leather chair behind his desk. With the shutters tightly closed and no lamps on except the one with the stained-glass shade, the corners of the room seemed to recede farther than the dimensions of the walls allowed, as if it were a place in a dream.

Because the motif of the lamp shade was fruit, the protective glass on the desk top reflected luminous ovals and circles of cherry-red, plum-purple, grape-green, lemon-yellow, and berry-blue. In its polished metal and Plexiglas surfaces, the cassette recorder, which lay on the glass, also reflected the bright mosaic, glimmering as if encrusted with jewels. When he reached for the recorder, Marty saw that his hand appeared to be sheathed in the pebbly, iridescent rainbow skin of an exotic lizard.

He hesitated, studying the faux scales on the back of his hand and the phantom jewels on the recorder. Real life was as layered with illusion as any piece of fiction.

He picked up the recorder and pressed the rewind button for a second or two, seeking the last few words of the unfinished letter to his editor. The thin, high-speed whistle-shriek of his voice in reverse issued like an alien language from the small, tinny speaker.

When he thumbed the play button, he found that he had not reversed far enough: *". . . I need . . . I need . . . I need . . ."*

Frowning, he switched the machine to rewind, taking the tape back twice as far as before.

But still: *". . . I need . . . I need . . ."*

Rewind. Two seconds. Five. Ten. Stop. Play.

". . . I need . . . I need . . . I need . . ."

After two more attempts, he found the letter: *". . . so I should be able to have the final draft of the new book in your hands in about a month. I think this one is . . . this one is . . . uh . . . this one . . ."*

The dictation stopped. Silence unreeled from the tape—and the sound of his breathing.

By the time the two-word chant finally began to issue from the speaker, Marty had leaned forward tensely on the edge of the chair, frowning at the recorder in his hand.

". . . I need . . . I need . . ."

He checked his watch. Not quite six minutes past four o'clock.

Initially the dreamy murmur was the same as when he'd first come to his senses and heard soft chanting like the responses to an interminable, unimaginative religious litany. After about half a minute, however, his voice on the tape changed, became sharp with urgency, swelled with anguish, then with anger.

". . . I NEED . . . I NEED . . . I NEED . . ."

Frustration seethed through those two words.

The Marty Stillwater on the tape—who might as well have been a total stranger to the listening Marty Stillwater—sounded in acute emotional pain for want of something that he could neither describe nor imagine.

Mesmerized, he scowled at the notched white spools of the cassette player turning relentlessly behind the plastic view window.

Finally the voice fell silent, the recording ended, and Marty consulted his watch again. More than twelve minutes past four.

He had assumed that he'd lost his concentration for only a few seconds, slipped into a brief daydream. Instead, he'd sat with the recorder gripped in his hand, the letter to his editor forgotten, repeating those two words for seven minutes or longer.

Seven minutes, for God's sake.

And he had remembered none of it. As if in a trance.

Now he stopped the tape. His hand was trembling, and when he put the cassette recorder on the desk, it rattled against the glass.

He looked around the office, where he had passed so many solitary hours in the concoction and solution of so many mysteries, where he had put uncounted characters through enormous travail and challenged them to find their way out of mortal danger. The room was so familiar: the overflowing bookshelves, a dozen original paintings that had been featured on the dust jackets of his novels, the couch that he had bought in anticipation of lazy plotting sessions but on which he had never had the time or inclination to lie, the computer with its oversize monitor.

But that familiarity was not comforting any more, because now it was tainted by the strangeness of what had happened minutes ago.

He blotted his damp palms on his jeans.

Having briefly lifted from him, dread settled again in the manner of Poe's mysterious raven perching above a chamber door.

Waking from the trance, perceiving danger, he had expected to find the threat outside in the street or in the form of a burglar roaming through the rooms below. But it was worse than that. The threat was not external. Somehow, the wrongness was within him.

2.

The night is deep and free of turbulence.

Below, the clotted clouds are silver with reflected moonlight, and for a while the shadow of the plane undulates across that vaporous sea.

The killer's flight from Boston arrives on time in Kansas City, Missouri. He goes directly to the baggage-claim area. Thanksgiving-holiday travelers will not head home until tomorrow, so the airport is quiet. His two pieces of luggage—one of which contains a Heckler & Koch P7 pistol, detachable silencer, and expanded magazines loaded with 9mm ammunition—are first and second to drop onto the carrousel.

At the rental-agency counter he discovers that his reservation has not been misplaced or misrecorded, as often happens. He will receive the large Ford sedan that he requested, instead of being stuck with a subcompact.

The credit card in the name of John Larrington is accepted by the clerk and by the American Express verifying machine with no problem, although his name is not John Larrington.

When he receives the car, it runs well and smells clean. The heater actually works.

Everything seems to be going his way.

Within a few miles of the airport he checks into a pleasant if anonymous four-story motor hotel, where the red-haired clerk at the reception counter tells him that he may have a complimentary breakfast—pastries, juice, and coffee—delivered in the morning simply by requesting it. His Visa card in the name of Thomas E. Jukovic is accepted, although Thomas E. Jukovic is not his name.

His room has burnt-orange carpet and striped blue wallpaper. However, the mattress is firm, and the towels are fluffy.

The suitcase containing the automatic pistol and ammunition remains locked in the trunk of the car, where it will offer no temptation to snooping motel employees.

After sitting in a chair by the window for a while, staring at Kansas City by starlight, he goes down to the coffee shop to have dinner. He is six feet tall, weighs a hundred and eighty pounds, but eats as heartily as a much larger man. A bowl of vegetable soup with garlic toast. Two cheeseburgers, french fries. A slice of apple pie with vanilla ice cream. Half a dozen cups of coffee.

He always has a big appetite. Often he is ravenous; at times his hunger seems almost insatiable.

While he eats, the waitress stops by twice to ask if the food is prepared well and if he needs anything else. She is not merely attentive but flirting with him.

Although he is reasonably attractive, his looks don't rival those of any movie star. Yet women flirt with him more frequently than with other men who are handsomer and better dressed than he. Consisting of Rockport walking shoes, khaki slacks, a dark-green crew-neck sweater, no jewelry, and an inexpensive wristwatch, his wardrobe is unremarkable, unmemorable. Which is the idea. The waitress has no reason to mistake him for a man of means. Yet here she is again, smiling coquettishly.

Once, in a Miami cocktail lounge where he had picked her up, a blonde with whiskey-colored eyes had assured him that an intriguing aura surrounded him. A compelling magnetism arose, she said, from his preference for silence and from the stony expression that usually occupied his face. "You are," she'd insisted playfully, "the epitome of the strong silent type. Hell, if you were in a movie with Clint Eastwood and Stallone, there wouldn't be any dialogue at all!"

Later he had beaten her to death.

He had not been angered by anything she'd said or done. In fact, sex with her had been satisfying.

But he had been in Florida to blow the brains out of a man named Parker Abbotson, and he'd been concerned that the woman might somehow later connect him with the assassination. He hadn't wanted her to be able to give the police a description of him.

After wasting her, he had gone to see the latest Spielberg picture, and then a Steve Martin flick.

He likes movies. Aside from his work, movies are the only life he has. Sometimes it seems his real home is a succession of movie theaters in different cities yet so alike in their shopping-center multiplexity that they might as well be the same dark auditorium.

Now he pretends to be unaware that the coffee-shop waitress is interested in him. She is pretty enough, but he wouldn't dare kill an employee of the restaurant in the very motel where he's staying. He needs to find a woman in a place to which he has no connections.

He tips precisely fifteen percent because either stinginess or extravagance is a sure way to be remembered.

After returning briefly to his room for a wool-lined leather jacket suitable to the late-November night, he gets in the rental Ford and drives in steadily widening circles through the surrounding commercial district. He is searching for the kind of establishment in which he will have a chance to find the right woman.

3.

Daddy wasn't Daddy.

He had Daddy's blue eyes, Daddy's dark brown hair, Daddy's too-big ears, Daddy's freckled nose; he was a dead-ringer for the Martin Stillwater pictured on the dustjackets of his books. He sounded just like Daddy when Charlotte and Emily and their mother came home and found him in the kitchen, drinking coffee, because he said, "There's no use pretending you went shopping at the mall after the movie. I had you followed by a private detective. I know you were at a poker parlor in Gardena, gambling and smoking cigars." He stood, sat, and moved like Daddy.

Later, when they went out to Islands for dinner, he even drove like Daddy. Which was too fast, according to Mom. Or simply "the confident, skillful technique of a master motorman" if you saw things Daddy's way.

But Charlotte knew something was wrong, and she fretted.

Oh, he hadn't been taken over by an alien who crawled out of a big seed pod from outer space or anything so extreme. He wasn't *that* different from the Daddy she knew and loved.

Mostly, the differences were minor. Though usually relaxed and easy-going, he was slightly tense. He held himself stiffly, as if balancing eggs on his head . . . or as if maybe he expected to be hit at any moment by someone, something. He didn't smile as quickly or as often as usual, and when he *did* smile, he seemed to be pretending.

Before he backed the car out of the driveway, he turned and checked on Charlotte and Emily to be sure they were using seatbelts, but he didn't say "the Stillwater rocket to Mars is about to blast off" or "if I take the turns too fast and you have to puke, please throw up neatly in your jacket pockets, not on my nice upholstery" or "if we build up enough speed to go back in time, don't shout insults at the dinosaurs" or any of the other silly things he usually said.

Charlotte noticed and was troubled.

The restaurant, Islands, had good burgers, great fries—which could be ordered well-done—salads, and soft tacos. Sandwiches and french fries were served in baskets, and the ambiance was Caribbean.

"Ambiance" was a new word for Charlotte. She liked the sound of it so much, she used it every chance she got—though Emily, hopeless child, was always confused and said "what ambulance, I don't see an ambulance" every time Charlotte used it. Seven-year-olds could be such a tribulation. Charlotte was ten—or would be in six weeks—and Emily had *just* turned seven in October. Em was a good sister, but of course seven-year-olds were so . . . so *sevenish.*

Anyway, the ambiance was tropical: bright colors, bamboo on the ceiling, wooden blinds, and lots of potted palms. Both the boy and girl waitresses wore shorts and bright Hawaiian-type shirts.

The place reminded her of Jimmy Buffet music, which was one of those things her parents loved but which Charlotte didn't get at all. At least the ambiance *was* cool, and the french fries were the best.

They sat in a booth in the non-smoking section, where the ambiance was even nicer. Her parents ordered Corona, which came in frosted mugs. Charlotte had a Coke, and Emily ordered root beer.

"Root beer is a grown-up drink," Em said. She pointed to Charlotte's Coke. "When are you going to stop drinking kid stuff?"

Em was convinced that root beer could be as intoxicating as real beer. Sometimes she pretended to be smashed after two glasses, which was stupid and embarrassing. When Em was doing her weaving-burping-drunk routine and strangers turned to stare, Charlotte explained that Em was seven. Everyone was understanding—from a seven-year-old, what else could be expected?—but it was embarrassing nonetheless.

By the time the waitress brought dinner, Mom and Daddy were talking about some people they knew who were getting a divorce—boring adult talk that could ruin an ambiance fast if you paid any attention. And Em was stacking french fries in peculiar piles, like miniature versions of modern sculptures they'd seen in a museum last summer; she was absorbed by the project.

With everyone distracted, Charlotte unzipped the deepest pocket on her denim jacket, withdrew Fred, and put him on the table.

He sat motionless under his shell, stumpy legs tucked in, headless, as big around as a man's wristwatch. Finally his beaky little nose appeared. He sniffed the air cautiously, and then he stretched his head out of the fortress that he carried on his back. His dark shiny turtle eyes regarded his new surroundings with great interest, and Charlotte figured he must be amazed by the ambiance.

"Stick with me, Fred, and I'll show you places no turtle has ever before seen," she whispered.

She glanced at her parents. They were still so involved with each other that they had not noticed when she'd slipped Fred out of her pocket. Now he was hidden from them by a basket of french fries.

In addition to fries, Charlotte was eating soft tacos stuffed with chicken, from which she extracted a ribbon of lettuce. The turtle sniffed it, turned his head away in disgust. She tried chopped tomato. *Are you serious?* he seemed to say, refusing the tidbit.

Occasionally, Fred could be moody and difficult. That was her fault, she supposed, because she had spoiled him.

She didn't think chicken or cheese would be good for him, and she was not going to offer him any tortilla crumbs until he ate his vegetables, so she nibbled on the crisp french fries and gazed around the restaurant as if fascinated by the other customers, ignoring the rude little reptile. He had rejected the lettuce and tomato merely to annoy her. If he thought she didn't give a hoot whether he ate or not, then he would probably eat. In turtle years, Fred was seven.

She actually became interested in a heavy-metal couple with leather clothes and strange hair. They distracted her for a few minutes, and she was startled by her mother's soft squeak of alarm.

"Oh," said her mother after she squeaked, "it's only Fred."

The ungrateful turtle—after all, Charlotte could have left him at home—was not beside her plate where he'd been left. He had crawled around the basket of fries to the other side of the table.

"I only got him out to feed him," Charlotte said defensively.

Lifting the basket so Charlotte could see the turtle, Mom said, "Honey, it's not good for him to be in your pocket all day."

"Not all day." Charlotte took possession of Fred and returned him to her pocket. "Just since we left the house for dinner."

Mom frowned. "What other livestock do you have with you?"

"Just Fred."

"What about Bob?" Mom asked.

"Oh, yuch," Emily said, making a face at Charlotte. "You got Bob in your pocket? I hate Bob."

Bob was a bug, a slow-moving black beetle as large as the last joint of Daddy's thumb, with faint blue markings on his carapace. She kept him in a big jar at home, but sometimes she liked to take him out and watch him crawl in his laborious way across a countertop or even over the back of her hand.

"I'd never bring Bob to a restaurant," Charlotte assured them.

"You also know better than to bring Fred," her mother said.

"Yes, ma'am," Charlotte said, genuinely embarrassed.

"Dumb," Emily advised her.

To Emily, Mom said, "No dumber than using french fries as if they're Lego blocks."

"I'm making art." Emily was always making art. She was weird sometimes even for a seven-year-old. *Picasso reincarnate,* Daddy called her.

"Art, huh?" Mom said. "You're making art out of your food, so then what are you going to eat? A painting?"

"Maybe," Em said. "A painting of a chocolate cake."

Charlotte zipped shut her jacket pocket, imprisoning Fred.

"Wash your hands before you go on eating," Daddy said.

Charlotte said, "Why?"

"What were you just handling?"

"You mean Fred? But Fred's clean."

"I said, wash your hands."

Her father's snappishness reminded Charlotte that he was not himself. He rarely spoke harshly to her or Em. She behaved not out of fear that he'd spank her or shout at her, but because it was important not to disappoint him or Mom. It was the best feeling in the world when she got a good grade in school or performed well at a piano recital and made them proud of her. And absolutely nothing was worse than messing up—and seeing a sad look of disappointment in their eyes, even when they didn't punish her or say anything.

The sharpness of her father's voice sent her directly to the ladies' room, blinking back tears every step of the way.

✳   ✳   ✳

Later, on the way home from Islands, when Daddy got a lead foot, Mom said, "Marty, this isn't the Indianapolis Five Hundred."

"You think this is fast?" Daddy asked, as if astonished. "This isn't fast."

"Even the caped crusader himself can't get the Batmobile up to speeds like this."

"I'm thirty-three, never had an accident. Spotless record. No tickets. Never been stopped by a cop."

"Because they can't catch you," Mom said.

"Exactly."

In the back seat, Charlotte and Emily grinned at each other.

For as long as Charlotte could remember, her parents had been having jokey conversations about his driving, though her mother was serious about wanting him to go slower.

"I've never even had a parking ticket," Daddy said.

"Well, of course, it's not easy to get a parking ticket when the speedometer needle is always pegged out."

In the past their back-and-forth had always been good-humored. But now, he suddenly spoke sharply to Mom: "For God's sake, Paige, I'm a good driver, this is a safe car, I spent more money on it than I should have precisely because it's one of the safest cars on the road, so will you just give this a rest?"

"Sure. Sorry," Mom said.

Charlotte looked at her sister. Em was wide-eyed with disbelief.

Daddy was not Daddy. Something was wrong. Big-Time wrong.

They had gone only a block before he slowed down and glanced at Mom and said, "Sorry."

"No, you were right, I'm too much of a worrier about some things," Mom told him.

They smiled at each other. It was all right. They weren't going to get divorced like those people they'd been talking about at dinner. Charlotte couldn't recall them ever being angry with each other for longer than a few minutes.

However, she was still worried. Maybe she *should* check around the house and outside behind the garage to see if she could find a giant empty seed pod from outer space.

4.

Like a shark cruising cold currents in a night sea, the killer drives.

This is his first time in Kansas City, but he knows the streets. Total mastery of the layout is part of his preparation for every assignment, in case he becomes the subject of a police pursuit and needs to make a hasty escape under pressure.

Curiously, he has no recollection of having seen—let alone studied—a map, and he can't imagine from where this highly detailed information was acquired. But he doesn't like to consider the holes in his memory because thinking about them opens the door on a black abyss that terrifies him.

So he just drives.

Usually he likes to drive. Having a powerful and responsive machine at his command gives him a sense of control and purpose.

But once in a while, as happens now, the motion of the car and the sights of a strange city—regardless of how familiar he may be with the layout of its streets—make him feel small, alone, adrift. His heart begins to beat fast. His palms are suddenly so damp, the steering wheel slips through them.

Then, as he brakes at a traffic light, he looks at the car in the lane beside him and sees a family revealed by the street lamps. The father is driving. The mother sits in the passenger seat, an attractive woman. A boy of about ten and a girl of six or seven are in the back seat. On their way home from a night out. Maybe a movie. Talking, laughing, parents and children together, sharing.

In his deteriorating condition, that sight is a merciless hammer blow, and he makes a thin wordless sound of anguish.

He pulls off the street, into the parking lot of an Italian restaurant. Slumps in his seat. Breathes in quick shallow gasps.

The emptiness. He dreads the emptiness.

And now it is upon him.

He feels as if he is a hollow man, made of the thinnest blown glass, fragile, only slightly more substantial than a ghost.

At times like this, he desperately needs a mirror. His reflection is one of the few things that can confirm his existence.

The restaurant's elaborate red and green neon sign illuminates the interior of the Ford. When he tilts the rearview mirror to look at himself, his skin has a cadaverous cast, and his eyes are alight with changing crimson shapes, as if fires burn within him.

Tonight, his reflection is not enough to diminish his agitation. He feels less substantial by the moment. Perhaps he will breathe out one last time, expelling the final thin substance of himself in that exhalation.

Tears blur his vision. He is overwhelmed by his loneliness, and tortured by the meaninglessness of his life.

He folds his arms across his chest, hugs himself, leans forward, and rests his forehead against the steering wheel. He sobs as if he is a small child.

He doesn't know his name, only the names he will use while in Kansas City. He wants so much to have a name of his own that is not as counterfeit as the credit cards on which it appears. He has no family, no friends, no home. He cannot recall who gave him this assignment—or any of the jobs before it—and he doesn't know why his targets must die. Incredibly, he has no idea who pays him, does not remember where he got the money in his wallet or where he bought the clothes he wears.

On a more profound level, he does not know *who* he is. He has no memory of a time when his profession was anything other than murder. He has no politics, no religion, no personal philosophy whatsoever. Whenever he tries to take an interest in current affairs, he finds himself unable to retain what he reads in the newspapers; he can't even focus his attention on television news. He is intelligent, yet he permits himself—or is permitted—only satisfactions of a physical nature: food, sex, the savage exhilaration of homicide. Vast regions of his mind remain uncharted.

A few minutes pass in green and red neon.

His tears dry. Gradually he stops trembling.

He will be all right. Back on the rails. Steady, controlled.

In fact he ascends with remarkable speed from the depths of despair. Surprising, how readily he is willing to continue with his latest assignment—and with the mere shadow of a life that he leads. Sometimes it seems to him that he operates as if programmed in the manner of a dumb and obedient machine.

On the other hand, if he were not to continue, what else would he do? This shadow of a life is the only life he has.

5.

While the girls were upstairs, brushing their teeth and preparing for bed, Marty methodically went from room to room on the first floor, making sure all of the doors and windows were locked.

He had circled half the downstairs—and was testing the latch on the window above the kitchen sink—before he realized what a peculiar task he had set for himself. Prior to turning in every night, he checked the front and back doors, of course, plus the sliding doors between the family room and patio, but he did not ordinarily verify that any particular window was secure unless he knew that it had been open for ventilation during the day. Nevertheless, he was confirming the integrity of the house perimeter as conscientiously as a sentry might certify the outer defenses of a fortress besieged by enemies.

As he was finishing in the kitchen, he heard Paige enter, and a moment later she slid both arms around his waist, embracing him from behind. "You okay?" she asked.

"Yeah, well . . ."

"Bad day?"

"Not really. Just one bad moment."

Marty turned in her arms to embrace her. She felt wonderful, so warm and strong, so *alive.*

That he loved her more now than when they had met in college was no surprise. The triumphs and failures they had shared, the years of daily struggle to make a place in the world and to seek the meaning of it, was rich soil in which love could grow.

However, in an age when ideal beauty was supposedly embodied in nineteen-year-old professional cheerleaders for major-league football teams, Marty knew a lot of guys who would be surprised to hear he'd found his wife increasingly attractive as she had aged from nineteen to thirty-three. Her eyes were no bluer than they had been when he'd first met her; her hair was not a richer shade of gold, and her skin was neither smoother nor more supple. Nevertheless, experience had given her character, depth. Corny as it sounded in this era of knee-jerk cynicism, she sometimes seemed to shine with an inner light, as radiant as the venerated subject of a painting by Raphael.

So, yeah, maybe he had a heart as soft as butter, maybe he was a sucker for romance, but he found her smile and the challenge of her eyes infinitely more exciting than a six-pack of naked cheerleaders.

He kissed her brow.

She said, "One bad moment? What happened?"

He hadn't decided how much he should tell her about those seven lost minutes. For now it might be best to minimize the deep weirdness of the experience, see the doctor Monday morning, and even have some tests done. If he was in good health, what had happened in the office this afternoon might prove to be an inexplicable singularity. He didn't want to alarm Paige unnecessarily.

"Well?" she persisted.

With the inflection she gave that single word, she reminded him that twelve years of marriage forbade serious secrets, no matter what good intentions motivated his reticence.

He said, "You remember Audrey Aimes?"

"Who? Oh, you mean in *One Dead Bishop?*"

One Dead Bishop was a novel he had written. Audrey Aimes was the lead character.

"Remember what her problem was?" he asked.

"She found a dead priest hanging on a hook in her foyer closet."

"Aside from that."

"She had *another* problem? Seems like a dead priest is enough. Are you sure you're not over-complicating your plots?"

"I'm serious," he said, though aware of how odd it was that he should choose to inform his wife of a personal crisis by comparing it to the experiences of a mystery-novel heroine whom *he* had created.

Was the dividing line between life and fiction as hazy for other people as it sometimes was for a writer? And if so—was there a book in that idea?

Frowning, Paige said, "Audrey Aimes . . . Oh, yeah, you're talking about her blackouts."

"Fugues," he said.

A fugue was a serious personality dissociation. The victim went places, talked to people, and engaged in varied activities while appearing normal—yet later could not recall where he had been or what he had done during the blackout, as if the time had passed in deepest sleep. A fugue could last minutes, hours, or even days.

Audrey Aimes had suddenly begun to suffer from fugues when she was thirty, because repressed memories of childhood abuse had begun to surface after more than two decades, and she had retreated from them psychologically. She'd been certain she'd killed the priest while in a fugue state, although of course someone else had murdered him and stuffed him in her closet, and the entire bizarre homicide was connected to what had happened to her when she was a little girl.

In spite of being able to earn a living by spinning elaborate fantasies out of thin air, Marty had a reputation for being as emotionally stable as the Rock of Gibraltar and as easy-going as a golden retriever on Valium, which was probably why Paige still smiled at him and appeared reluctant to take him seriously.

She stood on her toes, kissed his nose, and said, "So you forgot to take out the garbage, and now you're going to claim it's because you're suffering a personality breakdown due to long-forgotten, hideous abuses when you were six years old. Really, Marty. Shame on you. Your mom and dad are the sweetest people I've ever met."

He let go of her, closed his eyes, and pressed one hand against his forehead. He was developing a fierce headache.

"I'm serious, Paige. This afternoon, in the office . . . for seven minutes . . . well, I only know what the hell I was doing during that time because I've got it on a tape recorder. I don't remember any of it. And it's creepy. Seven creepy minutes."

He felt her body tense against his, as she realized that he was not engaged in some complex joke. And when he opened his eyes, he saw that her playful smile was gone.

"Maybe there's a simple explanation," he said. "Maybe there's no reason to be concerned. But I'm scared, Paige. I feel stupid, like I should just shrug and forget about it, but I'm scared."

6.

In Kansas City, a chill wind polishes the night until the sky seems to be an infinite slab of clear crystal in which stars are suspended and behind which is pent a vast reservoir of darkness.

Beneath that enormous weight of space and blackness, the Blue Life Lounge huddles like a research station on the floor of an ocean trench, pressurized to resist implosion. The facade is covered in a shiny aluminum skin reminiscent of Airstream travel trailers and roadside diners from the 1950s. Blue and green neon spells the name in lazy script and outlines the structure, glimmering in the aluminum and beckoning with as much allure as the lamps of Neptune.

Inside, where an amplified combo blasts out rock-'n'-roll from the past two decades, the killer moves toward the huge horseshoe bar in the center of the room. The air is thick with cigarette smoke, beer fumes, and body heat; it almost resists him, as if it's water.

The crowd offers radically different images from the traditional Thanksgiving scenes flooding television screens during this holiday weekend. At the tables the customers are mostly raucous young men in groups with too much energy and testosterone for their own good. They shout to be heard above the thundering music, grab at waitresses to get their attention, whoop in approval when the guitarist gets off a good riff.

Their determination to enjoy themselves has the frantic quality of insectile frenzy.

A third of the men at the tables are accompanied by young wives or girlfriends of the big-hair and heavy-makeup persuasion. They are as rowdy as the men—and would be as out of place at a hearthside family gathering as screeching bright-plumed parrots would be out of place at the bedside of a dying nun.

The horseshoe-shaped bar encircles an oval stage, bathed in red and white spotlights, where two young women with exceptionally firm bodies thrash to the music and call it dancing. They wear cowgirl costumes designed to tease, all fringe and spangles, and one of them elicits whistles and hoots when she removes her halter top.

The men on the bar stools are all ages and, unlike the customers at the tables, each appears to be alone. They sit in silence, staring up at the two smooth-skinned dancers. Many sway slightly on their stools or move their heads dreamily from side to side in time to some other music far less driving than the tunes the band is actually playing; they are like a colony of sea anemones, stirred by slow deep currents, waiting dumbly for a morsel of pleasure to drift to them.

He sits on one of only two empty stools and orders a bottle of Beck's dark from a bartender who could crack walnuts in the crooks of his arms. All three bartenders are tall and muscular, no doubt hired for their ability to double as bouncers if the need arises.

The dancer at the far end of the stage, the one whose breasts bounce unfettered, is a striking brunette with a thousand-watt smile. She is into the music and genuinely seems to enjoy performing.

Although the nearest dancer, a leggy blonde, is even more attractive than the brunette, her routine is mechanical, and she seems to be numbed either by drugs or disgust. She neither smiles nor looks at anyone, but gazes at some far place only she can see.

She seems haughty, disdainful of the men who stare at her, the killer included. He would derive a lot of pleasure from drawing his pistol and pumping several rounds into her exquisite body—one for good measure in the center of her pouting face.

An intense thrill shakes him at the mere contemplation of taking her beauty from her. The theft of her beauty appeals to him more than taking her life. He places little value on life but a great deal on beauty because his own life is often unbearably bleak.

Fortunately, the pistol is in the trunk of the rented Ford. He has left the gun in the car precisely to avoid a temptation like this, when he feels compelled toward violence.

As often as two or three times a day, he is gripped by a desire to destroy anyone who happens to be near him—men, women, children, it makes no difference. In the thrall of these dark seizures, he hates every last human being on the face of the earth—whether they are beautiful or ugly, rich or poor, smart or stupid, young or old.

Perhaps, in part, his hatred arises from the knowledge that he is different from them. He must always live as an outsider.

But simple alienation is not the primary reason he frequently contemplates random slaughter. He needs something from other people which they are unwilling to provide, and, because they withhold it, he hates them with such passion that he is capable of any atrocity—even though he has no idea what he expects to receive from them.

This mysterious need is sometimes so intense that it becomes painful. It is a hunger akin to starvation—but not a hunger for food. Often he finds himself on the trembling edge of a revelation; he realizes that the answer is astonishingly simple if only he can open himself to it, but enlightenment always eludes him.

The killer takes a long pull on the bottle of Beck's. He wants the beer, but he does not need it. Want is not need.

On the elevated stage, the blonde slips off her halter, exposing pale upswept breasts.

If he retrieves the pistol and expanded magazines of ammo from the trunk of the car, he will have ninety rounds. When the arrogant blonde is dead, he can kill the other dancer. Then the three muscle-bound bartenders with three headshots. He is well trained in the use of firearms—though he has no recollection of who trained him. With those five dead, he can target the fleeing crowd. Many who don't die from gunfire will perish when trampled in the panic to escape.

The prospect of slaughter excites him, and he knows that blood can make him forget, at least for a short while, the aching need that plagues him. He has experienced the pattern before. Need fosters frustration; frustration grows into anger; anger leads to hatred; hatred generates violence—and violence sometimes soothes.

He drinks more beer and wonders if he is insane.

He remembers a movie in which a psychiatrist assures the hero that only sane people question their sanity. Genuine madmen are always firmly convinced of their rationality. Therefore, he must be sane even to be able to doubt himself.

7.

Marty leaned against the door frame and watched while the girls took turns sitting on their bedroom vanity bench to let Paige brush their hair. Fifty strokes each.

Perhaps it was the easy rhythmic motion of the hairbrush or the tranquilizing domesticity of the scene that soothed Marty's headache. Whatever the reason, the pain faded.

Charlotte's hair was golden, just like her mother's, and Emily's was so dark brown that it was almost black, like Marty's. Charlotte chatted nonstop with Paige throughout her brushing; but Emily kept silent, arched her back, closed her eyes, and took an almost catlike pleasure in the grooming.

The contrasting halves of their shared room attested to other differences between the sisters. Charlotte liked posters full of motion: colorful hot-air balloons against a desert twilight; a ballet dancer in mid-entrechat; sprinting gazelles. Emily preferred posters of autumn leaves, evergreens hung with heavy snow, and moonlight-silvered surf breaking on a pale beach. Charlotte's bedspread was green, red, and yellow; Emily's was a beige chenille. Disorder ruled in Charlotte's domain, while Emily prized neatness.

Then there was the matter of pets. On Charlotte's side of the room, built-in bookshelves housed the terrarium that was home to Fred the Turtle, the wide-mouthed gallon jar where Bob the Bug made his home in dead leaves and grass, the cage that housed Wayne the Gerbil, another terrarium in which Sheldon the Snake was the tenant, a second cage in which Whiskers the Mouse spent a lot of time keeping an eye on Sheldon in spite of the glass and wire that separated them, and a final terrarium occupied by Loretta the Chameleon. Charlotte had rejected the suggestion that a kitten or puppy was a more appropriate pet. "Dogs and cats run around loose all the time, you can't keep them in a nice safe little home and protect them," she explained.

Emily had only one pet. Its name was Peepers. It was a stone the size of a small lemon, smoothed by decades of running water in the Sierra creek from which she had retrieved it during their summer vacation a year ago. She had painted two soulful eyes on it, and insisted, "Peepers is the best pet of all. I don't have to feed him or clean up after him. He's been around forever, so he's real smart and real wise, and when I'm sad or maybe mad, I just tell him what I'm hurting about, and he takes it all in and worries about it so I don't have to think about it any more and can be happy."

Emily was capable of expressing ideas that were, on the surface, entirely childlike but, on reflection, seemed deeper and more mature than anything expected from a seven-year-old. Sometimes, when he looked into her dark eyes, Marty felt she was seven going on four hundred, and he could hardly wait to see just how interesting and complex she was going to be when she was all grown-up.

After their hair was brushed, the girls climbed into the twin beds, and their mother tucked the covers around them, kissed them, and wished them sweet dreams. "Don't let the bedbugs bite," she warned Emily because the line always elicited a giggle.

As Paige retreated to the doorway, Marty moved a straight-backed chair from its usual place against the wall and positioned it at the foot of—and exactly between—the two beds. Except for a miniature battery-powered reading lamp clipped to his open notebook and a low-wattage Mickey Mouse luminaria plugged into a wall socket near the floor, he switched off all the lights. He sat in the chair, held the notebook at reading distance, and waited until the silence had acquired that same quality of pleasurable expectation that filled a theater in the moment when the curtain started to rise.

The mood was set.

This was the happiest part of Marty's day. Story time. No matter what else might happen after rising to meet the morning, he could always look forward to story time.

He wrote the tales himself in a notebook labeled *Stories for Charlotte and Emily,* which he might actually publish one day. Or might not. Every word was a gift to his daughters, so the decision to share the stories with anyone else would be entirely theirs.

Tonight marked the beginning of a special treat, a story in verse, which would continue through Christmas Day. Maybe it would go well enough to help him forget the unsettling events in his office.

> *"Well, now Thanksgiving is safely past,*
> *more turkey eaten this year than last—"*

"It rhymes!" Charlotte said with delight.

"Sssshhhhh!" Emily admonished her sister.

The rules of story time were few but important, and one of them was that the two-girl audience could not interrupt mid-sentence or, in the case of a poem, mid-stanza. Their feedback was valued, their reactions cherished, but a storyteller must receive his due respect.

He began again:

> *"Well, now Thanksgiving is safely past,*
> *more turkey eaten this year than last,*
> *more stuffing stuffed, more yams jammed*
> *into our mouths, and using both hands,*
> *coleslaw in slews, biscuits by twos,*
> *all of us too fat to fit in our shoes."*

The girls were giggling just where he wanted them to giggle, and Marty could barely restrain himself from turning around in his chair to see how Paige liked it so far, as she had heard none of it until this moment. But no one would respond to a storyteller who couldn't wait until the end for his plaudits; an unshakable air of confidence, whether faked or genuinely felt, was essential to success.

> *"So let's look ahead to the big holiday*
> *that's coming, coming, coming our way.*
> *I'm sure you know just what day I mean.*
> *It's not Easter Sunday, not Halloween.*
> *It's not a day to be sad and listless.*
> *I ask you, young ladies, what is it—?"*

"It's Christmas!" Charlotte and Emily answered in unison, and their immediate response confirmed that he had them in his spell.

> *"Someday soon, we'll put up a tree.*
> *Why only one? Maybe two, maybe three!*
> *Deck it with tinsel and baubles bright.*
> *It'll be an amazing and wonderful sight.*
> *String colored lights out on the roof—*
> *pray none are broken by anything's hoof.*
> *Salt down the shingles to melt the ice.*
> *If Santa fell, it just wouldn't be nice.*
> *He might fracture a leg or get a cut,*
> *perhaps even break his big jolly butt."*

He glanced at the girls. Their faces seemed to shine in the shadows. Without saying a word, they told him: *Don't stop, don't stop!*

God, he loved this. He loved *them.*

If heaven existed, it was exactly like this moment, this place.

> *"Oh, wait! I just heard terrible news.*
> *Hope it won't give you Christmas blues.*
> *Santa was drugged, tied up, and gagged,*
> *blindfolded, ear-stoppled, and bagged.*
> *His sleigh is waiting out in the yard,*
> *and someone has stolen Santa's bank card.*
> *Soon his accounts will be picked clean*
> *by the use of automatic-teller machines."*

"Uh-oh," Charlotte said, snuggling deeper into her covers, "it's going to be scary."

"Well, of course it is," Emily said. "Daddy wrote it."

"Will it be *too* scary?" Charlotte asked, pulling the blankets up to her chin.

"Are you wearing socks?" Marty asked.

Charlotte usually wore socks to bed except in summer, because otherwise her feet got cold.

"Socks?" she said. "Yeah? So?"

Marty leaned forward in his chair and lowered his voice to a spooky whisper: "Because this story won't end until Christmas Day, and by then it's gonna scare your socks off maybe a dozen times."

He made a wicked face.

Charlotte pulled the covers up to her nose.

Emily giggled and demanded: "Come on, Daddy, what's next?"

> *"Hark, the sound of silver sleigh bells*
> *echoes over the hills and the dells.*
> *And look—reindeer high up in the sky!*
> *Some silly goose has taught them to fly.*
> *The driver giggles quite like a loon—*
> *madman, goofball, a thug, and a goon.*
> *Something is wrong—any fool could tell.*
> *If this is Santa, then Santa's not well.*
> *He hoots, gibbers, chortles, and spits,*
> *and seems to be having some sort of fits.*
> *His mean little eyes spin just like tops.*
> *So somebody better quick call the cops.*
> *A closer look confirms his psychosis.*
> *And—oh, my dears—really bad halitosis!"*

"Oh, jeez," Charlotte said, pulling the covers up just below her eyes. She professed to dislike scary stories, but she was the quickest to complain if something frightening didn't happen in a tale sooner or later.

"So who is it?" Emily asked. "Who tied Santa up and robbed him and ran off in his sleigh?"

> *"Beware when Christmas comes this year,*
> *because there's something new to fear.*
> *Santa's twin—who is evil and mean—*
> *stole the sleigh, will make the scene,*
> *pretending to be his good brother.*
> *Guard your beloved children, mother!*
> *Down the chimney, into your home,*
> *here comes that vile psychotic gnome!"*

"Eeep!" Charlotte cried, and pulled the covers over her head.

Emily said, "What made Santa's twin so evil?"

"Maybe he had a bad childhood," Marty said.

"Maybe he was *born* that way," Charlotte said under her covers.

"Can people be born bad?" Emily wondered. Then she answered her own question before Marty could respond. "Well, sure, they can. 'Cause some people are born good, like you and Mommy, so then some people must be born bad."

Marty was soaking up the girls' reactions, loving it. On one level, he was a writer, storing away their words, the rhythms of their speech, expressions, toward the day when he might need to use some of this for a scene in a book. He supposed it wasn't admirable to be so constantly aware that even his own children were material; it might be morally repugnant, but he couldn't change. He was what he was. He was also a father, however, and he reacted primarily on that level, mentally preserving the moment because one day memories were all he would have of their childhood, and he wanted to be able to recall *everything,* the good and the bad, simple moments and big events, in Technicolor and Dolby sound and with perfect clarity, because it was all too precious to him to be lost.

Emily said, "Does Santa's evil twin have a name?"

"Yes," Marty said, "he does, but you'll have to wait until another night to hear it. We've reached our first stopping place."

Charlotte poked her head out from beneath the covers, and both girls insisted that he read the first part of the poem again, as he had known they would. Even the second time through, they would be too involved to be ready to sleep. They would demand a third reading, and he would oblige, for then they would be familiar enough with the words to settle down. Later, by the end of the third reading, they finally would be either deep in sleep or on the drowsy edge of it.

As he started with the first line again, Marty heard Paige turn out of the doorway and walk toward the stairs. She would be waiting for him in the family room, perhaps with flames crackling in the fireplace, perhaps with red wine and a snack of some kind, and they would curl up together and tell each other about their day.

Any five minutes of the evening, now or later, would be more interesting to him than a trip around the world. He was a hopeless homebody. The charms of hearth and family had more allure than the enigmatic sands of Egypt, the glamour of Paris, and the mystery of the Far East combined.

Winking at each of his daughters, reciting again, "Well, now Thanksgiving is safely past," he had for the moment forgotten that something disturbing had happened earlier in his office and that the sanctity of his home had been violated.

8.

In the Blue Life Lounge, a woman brushes against the killer and slides onto the bar stool beside him. She is not as beautiful as the dancers, but she is attractive enough for his purposes. Wearing tan jeans and a tight red T-shirt, she could be just another customer, but she is not. He knows her type—a discount Venus with the skills of a natural-born accountant.

They conduct a conversation by leaning close to each other to be heard above the band, and soon their heads are almost touching. Her name is Heather, or so she says. She has wintermint breath.

By the time the dancers retreat and the band takes a break, Heather has decided he isn't a vice cop on stakeout, so she grows bolder. She knows what he wants, she has what he wants, and she lets him know that he is a buyer in a seller's market.

Heather tells him that across the highway from the Blue Life Lounge is a motel where, if a girl is known to the management, rooms can be rented by the hour. This is no surprise to him, for there are laws of lust and economics as immutable as the laws of nature.

She pulls on her lambskin-lined jacket, and together they go out into the chilly night, where her wintermint breath turns to steam in the crisp air. They cross the parking lot and then the highway, hand-in-hand as if they are high school sweethearts.

Though she knows what he wants, she does not know what he needs any more than he does. When he gets what he wants, and when it does not quench the hot need in him, Heather will learn the pattern of emotion that is now so familiar to him: need fosters frustration; frustration grows into anger; anger leads to hatred; hatred generates violence—and violence sometimes soothes.

The sky is a massive slab of crystal-clear ice. The trees stand leafless and sere at the end of barren November. The wind makes a cold, mournful sound as it sweeps off the vast surrounding prairie, through the city. And violence sometimes soothes.

*   *   *

Later, having spent himself in Heather more than once, no longer in the urgent grip of lust, he finds the shabbiness of the motel room to be an intolerable reminder of the shallow, grubby nature of his existence. His immediate desire is sated, but his desire for more of a life, for direction and meaning, is undiminished.

The naked young woman, on top of whom he still lies, seems ugly now, even disgusting. The memory of intimacy with her repels him. She can't or won't give him what he needs. Living on the edge of society, selling her body, she is an outcast herself, and therefore an infuriating symbol of his own alienation.

She is taken by surprise when he punches her in the face. The blow is hard enough to stun her. As Heather goes limp, nearly unconscious, he slips both hands around her throat and chokes her with all the force of which he is capable.

The struggle is quiet. The blow, followed by extreme pressure on her windpipe and diminishment of the blood supply to her brain through the carotid arteries, renders her incapable of resistance.

He is concerned about drawing the unwanted attention of other motel guests. But a minimum of noise is also important because quiet murder is more personal, more intimate, more deeply satisfying.

So quietly does she succumb that he is reminded of nature films in which certain spiders and mantises kill their mates subsequent to a first and final act of intercourse, always without a sound from either assailant or victim. Heather's death is marked by a cold and solemn ritual equal to the stylized savagery of those insects.

Minutes later, after showering and dressing, he crosses the highway from the motel to the Blue Life Lounge and gets in his rental car. He has business to conduct. He was not sent to Kansas City to murder a whore named Heather. She was merely a diversion. Other victims await him, and now he is sufficiently relaxed and focused to deal with them.

9.

In Marty's office, by the party-colored light of the stained-glass lamp, Paige stood beside the desk, staring at the small tape recorder, listening to her husband chant two unsettling words in a voice that ranged from a melancholy whisper to a low snarl of rage.

After less than two minutes, she couldn't tolerate it any longer. His voice was simultaneously familiar and strange, which made it far worse than if she'd been unable to recognize it at all.

She switched off the recorder.

Realizing she was still holding the glass of red wine in her right hand, she took too large a swallow. It was a good California cabernet that merited leisurely sipping, but suddenly she was more interested in its effect than its taste.

Standing across the desk from her, Marty said, "There's at least five more minutes of the same thing. Seven minutes in all. After it happened, before you and the girls came home, I did some research." He gestured toward the bookshelves that lined one wall. "In my medical references."

Paige did not want to hear what he was going to tell her. The possibility of serious illness was unthinkable. If anything happened to Marty, the world would be a far darker and less interesting place.

She was not sure that she could deal with the loss of him. She realized her attitude was peculiar, considering that she was a child psychologist who, in her private practice and during the hours she donated to child-welfare groups, had counseled dozens of children about how to conquer grief and go on after the death of a loved one.

Coming around the desk toward her, his own wine glass already empty, Marty said, "A fugue can be symptomatic of several things. Early-stage Alzheimer's disease, for instance, but I believe we can rule that out. If I've got Alzheimer's at thirty-three, I'd probably be the youngest case on record by about a decade."

He put his glass on the desk and went to the window to stare out at the night between the slats of the plantation shutters.

Paige was struck by how vulnerable he suddenly appeared. Six feet tall, a hundred and eighty pounds, with his easy-going manner and limitless enthusiasm for life, Marty had always before struck her as being more solid and permanent than anything in the world, oceans and mountains included. Now he seemed as fragile as a pane of glass.

With his back toward her, still studying the night, he said, "Or it might have been an indication of a small stroke."

"No."

"Though according to the references I checked, the most likely cause is a brain tumor."

She raised her glass. It was empty. She could not remember having finished the wine. A little fugue of her own.

She set the glass on the desk. Beside the hateful cassette recorder. Then she went to Marty and put a hand on his shoulder.

When he turned to her, she kissed him lightly, quickly. She laid her head against his chest and hugged him, and he put his arms around her. Because of Marty, she had learned that hugs were as essential to a healthy life as were food, water, sleep.

Earlier, when she had caught him systematically checking window locks, she'd insisted, with only a scowl and a single word—*"Well?"*—that he not hide anything. Now she wished she hadn't insisted on hearing about his one bad moment in an otherwise fine day.

She looked up and met his eyes at last, still embracing him, and said, "It might be nothing."

"It's something."

"But I mean, nothing physical."

He smiled ruefully. "It's so comforting to have a psychologist in the house."

"Well, it could be psychological."

"Somehow, it doesn't help that maybe I'm just crazy."

"Not crazy. Stressed."

"Ah, yes, stress. *The* twentieth-century excuse, the favorite of goldbrickers filing fake disability claims, politicians trying to explain why they were drunk in a motel with naked teenage girls—"

She let go of him, turned away, angry. She wasn't upset with Marty, exactly, but with God or fate or whatever force had suddenly brought turbulent currents into their smoothly flowing lives.

She started toward the desk to get her glass of wine before she remembered she had already drunk it. She turned to Marty again.

"All right . . . except when Charlotte was so sick that time, you've always been about as stressed out as a clam. But maybe you're just a *secret* worrier. And lately, you've had a lot of pressures."

"I have?" he asked, raising his eyebrows.

"The deadline on this book is tighter than usual."

"But I've still got three months, and I think I'll need one."

"All the new career expectations—your publisher and agent and everyone in the business watching you in a different way now."

The paperback reprints of his two most recent novels had placed on the *New York Times* bestseller list, each for eight weeks. He had not yet enjoyed a hardcover bestseller, but that new level of success seemed imminent with the release of his new novel in January.

The sudden sales growth was exciting but also daunting. Though Marty wanted a larger audience, he also was determined not to tailor his writing to have wider appeal and thereby lose what made his books fresh. He knew he was in danger of *unconsciously* modifying his work, so lately he was being unusually hard on himself, even though he had *always* been his own toughest critic and had always revised each page of a story as many as twenty and thirty times.

"Then there's *People* magazine," she said.

"That's not stressful. It's over and done with."

A writer for *People* had come to the house a few weeks ago, and a photographer followed two days later for a ten-hour shoot. Marty being Marty, he liked them and they liked him, although first he had desperately resisted his publisher's entreaties to do the piece.

Given his friendly relationship with the *People* people, he had no reason to think the article would be negative, but even favorable publicity usually made him feel cheap and grasping. To him, the books were what mattered, not the person who wrote them, and he did not want to be, as he put it, "the Madonna of the mystery novel, posing nude in a library with a snake in my teeth to hype sales."

"It's not over and done with," Paige disagreed. The issue with the article about Marty would not hit the newsstands until Monday. "I know you're dreading it."

He sighed. "I don't want to be—"

"Madonna with a snake in your teeth. I know, baby. What I'm saying is, you're more stressed about the magazine than you realize."

"Stressed enough to black out for seven minutes?"

"Sure. Why not? I'll bet that's what the doctor will say."

Marty looked skeptical.

Paige moved into his arms again. "Everything's been going so well for us lately, almost too well. There's a tendency to get a little superstitious about it. But we worked hard, we earned all of this. Nothing's going to go wrong. You hear me?"

"I hear you," he said, holding her close.

"Nothing's going to go wrong," she repeated. "Nothing."

10.

After midnight.

The neighborhood boasts big lots, and the large houses are set far back from the front property lines. Huge trees, so ancient they seem almost to have acquired nascent intelligence, stand sentinel along the streets, watching over the prosperous residents, autumn-stripped black limbs bristling like high-tech antennae, gathering information about potential threats to the well-being of those who sleep beyond the brick and stone walls.

The killer parks around the corner from the house in which his work awaits. He walks the rest of the way, softly humming a cheery tune of his own creation, acting as if he has trod these sidewalks ten thousand times before.

Furtive behavior is always noticed and, when noticed, inevitably raises an alarm. On the other hand, a man acting boldly and directly is viewed as honest and harmless, is not remarked upon, and is later forgotten altogether.

A cold northwest breeze.

A moonless sky.

A suspicious owl monotonously repeats his single question.

The house is Georgian, brick with white columns. The property is encircled by a spear-point iron fence.

The driveway gate stands open and appears to have been left in that position for many years. The pace and peaceful quality of life in Kansas City cannot long sustain paranoia.

As if he owns the place, he follows the circular driveway to the portico at the main entrance, climbs the steps, and pauses at the front door to unzip a small breast pocket in his leather jacket. From the pocket he extracts a key.

Until this moment, he was not aware that he was carrying it. He doesn't know who gave it to him, but at once he knows its purpose. This has happened to him before.

The key fits the dead-bolt lock.

He opens the door on a dark foyer, steps across the threshold into the warm house, and withdraws the key from the lock. He closes the door softly behind him.

After putting the key away, he turns to a lighted alarm-system programming board next to the door. He has sixty seconds from the moment he opened the door to punch in the correct code to disarm the system; otherwise, police will be summoned. He remembers the six-digit disarming sequence just when it's required, punches it in.

He withdraws another item from his jacket, this time from a deep inside pocket: a pair of extremely compact night-vision goggles of a type manufactured for the military and unavailable for purchase by private citizens. They amplify even the meager available light so efficiently, by a factor of ten thousand, that he is able to move through dark rooms as confidently as if all of the lamps were lit.

Ascending the stairs, he removes the Heckler & Koch P7 from the oversize shoulder holster under his jacket. The extended magazine contains eighteen cartridges.

A silencer is tucked into a smaller sleeve of the holster. He frees it, and then quietly screws it onto the muzzle of the pistol. It will guarantee eight to twelve relatively quiet shots, but it will deteriorate too fast to allow him to expend the entire magazine without waking others in the house and neighborhood.

Eight shots should be more than he needs.

The house is large, and ten rooms open off the T-shaped second-floor hall, but he does not have to search for his targets. He is as familiar with this floor plan as with the street layout of the city.

Through the goggles, everything has a greenish cast, and white objects seem to glow with a ghostly inner light. He feels as if he is in a science-fiction movie, an intrepid hero exploring another dimension or an alternate earth that is identical to ours in all but a few crucial respects.

He eases open the master-bedroom door, enters. He approaches the king-size bed with its elaborate Georgian headboard.

Two people are asleep under the glowing greenish blankets, a man and woman in their forties. The husband lies on his back, snoring. His face is easily identifiable as that of the primary target. The wife is on her side, face half buried in her pillow, but the killer can see enough to ascertain that she is the secondary target.

He puts the muzzle of the P7 against the husband's throat.

The cold steel wakes the man, and his eyes pop open as if they have the counter-balanced lids of a doll's eyes.

The killer pulls the trigger, blowing out the man's throat, raises the muzzle, and fires two rounds pointblank in his face. The gunfire sounds like the soft spitting of a cobra.

He walks around the bed, making no sound on the plush carpet.

Two bullets in the wife's exposed left temple complete his assignment, and she never wakes at all.

For a while he stands by the bed, enjoying the incomparable tenderness of the moment. Being present at a death is to share one of the most intimate experiences anyone will ever know in this world. After all, no one except treasured family members and beloved friends are welcome at a deathbed, to witness a dying person's final breath. Therefore, the killer is able to rise above his gray and miserable existence only in the act of execution, for then he has the honor of sharing that most profound of all experiences, more solemn and significant than birth. In those precious magic moments when his targets perish, he establishes relationships, meaningful bonds with other human beings, *connections* that briefly banish his alienation and make him feel included, needed, loved.

Although these victims are always strangers to him—and in this case, he does not even know their names—the experience can be so poignant that tears fill his eyes. Tonight he manages to remain in complete control of himself.

Reluctant to let the brief connection end, he places one hand tenderly against the woman's left cheek, which is unsoiled by blood and still pleasantly warm. He walks around the bed again and gives the dead man's shoulder a gentle squeeze, as if to say, *Goodbye, old friend, goodbye.*

He wonders who they were. And why they had to die.

Goodbye.

Down he goes through the ghostly green house full of green shadows and radiant green forms. In the foyer he pauses to unscrew the silencer from the weapon and to holster both pieces.

He removes the goggles with dismay. Without the lenses, he is transported from that magical alternate earth, where for a brief while he felt a kinship with other human beings, to this world in which he strives so hard to belong but remains forever a man apart.

Exiting the house, he closes the door but doesn't bother locking it. He doesn't wipe off the brass knob, for he isn't concerned about leaving fingerprints.

The cold breeze soughs and whistles through the portico.

With ratlike scraping and rustling, crisp dead leaves scurry in packs along the driveway.

The sentinel trees now seem to be asleep at their posts. The killer senses that no one watches him from any of the blank black windows along the street. And even the interrogatory voice of the owl is silenced.

Still moved by what he has shared, he does not hum his little nonsense tune on the return trip to the car.

By the time he drives to the motor hotel where he is staying, he feels once more the weight of the oppressive apartheid in which he exists. Separate. Shunned. A solitary man.

In his room he slips off the shoulder holster and puts it on the nightstand. The pistol is still in the clasp of that nylon-lined leather sleeve. He stares at the weapon for a while.

In the bathroom he takes a pair of scissors from his shaving kit, closes the lid on the toilet, sits in the harsh fluorescent glare, and meticulously destroys the two bogus credit cards that he has used thus far on the assignment. He will fly out of Kansas City in the morning, employing yet another name, and on the drive to the airport he will scatter the tiny fragments of the cards along a few miles of highway.

He returns to the nightstand.

Stares at the pistol.

After leaving the dead bodies at the job site, he should have broken the weapon down into as many pieces as possible. He should have disposed of its parts in widely separated locations: the barrel in a storm drain perhaps, half the frame in a creek, the other half in a Dumpster . . . until nothing was left. That is standard procedure, and he is at a loss to understand why he disregarded it this time.

A low-grade guilt attends this deviation from routine, but he is not going to go out again and dispose of the weapon. In addition to the guilt, he feels . . . rebellious.

He undresses and lies down. He turns off the bedside lamp and stares at the layered shadows on the ceiling.

He is not sleepy. His mind is restless, and his thoughts jump from subject to subject with such unnerving rapidity that his hyperactive mental state soon translates into physical agitation. He fidgets, pulling at the sheets, readjusting blankets, pillows.

Out on the interstate highway, large trucks roll ceaselessly toward far destinations. The singing of their tires, the grumble of their engines, and the *whoosh* of the air displaced by their passage form a background white noise that is usually soothing. He has often been lulled to sleep by this Gypsy music of the open road.

Tonight, however, a strange thing happens. For reasons he can't understand, this familiar mosaic of sound isn't a lullaby but a siren song. He cannot resist it.

He gets out of bed and crosses the dark room to the only window. He has an obscure night view of a weedy hillside and above it a slab of sky—like the halves of an abstract painting. Atop the slope, separating sky and hill, the sturdy pickets of a highway guardrail are flickeringly illuminated by passing headlights.

He stares up, half in a trance, straining for glimpses of the westbound vehicles.

Usually melancholy, the highway cantata is now enticing, calling him, making a mysterious promise which he does not understand but which he feels compelled to explore.

He dresses, and packs his clothes.

Outside, the motor courtyard and walkways are deserted. Faced toward the rooms, cars wait for morning travel. In a nearby vending-machine alcove, a soft-drink dispenser clicks-clinks as if conducting repairs upon itself. The killer feels as if he is the only living creature in a world now run by—and for the benefit of—machines.

Moments later, he is on Interstate 70, heading toward Topeka, the pistol on the seat beside him but covered with a motel towel.

Something west of Kansas City calls him. He doesn't know what it is, but he feels inexorably drawn westward in the way that iron is pulled toward a magnet.

Strange as it might be, none of this alarms him, and he accedes to this compulsion to drive west. After all, for as long as he can remember, he has gone places without knowing the purpose of his trip until he has reached his destination, and he has killed people with no clue as to why they have to die or for whom the killing is done.

He is certain, however, that this sudden departure from Kansas City is not expected of him. He is supposed to stay at the motel until morning and catch an early flight out to . . . Seattle.

Perhaps in Seattle he would have received instructions from the bosses he cannot recall. But he will never know what might have happened because Seattle is now stricken from his itinerary.

He wonders how much time will pass before his superiors—whatever their names and identities—will realize that he has gone renegade. When will they start looking for him, and how will they ever find him if he is no longer operating within his program?

At two o'clock in the morning, traffic is light on Interstate 70, mostly trucks, and he speeds across Kansas in advance of some of the big rigs and in the blustery wakes of others, remembering a movie about Dorothy and her dog Toto and a tornado that plucked them out of that flat farmland and dropped them in a far stranger place.

With both Kansas City, Missouri, and Kansas City, Kansas, behind him, the killer realizes he's muttering to himself: *"I need, I need."*

This time he feels close to a revelation that will identify the precise nature of his longing.

"I need . . . to be . . . I need to be . . . I need to be . . ."

As the suburbs and finally the dark prairie flash past on both sides, excitement builds steadily in him. He trembles on the brink of an insight that, he senses, will change his life.

"I need to be . . . to be . . . I need to be someone."

At once, he understands the meaning of what he has said. By "to be someone," he does not mean what another man might intend to say with those same three words; he does not mean that he needs to be someone famous or rich or important. Just someone. Someone with a real name. Just an ordinary Joe, as they used to say in the movies of the forties. Someone who has more substance than a ghost.

The pull of the unknown lodestar in the west grows stronger by the mile. He leans forward slightly, hunching over the steering wheel, peering intently into the night.

Beyond the horizon, in a town he can't yet envision, a life awaits him, a place to call home. Family, friends. Somewhere there are shoes into which he can step, a past he can wear comfortably, purpose. And a future in which he can be like other people—accepted.

The car speeds westward, cleaving the night.

11.

Half past midnight, on his way to bed, Marty Stillwater stopped by the girls' room, eased open the door, and stepped silently across the threshold. In the butterscotch-yellow glow of the Mickey Mouse nightlight, he could see both of his daughters sleeping peacefully.

Now and then he liked to watch them for a few minutes while they slept, just to convince himself that they were real. He'd had more than his share of happiness and prosperity and love, so it followed that some of his blessings might prove transitory or even illusory; fate might intervene to balance the scales.

To the ancient Greeks, Fate was personified in the form of three sisters: Clotho, who spun the thread of life; Lachesis, who measured the length of the thread; and Atropos, smallest of the three but the most powerful, who snipped the thread at her whim.

Sometimes, to Marty, that seemed a logical way to look at things. He could imagine the faces of those white-robed women in more detail than he could recall his own Mission Viejo neighbors. Clotho had a kind face with merry eyes, reminiscent of the actress Angela Lansbury, and Lachesis was as cute as Goldie Hawn but with a saintly aura. Ridiculous, but that's how he saw them. Atropos was a bitch, beautiful but cold—pinched mouth, anthracite-black eyes.

The trick was to remain in the good graces of the first two sisters without drawing the attention of the third.

Five years ago, in the guise of a blood disorder, Atropos had descended from her celestial home to take a whack at the thread of Charlotte's life and, thankfully, had failed to cut it all the way through. But this goddess answered to many names besides Atropos: cancer, cerebral hemorrhage, coronary thrombosis, fire, earthquake, poison, homicide, and countless others. Now perhaps she was paying them a return visit under one of her many pseudonyms, with Marty as her target instead of Charlotte.

Frequently, the vivid imagination of a novelist was a curse.

A whirring-clicking noise suddenly arose from the shadows on Charlotte's side of the room, startling Marty. As low and menacing as a rattlesnake's warning. Then he realized what it was: one half of the gerbil's big cage was occupied by an exercise wheel, and the restless rodent was running furiously in place.

"Go to sleep, Wayne," he said softly.

He took one more look at his girls, then stepped out of the room and pulled the door shut quietly behind him.

12.

He reaches Topeka at three o'clock in the morning.

He is still drawn toward the western horizon as a migrating creature might be pulled relentlessly southward with the approach of winter, answering a call that is soundless, a beacon that can't be seen, as though it is the trace of iron in his very blood that responds to the unknown magnet.

Exiting the freeway on the outskirts of the city, he scouts for another car.

Somewhere there are people who know the name John Larrington, the identity under which he rented the Ford. When he does not show up in Seattle for whatever job awaits him, his strange and faceless superiors will no doubt come looking for him. He suspects they have substantial resources and influence; he must shed every connection with his past and leave the hunters with no means of tracking him.

He parks the rental Ford in a residential neighborhood and walks three blocks, trying the doors of the cars at the curb. Only half are locked. He is prepared to hot-wire a car if it comes to that, but in a blue Honda he finds the keys tucked behind the sun visor.

After driving back to the Ford and transferring his suitcases and the pistol to the Honda, he cruises in ever-widening circles, searching for a twenty-four-hour-a-day convenience store.

He has no map of Topeka in his head because no one expected him to go there. Unnerved to see street signs on which all of the names are unfamiliar, he has no knowledge of where any route will lead.

He feels more of an outcast than ever.

Within fifteen minutes he locates a convenience store and nearly empties the shelves of Slim Jims, cheese crackers, peanuts, miniature doughnuts, and other food that will be easy to eat while driving. He is already starved. If he is going to be on the road for as much as another two days—assuming he might be drawn all the way to the coast—he will need considerable supplies. He does not want to waste time in restaurants, yet his accelerated metabolism requires him to eat larger meals and more frequently than other people eat.

After adding three six-packs of Pepsi to his purchase, he goes to the checkout counter, where the sole clerk says, "You must be having an all-night party or something."

"Yeah."

When he pays the bill, he realizes the three hundred bucks in his wallet—the amount of cash he *always* has with him on a job—will not take him far. He can no longer use the phony credit cards, of which he still has two, because someone will surely be able to track him through his purchases. He will need to pay cash from now on.

He takes the three large bags of supplies to the Honda and returns to the store with the Heckler & Koch P7. He shoots the clerk once in the head and empties the register, but all he gets is his own money back plus fifty dollars. Better than nothing.

At an Arco service station, he fills the tank of the Honda with gasoline and buys a map of the United States.

Parked at the edge of the Arco lot, under a sodium-vapor light that colors everything sickly yellow, he eats Slim Jims. He's ravenous.

By the time he switches from sausages to doughnuts, he begins to study the map. He could continue westward on Interstate 70—or instead head southwest on the Kansas Turnpike to Wichita, keep going to Oklahoma City, and then turn directly west again on Interstate 40.

He is not accustomed to having choices. He usually does what he is . . . programmed to do. Now, faced with alternatives, he finds decision-making unexpectedly difficult. He sits irresolute, increasingly nervous, in danger of being paralyzed by indecision.

At last he gets out of the Honda and stands in the cool night air, seeking guidance.

The wind vibrates the telephone wires overhead—a haunting sound, as thin and bleak as the frightened crying of dead children wandering in a dark Beyond.

He turns westward as inexorably as a compass needle seeks magnetic north. The attraction feels psychic, as if a presence out there calls to him, but the connection is less sophisticated than that, more biological, reverberating in his blood and marrow.

Behind the wheel of the car again, he finds the Kansas Turnpike and heads toward Wichita. He is still not sleepy. If he has to, he can go two or even three nights without sleep and lose none of his mental or physical edge, which is only one of his special strengths. He is so excited by the prospect of being someone that he might drive nonstop until he finds his destiny.

13.

Paige knew that Marty half expected to be stricken by another blackout, this time in public, so she admired his ability to maintain a carefree facade. He seemed as lighthearted as the kids.

From the girls' point of view, Sunday was a perfect day.

Late-morning, Paige and Marty took them to the Ritz-Carlton Hotel in Dana Point for the Thanksgiving-weekend brunch. It was a place they went only on special occasions.

As always, Emily and Charlotte were enchanted by the lushly landscaped grounds, beautiful public rooms, and impeccable staff in crisp uniforms. In their best dresses, with ribbons in their hair, the girls had great fun playing at being cultured young ladies—almost as much fun as raiding the dessert buffet twice each.

In the afternoon, because it was unseasonably warm, they changed clothes and visited Irvine Park. They walked the picturesque trails, fed the ducks in the pond, and toured the small zoo.

Charlotte loved the zoo because the animals were, like her menagerie at home, kept in enclosures where they were safe from harm. There were no exotic specimens—all the animals were indigenous to the region—but in her typical exuberance, Charlotte found each to be the most interesting and cutest creature she had ever seen.

Emily got into a staring contest with a wolf. Large, amber-eyed, with a lustrous silver-gray coat, the predator met and intensely held the girl's gaze from his side of a chain-link fence.

"If you look away first," Emily calmly and somberly informed them, "then a wolf will just eat you all up."

The confrontation went on so long that Paige became uneasy in spite of the sturdy fence. Then the wolf lowered his head, sniffed the ground, yawned elaborately to show he had not been intimidated but had merely lost interest, and sauntered away.

"If he couldn't get the three little pigs with all his huffing and puffing," Emily said, "then I *knew* he couldn't get me, 'cause I'm smarter than pigs."

She was referring to the Disney cartoon, the only version of the fairy tale with which she was familiar.

Paige resolved never to let her read the Brothers Grimm version, which was about seven little goats instead of three pigs. The wolf swallowed six of them whole. They were saved from digestion at the last minute when their mother cut open the wolf's belly to pull them from his steaming innards.

Paige glanced back at the wolf as they walked away. It was watching Emily again.

14.

Sunday is a full day for the killer.

In Wichita, just before dawn, he gets off the turnpike. In another residential neighborhood rather like the one in Topeka, he swaps the license plates on the Honda for those on a Chevy, making his stolen vehicle more difficult to locate.

Shortly after nine Sunday morning he arrives in Oklahoma City, Oklahoma, where he stops long enough to fill the tank with gasoline.

A shopping mall is across the road from the service station. In one corner of the huge deserted parking lot stands an unmanned Goodwill Industries collection box, as large as a garden shed. After tanking up, he leaves his suitcases and their contents with Goodwill. He keeps only the clothes he's wearing and the pistol.

During the night, on the highway, he had time to think about his peculiar existence—and to wonder if he might be carrying a compact transmitter that would help his superiors locate him. Perhaps they anticipated that one day he would go renegade on them.

He knows that a moderately powerful transmitter, operating off a tiny battery, can be hidden in an extremely small space. Such as the walls of a suitcase.

As he turns directly west on Interstate 40, a coal-dark sludge of clouds seeps across the sky. Forty minutes later, when the rain comes, it is molten silver, and it instantly washes all of the color out of the vast empty land that flanks the highway. The world is twenty, forty, a hundred shades of gray, without even lightning to relieve the oppressive dreariness.

The monochromatic landscape provides no distraction, so he has time to worry further about the faceless hunters who might be close behind him. Is it paranoid to wonder if a transmitter could be woven into his clothing? He doubts it could be concealed in the material of his pants, shirt, sweater, underwear, or socks without being detectable by its very weight or upon casual inspection. Which leaves his shoes and leather jacket.

He rules out the pistol. They wouldn't build anything into the P7 that might interfere with its function. Besides, he was expected to discard it soon after the murders for which it was provided.

Halfway between Oklahoma City and Amarillo, east of the Texas border, he pulls off the interstate into a rest area, where ten cars, two big trucks, and two motorhomes have taken refuge from the storm.

In a surrounding grove of evergreens, the boughs of the trees droop as if sodden with rain, and they appear charcoal gray instead of green. The large pinecones are tumorous and strange.

A squat block building houses restrooms. He hurries through the cold downpour to the men's facilities.

While the killer is at the first of three urinals, rain drumming loudly on the metal roof and the humid air heavy with the limy smell of damp concrete, a man in his early sixties enters. At a glance: thick white hair, deeply seamed face, bulbous nose patterned with broken capillaries. He goes to the third of the urinals.

"Some storm, huh?" the stranger says.

"A real rat drowner," the killer answers, having heard that phrase in a movie.

"Hope it blows over soon."

The killer notices that the older man is about his height and build. As he zips up his pants, he says, "Where you headed?"

"Right now, Las Vegas, but then somewhere else and somewhere else after that. Me and the wife, we're retired, we pretty much live in that motorhome. Always wanted to see the country, and we sure in blue blazes are seeing it now. Nothing like life on the road, new sights every day, pure freedom."

"Sounds great."

At the sink, washing his hands, the killer stalls, wondering if he dares take the jabbering old fool right now, jam the body in a toilet stall. But with all the people in the parking lot, somebody might walk in unexpectedly.

Closing his fly, the stranger says, "Only problem is, Frannie—that's my wife—she hates for me to drive in the rain. Anything more than the tiniest drizzle, she wants to pull over and wait it out." He sighs. "This won't be a day we make a lot of miles."

The killer dries his hands under a hot-air machine. "Well, Vegas isn't going anywhere."

"True. Even when the good Lord comes on Judgment Day, there'll be blackjack tables open."

"Hope you break the bank," the killer says, and leaves as the older man goes to the sink.

In the Honda again, wet and shivering, he starts the engine and turns on the heater. But he doesn't put the car in gear.

Three motorhomes are parked in the deep spaces along the curb.

A minute later, Frannie's husband comes out of the men's room. Through the rippling rain on the windshield, the killer watches the white-haired man sprint to a large silver-and-blue Road King, which he enters through the driver's door at the front. Painted on the door is the outline of a heart, and in the heart are two names in fancy script: Jack and Frannie.

Luck is not with Jack, the Vegas-bound retiree. The Road King is only four spaces away from the Honda, and this proximity makes it easier for the killer to do what must be done.

The sky is purging itself of an entire ocean. The water falls straight down through the windless day, continuously shattering the mirrorlike puddles on the blacktop, gushing along the gutters in seemingly endless torrents.

Cars and trucks come in off the highway, park for a while, leave, and are replaced by new vehicles that pull in between the Honda and the Road King.

He is patient. Patience is part of his training.

The engine of the motorhome is idling. Crystallized exhaust plumes rise from the twin tail pipes. Warm amber light glows at the curtained windows along the side.

He envies their comfortable home on wheels, which looks cozier than any home he can yet hope to have. He also envies their long marriage. What would it be like to have a wife? How would it feel to be a beloved husband?

After forty minutes, the rain still isn't easing off, but a flock of cars leaves. The Honda is the only vehicle parked on the driver's side of the Road King.

Taking the pistol, he gets out of the car and walks quickly to the motorhome, watching the side windows in case Frannie or Jack parts the curtains and peers out at this most inopportune moment.

He glances toward the restrooms. No one in sight.

Perfect.

He grips the cold chrome door handle. The lock isn't engaged. He scrambles inside, up the steps, and looks over the driver's seat.

The kitchen is immediately behind the open cab, a dining nook beyond the kitchen, then the living room. Frannie and Jack are in the nook, eating, the woman with her back toward the killer.

Jack sees him first, starts simultaneously to rise and slide out of the narrow booth, and Frannie looks back over her shoulder, more curious than alarmed. The first two rounds take Jack in the chest and throat. He collapses over the table. Spattered with blood, Frannie opens her mouth to scream, but the third hollow-point round drastically reshapes her skull.

The silencer is attached to the muzzle, but it isn't effective any more. The baffles have been compressed. The sound accompanying each shot is only slightly quieter than regular gunfire.

The killer pulls the driver's door shut behind him. He looks out at the sidewalk, the rainswept picnic area, the restrooms. No one in sight.

He climbs over the gear-shift console, into the passenger's seat, and peers out the front window on that side. Only four other vehicles share the parking lot. The nearest is a Mack truck, and the driver must be in the men's room because no one is in the cab.

It's unlikely that anyone could have heard the shots. The roar of the rain provides ideal cover.

He swivels the command chair around, gets up, and walks back through the motorhome. He stops at the dead couple, touches Jack's back . . . then Frannie's left hand, which lies on the table in a puddle of blood beside her lunch plate.

"Goodbye," he says softly, wishing he could take more time to share this special moment with them.

Having come this far, however, he is nearly frantic to exchange his clothes for those of Frannie's husband and get on the road again. He has convinced himself that a transmitter is, indeed, concealed in the rubber heels of his Rockport shoes, and that its signal is even now leading dangerous people to him.

Beyond the living room is a bathroom, a large closet crammed with Frannie's clothes, and a bedroom with a smaller closet filled with Jack's wardrobe. In less than three minutes he strips naked and dresses in new underwear, white athletic socks, jeans, a red-and-brown-checkered shirt, a pair of battered sneakers, and a brown leather jacket to replace his black one. The inseam of the pants is just right; the waist is two inches too big, but he cinches it in with a belt. The shoes are slightly loose though wearable, and the shirt and jacket fit perfectly.

He carries the Rockport shoes into the kitchen. To confirm his suspicion, he takes a serrated bread knife from a drawer and saws off several thin layers of the rubber heel on one shoe until he discovers a shallow cavity packed tightly with electronics. A miniaturized transmitter is connected to a series of watch batteries that seems to extend all the way around the heel and perhaps the sole as well.

Not paranoid after all.

They're coming.

Abandoning the shoes in a litter of rubber shavings on the kitchen counter, he urgently searches Jack's body and takes the money out of the old man's wallet. Sixty-two bucks. He searches for Frannie's purse, finds it in the bedroom. Forty-nine dollars.

When he leaves the motorhome, the mottled gray-black sky is convex, bent low with the weight of the thunderheads. Rain by the megaton batters the earth.

Coils of fog serpentine among the trunks of the pine trees and seem to be reaching for him as he splashes to the Honda.

On the interstate again, speeding through the perpetual twilight beneath the storm, he turns the car heater to its highest setting and soon crosses the state line into Texas, where the flat land becomes impossibly flatter.

Having shed the last of the meager belongings from his old life, he feels liberated. Soaked by the cold rain, he shivers uncontrollably, but he is also trembling with anticipation and excitement.

His destiny lies somewhere to the west.

He peels the plastic wrapper off a Slim Jim and eats while he drives. A subtle flavor, threaded through the primary taste of the cured meat, reminds him of the metallic odor of blood in the house in Kansas City, where he left the nameless dead couple in their enormous Georgian bed.

The killer pushes the Honda as fast as he dares on the rain-slick highway, prepared to kill any cop who pulls him over. Reaching Amarillo, Texas, just after dusk on Sunday evening, he discovers that the Honda is virtually running on empty. He pulls into a truckstop only long enough to tank up, use the bathroom, and buy more food to take with him.

After Amarillo, rocketing westward into the night, he passes Wildorado, with the New Mexico border ahead, and suddenly he realizes that he is crossing the badlands, in the heart of the Old West, where so many wonderful movies have been set. John Wayne and Montgomery Clift in *Red River,* Walter Brennan stealing scenes left and right. *Rio Bravo.* And *Shane* was set back there in Kansas—wasn't it?—Jack Palance blowing away Elisha Cook, Jr. decades before Dorothy took the tornado to Oz. *Stagecoach, The Gunfighter, True Grit, Destry Rides Again, The Unforgiven, High Plains Drifter, Yellow Sky,* so many great movies, not all of them set in Texas but at least in the *spirit* of Texas, with John Wayne and Gregory Peck and Jimmy Stewart and Clint Eastwood, legends, mythical places now made real and waiting out there beyond the highway, obscured by rain and mist and darkness. It was almost possible to believe that those stories were being played out right now, in the frontier towns he was passing, and that he was Butch Cassidy or the Sundance Kid or some other gunman of an earlier century, a killer but not really a bad guy, misunderstood by society, forced to kill because of what had been done to him, a posse on his trail . . .

Memories from theater screens and late-night movies on TV—which constitute by far the largest portion of the memories he possesses—flood his troubled mind, soothing him, and for a while he is lost so completely in those fantasies that he pays too little attention to his driving. Gradually he becomes aware that his speed has fallen to forty miles an hour. Trucks and cars explode past him, the wind of their passage buffeting the Honda, splashing dirty water across his windshield, their red taillights swiftly receding into the gloom.

Assuring himself that his mysterious destiny will prove to be as great as any that John Wayne pursued in films, he accelerates.

Empty and half-empty packages of food, crumpled and smeary and full of crumbs, are heaped on the passenger seat. They cascade onto the floor, under the dashboard, completely filling the leg space on that side of the car.

From the litter, he extracts a new box of doughnuts. To wash them down he opens a warmish Pepsi.

Westward. Steadily westward.

An identity awaits him. He is going to be someone.

15.

Later Sunday, at home, after huge bowls of popcorn and two videos, Paige tucked the girls into bed, kissed them goodnight, and retreated to the open doorway to watch Marty as he settled down for that moment of the day he most cherished. Story time.

He continued with the poem about Santa's evil twin, and the girls were instantly enraptured.

> *"Reindeer sweep down out of the night.*
> *See how each is brimming with fright?*
> *Tossing their heads, rolling their eyes,*
> *these gentle animals are so very wise—*
> *they know this Santa isn't their friend,*
> *but an imposter and far 'round the bend.*
> *They would stampede for all they're worth,*
> *dump this nut off the edge of the earth.*
> *But Santa's bad brother carries a whip,*
> *a club, a harpoon, a gun at his hip,*
> *a blackjack, an Uzi—you better run!—*
> *and a terrible, horrible, wicked raygun."*

"Raygun?" Charlotte said. "Then he's an alien!"

"Don't be silly," Emily admonished her. "He's Santa's twin, so if he's an alien, Santa is an alien too, which he isn't."

With the smug condescension of a nine-year-old who had long ago discovered Santa Claus wasn't real, Charlotte said, "Em, you have a lot to learn. Daddy, what's the raygun do? Turn you to mush?"

"To stone," Emily said. She withdrew one hand from under the covers and revealed the polished stone on which she had painted a pair of eyes. "That's what happened to Peepers."

> "They land on the roof, quiet and sneaky.
> Oh, but this Santa is fearfully freaky.
> He whispers a warning to each reindeer,
> leaning close to make sure they hear:
> 'You have relatives back at the Pole—
> antlered, gentle, quite innocent souls.
> So if you fly away while I'm inside,
> back to the Pole on a plane I will ride.
> I'll have a picnic in the midnight sun:
> reindeer pie, pâté, reindeer in a bun,
> reindeer salad and hot reindeer soup,
> oh, all sorts of tasty reindeer goop.' "

"I *hate* this guy," Charlotte announced emphatically. She pulled her covers up to her nose as she had done the previous evening, but she wasn't genuinely frightened, just having a good time pretending to be spooked.

"This guy, he was just born bad," Emily decided. "For sure, he couldn't be this way just 'cause his mommy and daddy weren't as nice to him as they should've been."

Paige marveled at Marty's ability to strike the perfect note to elicit the kids' total involvement. If he'd given her the poem to review before he'd started reading it, Paige would have advised that it was a little too strong and dark to appeal to young girls.

So much for the question of which was superior—the insights of the psychologist or the instinct of the storyteller.

> "At the chimney, he looks down the bricks,
> but that entrance is strictly for hicks.

With all his tools, a way in can be found
for a fat bearded burglar out on the town.
From roof to yard to the kitchen door,
he chuckles about what he has in store
for the lovely family sleeping within.
He grins one of his most nasty grins.
Oh, what a creep, a scum, and a louse.
He's breaking into the Stillwater house."

"Our place!" Charlotte squealed.

"I knew!" Emily said.

Charlotte said, "You did not."

"Yes, I did."

"Did not."

"Did too. That's why I'm sleeping with Peepers, so he can protect me until after Christmas."

They insisted that their father read the whole thing from the beginning, all verses from both nights. As Marty began to oblige, Paige faded out of the doorway and went downstairs to put away the leftover popcorn and straighten up the kitchen.

The day had been perfect as far as the kids were concerned, and it had been good for her as well. Marty had not suffered another episode, which allowed her to convince herself that the fugue had been a singularity—frightening, inexplicable, but not an indication of a serious degenerative condition or disease.

Surely no man could keep pace with two such energetic children, entertain them, and prevent them from getting cranky for an entire busy day unless he was in extraordinarily good health. Speaking as the other half of the Fabulous Stillwater Parenting Machine, Paige was exhausted.

Curiously, after putting away the popcorn, she found herself checking window and door locks.

Last night Marty had been unable to explain his own heightened sense of a need for security. His trouble, after all, was internal.

Paige figured it had been simple psychological transference. He had been reluctant to dwell on the possibility of brain tumors and cerebral hemorrhages because those things were utterly beyond his control, so he had turned outward to seek enemies against which he might be able to take concrete action.

On the other hand, perhaps he had been reacting on instinct to a real threat beyond conscious perception. As one who incorporated some Jungian theory into her personal and professional worldview, Paige had room for such concepts as the collective unconscious, synchronicity, and intuition.

Standing at the French doors in the family room, staring across the patio to the dark yard, she wondered what threat Marty might have sensed out there in a world that, throughout her lifetime, had become increasingly fraught with danger.

16.

His attention deviates from the road ahead only for quick glances at the strange shapes that loom out of the darkness and the rain on both sides of the highway. Broken teeth of rock thrust from the sand and scree as if a behemoth just beneath the earth is opening its mouth to swallow whatever hapless animals happen to be on the surface. Widely spaced clusters of stunted trees struggle to stay alive in a stark land where storms are rare and drenching downpours rarer still; gnarled branches bristle out of the mist, as jagged and chitinous as the spiky limbs of insects, briefly illuminated by headlights, thrashing in the wind for an instant but then gone.

Although the Honda has a radio, the killer does not switch it on because he wants no distraction from the mysterious power which pulls him westward and with which he seeks communion. Mile by dreary mile, the magnetic attraction increases, and it is all that he cares about; he could no more turn away from it than the earth could reverse its rotation and bring tomorrow's sunrise in the west.

He leaves the rain behind and eventually passes from under the ragged clouds into a clear night with stars beyond counting. Along part of the horizon, luminous peaks and ridges can be seen dimly, so distant they might define the edge of the world, like alabaster ramparts protecting a fairy-tale kingdom, the walls of Shangri-la in which the light of last month's moon still glimmers.

Into the vastness of the Southwest he goes, past necklaces of light that are the desert towns of Tucumcari, Montoya, Cuervo, and then across the Pecos River.

Between Amarillo and Albuquerque, when he stops for oil and gasoline, he uses a service-station restroom reeking of insecticide, where two dead cockroaches lie in a corner. The yellow light and dirty mirror reveal a reflection recognizably his but somehow different. His blue eyes seem darker and more fierce than he has ever seen them, and the lines of his usually open and friendly face have hardened.

"I'm going to become someone," he says to the mirror, and the man in the mirror mouths the words in concert with him.

At eleven-thirty Sunday night, when he reaches Albuquerque, he fuels the Honda at another truckstop and orders two cheeseburgers to go. Then he is off on the next leg of his journey—three hundred and twenty-five miles to Flagstaff, Arizona—eating the sandwiches out of the white paper bags in which they came and into which drips fragrant grease, onions, and mustard.

This will be his second night without rest, yet he isn't sleepy. He is blessed with exceptional stamina. On other occasions he has gone seventy-two hours without sleep, yet has remained clear-headed.

From movies he has watched on lonely nights in strange towns, he knows that sleep is the one unconquerable enemy of soldiers desperate to win a tough battle. Of policemen on stakeout. Of those who must valiantly stand guard against vampires until dawn brings the sun and salvation.

His ability to call a truce with sleep whenever he wishes is so unusual that he shies away from thinking about it. He senses there are things about himself that he is better off not knowing, and this is one of them.

Another lesson he has learned from movies is that every man has secrets, even those he keeps from himself. Therefore, secrets merely make him like all other men. Which is precisely the condition he most desires. To be like other men.

❊   ❊   ❊

In the dream, Marty stood in a cold and windswept place, in the grip of terror. He was aware that he was on a plain as featureless and flat as one of those vast valley floors out in the Mojave Desert on the drive to Las Vegas, but he couldn't actually see the landscape because the darkness was as deep as death. He knew something was rushing toward him through the gloom, something inconceivably strange and hostile, immense and deadly yet utterly silent, *knew* in his bones that it was coming, dear God, yet had no idea of the direction of its approach. Left, right, in front, behind, from the ground beneath his feet or from out of the sable-black sky above, it was coming. He could *feel* it, an object of such colossal size and weight that the atmosphere was compressed in its path, the air thickening as the unknown danger drew nearer. Closing on him so rapidly, faster, faster, and nowhere to hide. Then he heard Emily pleading for help somewhere in the unrelenting blackness, calling for her daddy, and Charlotte calling, too, but he could not get a fix on them. He ran one way, then another, but their increasingly frantic voices always seemed to be behind him. The unknown threat was closer, closer, the girls frightened and crying, Paige shouting his name in a voice so freighted with terror that Marty began to weep with frustration at his inability to find them, oh dear Jesus, and it was almost on top of him, the thing, whatever it was, as unstoppable as a falling moon, worlds colliding, a weight beyond measure, a force as primal as the one that had created the universe, as destructive as the one that would someday end it, Emily and Charlotte screaming, screaming—

❋   ❋   ❋

West of the Painted Desert, outside Flagstaff, Arizona, shortly before five o'clock Monday morning, flurries of snow swirl out of the pre-dawn sky, and the cold air is a penetrating scalpel that scrapes his bones. The brown leather jacket that he took from the dead man's closet in the motorhome less than sixteen hours ago in Oklahoma is not heavy enough to keep him warm in the early-morning bitterness. He shivers as he fills the tank of the Honda at a self-service pump.

On Interstate 40 again, he begins the three-hundred-fifty-mile trip to Barstow, California. His compulsion to keep moving westward is so irresistible that he is as helpless in its grip as an asteroid captured by the earth's tremendous gravity and pulled inexorably toward a cataclysmic impact.

❋   ❋   ❋

Terror propelled him out of the dream of darkness and unknown menace: Marty Stillwater sat straight up in bed. His first waking breath was so explosive, he was sure he had awakened Paige, but she slept on undisturbed. He was chilled yet sheathed in sweat.

Gradually his heart stopped pounding so fearfully. With the glowing green numerals on the digital clock, the red cable-box light on top of the television, and the ambient light at the windows, the bedroom was not nearly as black as the plain in his dream.

But he could not lie down. The nightmare had been more vivid and unnerving than any he'd ever known. Sleep was beyond his reach.

Slipping out from under the covers, he padded barefoot to the nearest window. He studied the sky above the rooftops of the houses across the street, as if something in that dark vault would calm him.

Instead, when he noticed the black sky was brightening to a deep gray-blue along the eastern horizon, the approach of dawn filled him with the same irrational dread he had felt in his office on Saturday afternoon. As color crept into the heavens, Marty began to tremble. He tried to control himself, but his shivering grew more violent. It was not daylight that he feared, but something the day was bringing with it, an unnameable threat. He could feel it reaching for him, seeking him—which was crazy, damn it—and he shuddered so violently that he had to put one hand against the windowsill to steady himself.

"What's wrong with me?" he whispered desperately. "What's happening, what's wrong?"

❋　　❋　　❋

Hour after hour, the speedometer needle quivers between 90 and 100 on the gauge. The steering wheel vibrates under his palms until his hands ache. The Honda shimmies, rattles. The engine issues a thin unwavering shriek, unaccustomed to being pushed so hard.

Rust-red, bone-white, sulfur-yellow, the purple of desiccated veins, as dry as ashes, as barren as Mars, pale sand with reptilian spines of mottled rock, speckled with withered clumps of mesquite: the cruel fastness of the Mojave Desert has a majestic barrenness.

Inevitably, the killer thinks of old movies about settlers moving west in wagon trains. He realizes for the first time how much courage was required to make their journey in those rickety vehicles, trusting their lives to the health and stamina of dray horses.

Movies. California. He is in California, home of the movies.

Move, move, move.

From time to time, an involuntary mewling escapes him. The sound is like that of an animal dying of dehydration but within sight of a watering hole, dragging itself toward the pool that offers salvation but afraid it will perish before it can slake its burning thirst.

*   *   *

Paige and Charlotte were already in the garage, getting in the car, when they both cried, "Emily, hurry up!"

As Emily turned away from the breakfast table and started toward the open door that connected the kitchen to the garage, Marty caught her by the shoulder and turned her to face him. "Wait, wait, wait."

"Oh," she said, "I forgot," and puckered up for a smooch.

"That comes second," he said.

"What's first?"

"This." He dropped to one knee, bringing himself to her level, and with a paper towel he blotted away her milk mustache.

"Oh, gross," she said.

"It was cute."

"More like Charlotte."

He raised his eyebrows. "Oh?"

"She's the messy one."

"Don't be unkind."

"She knows it, Daddy."

"Nevertheless."

From the garage, Paige called again.

Emily kissed him, and he said, "Don't give your teacher any trouble."

"No more than she gives me," Emily answered.

Impulsively he pulled her against him, hugged her fiercely, reluctant to let her go. The clean fragrance of Ivory soap and baby shampoo clung to her; milk and the oaty aroma of Cheerios were on her breath. He had never smelled anything sweeter, better. Her back was frightfully small under the flat of his hand. She was so delicate, he could feel the beat of her young heart both through her chest—which pressed against him—and through her scapula and spine, against which his hand lay. He was overcome with the feeling that something terrible was going to happen and that he would never see her again if he allowed her to leave the house.

He had to let her go, of course—or explain his reluctance, which he could not do.

Honey, see, the problem is, something's wrong in Daddy's head, and I keep getting these scary thoughts, like I'm going to lose you and Charlotte and Mommy. Now, I know nothing's going to happen, not really, because the problem is all in my head, like a big tumor or something. Can you spell "tumor"? Do you know what it is? Well, I'm going to see a doctor and have it cut out, just cut out that bad old tumor, and then I won't be so frightened for no reason. . . .

He dared say nothing of the sort. He would only scare her.

He kissed her soft, warm cheek and let her go.

At the door to the garage, she paused and looked back at him. "More poem tonight?"

"You bet."

She said, "Reindeer salad . . ."

". . . reindeer soup . . ."

". . . all sorts of tasty . . ."

". . . reindeer goop," Marty finished.

"You know what, Daddy?"

"What?"

"You're *soooo* silly."

Giggling, Emily went into the garage. The *ca-chunk* of the door closing behind her was the most final sound Marty had ever heard.

He stared at the door, willing himself not to rush to it and jerk it open and shout at them to get back into the house.

He heard the big garage door rolling up.

The car engine turned over, chugged, caught, raced a little as Paige pumped the accelerator before shifting into reverse.

Marty hurried out of the kitchen, through the dining room, into the living room. He went to one of the front windows from which he could see the driveway. The plantation shutters were folded away from the window, so he stayed a couple of steps from the glass.

The white BMW backed down the driveway, out of the shadow of the house and into the late-November sunshine. Emily was riding up front with her mother, and Charlotte was in the rear seat.

As the car receded along the tree-lined street, Marty stepped so close to the living-room window that his forehead pressed against the cool glass. He tried to keep his family in view as long as possible, as if they were certain to survive *anything*—even falling airplanes and nuclear blasts—if he just did not let them out of his sight.

His last glimpse of the BMW was through a sudden veil of hot tears that he barely managed to repress.

Disturbed by the intensity of his emotional reaction to his family's departure, he turned away from the window and said savagely, "What the hell's the matter with me?"

After all, the girls were merely going to school and Paige to her office, where they went more days than not. They were following a routine that had never been dangerous before, and he had no logical reason to believe it was going to be dangerous today—or ever.

He looked at his wristwatch. 7:48.

His appointment with Dr. Guthridge was only slightly more than five hours away, but that seemed an interminable length of time. Anything could happen in five hours.

❄　　❄　　❄

Needles to Ludlow to Daggett.

Move, move, move.

9:04 Pacific Standard Time.

Barstow. Dry bleached town in a hard dry land. Stagecoaches stopped here long ago. Railroad yards. Waterless rivers. Cracked stucco, peeling paint. Green of trees faded by a perpetual layer of dust on the leaves. Motels, fast-food restaurants, more motels.

A service station. Gasoline. Men's room. Candy bars. Two cans of cold Coke.

Attendant too friendly. Chatty. Slow to make change. Little pig eyes. Fat cheeks. Hate him. Shut up, shut up, shut up.

Should shoot him. Should blow his head off. Satisfying. Can't risk it. Too many people around.

On the road again. Interstate 15. West. Candy bars and Coke at eighty miles an hour. Desolate plains. Hills of sand, shale. Volcanic rock. Many-armed Joshua trees standing sentinel.

As a pilgrim to a holy place, as a lemming to the sea, as a comet on its eternal course, westward, westward, trying to out-race the ocean-seeking sun.

* * *

Marty owned five guns.

He was not a hunter or collector. He didn't shoot skeet or take target practice for the fun of it. Unlike several people he knew, he hadn't armed himself out of fear of social collapse—though sometimes he saw signs of it everywhere. He could not even say that he *liked* guns, but he recognized the need for them in a troubled world.

He had purchased the weapons one by one for research purposes. As a mystery novelist, writing about cops and killers, he believed he had a responsibility to know whereof he wrote. Because he was not a gun hobbyist and had a finite amount of time to research all of the many backgrounds and subjects upon which each novel touched, minor mistakes were inevitable now and then, but he felt more comfortable writing about a weapon if he had fired it.

In his nightstand he kept an unloaded Korth .38 revolver and a box of cartridges. The Korth was a handmade weapon of the highest quality, produced in Germany. After learning to use it for a novel titled *The Deadly Twilight,* he had kept it for home defense.

Several times, he and Paige had taken the girls to an indoor shooting range to witness target practice, instilling in them a deep respect for the revolver. When Charlotte and Emily were old enough, he would teach them to use a gun, though one less powerful and with less recoil than the Korth. Firearm accidents virtually always resulted from ignorance. In Switzerland, where every male citizen was required to own a firearm to defend the country in times of trouble, gun instruction was universal and tragic accidents extremely rare.

He removed the .38 from the nightstand, loaded it, and took it to the garage, where he tucked it in the glove compartment of their second car, a green Ford Taurus. He wanted it for protection to and from his one-o'clock appointment with Dr. Guthridge.

A Mossberg 12-gauge shotgun, a Colt M16 A2 rifle, and two pistols—a Beretta Model 92 and a Smith & Wesson 5904—were stored in their original boxes inside a locked metal cabinet in one corner of the garage. There were also boxes of ammunition in every caliber required. He unpacked each weapon, which had been cleaned and oiled before being put away, and loaded it.

He put the Beretta in the kitchen, in an upper cabinet beside the stove, in front of a pair of ceramic casserole dishes. The girls would not happen upon it there before he called a family conference to explain the reasons for his extraordinary precautions—if he *could* explain.

The M16 went on an upper shelf in the foyer closet just inside the front door. He put the Smith & Wesson in his office desk, in the second drawer of the right-hand drawer bank, and slipped the Mossberg under the bed in the master bedroom.

Throughout his preparations, he worried that he was deranged, arming himself against a threat that did not exist. Considering the seven-minute fugue he had experienced on Saturday, messing around with weapons was the *last* thing he should be doing.

He had no proof of impending danger. He was operating sheerly on instinct, a soldier ant mindlessly constructing fortifications. Nothing like this had ever happened to him before. By nature he was a thinker, a planner, a brooder, and only last of all a man of action. But this was a *flood* of instinctual response, and he was swept away by it.

Then, just as he finished hiding the shotgun in the master bedroom, worries about his mental condition were abruptly outweighed by another consideration. The oppressive atmosphere of his recent dream was with him again, the feeling that some terrible weight was bearing down on him at a murderous speed. The air seemed to thicken. It was almost as bad as in the nightmare. And getting worse.

God help me, he thought—and was not sure if he was asking for protection from some unknown enemy or from dark impulses in himself.

✳   ✳   ✳

"I need . . ."

Dust devils. Dancing on the high desert.

Sunlight sparkling in broken bottles along the highway.

Fastest thing on the road. Passing cars, trucks. The landscape a blur. Scattered towns, all blurs.

Faster. Faster. As if being sucked into a black hole.

Past Victorville.

Past Apple Valley.

Through the Cajon Pass at forty-two hundred feet above sea level.

Then descending. Past San Bernardino. Onto the Riverside Freeway.

Riverside. Carona.

Through the Santa Ana Mountains.

"I need to be . . ."

South. The Costa Mesa Freeway.

The City of Orange. Tustin. In the southern California suburban maze.

Such powerful magnetism, pulling, pulling ruthlessly.

More than magnetism. Gravity. Down into the vortex of the black hole.

Switch to the Santa Ana Freeway.

Mouth dry. A bitter metallic taste. Heart pounding fiercely, pulse throbbing in his temples.

"I need to be someone."

Faster. As if tied to a massive anchor on an endless chain, plummeting into the lightless fathoms of a bottomless ocean trench.

Past Irvine, Laguna Hills, El Toro.

Into the dark heart of the mystery.

"*. . . need . . . need . . . need . . . need . . . need . . .*"

Mission Viejo. This exit. Yes.

Off the freeway.

Seeking the magnet. The enigmatic attractant.

All the way from Kansas City to find the unknown, to discover his strange and wondrous future. Home. Identity. Meaning.

Turn left here, two blocks, turn right. Unfamiliar streets. But to find the way, he needs only to give himself to the power that pulls him.

Mediterranean houses. Neatly trimmed lawns. Palm shadows on pale-yellow stucco walls.

Here.

That house.

To the curb. Stop. Half a block away.

Just a house like the others. Except. Something inside. Whatever he first sensed in faraway Kansas. Whatever draws him. Something.

The attractant.

Inside.

Waiting.

A wordless cry of triumph escapes him, and he shudders violently with relief. He no longer needs to seek his destiny. Although he does not yet know what it may be, he is certain that he's found it, and he sags in his seat, his sweaty hands slipping off the steering wheel, pleased to be at the end of the long journey.

He is more excited than he has ever been, filled with curiosity; however, released at last from the iron grip of compulsion, he loses his sense of urgency. His trip-hammering heart decelerates to a more normal number of beats per minute. His ears stop ringing, and he is able to breathe more deeply and evenly than he has for at least fifty miles. In startlingly short order, he is as outwardly calm and self-contained as he was in the big house in Kansas City, where he gratefully shared the tender intimacies of death with the man and woman in the antique Georgian bed.

✳　　✳　　✳

By the time Marty took the keys to the Taurus off the kitchen pegboard, stepped into the garage, locked the door to the house, and pushed the button to raise the automatic garage door, his awareness of impending danger was so acute and harrowing that he was on the edge of blind panic. In the feverish thrall of paranoia, he was convinced that he was being hunted by an uncanny enemy who employed not merely the usual five senses but paranormal means, a truly crazy notion, for God's sake, straight out of the *National Enquirer,* crazy yet inescapable because he actually could *feel* a presence . . . a violent stalking presence that was conscious of him, pressing him, probing. He felt as if a viscous fluid was squirting into his skull under tremendous pressure, compressing his brain, squeezing consciousness out of him. A very real physical effect was part of it, too, because he was as weighed down as a deep-sea diver under a crushing tonnage of water, joints aching, muscles burning, lungs reluctant to expand and accept new breath. Extreme sensitivity to every stimulant nearly incapacitated him: the hard clatter of the rising garage door was ear-splitting; intruding sunlight seared his eyes; and a musty odor—ordinarily too faint to be detected—exploded like a poisonous cloud of spores out of a corner of the garage, so pungent that it made him nauseous.

In an instant, the seizure passed, and he was in full control of himself. Although it had seemed as if his skull would burst, the internal pressure relented as abruptly as it had grown, and he no longer teetered on the brink of unconsciousness. The pain in his joints and muscles was gone, and the sunlight didn't sting his eyes. It was like snapping out of a nightmare—except he was awake on both sides of the snap.

Marty leaned against the Taurus. He was hesitant to believe that the worst was past, waiting tensely for another inexplicable wave of paranoid terror to batter him.

He looked out from the shadowy garage at the street, which was simultaneously familiar and strange, half expecting some monstrous phantasm to rise out of the pavement or descend through the sun-drenched air, a creature inhuman and merciless, ferocious and bent upon his destruction, the invisible specter of his nightmare now made flesh.

His confidence didn't return, and he couldn't stop shaking, but his apprehension gradually diminished to a tolerable level, until he was able to consider whether he dared to drive. What if a similarly disorienting spasm of fear hit him while he was behind the wheel? He would be virtually oblivious of stop signs, oncoming traffic, and hazards of all kinds.

More than ever, he needed to see Dr. Guthridge.

He wondered if he should go back into the house and call a taxi. But this wasn't New York City, streets aswarm with cabs; in southern California, the words "taxi service" were, more often than not, an oxymoron. By the time he could reach Guthridge's office by taxi, he might have missed his appointment.

He got in the car, started the engine. With wary concentration, he backed out of the garage and into the street, handling the wheel as stiffly as a ninety-year-old man acutely aware of the brittleness of his bones and the tenuous thread of his existence.

All the way to the doctor's office in Irvine, Marty Stillwater thought about Paige and Charlotte and Emily. By the treachery of his own weak flesh, he could be denied the satisfaction of seeing the girls become women, the pleasure of growing old at his wife's side. Although he believed in a world beyond death where eventually he might be reunited with those he loved, life was so precious that even the promise of a blissful eternity would not compensate for the loss of a few years on this side of the veil.

❋　　❋　　❋

From half a block away, the killer watches the car slowly back out of the garage.

As the Ford turns away from him and gradually recedes through the vinegar-gold autumn sunshine, he realizes the magnet which drew him from Kansas is in that car. Perhaps it is the dimly seen man behind the steering wheel—though it might not be a person at all but a talisman hidden elsewhere in the vehicle, a magical object beyond his understanding and to which his destiny is linked for reasons yet unclear.

The killer almost starts the Honda to follow the attractant, but decides the stranger in the Ford will return sooner or later.

He puts on his shoulder holster, slips the pistol into it, and shrugs into the leather jacket.

From the glove compartment, he removes the zippered leather case that contains his set of burglary tools. It includes seven spring-steel picks, an L-shaped tension tool, and a miniature aerosol can of graphite lubricant.

He gets out of the car and proceeds boldly along the sidewalk toward the house.

At the end of the driveway stands a white mailbox on which is stenciled a single name—STILLWATER. Those ten black letters seem to possess symbolic power. Still water. Calm. Peace. He has found still water. He has come through much turbulence, violent rapids and whirlpools, and now he has found a place where he can rest, where his soul will be soothed.

Between the garage and the property-line fence, he opens the gravity latch on a wrought-iron gate. He follows a walkway flanked by the garage on his left and a head-high eugenia hedge on his right, all the way to the rear of the house.

The shallow backyard is lushly planted. It boasts mature ficus trees and a continuation of the sideyard eugenia hedge, which screen him from the prying eyes of neighbors.

The patio is sheltered by an open-beam redwood cover through which thorny trailers of bougainvillea are densely intertwined. Even on this last day of November, clusters of blood-red flowers fringe the patio roof. The concrete floor is spattered with fallen petals, as though a hard-fought battle was waged here.

A kitchen door and large sliding glass door provide two possible entrances from the patio. Both are locked.

The sliding door, beyond which he can see a deserted family room with comfortable furniture and a large television, is further secured by a wooden pole wedged into the interior track. If he gets through the lock, he nevertheless will need to break the glass to reach inside and remove the pole.

He knocks sharply on the other door, although the window beside it reveals that no one is in the kitchen. When there is no response, he knocks again with the same result.

From his compact kit of burglary tools, he withdraws the can of graphite. Crouching before the door, he sprays the lubricant into the lock. Dirt, rust, or other contamination can bind the pin tumblers.

He trades the graphite spray for the tension tool and that pick known as a "rake." He inserts the L-shaped wrench first to maintain the necessary tension on the lock core. He pushes the rake into the key channel as deep as it will go, then brings it up until he feels it press against the pins. Squinting into the lock, he rapidly draws the rake out, but it does not raise all of the pin tumblers to their shear point, so he tries again, and again, and finally on the sixth try the channel seems to be clear.

He turns the knob.

The door opens.

He half expects an alarm to go off, but there is no siren. A quick scan of the header and jamb fails to reveal magnetic switches, so there must not be a silent alarm, either.

After he puts the tools away and zippers shut the leather case, he steps across the threshold and softly closes the door behind him.

He stands for a while in the cool, shadowy kitchen, absorbing the vibrations, which are good. This house welcomes him. Here, his future begins, and it will be immeasurably brighter than his confused and amnesia-riddled past.

As he moves out of the kitchen to explore the premises, he does not draw the P7 from his shoulder holster. He is sure that no one is at home. He senses no danger, only opportunity.

"I need to be someone," he tells the house, as if it is a living entity with the power to grant his wishes.

The ground floor offers nothing of interest. The usual rooms are filled with comfortable but unremarkable furniture.

Upstairs, he stops only briefly at each room, getting an overall picture of the second-floor layout before taking time for a thorough investigation. There's a master bedroom with attached bath, walk-in closet . . . a guest bedroom . . . kids' room . . . another bath . . .

The final bedroom at the end of the hall—which puts him at the front of the house—is used as an office. It contains a big desk and computer system, but it's more cozy than businesslike. A plump sofa stands under the shuttered windows, a stained-glass lamp on the desk.

One of the two longest walls is covered with paintings hung in a double row, frames almost touching. Although the pieces of the collection are obviously by more than one artist, the subject matter, without exception, is dark and violent, rendered with unimpeachable skill: twisted shadows, disembodied eyes wide with terror, a Ouija board on which stands a blood-spotted trivet, ink-black palm trees silhouetted against an ominous sunset, a face distorted by a funhouse mirror, the gleaming steel blades of sharp knives and scissors, a mean street where menacing figures lurk just beyond the sour-yellow glow of street lamps, leafless trees with coaly limbs, a hot-eyed raven perched upon a bleached skull, pistols, revolvers, shotguns, an ice pick, meat cleaver, hatchet, a queerly stained hammer lying obscenely on a silk negligee and lace-trimmed bed-sheet . . .

He likes this artwork.

It speaks to him.

This is life as he knows it.

Turning from the gallery wall, he clicks on the stained-glass lamp and marvels at its multi-hued luminous beauty.

In the clear sheet of glass that protects the top of the desk, the mirror-image circles and ovals and teardrops of color are still lovely but darker than when viewed directly. In some indefinable way, they are also foreboding.

Leaning forward, he sees the twin ovals of his eyes staring back at him from the polished glass. Glimmering with their own tiny reflections of the mosaic lamplight, they seem to be not eyes, in fact, but the luminous sensors of a machine—or, if eyes, then the fevered eyes of something soulless—and he quickly looks away from them before too much self-examination leads him to fearful thoughts and intolerable conclusions.

"I need to be someone," he says nervously.

His gaze falls upon a photograph in a silver frame, which also stands on the desk. A woman and two little girls. A pretty trio. Smiling.

He picks up the photograph to study it more closely. He presses one fingertip against the woman's face and wishes he could touch her for real, feel her warm and pliant skin. He slides his finger across the glass, first touching the blond-haired child, and then the dark-haired pixie.

After a minute or two, when he moves away from the desk, he carries the photograph with him. The three faces in the portrait are so appealing that he needs to be able to look at them again whenever the desire arises.

As he investigates the titles on the spines of the volumes in the book-cases, he makes a discovery that gives him an understanding, however incomplete, of why he was drawn from the gray autumnal plains of the Midwest to the post-Thanksgiving sun of California.

On a few of the shelves, the books—mystery novels—are by the same author: Martin Stillwater. The surname is the one he saw on the mailbox outside.

He puts aside the silver-framed portrait and withdraws a few of these novels from the shelves, surprised to see that some of the dustjacket illustrations are familiar because the original paintings are hanging on the gallery wall that so fascinated him. Each title appears in a variety of translations: French, German, Italian, Dutch, Swedish, Danish, Japanese, and several other languages.

But nothing is as interesting as the author's photo on the back of each jacket. He studies them for a long time, tracing Stillwater's features with one finger.

Intrigued, he peruses the copy on the jacket flaps. Then he reads the first page of a book, the first page of another, and another.

He happens upon a dedication page in the front of one book and reads what is printed there: *This opus is for my mother and father, Jim and Alice Stillwater, who taught me to be an honest man—and who can't be blamed if I am able to* think *like a criminal.*

His mother and father. He stares in astonishment at their names. He has no memory of them, cannot picture their faces or recall where they might live.

He returns to the desk to consult the Rolodex. He discovers Jim and Alice Stillwater in Mammoth Lakes, California. The street address means nothing to him, and he wonders if it is the house in which he grew up.

He must love his parents. He dedicated a book to them. Yet they are ciphers to him. So much has been lost.

He returns to the bookshelves. Opening the U.S. or British edition of every title in the collection to study the dedication, he eventually finds: *To Paige, my perfect wife, on whom all of my best female characters are based—excluding, of course, the homicidal psychopaths.*

And two volumes later: *To my daughters, Charlotte and Emily, with the hope they will read this book one day when they are grown up and will know that the daddy in this story speaks my own heart when he talks with such conviction and emotion about his feelings for his own little girls.*

Putting the books aside, he picks up the photograph once more and holds it in both hands with something like reverence.

The attractive blonde is surely Paige. A perfect wife.

The two girls are Charlotte and Emily, although he has no way of knowing which is which. They look sweet and obedient.

Paige, Charlotte, Emily.

At last he has found his life. This is where he belongs. This is home. The future begins now.

Paige, Charlotte, Emily.

This is the family toward which destiny has led him.

"I need to be Marty Stillwater," he says, and he is thrilled to have found, at last, his own warm place in this cold and lonely world.

TWO

1.

Dr. Paul Guthridge's office suite had three examination rooms. Over the years, Marty had been in all of them. They were identical to one another, indistinguishable from rooms in doctors' offices from Maine to Texas: pale-blue walls, stainless-steel fixtures, otherwise white-on-white; scrub sink, stool, an eye chart. The place had no more charm than a morgue—though a better smell.

Marty sat on the edge of a padded examination table that was protected by a continuous roll of paper sheeting. He was shirtless, and the room was cool. Though he was still wearing his pants, he felt naked, vulnerable. In his mind's eye, he saw himself having a catatonic seizure, being unable to talk or move or even blink, whereupon the physician would mistake him for dead, strip him naked, wire an ID tag to his big toe, tape his eyelids shut, and ship him off to the coroner for processing.

Although it earned him a living, a suspense writer's imagination made him more aware of the constant proximity of death than were most people. Every dog was a potential rabies carrier. Every strange van passing through the neighborhood was driven by a sexual psychopath who would kidnap and murder any child left unattended for more than three seconds. Every can of soup in the pantry was botulism waiting to happen.

He was not particularly afraid of doctors—though he was not comforted by them, either.

What troubled him was *the whole idea* of medical science, not because he distrusted it but because, irrationally, its very existence was a reminder that life was tenuous, death inescapable. He didn't need reminders. He already possessed an acute awareness of mortality, and spent his life trying to cope with it.

Determined not to sound like an hysteric while describing his symptoms to Guthridge, Marty recounted the odd experiences of the past three days in a quiet, matter-of-fact voice. He tried to use clinical rather than emotional terms, beginning with the seven-minute fugue in his office and ending with the abrupt panic attack he had suffered as he had been leaving the house to drive to the doctor's office.

Guthridge was an excellent internist—in part because he was a good listener—although he didn't look the role. At forty-five, he appeared ten years younger than his age, and he had a boyish manner. Today he wore tennis shoes, chinos, and a Mickey Mouse sweatshirt. In the summer, he favored colorful Hawaiian shirts. On those rare occasions when he wore a traditional white smock over slacks, shirt, and tie, he claimed to be "playing doctor" or "on strict probation from the American Medical Association's dress-code committee," or "suddenly overwhelmed by the godlike responsibilities of my office."

Paige thought Guthridge was an exceptional physician, and the girls regarded him with the special affection usually reserved for a favorite uncle.

Marty liked him too.

He suspected the doctor's eccentricities were not calculated entirely to amuse patients and put them at ease. Like Marty, Guthridge seemed morally offended by the very fact of death. As a younger man, perhaps he'd been drawn to medicine because he saw the physician as a knight battling dragons incarnated as illnesses and diseases. Young knights believe that noble intentions, skill, and faith will prevail over evil. Older knights know better—and sometimes use humor as a weapon to stave off bitterness and despair. Guthridge's quips and Mickey Mouse sweatshirts might relax his patients, but they were also his armor against the hard realities of life and death.

"Panic attack? You, of all people, suffering a panic attack?" Paul Guthridge asked doubtfully.

Marty said, "Hyperventilating, heart pounding, felt like I was going to explode—sounds like a panic attack to me."

"Sounds like sex."

Marty smiled. "Trust me, it wasn't sex."

"You could be right," Guthridge said with a sigh. "It's been so long, I'm not sure what sex was like exactly. Believe me, Marty, this is a bad decade to be a bachelor, so many really nasty diseases out there. You meet a new girl, date her, give her a chaste kiss when you take her home—and then wait to see if your lips are going to rot and fall off."

"That's a swell image."

"Vivid, huh? Maybe I should've been a writer." He began to examine Marty's left eye with an ophthalmoscope. "Have you been having unusually intense headaches?"

"One headache over the weekend. But nothing unusual."

"Repeated spells of dizziness?"

"No."

"Temporary blindness, noticeable narrowing of peripheral vision?"

"Nothing like that."

Turning his attention to Marty's right eye, Guthridge said, "As for being a writer—other doctors have done it, you know. Michael Crichton, Robin Cook, Somerset Maugham—"

"Seuss."

"Don't be sarcastic. Next time I have to give you an injection, I might use a horse syringe."

"It always feels like you do anyway. I'll tell you something, being a writer isn't half as romantic as people think."

"At least you don't have to handle urine samples," Guthridge said, setting aside the ophthalmoscope.

With squiggly ghost images of the instrument light still dancing in his eyes, Marty said, "When a writer's first starting out, a lot of editors and agents and movie producers treat him as if he *is* a urine sample."

"Yeah, but now you're a celebrity," Guthridge said, plugging his stethoscope ear tips in place.

"Far from it," Marty objected.

Guthridge pressed the icy steel of the stethoscope diaphragm against Marty's chest. "Okay, breathe deeply . . . hold . . . breathe out . . . and again." After listening to Marty's lungs as well as his heart, the doctor put the stethoscope aside. "Hallucinations?"

"No."

"Strange smells?"

"No."

"Things taste the way they should? I mean, you haven't been eating ice cream and it suddenly tasted bitter or oniony, nothing like that?"

"Nothing like that."

As he wrapped the pressure cuff of a sphygmomanometer around Marty's arm, Guthridge said, "Well, all I know is, to get into *People* magazine, you've got to be a celebrity of one kind or another—rock singer, actor, smarmy politician, murderer, or maybe the guy with the world's largest collection of ear wax. So if you think you aren't a celebrity author, then I want to know who you've killed and exactly how much damn ear wax you own."

"How'd you know about *People*?"

"We subscribe for the waiting room." He pumped air into the cuff until it was tight, then read the falling mercury on the gauge before he continued: "The latest copy was in this morning's mail. My receptionist showed it to me, really amused. She said you were the least likely Mr. Murder she could imagine."

Confused, Marty said, "Mr. Murder?"

"You haven't seen the piece?" Guthridge asked as he pulled off the pressure cuff, punctuating his question with the ugly sound of a Velcro seal tearing open.

"Not yet, no. They don't show it to you in advance. You mean, in the article, they call me Mr. Murder?"

"Well, it's sort of cute."

"Cute?" Marty winced. "I wonder if Philip Roth would think it was cute to be 'Mr. Litterateur' or Terry McMillan 'Ms. Black Saga.' "

"You know what they say—all publicity is good publicity."

"That was Nixon's first reaction to Watergate, wasn't it?"

"We actually take two subscriptions to *People*. I'll give you one of our copies when you leave." Guthridge grinned impishly. "You know, until I saw the magazine, I never realized what a really scary guy you are."

Marty groaned. "I was afraid of this."

"It's not bad really. Knowing you, I suspect you'll find it a little embarrassing. But it won't kill you."

"What *is* going to kill me, Doc?"

Frowning, Guthridge said, "Based on this exam, I'd say old age. From all outward signs, you're in good shape."

"The key word is 'outward,' " Marty said.

"Right. I'd like you to have some tests. It'll be on an out-patient basis at Hoag Hospital."

"I'm ready," Marty said grimly, though he was not ready at all.

"Oh, not today. They won't have an opening until at least tomorrow, probably Wednesday."

"What're you looking for with these tests?"

"Brain tumors, lesions. Severe blood chemistry imbalances. Or maybe a shift in the position of the pineal gland, putting pressure on surrounding brain tissue—which could cause symptoms similar to some of yours. Other things. But don't worry about it because I'm pretty sure we're going to draw a blank. Most likely, your problem is simply stress."

"That's what Paige said."

"See? You could've saved my fee."

"Be straight with me, Doc."

"I am being straight."

"I don't mind saying this scares me."

Guthridge nodded sympathetically. "Of course it does. But listen, I've seen symptoms far more bizarre and severe than yours—and it turns out to be stress."

"Psychological."

"Yes, but nothing long-term. You aren't going mad, either, if that's what you're worried about. Try to relax, Marty. We'll know where we stand by the end of the week." When he needed it, Guthridge could call upon a demeanor as reassuring—and a bedside manner as soothing—as that of any gray-haired medical eminence in a three-piece suit. He slipped Marty's shirt from one of the clothes hooks on the back of the door and handed it to him. The faint gleam in his eye betrayed another shift in mood: "Now, when I book time at the hospital, what patient name should I give to them? Martin Stillwater or Martin Murder?"

2.

He explores his home. He is eager to learn about his new family.

Because he is most intrigued by the thought of himself as a father, he begins in the girls' bedroom. For a while he stands just inside the door, studying the two distinctly different sides of the room.

He wonders which of his young daughters is the effervescent one who decorates her walls with posters of dazzlingly colorful hot-air balloons and leaping dancers, who keeps a gerbil and other pets in wire cages and glass terrariums. He still holds the photograph of his wife and children, but the smiling faces in it reveal nothing of their personalities.

The second daughter is apparently contemplative, favoring quiet landscapes on her walls. Her bed is neatly made, the pillows plumped just-so. Her storybooks are shelved in orderly fashion, and her corner desk is free of clutter.

When he slides open the mirrored closet door, he finds a similar division in the hanging clothes. Those to the left are arranged both according to the type of garment and color. Those to the right are in no particular order, askew on the hangers, and jammed against one another in a way that virtually assures wrinkling.

Because the smaller jeans and dresses are on the left side of the closet, he can be sure that the neat and contemplative girl is the younger of the two. He raises the photograph and stares at her. The pixie. So cute. He still does not know whether she is Charlotte or Emily.

He goes to the desk in the older daughter's side of the room and stares down at the clutter: magazines, schoolbooks, one yellow hair ribbon, a butterfly barrette, a few scattered sticks of Black Jack chewing gum, colored pencils, a tangled pair of pink kneesocks, an empty Coke can, coins, and a Game Boy.

He opens one of the textbooks, then another. Both of them have the same name penciled in front: Charlotte Stillwater.

The older and less disciplined girl is Charlotte. The younger girl who keeps her belongings neat is Emily.

Again, he looks at their faces in the photograph.

Charlotte is pretty, and her smile is sweet. However, if he is going to have trouble with either of his children, it will be with this one.

He will not tolerate disorder in his house. Everything must be perfect. Neat and clean and happy.

In lonely hotel rooms in strange cities, awake in the darkness, he has ached with need and has not understood what would satisfy his longing. Now he knows that being Martin Stillwater—father to these children, husband to this wife—is the destiny that will fill the terrible void and at last bring him contentment. He is grateful to whatever power has led him here, and he is determined to fulfill his responsibilities to his wife, his children, and society. He wants an ideal family like those he has seen in certain favorite movies, wants to be kind like Jimmy Stewart in *It's a Wonderful Life* and wise like Gregory Peck in *To Kill a Mockingbird* and revered like both of them, and he will do whatever is necessary to ensure a loving, harmonious, and orderly home.

He has seen *The Bad Seed,* too, and he knows that some children can destroy a home and all hope of harmony because they are seething with the potential for evil. Charlotte's slovenly habits and strange menagerie strongly indicate that she is capable of disobedience and possibly violence.

When snakes appear in movies, they are *always* symbols of evil, dangerous to the innocent; therefore, the snake in the terrarium is chilling proof of this child's corruption and her need for guidance. She keeps other reptiles as well, a couple of rodents, and an ugly black beetle in a glass jar—all of which the movies have taught him to associate with the powers of darkness.

He studies the photograph again, marveling at how innocent Charlotte looks.

But remember the girl in *The Bad Seed.* She appeared to be an angel yet was thoroughly evil.

Being Martin Stillwater may not prove as easy as he had first thought. Charlotte might be a real handful.

Fortunately, he has seen *Lean on Me* in which Morgan Freeman is a high school principal bringing order to a school overwhelmed by anarchy, and he has seen *The Principal* starring Jim Belushi, so he knows that even bad kids really want discipline. They will respond properly if adults have the guts to insist upon rules of behavior.

If Charlotte is disobedient and stubborn, he will punish her until she learns to be a good little girl. He will not fail her. At first she will hate him for denying her privileges, for confining her to her room, for hurting her if that becomes necessary, but in time she will see that he has her best interests at heart, and she will learn to love him and understand how wise he is.

In fact he can visualize the triumphant moment when, after so much struggle, her rehabilitation is ensured. Her realization that she has been wrong and that he has been a good father will culminate in a touching scene. They will both cry. She will throw herself in his arms, remorseful and ashamed. He will hug her very tightly and tell her it's all right, all right, don't cry. She will say, "Oh, Daddy," in a tremulous voice, and cling fiercely to him, and thereafter everything will be perfect between them.

He yearns for that sweet triumph. He can even hear the soaring and emotional music that will accompany it.

He turns away from Charlotte's side of the room, goes to his younger daughter's neat bed.

Emily. The pixie. She will never give him any trouble. She is the good daughter.

He will hold her on his lap and read to her from storybooks. He will take her to the zoo, and her little hand will be lost in his. He will buy her popcorn at the movies, and they will sit side by side in the darkness, laughing at the latest Disney animated feature.

Her big dark eyes will adore him.

Sweet Emily. Dear Emily.

Almost reverently, he pulls back the chenille bedspread. The blanket. The top sheet. He stares at the bottom sheet on which she slept last night, and the pillows on which her delicate head rested.

His heart swells with affection, tenderness.

He puts one hand against the sheet, slides it back and forth, back and forth, feeling the fabric on which her young body has so recently lain.

Every night he will tuck her into bed. She will press her small mouth to his cheek, such warm little kisses, and her breath will have the sweet peppermint aroma of toothpaste.

He bends down to smell the sheets.

"Emily," he says softly.

Oh, how he longs to be her father and to look into those dark yet limpid eyes, those huge and adoring eyes.

With a sigh, he returns to Charlotte's side of the room. He drops the silver-framed photograph of his family on her bed, and he studies the kept creatures housed on the bookless bookshelves.

Some of the wild things watch him.

He begins with the gerbil. When he unlatches the door and reaches into its cage, the timid creature cowers in a far corner, paralyzed with fear, sensing his intent. He seizes it, withdraws it from the cage. Although it tries to squirm free, he grips its body firmly in his right hand, its head in his left, and wrenches sharply, snapping its neck. A brittle, dry sound. Its cry is shrill but brief.

He throws the dead gerbil on the brightly colored bedspread.

This will be the beginning of Charlotte's discipline.

She will hate him for it. But only for a while.

Eventually she will realize that these are unsuitable pets for a little girl.

Symbols of evil. Reptiles, rodents, beetles. The sort of creatures witches use as their familiars, to communicate between them and Satan.

He has learned all about witches' familiars from horror movies. If there was a cat in the house he would kill it as well, without hesitation, because sometimes they are cute and innocent, just cats and nothing more, but sometimes they are the very spawn of Hell. By inviting such creatures into your home, you risk inviting the devil himself.

One day Charlotte will understand. And be grateful.

Eventually she will love him.

They will all love him.

He will be a good husband and father.

Much smaller than the gerbil, the frightened mouse quivers in his fist, its tail hanging below his clenched fingers, only its head protruding above. It empties its bladder. He grimaces at the warm dampness and, in disgust, squeezes with all his strength, crushing the life out of the filthy little beast.

He tosses it onto the bed beside the dead gerbil.

The harmless garden snake in the glass terrarium makes no effort to slither away from him. He holds it by the tail and snaps it as if it is a whip, snaps it again, then lashes it hard against the wall, again, and a third time. When he dangles it before his face, it is entirely limp, and he sees that its skull is crushed.

He coils it next to the gerbil and the mouse.

The beetle and the turtle make satisfying crunching sounds when he stomps them under the heel of his shoe. He arranges their oozing remains on the bedspread.

Only the lizard escapes him. When he slides the lid partway off its terrarium and reaches in for it, the chameleon scampers up his arm, quicker than the eye, and leaps off his shoulder. He spins around, searching for it, and sees it on the nearby vanity, where it skitters between a hairbrush and a comb, onto a jewelry box. There it freezes and begins to change color to match its background, but when he tries to snatch it up, it darts away, off the dresser, onto the floor, across the room, under Emily's bed, out of sight.

He decides to let it go.

This might be for the best. When Paige and the girls get home, the four of them will search for it together. When they find it, he will kill it in front of Charlotte or perhaps require her to kill it herself. That will be a good lesson. Thereafter, she will bring no more inappropriate pets into the Stillwater house.

3.

In the parking lot outside of the three-story, Spanish-style business complex where Dr. Guthridge had his offices, while a gusty wind harried dead leaves across the pavement, Marty sat in his car and read the article about himself in *People*. Two photographs and a page's worth of prose were spread over three pages of the magazine. At least for the few minutes he took to read the piece, all of his other worries were forgotten.

The black headline made him flinch even though he knew what it would be—**MR. MURDER**—but he was equally embarrassed by the subhead in smaller letters: IN SOUTHERN CALIFORNIA, MYSTERY NOVELIST MARTIN STILL-WATER SEES DARKNESS AND EVIL WHERE OTHERS SEE ONLY SUNSHINE.

He felt it portrayed him as a brooding pessimist who dressed entirely in black and lurked on beaches and among the palm trees, glowering at anyone who dared to have fun, tediously expounding on the inherent vileness of the human species. At best it implied he was a theatrical phony costuming himself in what he thought was the most commercial image for a mystery novelist.

Possibly he was over-reacting. Paige would tell him that he was too sensitive about these things. That was what she always said, and she usually made him feel better, whether he could bring himself to believe her or not.

He examined the photographs before reading the piece.

In the first and largest picture, he was standing in the yard behind the house, against a backdrop of trees and twilight sky. He looked demented.

The photographer, Ben Walenko, had been given instructions to induce Marty into a pose deemed fitting for a mystery novelist, so he had come with props he assumed Marty would brandish with suitable expressions of malevolent intent: an axe, an enormous knife, an ice pick, and a gun. When Marty politely declined to use the props and also refused to wear a trenchcoat with the collar turned up and a fedora pulled low on his forehead, the photographer agreed it was ludicrous for an adult to play dress-up, and suggested they avoid the usual clichés in favor of shots portraying him simply as a writer and an ordinary human being.

Now it was obvious that Walenko had been clever enough to get what he wanted without props, after lulling his subject into a false sense of security. The backyard had seemed an innocuous setting. However, through a combination of the deep shadows of dusk, looming trees, ominous clouds backlit by the final somber light of day, the strategic placement of studio lights, and an extreme camera angle, the photographer succeeded in making Marty appear weird. Furthermore, of the twenty exposures taken in the backyard, the editors had chosen the worst: Marty was squinting; his features were distorted; the photographer's lights were reflected in his slitted eyes, which seemed to be glowing like the eyes of a zombie.

The second photograph was taken in his study. He was sitting at his desk, facing the camera. He was recognizably himself in this one, though by now he preferred *not* to be recognizable, for it seemed that the only way he could maintain a shred of dignity was to have his true appearance remain a mystery; a combination of shadows and the peculiar light of the stained-glass lamp, even in a black-and-white shot, made him resemble a Gypsy fortuneteller who had glimpsed a portent of disaster in his crystal ball.

He was convinced that a lot of the modern world's problems could be attributed to the popular media's saturation of society and its tendency not merely to simplify all issues to the point of absurdity but to confuse fiction and reality. Television news emphasized dramatic footage over facts, sensationalism over substance, seeking ratings with the same tools employed by the producers of prime-time cop and courtroom dramas. Documentaries about real historical figures had become "docudramas" in which accurate details of famous lives and events were relentlessly subordinated to entertainment values or even to the personal fantasies of the show's creators, grossly distorting the past. Patent medicines were sold in TV commercials by performers who also played doctors in highly rated programs, as if they had in fact graduated from Harvard Medical School instead of merely having attended an acting class or two. Politicians made cameo appearances on episodes of situation comedies. Actors in those comedies appeared at political rallies. Not long ago the Vice-President of the United States engaged in a protracted argument with a fictional television reporter from a sitcom. The public confused actors *and* politicians with the roles they played. A mystery writer was supposed to be not merely like a character in one of his books but like the cartoonish archetype of the most common character in the entire genre. And year by troubled year, fewer people were able to think clearly about important issues or separate fantasy from reality.

Marty had been determined not to contribute to that sickness, but he had been suckered. Now he was fixed in the public mind as Martin Stillwater, creepy and mysterious author of creepy murder mysteries, preoccupied with the dark side of life, as brooding and strange as any of the characters about whom he wrote.

Sooner or later a disturbed citizen, having confused Marty's manipulation of fictional people in novels for the manipulation of actual people in real life, would arrive at his house in an old van decorated with signs accusing him of having killed John Lennon, John Kennedy, Rick Nelson, and God-alone-knew-who-else, even though he was an infant when Lee Harvey Oswald pulled the trigger on Kennedy (or when seventeen thousand and thirty-seven homosexual conspirators pulled the trigger, if you believed Oliver Stone's movie). Something similar had happened to Stephen King, hadn't it? And Salman Rushdie had sure experienced a few years as suspenseful as any endured by a character in a Robert Ludlum extravaganza.

Chagrined by the bizarre image the magazine had given him, flushed with embarrassment, Marty surveyed the parking lot to be sure no one was watching him as he read about himself. A couple of people were going to and from their cars, but they were paying no attention to him.

Clouds had crept into the previously sunny day. The wind spun dead leaves into a miniature tornado that danced across an empty expanse of blacktop.

He read the article, punctuating it with sighs and mutters. Although it contained a few minor errors, the text was generally factual. But the spin on it matched the photographs. Spooky old Marty Stillwater. What a dour and gloomy guy. Sees a criminal's wicked grin behind every smile. Works in a dimly lighted office, almost dark, and *says* he's just trying to reduce the glare on the computer screen (wink, wink).

His refusal to allow Charlotte and Emily to be photographed, based upon a desire to protect their privacy and to guard against their being teased by schoolmates, was interpreted as a fear of kidnappers lurking under every bush. After all, he had written a novel about a kidnapping a few years ago.

Paige, "as pretty and cerebral as a Martin Stillwater heroine," was said to be a "psychologist whose own job requires her to probe into the darkest secrets of her patients," as if she was engaged not in the counseling of children troubled by their parents' divorces or the death of a loved one but in the deep analysis of the era's most savage serial killers.

"Spooky old Paige Stillwater," he said aloud. "Well, why else would she have married me if she wasn't already a little weird?"

He told himself he was over-reacting.

Closing the magazine, he said, "Thank God I didn't let the girls participate. They'd have come out of it looking like the children in 'The Addams Family.' "

Again he told himself that he was over-reacting, but his mood didn't improve. He felt violated, trivialized; and the fact that he was talking aloud to himself seemed, annoyingly, to validate his new national reputation as an amusing eccentric.

He twisted the key in the ignition, started the engine.

As he drove across the parking lot toward the busy street, Marty was troubled by the feeling that his life had taken more than merely a temporary turn for the worse with the fugue on Saturday, that the magazine article was yet another signpost on this new dark route, and that he would travel a long distance on rough pavement before rediscovering the smooth highway that he had lost.

A whirlwind of leaves burst over the car, startling him. The dry foliage rasped across the hood and roof, like the claws of a beast determined to get inside.

4.

Hunger overcomes him. He has not slept since Friday night, has driven across half the country at high speed, in bad weather more than not, and has experienced an exciting and emotional hour and a half in the Stillwater house, confronting his destiny. His stores of energy are depleted. He is shaky and weak-kneed.

In the kitchen he raids the refrigerator, piling food on the oak breakfast table. He consumes several slices of Swiss cheese, half a loaf of bread, a few pickles, the better part of a pound of bacon, mixing it all together without actually bothering to make sandwiches, a bite of this and a bite of that, chewing the bacon raw because he doesn't want to waste time cooking it, eating fast and with single-minded fixation on the feast, ravenous, oblivious of manners, urgently washing down everything with big swallows of cold beer that foams over his chin. There is so much he wants to do before his wife and kids return home, and he doesn't know quite when to expect them. The fatty meat is cloying, so periodically he dips into a wide-mouth jar of mayonnaise and scoops out thick wads of the stuff, sucking it off his fingers to lubricate a mouthful of food that he finds hard to swallow even with the aid of another bottle of Corona. He concludes his meal with two thick slices of chocolate cake, washing those down with beer as well, whereafter he hastily cleans up the mess with paper towels and washes his hands at the sink.

He is revitalized.

With the silver-framed photograph in hand, he returns to the second floor, taking the stairs two at a time. He proceeds to the master bedroom, where he clicks on both nightstand lamps.

For a while he stares at the king-size bed, excited by the prospect of having sex with Paige. Making love. When it is done with someone for whom you truly care, it is called "making love."

He truly cares for her.

He *must* care.

After all, she is his wife.

He knows that her face is good, excellent, with a full mouth and fine bone structure and laughing eyes, but he can't tell much about her body from the photograph. He imagines that her breasts are full, belly flat, legs long and shapely, and he is eager to lie with her, deep inside of her.

At the dresser, he opens drawers until he finds her lingerie. He caresses a half-slip, the smooth cups of a brassiere, a lace-trimmed camisole. He removes a pair of silky panties from the drawer and rubs his face with them, breathing deeply while repeatedly whispering her name.

Making love will be unimaginably different from the sweaty sex he has known with sluts picked up in bars, because those experiences have always left him feeling empty, alienated, frustrated that his desperate need for true intimacy is unfulfilled. Frustration fosters anger; anger leads to hatred; hatred generates violence—and violence sometimes soothes. But that pattern will not apply when he makes love to Paige, for he belongs in her arms as he has belonged in no others. With her, his need will be satisfied every bit as much as will his desire. Together, they will achieve a union beyond anything he can imagine, perfect oneness, bliss, spiritual as well as physical consummation, all of which he has seen in countless movies, bodies bathed in golden light, ecstasy, a fierce intensity of pleasure possible only in the presence of love. Afterward, he will not have to kill her because then they will be as one, two hearts beating in harmony, no reason for killing anyone, transcendent, all needs gloriously satisfied.

The prospect of romance leaves him almost breathless.

"I will make you so happy, Paige," he promises her picture.

Realizing he hasn't bathed since Saturday, wanting to be clean for her, he returns her silken panties to the stack from which he had plucked them, closes the dresser drawer, and goes into his bathroom to shower.

He strips out of the clothes he took from the motorhome closet of the white-haired retiree, Jack, in Oklahoma on Sunday, hardly twenty-four hours ago. After wadding each garment into a tight ball, he stuffs it into a brass wastebasket.

The shower stall is spacious, and the water is wonderfully hot. He works up a heavy lather with the bar of soap, and soon the clouds of steam are laden with an almost intoxicating floral aroma.

After drying off on a yellow towel, he searches bathroom drawers until he finds his toiletries. He uses a roll-on deodorant and then combs his wet hair straight back from his forehead to let it dry naturally. He shaves with an electric razor, splashes on some lime-scented cologne, and brushes his teeth.

He feels like a new man.

In his half of the large walk-in closet, he selects a pair of cotton briefs, blue jeans, a blue-and-black-checkered flannel shirt, athletic socks, and a pair of Nikes. Everything fits perfectly.

It feels so good to be home.

5.

Paige stood at one of the windows and watched the gray clouds roll in from the west, driven by a Pacific wind. As they came, the earth below them darkened, and sun-mantled buildings put on cloaks of shadows.

The inner sanctum of her three-room, sixth-floor office suite had two large panes of glass that provided an uninspiring view of a freeway, a shopping center, and the jammed-together roofs of housing tracts that receded across Orange County apparently to infinity. She would have enjoyed a panoramic ocean vista or a window on a lushly planted courtyard, but that would have meant higher rent, which had been out of the question during the early years of Marty's writing career when she'd been their primary breadwinner.

Now, in spite of his growing success and impressive income, obligating herself to a pricier lease at a new location was still imprudent. Even a prospering literary career was an uncertain living. The owner of a fresh-produce store, when ill, had employees who would continue to sell oranges and apples in his absence, but if Marty became ill, the entire enterprise screeched to a halt.

And Marty was ill. Perhaps seriously.

No, she wouldn't think about that. They knew nothing for sure. It was more like the old Paige, the pre-Marty Paige, to worry about mere possibilities instead of about only what was already fact.

Appreciate the moment, Marty would tell her. He was a born therapist. Sometimes she thought she'd learned more from him than from the courses she had taken to earn her doctorate in psychology.

Appreciate the moment.

In truth the constant bustle of the scene beyond the window was invigorating. And whereas she had once been so predisposed to gloom that bad weather could negatively affect her mood, all of these years with Marty and his usually unshakable good cheer had made it possible for her to see the somber beauty in an oncoming storm.

She had been born and raised in a loveless house as grim and cold as any arctic cavern. But those days were far behind her, and the effect of them had long ago diminished.

Appreciate the moment.

Checking her watch, she pulled the drapes shut because the mood of her next two clients was not likely to be immune to the influence of gray weather.

When the windows were covered, the place was as cozy as any parlor in a private home. Her desk, books, and files were in the third office, rarely seen by those she counseled. She always met with them in this more welcoming room. The floral-pattern sofa with its variety of throw pillows lent a lot of charm, and each of three plushly upholstered armchairs was commodious enough to permit young guests to curl up entirely on the seat with their legs tucked under them if they wished. Celadon lamps with fringed silk shades cast a warm light that glimmered in the bibelots on the end tables and in the glazes of Lladro porcelain figurines in the mahogany breakfront.

Paige usually offered hot chocolate and cookies, or pretzels with a cold glass of cola, and conversation was facilitated because the overall effect was like being at Grandma's house. At least it was how Grandma's house had been in the days when no grandma ever underwent plastic surgery, had herself reconfigured by liposuction, divorced Grandpa, went on singles' cruises to Cabo San Lucas, or flew to Vegas with her boyfriend for the weekend.

Most clients, on their first visit, were astonished not to find the collected works of Freud, a therapy couch, and the too-solemn atmosphere of a psychiatrist's office. Even when she reminded them that she was not a psychiatrist, not a medical doctor at all, but a counselor with a degree in psychology who saw "clients" rather than "patients," people with communication problems rather than neuroses or psychoses, they remained bewildered for the first half an hour or so. Eventually the room—and, she liked to think, her relaxed approach—won them over.

Paige's two o'clock appointment, the last of the day, was with Samantha Acheson and her eight-year-old son, Sean. Samantha's first husband, Sean's father, had died shortly after the boy's fifth birthday. Two and a half years later, Samantha remarried, and Sean's behavioral problems began virtually on the wedding day, an obvious result of his misguided conviction that she had betrayed his dead father and might one day betray him as well. For five months, Paige had met twice a week with the boy, winning his trust, opening lines of communication, so they could discuss the pain and fear and anger he was unable to talk about with his mother. Today, Samantha was to participate for the first time, which was an important step because progress was usually swift once the child was ready to say to the parent what he had said to his counselor.

She sat in the armchair she reserved for herself and reached to the end table for the reproduction-antique telephone, which was both a working phone and an intercom to the reception lounge. She intended to ask Millie, her secretary, to send in Samantha and Sean Acheson, but the intercom buzzed before she lifted the receiver.

"Marty's on line one, Paige."

"Thank you, Millie." She pressed line one. "Marty?"

He didn't respond.

"Marty, are you there?" she asked, looking to see if she had punched the correct button.

Line one was lit, but there was only silence on it.

"Marty?"

"I like the sound of your voice, Paige. So melodic."

He sounded . . . odd.

Her heart began to knock against her ribs, and she struggled to suppress the fear that swelled in her. "What did the doctor say?"

"I like your picture."

"My picture?" she said, baffled.

"I like your hair, your eyes."

"Marty, I don't—"

"You're what I need."

Her mouth had gone dry. "Is something wrong?"

Suddenly he spoke very fast, running sentences together: "I want to kiss you, Paige, kiss your breasts, hold you against me, make love to you, I will make you very happy, I want to be in you, it will be just like the movies, bliss."

"Marty, honey, what—"

He hung up, cutting her off.

As surprised and confused as she was worried, Paige listened to the dial tone before returning the handset to the cradle.

What the hell?

It was two o'clock, and she doubted that his appointment with Guthridge had lasted an hour; therefore, he hadn't phoned her from the doctor's office. On the other hand, he wouldn't have had time to drive all the way home, which meant he had called her en route.

She lifted the handset and punched in the number of his car phone. He answered on the second ring, and she said, "Marty, what the hell's wrong?"

"Paige?"

"What was that all about?"

"What was *what* all about?"

"Kissing my breasts, for God's sake, just like the movies, bliss."

He hesitated, and she could hear the faint rumble of the Ford's engine, which meant he was in transit. After a beat he said, "Kid, you've lost me."

"A minute ago, you call here, acting as if—"

"No. Not me."

"You *didn't* call here?"

"Nope."

"Is this a joke?"

"You mean, somebody called, said he was me?"

"Yes, he—"

"Did he sound like me?"

"Yes."

"Exactly like me?"

Paige thought about that for a moment. "Well, not exactly. He sounded a lot like you and then . . . not quite like you. It's hard to explain."

"I hope you hung up on him when he got obscene."

"You—" She corrected herself: "*He* hung up first. Besides, it wasn't an obscene call."

"Oh? What was that about kissing your breasts?"

"Well, it didn't seem obscene 'cause I thought he was you."

"Paige, refresh my memory—when was the last time I called you at work to talk about kissing your breasts?"

She laughed. "Well . . . never, I guess," and when he laughed, too, she added, "but maybe it wouldn't be a bad idea now and then, liven up the day a little."

"They are very kissable."

"Thank you."

"So's your tush."

"You've got me blushing," she said, and it was true.

"So's your—"

"Now *this* is getting obscene," she said.

"Yeah, but I'm the victim."

"How do you figure?"

"*You* called *me* and pretty much demanded that I talk dirty."

"I guess I did. Women's liberation, you know."

"Where will it all end?"

A disturbing possibility had occurred to Paige, but she was reluctant to express it: Perhaps the call *had* been from Marty, made on his car phone while he was in a fugue state similar to the one on Saturday afternoon when he'd monotonously repeated those two words into a tape recorder for seven minutes and later had no memory of it.

She suspected the same thought had just occurred to him because his sudden reticence matched hers.

At last Paige broke the silence. "What did Paul Guthridge have to say?"

"He thinks it's probably stress."

"Thinks?"

"He's setting up tests for tomorrow or Wednesday."

"But he wasn't worried?"

"No. Or he pretended he wasn't."

Paul's informal style was not reflected in the way he imparted essential information to his patients. He was always direct and to the point. Even when Charlotte had been so ill, when some doctors might have soft-pedaled the more alarming possibilities to let the parents adjust slowly to the worst-case scenario, Paul had bluntly assessed her situation with Paige and Marty. He knew that no half-truth or false optimism should ever be mistaken for compassion. If Paul didn't appear to be more than ordinarily concerned about Marty's condition and symptoms—that was good news.

"He gave me his spare copy of the new *People,*" Marty said.

"Uh-oh. You say that as if he handed you a bag of dog poop."

"Well, it isn't what I was hoping for."

"It's not as bad as you think," she said.

"How do you know? You haven't even seen it yet."

"But I know you and how you are about these things."

"In the one photo, I look like the Frankenstein monster with a bad hangover."

"I've always loved Boris Karloff."

He sighed. "I suppose I can change my name, have some plastic surgery, and move to Brazil. But before I book a flight to Rio, do you want me to pick up the kids at school?"

"I'll get them. They'll be an hour later today."

"Oh, that's right, Monday. Piano lessons."

"We'll be home by four-thirty," she said. "You can show me *People* and spend the evening crying on my shoulder."

"To hell with that. I'll show you *People* and spend the evening kissing your breasts."

"You're special, Marty."

"I love you, too, kid."

When she hung up, Paige was smiling. He could always make her smile, even in darker moments.

She refused to think about the strange phone call, about illness or fugues or pictures that made him look like a monster.

Appreciate the moment.

She did just that for a minute or so, then called Millie on the intercom and asked her to send in Samantha and Sean Acheson.

6.

In his office, he sits in the executive chair behind the desk. It is comfortable. He can almost believe he has sat in it before.

Nevertheless, he is nervous.

He switches on the computer. It is an IBM PC with substantial harddisk storage. A good machine. He can't remember purchasing it.

After the system runs a data-management program, the oversize screen presents him with a "Main Selection Menu" that includes eight choices, mostly word-processing software. He chooses WordPerfect 5.1, and it is loaded.

He doesn't recall being instructed in the operation of a computer or in the use of WordPerfect. This training is cloaked in amnesiac mists, as is his training in weaponry and his uncanny familiarity with the street systems of various cities. Evidently, his superiors believed he would need to understand basic computer operation and be familiar with certain software programs in order to carry out his assignments.

The screen clears.

Ready.

In the lower right-hand corner of the blue screen, white letters and numbers tell him that he is in document one, on page one, at line one, in the tenth position.

Ready. He is ready to write a novel. His work.

He stares at the blank monitor, trying to start. Beginning is more difficult than he had expected.

He has brought a bottle of Corona from the kitchen, suspecting he might need to lubricate his thoughts. He takes a long swallow. The beer is cold, refreshing, and he knows that it is just the thing to get him going.

After finishing half the bottle, confidence renewed, he begins to type. He bangs out two words, then stops:

The man

The man what?

He stares at the screen for a minute, then types "entered the room." But what room? In a house? An office building? What does the room look like? Who else is in it? What is this man doing in this room, why is he here? Does it have to be a room? Could he be entering a train, a plane, a graveyard?

He deletes "entered the room" and replaces it with "was tall." So the man is tall. Does it matter that he is tall? Will tallness be important to the story? How old is he? What color are his eyes, his hair? Is he Caucasian, black, Asian? What is he wearing? As far as that goes, does it have to be a man at all? Couldn't it be a woman? Or a child?

With these questions in mind, he clears the screen and starts the story from the beginning:

The

He stares at the screen. It is terrifyingly blank. Infinitely blanker than it was before, not just three letters blanker with the deletion of "man." The choices to follow that simple article, "the," are limitless, which makes the selection of the second word a great deal more daunting than he would have supposed before he sat in the black leather chair and switched on the machine.

He deletes "The."

The screen is clear.

Ready.

He finishes the bottle of Corona. It is cold and refreshing, but it does not lubricate his thoughts.

He goes to the bookshelves and pulls off eight of the novels bearing his name, Martin Stillwater. He carries them to the desk, and for a while he sits and reads first pages, second pages, trying to kick-start his brain.

His destiny is to be Martin Stillwater. That much is perfectly clear.

He will be a good father to Charlotte and Emily.

He will be a good husband and lover to the beautiful Paige.

And he will write novels. Mystery novels.

Evidently, he has written them before, at least a dozen, so he can write them again. He simply has to re-acquire the feeling for how it is done, relearn the habit.

The screen is blank.

He puts his fingers on the keys, ready to type.

The screen is so blank. Blank, blank, blank. Mocking him.

Suspecting that he is merely inhibited by the soft persistent hum of the monitor fan and the demanding electronic-blue field of document one, page one, he switches off the computer. The resultant silence is a blessing, but the flat gray glass of the monitor is even more mocking than the blue screen; turning the machine off seems like an admission of defeat.

He needs to be Martin Stillwater, which means he needs to write.

The man. The man was. The man was tall with blue eyes and blond hair, wearing a blue suit and white shirt and red tie, about thirty years old, and he didn't know what he was doing in the room that he entered. Damn. No good. The man. The man. The man . . .

He needs to write, but every attempt to do so leads quickly to frustration. Frustration soon spawns anger. The familiar pattern. Anger generates a specific hatred for the computer, a *loathing* of it, and also a less focused hatred of his unsatisfactory position in the world, of the world itself and every one of its inhabitants. He needs so little, so pathetically little, just to belong, to be like other people, to have a home and a family, to have a purpose that he understands. Is that so much? Is it? He does not want to be rich, rub elbows with the high and mighty, dine with socialites. He is not asking for fame. After much struggle, confusion, and loneliness, he now has a home and wife and two children, a sense of direction, a destiny, but he feels it slipping away from him, through his fingers. He needs to be Martin Stillwater, but in order to be Martin Stillwater, he needs to be able to *write,* and he can't write, can't write, damn it all, can't write. He knows the street layout of Kansas City, other cities, and he knows all about weaponry, about picking locks, because they seeded that knowledge in him—whoever "they" are—but they haven't seen fit also to implant the knowledge of how to write mystery novels, which he needs, oh so desperately *needs,* if he is ever to be Martin Stillwater, if he is to keep his lovely wife, Paige, and his daughters and his new destiny, which is slipping, slipping, slipping through his fingers, his one chance at happiness swiftly evaporating, because they are against him, all of them, the whole world, set against him, determined to keep him alone and confused. And why? *Why?* He hates them and their schemes and their faceless power, despises them and their machines with such bitter intensity that—

—with a shriek of rage, he slams his fist through the dark screen of the computer, striking out at his own fierce reflection almost as much as at the machine and all that it represents. The sound of shattering glass is loud in the silent house, and the vacuum inside the monitor pops simultaneously with a brief hiss of invading air.

He withdraws his hand from the ruins even as fragments of glass are still clinking onto the keyboard, and he stares at his bright blood. Sharp slivers bristle from the webs between his fingers and from a couple of knuckles. An elliptical shard is embedded in the meat of his palm.

Although he is still angry, he is gradually regaining control of himself. Violence sometimes soothes.

He swivels the chair away from the computer to face the opposite side of the U-shaped work area, where he leans forward to examine his wounds in the light of the stained-glass lamp. The glass thorns in his flesh sparkle like jewels.

He is experiencing only mild pain, and he knows it will soon pass. He is tough and resilient; he enjoys splendid recuperative powers.

Some of the fragments of the screen have not pierced his hand deeply, and he is able to pry them out with his fingernails. But others are firmly wedged in the flesh.

He pushes the chair away from the desk, gets to his feet, and heads for the master bathroom. He will need tweezers to extract the more stubborn splinters.

Although he bled freely at first, already the flow is subsiding. Nevertheless he holds his arm in the air, his hand straight up, so the blood will trickle down his wrist and under the sleeve of his shirt rather than drip on the carpet.

After he has plucked out the glass, perhaps he will telephone Paige at work again.

He was so excited when he found her office number on the Rolodex in his study, and he was thrilled to speak with her. She sounded intelligent, self-assured, gentle. Her voice had a slightly throaty timbre that he found sexy.

It will be a wonderful bonus if she is sexy. Tonight, they will share a bed. He will take her more than once. Recalling the face in the photograph and the husky voice on the phone, he is confident that she will satisfy his needs as they have never been satisfied before, that she will not leave him unfulfilled and frustrated as have so many other women.

He hopes she matches or exceeds his expectations. He hopes there will be no reason to hurt her.

In the master bathroom, he locates a pair of tweezers in the drawer where Paige keeps her makeup, cuticle scissors, nail files, emery boards, and other grooming aids.

At the sink, he holds his hand over the basin. Although he has already stopped bleeding, the flow starts again at each point from which he works loose a piece of glass. He turns on the hot water so the dripping blood will be sluiced down the drain.

Maybe tonight, after sex, he will talk with Paige about his writer's block. If he has been blocked before, she might remember what steps he took on other occasions to break the creative impasse. Indeed, he is sure she will know the solution.

Pleasantly surprised and with a sense of relief, he realizes that he no longer has to deal with his problems alone. As a married man, he has a devoted partner with whom to share the many troubles of the day.

Raising his head, looking at his reflection in the mirror behind the sink, he grins and says, "I have a wife now."

He notices a spot of blood on his right cheek, another on the side of his nose.

Laughing softly, he says, "You're such a slob, Marty. You've got to clean up your act. You have a wife now. Wives like their husbands to be neat."

He returns his attention to his hand and, with the tweezers, picks at the last of the prickling glass.

In an increasingly good mood, he laughs again and says, "Gonna have to go out and buy a new computer monitor first thing tomorrow."

He shakes his head, amazed by his own childish behavior.

"You're something else, Marty," he says. "But I guess writers are *supposed* to be temperamental, huh?"

After easing the final splinter of glass from the web between two fingers, he puts down the tweezers and holds his wounded hand under the hot water.

"Can't carry on like this any more. Not any more. You'll scare the bejesus out of little Emily and Charlotte."

He looks in the mirror again, shakes his head, grinning. "You nut," he says to himself, as if speaking with affection to a friend whose foibles he finds charming. "What a nut."

Life is good.

7.

The leaden sky settled lower under its own weight. According to a radio report, rain would fall by dusk, ensuring rush-hour commuter jam-ups that would make Hell preferable to the San Diego Freeway.

Marty should have gone directly home from Guthridge's office. He was close to finishing his current novel, and in the final throes of a story, he usually spent as much time as possible at work because distractions were ruinous to the narrative momentum.

Besides, he was uncharacteristically apprehensive about driving. When he thought back, he could account for the time minute by minute since he'd left the doctor and was sure he hadn't called Paige while in a fugue behind the wheel of the Ford. Of course, a fugue victim had no memory of being afflicted, so even a meticulous reconstruction of the past hour might not reveal the truth. Researching *One Dead Bishop,* he'd learned of victims who traveled hundreds of miles and interacted with dozens of people while in a disassociative condition yet later could recall nothing they'd done. The danger wasn't as grave as drunken driving . . . though operating a ton and a half of steel at high speed in an altered state of consciousness wasn't smart.

Nevertheless, instead of going home, he went to the Mission Viejo Mall. Much of the workday was already shot. And he was too restless to read or watch TV until Paige and the girls got home.

When the going gets tough, the tough go shopping, so he browsed for books and records, buying a novel by Ed McBain and a CD by Alan Jackson, hoping that such mundane activities would help him forget his troubles. He strolled past the cookie shop twice, coveting the big ones with chocolate chips and pecans but finding the will power to resist their allure.

The world is a better place, he thought, if you're ignorant of good nutrition.

When he left the mall, sprinkles of cold rain were painting camouflage patterns on the concrete sidewalk. Lightning flashed as he ran for the

Ford, caissons of thunder rolled across the embattled sky, and the sprinkles became heavy volleys just as he pulled the door shut and settled behind the steering wheel.

Driving home, Marty took considerable pleasure in the glimmer of rain-silvered streets, the burbling splash of the tires churning through deep puddles—and the sight of swaying palm fronds, which seemed to be combing the gray tresses of the stormy sky and which reminded him of certain Somerset Maugham stories and an old Bogart film. Because rain was an infrequent visitor to drought-stricken California, the benefit and novelty outweighed the inconvenience.

He parked in the garage and entered the house by the connecting door to the kitchen, enjoying the damp heaviness of the air and the scent of ozone that always accompanied the start of a storm.

In the shadowy kitchen, the luminous green display of the electronic clock on the stove read 4:10. Paige and the girls might be home in twenty minutes.

He switched on lamps and sconces as he moved from room to room. The house never felt homier than when it was warm and well lighted while rain drummed on the roof and the gray pall of a storm veiled the world beyond every window. He decided to start the gas-log fire in the family-room fireplace and to lay out all of the fixings for hot chocolate so it could be made immediately after Paige and the girls arrived.

First, he went upstairs to check the fax and answering machines in his office. By now Paul Guthridge's secretary should have called with a schedule of test appointments at the hospital.

He also had a wild hunch his literary agent had left a message about a sale of rights in one foreign territory or another, or maybe news of an offer for a film option, a reason to celebrate. Curiously, the storm had improved his mood instead of darkening it, probably because inclement weather tended to focus the mind on the pleasures of home, though it was always his nature to find reasons to be upbeat even when common sense suggested pessimism was a more realistic reaction. He was never able to stew in gloom for long; and since Saturday he'd had enough negative thoughts to last a couple of years.

Entering his office, he reached for the wall switch to flick on the overhead light but left it untouched, surprised that the stained-glass lamp and a work lamp were aglow. He always extinguished lights when leaving the house. Before he'd gone to the doctor's office, however, he'd been inexplicably oppressed by the bizarre feeling of being in the path of an unknown Juggernaut, and evidently he'd not had sufficient presence of mind to switch off the lamps.

Remembering the panic attack at its worst, in the garage, when he'd been nearly incapacitated by terror, Marty felt some of the air bleeding out of his balloon of optimism.

The fax and answering machines were on the back corner of the U-shaped work area. The red message light was blinking on the latter, and a couple of flimsy sheets of thermal paper were in the tray of the former.

Before he reached either machine, Marty saw the shattered video display, glass teeth bristling from the frame. A black maw gaped in the center. A piece of glass crunched under his shoe as he pushed his office chair aside and stared down at the computer in disbelief.

Jagged pieces of the screen littered the keyboard.

A twist of nausea knotted his stomach. Had he done this, too, in a fugue? Picked up some blunt object, hammered the screen to pieces? His life was disintegrating like the ruined monitor.

Then he noticed something else on the keyboard in addition to the glass. In the dim light he thought he was looking at drops of melted chocolate.

Frowning, Marty touched one of the splotches with the tip of his index finger. It was still slightly tacky. Some of it stuck to his skin.

He moved his hand under the work lamp. The sticky substance on his fingertip was dark red, almost maroon. Not chocolate.

He raised his stained finger to his nose, seeking a defining scent. The odor was faint, barely detectable, but he knew at once what it was, probably had known from the moment he touched it, because on a deep primitive level he was programmed to recognize it. Blood.

Whoever destroyed the monitor had been cut.

Marty's hands were free of lacerations.

He was utterly still, except for a crawling sensation along his spine, which left the nape of his neck creped with gooseflesh.

Slowly he turned, expecting to find that someone had entered the room behind him. But he was alone.

Rain pummeled the roof and gurgled through a nearby downspout. Lightning flickered, visible through the cracks between the wide slats of the plantation shutters, and peals of thunder reverberated in the window glass.

He listened to the house.

The only sounds were those of the storm. And the rapid thud of his heartbeat.

He stepped to the bank of drawers on the right-hand side of the desk, slid open the second one. This morning he had placed the Smith & Wesson 9mm pistol in there, on top of some papers. He expected it to be missing, but again his expectations were not fulfilled. Even in the soft and beguiling light of the stained-glass lamp, he could see the handgun gleaming darkly.

"I need my life."

The voice startled Marty, but its effect was nothing compared to the paralytic shock that seized him when he looked up from the gun and saw the identity of the speaker. The man was just inside the hallway door. He was wearing what might have been Marty's own jeans and flannel shirt, which fit him well because he was a dead-ringer for Marty. In fact, but for the clothes, the intruder might have been a reflection in a mirror.

"I need my life," the man repeated softly.

Marty had no brother, twin or otherwise. Yet only an identical twin could be so perfectly matched to him in every detail of face, height, weight, and body type.

"Why have you stolen my life?" the intruder asked with what seemed to be genuine curiosity. His voice was level and controlled, as if the question was not entirely insane, as if it was actually possible, at least in his experience, to steal a life.

Realizing that the intruder *sounded* like him, too, Marty closed his eyes and tried to deny what stood before him. He assumed he was hallucinating and was, himself, speaking for the phantom in a sort of unconscious ventriloquism. Fugues, an unusually intense nightmare, a panic attack, now hallucinations. But when he opened his eyes, the doppelganger was still there, a stubborn illusion.

"Who are you?" the double asked.

Marty could not speak because his heart felt as if it had moved into his throat, each fierce beat almost choking him. And he didn't *dare* to speak because to engage in conversation with an hallucination would surely be to lose his final tenuous grasp on sanity and descend entirely into madness.

The phantom refined its question, still speaking in a tone of wonder and fascination but nonetheless menacing for its hushed voice: *"What* are you?"

With none of the eerie fluidity and ghostly shimmer of either a psychological or supernatural apparition, neither transparent nor radiant, the double took another step into the room. When he moved, shadows and light played over him in the same manner as they would have caressed any three-dimensional object. He seemed as solid as a real man.

Marty noticed the pistol in the intruder's right hand. Held against his thigh. Muzzle pointed at the floor.

The double advanced one more step, stopping no more than eight feet from the other side of the desk. With a half-smile that was more unnerving than any glower could have been, the gunman said, "How does this happen? What now? Do we somehow become one person, fade into each other, like in some crazy science-fiction movie—"

Terror had sharpened Marty's senses. As if looking at his doppelganger through a magnifying glass, he could see every contour, line, and pore of its face. In spite of the dim light, the furniture and books in the shadowed areas were as clearly detailed as those items on which the glow of lamps fell. Yet with all his heightened powers of observation, he did not recognize the make of the other's pistol.

"—or do I just kill you and take your place?" the stranger continued. "And if I kill you—"

It seemed that any hallucination he conjured would be carrying a weapon with which he was familiar.

"—do the memories you've stolen from me become mine again when you're dead? If I kill you—"

After all, if this figure was merely a symbolic threat spewed up by a diseased psyche, then everything—the phantom, his clothes, his armament—had to come from Marty's experience and imagination.

"—am I made whole? When you're dead, will I be restored to my family? And will I know how to write again?"

Conversely, if the gun was real, the double was real.

Cocking his head, leaning forward slightly, as if intensely interested in Marty's response, the intruder said, "I need to write if I'm going to be what I'm meant to be, but the words won't come."

The one-sided conversation repeatedly surprised Marty with its twists and turns, which didn't support the notion that his troubled psyche had fabricated the intruder.

Anger entered the double's voice for the first time, bitterness rather than hot fury but rapidly growing fiery: "You've stolen that too, the words, the talent, and I need it back, need it now so bad I ache. A purpose, meaning. Do you know? You understand? Whatever you are, *can* you understand?

The terrible emptiness, hollowness, God, such a deep, dark hollowness."
He was spitting out the words now, and his eyes were fierce. "I want what's
mine, mine, damn it, my life, mine, I want my life, my destiny, my Paige,
she's mine, my Charlotte, my Emily—"

The width of the desk and eight feet beyond, eleven feet in all: point-
blank range.

Marty pulled the 9mm pistol from the desk drawer, grasping it in both
hands, thumbing off the safety, squeezing the trigger even as he raised the
muzzle. He didn't care if the target was real or some form of spirit. All he
cared about was obliterating it before it killed him.

The first shot tore a chunk out of the far edge of the desk, and wood
splinters exploded like a swarm of angry wasps bursting into flight. The
second and third rounds hit the other Marty in the chest. They neither
passed through him as if he were ectoplasm nor shattered him as if he were
a reflection in a mirror, but instead catapulted him backward, off his feet,
taking him by surprise before he could raise his own gun, which flew out
of his hand and hit the floor with a hard thud. He crashed against a
bookcase, clawing at a shelf with one hand, pulling a dozen volumes to the
floor, blood spreading across his chest—sweet Jesus, so much blood—eyes
wide with shock, no cry escaping him except for one hard low "uh" that
was more a sound of surprise than pain.

The bastard should have fallen like a rock down a well, but he stayed
on his feet. In the same moment that he slammed into the bookcase, he
pushed away from it, staggered-plunged through the open doorway, into
the upstairs hall, out of sight.

Stunned more by the fact that he'd actually pulled the trigger on someone than that the "someone" was the mirror image of himself, Marty
sagged against the desk, gasping for breath as desperately as if he hadn't
inhaled since the double had first walked into the room. Maybe he hadn't.
Shooting a man for real was a whole hell of a lot different from shooting
a character in a novel; it almost seemed as if, in some magical fashion, part
of the impact of the bullets on the target redounded on the shooter
himself. His chest ached, he was dizzy, and his peripheral vision briefly
succumbed to a thick seeping darkness which he pressed back with an act
of will.

He didn't dare pass out. He thought the other Marty must be badly
wounded, dying, maybe dead. *God, the spreading blood on his chest, scarlet
blossoms, sudden roses.* But he didn't know for sure. Maybe the wounds

only looked mortal, maybe the brief glimpse he'd had was misleading, and maybe the double was not only still alive but strong enough to get out of the house and away. If the guy escaped and lived, sooner or later he'd be back, just as weird and crazy but even angrier, better prepared. Marty had to finish what he started before his double had a chance to do the same.

He glanced at the phone. Dial 911. Get the police, then go after the wounded man.

But the desk clock was beside the phone, and he saw the time—4:26. Paige and the girls. On their way home from school, later than usual, delayed by piano lessons. Oh, my God. If they came into the house and saw the other Marty, or found him in the garage, they'd think he was *their* Marty, and they'd run to him, frightened by his wounds, wanting to help, and maybe he would still be strong enough to harm them. Was the pistol that he dropped his only weapon? Can't make that assumption. Besides, the son of a bitch could get a knife out of the rack in the kitchen, the butcher's knife, hide it against his side, behind his back, let Emily get close, then jam it through her throat, or deep into Charlotte's belly.

Every second counted. Forget 911. Waste of time. The cops wouldn't get there before Paige.

As Marty rounded the desk, his legs were wobbly, but less so as he crossed the room toward the hallway. He saw blood splattered on the wall, oozing down the spines of his own books, staining his name. A creeping tide of darkness lapped at the edges of his vision again. He clenched his teeth and kept going.

When he reached the double's pistol, he kicked it deeper into the room, farther from the doorway. That simple act gave him a surge of confidence because it seemed like something a cop would have the presence of mind to do—make it harder for the perp to regain his weapon.

Maybe he could handle this, get through it, as strange and scary as it was, the blood and all. Maybe he would be okay.

So nail the guy. Make sure he's down, all the way down and all the way out.

To write his mystery novels, he'd done a lot of research into police procedures, not merely studying police-academy textbooks and training films but riding with uniformed cops on night patrols and hanging out with plainclothes detectives on and off the job. He knew perfectly well how best to go through a doorway under these circumstances.

Don't be too confident. Figure the creep has another weapon besides the one he dropped, gun or knife. Stay low, clear that doorway fast. Easier to die in a doorway than anywhere else because every door opens on the unknown. Keep your gun in both hands as you move, arms in front of you, straight and locked, sweep left and right as you cross the threshold, swinging the gun to cover both flanks. Then slip to one side or the other and keep your back against the wall as you move, so you always know your back is safe, only three sides to worry about.

All of that wisdom flashed through his mind, as it might have passed through the mind of one of his hard-nosed police characters—yet he behaved like any panicked civilian, stumbling heedlessly into the upstairs hall, holding the pistol in only his right hand, arms loose, breathing explosively, making more of a target than a threat of himself, because when you came right down to it, he *wasn't* a cop, only an asshole who sometimes wrote about them. No matter how long you indulged the fantasy, you couldn't *live* the fantasy, you couldn't act like a cop in a pressurized situation unless you had trained like a cop. He had been as guilty as anyone of confusing reality and fiction, thinking he was as invincible as the hero on a printed page, and he'd been damned lucky the *other* Marty hadn't been waiting for him. The upstairs hall was deserted.

He looked exactly like me.

Couldn't think about that now, no time for it yet. Concentrate on staying alive, wasting the bastard before he hurt Paige or the girls. If you survive, there'll be time to seek an explanation for that astonishing resemblance, solve the mystery, but not now.

Listen. Movement?

Maybe.

No. Nothing.

Keep the gun up, muzzle aimed ahead.

Just outside the office doorway, a smeary handprint in wet blood marred the wall. A horrid amount of blood was puddled on the light-beige carpet there. At least part of the time when Marty had stood behind his desk, stunned and temporarily immobilized by the violence, the wounded man had leaned against this hallway wall, perhaps trying unsuccessfully to staunch his bleeding wounds.

Marty was sweating, nauseated and afraid. Perspiration trickled into the corner of his left eye, stinging, blurring his vision. He blotted his slick forehead with his shirt sleeve, blinked furiously to wash the salt out of his eye.

When the intruder had shoved away from the wall and started moving—perhaps while Marty was still frozen behind his desk—he had walked through his own pooled blood. His route was marked by fragmentary red imprints of the ridged patterns on athletic-shoe soles as well as by a continuous scarlet drizzle.

Silence in the house. With a little luck, maybe it was the silence of the dead.

Shivering, Marty cautiously followed the repulsive trail past the hall bath, around the corner, past the double-door entrance to the dark master bedroom, past the head of the stairs. He stopped at that point where the second-floor hall became a gallery overlooking the living room.

On his right was a bleached oak railing, beyond which hung the brass chandelier that he'd switched on when he'd passed through the foyer earlier. Below the chandelier were the descending stairs and the two-story, tile-floored entrance foyer that flowed directly into the two-story living room.

To his left and a few feet farther along the gallery was the room Paige used as a home office. One day it would become another bedroom for Charlotte or Emily when they decided they were ready to sleep separately. The door stood half open. Bat-black shadows swarmed beyond, relieved only by the gray storm light of the waning day, which hardly penetrated the windows.

The blood trail led past that office to the end of the gallery, directly to the door of the girls' bedroom, which was closed. The intruder was in there, and it was infuriating to think of him among the girls' belongings, touching things, tainting their room with his blood and madness.

He recalled the angry voice, touched with lunacy yet so like his own voice: *My Paige, she's mine, my Charlotte, my Emily . . .*

"Like hell, they're yours," Marty said, keeping the Smith & Wesson aimed squarely at the closed door.

He glanced at his wristwatch.

4:28.

Now what?

He could stay there in the hallway, ready to blow the bastard to Hell if the door opened. Wait for Paige and the kids, shout to them when they came in, tell Paige to call 911. Then she could hustle the kids across the street to Vic and Kathy Delorio's house, where they'd be safe, while he covered the door until the police arrived.

That plan sounded good, responsible, cool and calm. Briefly, the knocking of his heart against his ribs became less insistent, less punishing.

Then the curse of a writer's imagination hit him hard, a black whirlpool sucking him down into dark possibilities, the curse of what if, what if, *what if.* What if the other Marty was still strong enough to push open the window in the girls' room, climb out onto the patio cover at the back of the house, and jump down to the lawn from there? What if he fled along the side of the house and out to the street just as Paige was pulling into the driveway with the girls?

It might happen. Could happen. *Would* happen. Or something else just as bad would happen, worse. The whirlpool of reality spun out more terrible possibilities than the darkest thoughts of any writer's mind. In this age of social dissolution, even on the most peaceful streets in the quietest neighborhoods, unexpected acts of grotesque savagery could occur, whereupon people were shocked and horrified but *not* surprised.

He might be guarding the door to a deserted room.

4:29.

Paige might be turning the corner two blocks away, entering their street.

Maybe the neighbors had heard the gunshots and had already called the police. Please, God, let that be the case.

He had no conscionable choice but to throw open the door to the girls' room, go in, and confirm whether The Other was there or not.

The Other. In his office, when the confrontation had begun, he'd quickly dismissed his initial thought that he was dealing with something supernatural. A spirit could not be as solid and three-dimensional as this man was. If they existed at all, creatures from the other side of the line between life and death would not be vulnerable to bullets. Yet a feeling of the uncanny persisted, weighed heavier on him moment by moment. Although he suspected that the nature of this adversary was far stranger than ghosts or shape-changing demons, that it was simultaneously more terrifying and more mundane, that it was born of this world and no other, he nevertheless could not help but think of it in terms usually reserved for stories of haunting spirits: Ghost, Phantom, Revenant, Apparition, Specter, The Uninvited, The Undying, The Entity.

The Other.

The door waited.

The silence of the house was deeper than death.

Already focused narrowly on the pursuit of The Other, Marty's attention constricted further, until he was oblivious of his own heartbeat, blind to everything but the door, deaf to all sounds except those that might come from the girls' room, conscious of no sensation except the pressure of his finger on the trigger of the pistol.

The blood trail.

Red fragments of shoeprints.

The door.

Waiting.

He was rooted in indecision.

The door.

Something suddenly clattered above him. He snapped his head back and looked at the ceiling. He was directly under the three-foot-square, seven-foot-deep shaft that soared up to a dome-shaped Plexiglas skylight. Rain was beating against the Plexiglas. Only rain, the clatter of rain.

As if the strain of indecision had snapped him back to the full spectrum of reality, he was abruptly deluged by all the voices of the storm, of which he'd been utterly unaware while tracking The Other. He'd been intently listening *through* the background racket for the stealthier sounds of his quarry. Now the wind's gibbering-hooting-moaning, the rataplan of rain, fulminant thunder, the bony scraping of a tree limb against one side of the house, the tinny rattle of a loose section of rain gutter, and less identifiable noises flooded over him.

The neighbors couldn't have heard gunshots above the raging storm. So much for that hope.

Marty seemed to be swept forward by the tumult, along the blood trail, one hesitant step, then another, inexorably toward the waiting door.

8.

The storm ushered in an early twilight, bleak and protracted, and Paige had the headlights on all the way home from the girls' school. Though turned to the highest speed, the windshield wipers could barely cope with the cataracts that poured out of the draining sky. Either the latest drought would be broken this rainy season or nature was playing a cruel trick by raising expectations she would not fulfill. Intersections were flooded. Gutters overflowed. The BMW spread great white wings of water as it passed through one deep puddle after another. And out of the misty murk, the headlights of oncoming cars swam at them like the searching lamps of bathyscaphes probing deep ocean trenches.

"We're a submarine," Charlotte said excitedly from the passenger seat beside Paige, looking out of the side window through plumes of tire spray, "swimming with the whales, Captain Nemo and the *Nautilus* twenty thousand leagues beneath the sea, giant squids stalking us. Remember the giant squid, Mom, from the movie?"

"I remember," Paige said without taking her eyes from the road.

"Up periscope," Charlotte said, gripping the handles of that imaginary instrument, squinting through the eyepiece. "Raiding the sea lanes, ramming ships with our super-strong steel bow—*boom!*—and the crazy captain playing his huge pipe organ! You remember the pipe organ, Mom?"

"I remember."

"Diving deeper, deeper, the pressure hull starting to crack, but the crazy Captain Nemo says *deeper,* playing his pipe organ and saying *deeper,* and all the time here comes the squid." She broke into the shark's theme from the movie *Jaws: "Dum-dum, dum-dum, dum-dum, dum-dum, da-da-dum!"*

"That's silly," Emily said from the rear seat.

Charlotte turned in her shoulder harness to look back between the front seats. "What's silly?"

"Giant squid."

"Oh, is that so? Maybe you wouldn't think they were so silly if you were swimming and one of them came up under you and bit you in half, ate you in two bites, then spit out your bones like grape seeds."

"Squid don't eat people," Emily said.

"Of course they do."

"Other way around."

"Huh?"

"People eat squid," Emily said.

"No way."

"Way."

"Where'd you get a dumb idea like that?"

"Saw it on a menu at a restaurant."

"What restaurant?" Charlotte asked.

"Couple different restaurants. You were there. Isn't it true, Mom—don't people eat squid?"

"Yes, they do," Paige agreed.

"You're just agreeing with her so she won't look like a dumb seven-year-old," Charlotte said skeptically.

"No, it's true," Paige assured her. "People eat squid."

"How?" Charlotte asked, as if the very thought beggared her imagination.

"Well," Paige said, braking for a red traffic light, "not all in one piece, you know."

"I guess not!" Charlotte said. "Not a *giant* squid, anyway."

"You can slice the tentacles and sauté them in garlic butter for one thing," Paige said, and looked at her daughter to see what impact that bit of culinary news would have.

Charlotte grimaced and faced forward again. "You're trying to gross me out."

"Tastes good," Paige insisted.

"I'd rather eat dirt."

"Tastes better than dirt, I assure you."

Emily piped up from the back seat again: "You can also slice their tentacles and french-fry 'em."

"That's right," Paige said.

Charlotte's judgment was simple and direct: "Yuch."

"They're like little onion rings, only squid," Emily said.

"This is sick."

"Little gummy french-fried squid rings dripping gooey squid ink," Emily said, and giggled.

Turning in her seat again to look at her sister, Charlotte said, "You're a disgusting troll."

"Anyway," Emily said, "we're not in a submarine."

"Of course we're not," Charlotte said. "We're in a car."

"No, we're in a hypofoil."

"A *what?*"

Emily said, "Like we saw on TV that time, the boat that goes between England and somewhere, and it rides on top of the water, really zooooom-ing along."

"Honey, you mean 'hydrofoil,'" Paige said, taking her foot off the brake when the light turned green, and accelerating cautiously across the flooded intersection.

"Yeah," Emily said. "Hyderfoil. We're in a hyderfoil, going to England to meet the queen. I'm going to have tea with the queen, drink tea and eat squid and talk about the family jewels."

Paige almost laughed out loud at that one.

"The queen doesn't serve squid," Charlotte said exasperatedly.

"Bet she does," said Emily.

"No, she serves crumpets and scones and trollops and stuff," Charlotte said.

This time Paige *did* laugh out loud. She had a vivid image in her head: The very proper and gracious Queen of England inquiring of a gentleman guest if he would like a trollop with his tea, and indicating a garish hooker waiting nearby in Frederick's of Hollywood lingerie.

"What's so funny?" Charlotte asked.

Stifling her laugh, Paige lied: "Nothing, I was just thinking about something, something else, happened a long time ago, wouldn't seem funny to you now, just an old Mommy memory."

The last thing she wanted was to inhibit their conversation. When she was in the car with them, she rarely turned on the radio. Nothing on the dial was half as entertaining as the Charlotte and Emily Show.

As the rain began to fall harder than ever, Emily proved to be in one of her more loquacious moods. "It's a lot more fun going on a hyderfoil to see the queen than being in a submarine with a giant squid chomping on it."

"The queen is boring," Charlotte said.

"Is not."

"Is too."

"She has a torture chamber under the palace."

Charlotte turned in her seat again, interested in spite of herself. "She does?"

"Yeah," Emily said. "And she keeps a guy down there in an iron mask."

"An iron mask?"

"An iron mask," Emily repeated somberly.

"Why?"

"He's *real* ugly," Emily said.

Paige decided both of them were going to grow up to be writers. They had inherited Marty's vivid and restless imagination. They would probably be as driven to exercise it as he was, although what they wrote would be quite different from their father's novels, and *far* different from the work of each other.

She couldn't wait to tell Marty about submarines, hyderfoils, giant squids, french-fried tentacles, and trollops with the queen.

She had decided to take Paul Guthridge's preliminary diagnosis to heart, attribute Marty's unnerving symptoms to nothing but stress, and stop worrying—at least until they got test results revealing something worse. Nothing was going to happen to Marty. He was a force of nature, a deep well of energy and laughter, indomitable and resilient. He would bounce back just as Charlotte had bounced off her deathbed five years ago. Nothing was going to happen to *any* of them because they had too much living to do, too many good times ahead of them.

A fierce bolt of lightning—which seldom accompanied storms in southern California but which blazed in plenitude this time—crackled across the sky, pulling after it a bang of thunder, as incandescent as any celestial chariot that might carry God out of the heavens on Judgment Day.

9.

Marty was only six or eight feet from the girls' bedroom door. He approached from the hinged side, so he could reach across for the knob, hurl the door inward, and avoid silhouetting himself squarely in the frame.

Trying not to tread in the blood, he glanced down for just a second at the carpet, where the spatters of gore were smaller and fewer than at other points along the hall. He glimpsed an anomaly that registered only subconsciously at first, and he eased forward another step with his gaze riveted on the door again before fully realizing what he'd seen: an impression of the forward half of a shoe sole, faintly inked in red, like twenty or thirty others he'd already passed, except that the narrow portion of this imprint, the toe, was pointed differently from all the others, in the wrong direction, back the way he had come.

Marty froze as he grasped the import of the shoeprint.

The Other had gone as far as the girls' bedroom but not into it. He had turned back, having somehow reduced the flow of blood so dramatically that he was no longer clearly marking his trail—except for one telltale shoeprint and perhaps a couple that Marty hadn't noticed.

Swinging around, holding the gun in both hands, Marty cried out at the sight of The Other coming at him from Paige's office, moving much too fast for a man with chest wounds and minus a pint or two of blood. He hit Marty hard, smashing in under the pistol, driving him into the gallery railing and forcing his arms up.

Marty pulled the trigger reflexively while he was being carried backward, but the bullet ploughed into the hallway ceiling. The sturdy handrail slammed the small of his back, and a half-strangled scream escaped him as white-hot pain shot horizontally across his kidneys and played spike-shoed hopscotch up the knuckled staircase of his spine.

Even as he screamed, he lost the gun. It popped out of his hands and arced back over his head into the empty vaulted space behind him.

The tortured oak railing shuddered, a loud dry crack signaled imminent collapse, and Marty was sure they were going to crash into the stairwell. But the balusters did not give way, and the handrail held fast to the newel post at each end.

Pressing relentlessly forward, The Other bent Marty backward and over the balustrade, trying to strangle him. Hands of iron. Fingers like hydraulic pincers driven by a powerful motor. Compressing the carotid arteries.

Marty rammed a knee into his assailant's crotch, but it was blocked. The attempt left him unbalanced, with just one foot on the floor, and he was shoved farther across the balustrade, until he was both pinned against and balanced on the handrail.

Choking, unable to breathe, aware that the worst danger was the diminution of blood to his brain, Marty clasped his hands in a wedge and drove them upward between The Other's arms, trying to spread them wider and break the strangulating grip. The assailant redoubled his efforts, determined to hold tight. Marty strained harder, too, and his overworked heart pounded painfully against his breastbone.

They should have been equally matched, damn it, they were the same height, same weight, same build, in the same physical condition, to all appearances the same *man.*

Yet The Other, though suffering two potentially mortal bullet wounds, was the stronger, and not merely because he had the advantage of a superior position, better leverage. He seemed to possess inhuman power.

Face to face with his duplicate, washed by each hot explosive breath, Marty might have been gazing into a mirror, though the savage reflection before him was contorted by expressions he'd never seen on his own face. Bestial rage. Hatred as purely toxic as cyanide. Spasms of maniacal pleasure twisted the familiar features as the strangler thrilled to the act of murder.

With lips peeled back from his teeth, spittle flying as he spoke, impossibly but repeatedly tightening his stranglehold to emphasize his words, The Other said, "Need my life now, my life, mine, mine, *now*. Need my family, now, mine, now, now, now, need *it, NEED IT!*"

Negative fireflies swooped and darted across Marty's field of vision, negative because they were the photo-opposite of the lantern-bearing fireflies on a warm summer night, not pulses of light in the darkness but pulses of darkness in the light. Five, ten, twenty, a hundred, a teeming swarm. The looming face of The Other vanished in sections under the blinking black swarm.

Despairing of breaking the assailant's grip, Marty clawed at the hate-filled face. But he couldn't quite reach it. His every effort seemed feeble, hopeless.

So many negative fireflies.

Glimpsed between them: the vicious and wrathful face of his wife's demanding new husband, the domineering face of his daughters' stern new father.

Fireflies. Everywhere, everywhere. Spreading their wings of obliteration.

Bang. Loud as a rifle shot. Second, third, fourth explosions—one right after another. Balusters breaking.

The handrail cracked. Sagged backward. It no longer received support from the balusters that had gone to splinters under it.

Marty stopped resisting the attacker and frantically tried to wrap his legs and arms around the railing in the hope of clinging to the anchored remains instead of hurtling out through the opening gap. But the center section of the balustrade disintegrated so completely, so swiftly, he couldn't find purchase in its crumbling elements, and the weight of his clutching assailant lent gravity more assistance than it required. As they teetered on the brink, however, Marty's actions altered the dynamics of their struggle just enough so The Other rolled past him and fell first. The assailant let go of Marty's throat but dragged him along in the top position. They dropped into the stairwell, crashed through the outer railing, instantly making kindling of it, and slammed into the Mexican-tile floor of the foyer.

The drop had been sixteen feet, not a tremendous distance, probably not even a lethal distance, and their momentum had been broken by the lower railing. Yet the impact knocked out what little breath Marty had drawn on the way down, even though he was cushioned by The Other, who hit the Mexican tiles back-first with the resounding *thwack* of a sledgehammer.

Gasping, coughing, Marty pushed away from his double and tried to scramble out of reach. He was breathless, lightheaded, and not sure if he had broken any bones. When he gasped, the air stung his raw throat, and when he coughed, the pain might not have been worse if he'd tried to swallow a tangled wad of barbed wire and bent nails. Scrambling cat-quick, which was what he had in mind, actually proved to be out of the question, and he could only drag himself across the foyer floor, hitching and shuddering like a bug that had been squirted with insecticide.

Blinking away tears squeezed out of him by the violent coughing, he spotted the Smith & Wesson. It was about fifteen feet away, well beyond the point at which the transition from tile floor to hardwood marked the end of the entrance foyer and the beginning of the living room. Considering the intensity with which he focused on it and the dedication with which he dragged his half-numb and aching body toward it, the pistol might have been the Holy Grail.

He became aware of a rumble separate from the sounds of the storm, followed by a thump, which he blearily assumed had something to do with The Other, but he didn't pause to look back. Maybe what he heard was a death twitch, heels drumming on the floor, one final convulsion. At the very *least* the bastard must be gravely injured. Crippled and dying. But Marty wanted to get his trembling hands on the gun before celebrating his own survival.

He reached the pistol, clutched it, and let out a grunt of weary triumph. He flopped on his side, eeled around, and aimed back toward the foyer, prepared to discover that his dogged pursuer was looming over him.

But The Other was still flat on his back. Legs splayed out. Arms at his sides. Motionless. Might even be dead. No such luck. His head lolled toward Marty. His face was pale, glazed with sweat, as white and shiny as a porcelain mask.

"Broke," he wheezed.

He seemed able to move only his head and the fingers of his right hand, though not the hand itself. A grimace of effort, rather than pain, contorted his features. He lifted his head off the floor, and the still-vital fingers curled and uncurled like the legs of a dying tarantula, but he appeared incapable of sitting up or bending either leg at the knee.

"Broke," he repeated.

Something in the way the word was spoken made Marty think of a toy soldier, bent springs, and ruined gears.

Steadying himself against the wall with one hand, Marty got to his feet.

"Gonna kill me?" The Other asked.

The prospect of putting a bullet in the brain of an injured and defenseless man was repulsive in the extreme, but Marty was tempted to commit the atrocity and worry about the psychological and legal consequences later. He was restrained as much by curiosity as by moral considerations.

"Kill you? Love to." His voice was hoarse and no doubt would be so for a day or two, until he recovered from the strangulation attempt. "Who the hell are you?" Every raspy word reminded him of how fortunate he was to have lived to ask the question.

The low rumble came again, the same noise he had heard when he'd been crawling toward the pistol. This time he recognized it: not the convulsions and drumming heels of a dying man, but simply the vibrations of the automatic garage door, which had been going up the first time, and which now was coming down.

Voices arose in the kitchen as Paige and the girls entered the house from the garage.

Less shaky by the second, and having caught his breath, Marty hurried across the living room, toward the dining room, eager to stop the kids before they saw anything of what had happened. For a long time to come, they would have trouble feeling comfortable in their own home, knowing an intruder had gotten in and had tried to kill their father. But they would be more seriously traumatized if they saw the destruction and the bloodstained man lying paralyzed on the foyer floor. Considering the macabre fact that the intruder was also a dead-ringer for their father, they might never sleep well in this house again.

When Marty burst into the kitchen from the dining room, letting the swinging door slap back and forth behind him, Paige turned in surprise from the rack where she was hanging her raincoat. Still in their yellow slickers and floppy vinyl hats, the girls grinned and tilted their heads expectantly, probably figuring that his explosive entrance was the start of a joke or one of Daddy's silly impromptu performances.

"Get them out of here," he croaked at Paige, trying to sound calm, defeated by his coarse voice and all-too-evident tension.

"What's happened to you?"

"Now," he insisted, "right away, take them across the street to Vic and Kathy's."

The girls saw the gun in his hand. Their grins vanished, and their eyes widened.

Paige said, "You're bleeding. What—"

"Not me," he interrupted, belatedly realizing that he'd gotten the blood of The Other all over his shirt when he'd fallen atop the man. "I'm okay."

"What's happened?" Paige demanded.

Yanking open the connecting door to the garage, he said, "We've had a thing here." His throat hurt when he talked, yet he was all but babbling in his urgent desire to get them safely out of the house, incoherent for perhaps the first time in his word-obsessed life. "A problem, a thing, Jesus, you know, like a thing that happened, some trouble—"

"Marty—"

"Come on, over to the Delorios' place, all of you." He stepped across the threshold, into the dark garage, hit the Genie button, and the big door rumbled upward. He met Paige's eyes. "They'll be safe at the Delorios' place."

Not bothering to pull her coat off the rack, Paige shepherded the girls past him, into the garage, toward the rising door.

"Call the police," he shouted after her, wincing at the pain that a shout cost him.

She glanced back at him, her face lined with worry.

He said, "I'm all right, but we got a guy here, shot bad."

"Come with us," she pleaded.

"Can't. Call the police."

"Marty—"

"Go, Paige, just go!"

She moved between Charlotte and Emily, took each of them by the hand, and led them out of the garage, into the downpour, turning to look back at him only once more.

He watched until they reached the end of the driveway, checked left and right for traffic, and then started across the street. Step by step, as they moved away through the silver curtains of rain, they looked less like real people and more like three retreating spirits. He had the disconcertingly prescient feeling that he would never see them alive again; he knew it was nothing more than an irrational adrenaline-hyped reaction to what he'd been through, but the fear took root in him and grew nevertheless.

A cold wet wind invaded the deepest reaches of the garage, and the perspiration on Marty's face felt as if it had been instantly transformed into ice.

He stepped back into the kitchen and pushed the door shut.

Though he was shivering, half freezing, he craved a cold drink because his throat burned as if it harbored a kerosene fire.

Maybe the man in the foyer was dying, having convulsions right that second, or a heart attack. He was in damned bad shape. So it would be a good idea to get in there and watch over him, in case CPR was necessary before the authorities arrived. Marty didn't care if the guy died—*wanted* him dead—but not until a lot of questions were answered and these recent events made at least *some* sense.

But before he did anything else, he had to get a drink to soothe his throat. Right now, every swallow was torture. When the cops arrived, he would have to be prepared to do a lot of talking.

Tap water didn't seem cold enough to do the trick, so he opened the refrigerator, which he could have sworn was a lot emptier than it had been earlier in the day, and grabbed a carton of milk. No, the idea of milk made him gag. Milk reminded him of blood because it was a bodily fluid, which was ridiculous, of course; but the events of the past hour were irrational, so it followed that some of his reactions would be irrational as well. He returned the carton to the shelf, reached for the orange juice, then saw the bottles of Corona and sixteen-ounce cans of Coors. Nothing had ever looked more desirable than those chilled beers. He grabbed one of the cans because it contained one-third more ounces than a bottle of Corona.

The first long swallow fueled the fire in his throat instead of quenching it. The second hurt slightly less than the first, the third less than the second, and thereafter every sip was as soothing as medicated honey.

With the pistol in one hand and the half-empty can of Coors in the other, shivering more at the memory of what had happened and at the prospect of what lay ahead than because of the icy beer, he went back through the house to the foyer.

The Other was gone.

Marty was so startled, he dropped the Coors. The can rolled behind him, spilling foamy beer on the hardwood floor of the living room. Although the can had slipped out of his grasp so easily, nothing short of hydraulic prybars could have forced him to let go of the gun.

Broken balusters, a section of handrail, and splinters littered the foyer floor. Several Mexican tiles were cracked and chipped from the impact of hard oak and Smith & Wesson steel. No body.

From the moment the double entered Marty's office, the waking day had drifted into nightmare without the usual prerequisite of sleep. Events had slipped the chains of reality, and his own home had become a dark dreamscape. As surreal as the confrontation had been, he hadn't seriously doubted its actuality while it had been playing out. And he didn't doubt it now, either. He hadn't shot a figment of the mind, been strangled by an illusion, or plunged alone through the gallery railing. Lying incapacitated in the foyer, The Other had been as real as the shattered balustrade still scattered on the tiles.

Alarmed by the possibility that Paige and the girls had been attacked in the street before they had gotten to the Delorios' house, Marty turned to the front door. It was locked. From the inside. The security chain was in place. The madman hadn't left the house by that route.

Hadn't left it at all. How could he, in his condition? Don't panic. Be calm. Think it through.

Marty would have bet a year of his life that The Other's catastrophic injuries had been real, not pretense. The bastard's back *had* been broken. His inability to move more than his head and the fingers of one hand meant his spine probably had been severed, as well, when he had done his gravity dance with the floor.

So where was he?

Not upstairs. Even if his spine hadn't been damaged, even if he'd escaped quadriplegia, he couldn't have dragged his battered body up to the second floor during the short time Marty had been in the kitchen.

Opposite the entrance to the living room, a small den opened off the study. The dishwater-gray light of the storm-washed dusk seeped between the open slats of the shutters, illuminating nothing. Marty stepped through the doorway, snapped on the lights. The den was deserted. At the closet, he slid open the mirrored door, but The Other wasn't hiding in there, either.

Foyer closet. Nothing. Powder bath. Nothing. The deep closet under the stairs. Laundry. Family room. Nothing, nothing, nothing.

Marty searched frantically, recklessly, heedless of his safety. He expected to discover his would-be killer nearby and essentially helpless, perhaps even dead, this feeble attempt at escape having depleted the last of the man's resources.

Instead, in the kitchen, he found the back door standing open to the patio. A gust of cold wind swept in from outside, rattling the cupboard doors. On the rack by the entrance to the garage, Paige's raincoat billowed with false life.

While Marty had been returning to the foyer via the dining room and living room, The Other had headed for the kitchen by another route. He must have gone along the short hall that led from the foyer past the powder bath and laundry, and then crossed one end of the family room. He couldn't have crawled that far so quickly. He had been on his feet, perhaps unsteady, but on his feet nonetheless.

No. It wasn't possible. Okay, maybe the guy didn't have a severed spine, after all. Maybe not even a fractured spine. But his back *had* to have been broken. He couldn't simply have sprung to his feet and capered off.

The waking nightmare had displaced reality again. It was time once more to stalk—and be stalked—by something which enjoyed the regenerative powers of a monster in a dream, something which said it had come looking for a life and which seemed fearfully equipped to take it.

Marty stepped through the open door onto the patio.

Renewed fear lifted him to a higher state of awareness in which colors were more intense, odors were more pungent, and sounds were clearer and more refined than ever before. The feeling was akin to the inexpressibly keen sensations of certain childhood and adolescent dreams—especially those in which the dreamer travels the skies as effortlessly as a bird, or experiences sexual communion with a woman of such exquisite form that, later, neither her face nor body can be recalled but only the essential radiance of perfect beauty. Those special dreams seemed not to be fantasies at all but glimpses of a greater and more detailed reality beyond the reality of the waking world. Stepping through the kitchen door, passing out of the warm house into the cold realm of nature, Marty was strangely reminded of the ravishing vividness of those long-forgotten visions, for now he experienced similarly acute sensations, alert to every nuance of what he saw-heard-smelled-touched.

From the thick thatching of bougainvillea overhead, scores of drips and drizzles splashed into puddles as black as oil in the fading light. Upon that liquid blackness floated crimson blossoms in patterns that, though random, seemed consciously mysterious, as portentous and full of meaning as the ancient calligraphy of some long-dead Chinese mystic.

Around the perimeter of the backyard—small and walled, as in most southern California neighborhoods—Indian laurels and clustered eugenias shivered miserably in the brisk wind. Near the northwest corner, the long and tender trailers of a pair of red-gum eucalyptus lashed the air, shedding oblong leaves as smoky-silver as the wings of dragonflies. In the shadows cast by the trees—and behind several of the larger shrubs—were places in which a man could hide.

Marty had no intention of searching there. If his quarry had dragged himself out of the house to cower in a chilly, sodden nest of jasmine and agapanthus, weak from loss of blood—which was most likely the case—finding him was not urgent. It was more important to be sure he was not at that moment escaping unpursued.

Long adapted to dry conditions and accustomed to only the water provided by the sprinkler system, choruses of toads sang from their hidden niches, scores of shrill voices that were usually charming but seemed eerie and threatening now. Above their aria rose the wail of distant but approaching sirens.

If the intruder was trying to get away before the police came, the possible routes of escape were few. He could have climbed one of the property walls, but that seemed unlikely because, regardless of how miraculous his recovery, he simply hadn't had sufficient time to cross the lawn, push through the shrubs, and clamber into one of the neighbors' yards.

Marty turned right and ran out from under the dripping patio cover. Soaked to the skin in half a dozen steps, he followed the rear walkway along the house, then hurried past the back of the attached garage.

The downpour had lured snails from moist and shadowy retreats where they usually remained until well after nightfall. Their pale, jellied bodies were stretched most of the way out of their shells, thick feelers questing ahead. Unavoidably, he stepped on a few, smashed them to pulp, and through his mind flashed the superstitious notion that a cosmic entity would at any second crush him underfoot with equal callousness.

When he turned the corner onto the service walkway flanked by a garage wall and eugenia hedge, he expected to see the look-alike limping toward the front of the property. The walkway was deserted. The gate at the end stood half open.

The sirens were much louder by the time Marty sprinted into the driveway in front of the house. He sloshed through a gutter filled with four or five inches of fast-flowing water as cold as the Styx, stepped into the street, looked left and right, but as yet no police cars were in sight.

The Other was nowhere to be seen, either. Marty was alone on the street.

In the next block south, too far off for him to recognize the make and model, a car was speeding away. In spite of the fact that it was moving too fast for weather conditions, he doubted it was driven by the look-alike. He was still hard-pressed to believe the injured man had been able to walk, let alone reach his car and drive away so quickly. Surely they would find the son of a bitch nearby, lying in shrubbery, unconscious or dead. The car turned the corner much too fast; the thin squeal of its protesting tires was audible above the plink, plop, and susurration of the rain. Then it was gone.

From the north, the banshee shriek of sirens abruptly swelled much louder, and Marty turned to see a black-and-white police sedan negotiate that corner almost as fast as the other car had rounded the corner to the south. Revolving red and blue emergency beacons threw bright Frisbees of light through the gray rain and across the blacktop. The siren cut off as the sedan fishtailed to a stop twenty feet from Marty in the center of the street, with stunt-driver dramatics that seemed excessive even under the circumstances.

The siren of a backup cruiser warbled in the distance as the front doors of the first black-and-white flew open. Two uniformed officers came out of the cruiser, staying low, sheltering behind the doors, shouting, "Drop it! Now! Do it! Drop it right now or die, asshole! *Now!*"

Marty realized he was still holding the 9mm pistol. The cops knew nothing more than what Paige had told them when she'd called 911, that a man had been shot, so of course they figured *he* was the perp. If he didn't do exactly what they demanded, and do it fast, they would shoot him and be justified in doing so.

He let the gun fall out of his hand.

It clattered on the pavement.

They ordered him to kick it away from himself. He complied.

As they rose from behind the open car doors, one of the cops shouted, "On the ground, facedown, hands behind your back!"

He knew better than to try to make them understand that he was the victim rather than the perpetrator. They wanted obedience first, explanations later, and if their positions had been reversed he would have expected the same thing of them.

He dropped to his hands and knees, then stretched full length on the street. Even through his shirt, the wet blacktop was so cold that it took his breath away.

Vic and Kathy Delorio's house was directly across the street from where he was lying, and Marty hoped Charlotte and Emily had been kept away from the front windows. They shouldn't have to see their father flat on the ground, under the guns of policemen. They were already scared. He remembered their wide-eyed stares when he'd burst into the kitchen with the gun in his hand, and he didn't want them frightened further.

The cold leached into his bones.

The second siren suddenly grew much louder from one second to the next. He guessed the backup black-and-white had turned a corner to the south and was approaching from that end of the block. The piercing wail was as cold as a sharp icicle in the ear.

With one side of his face to the pavement, blinking rain out of his eyes, he watched the cops approach. They kept their guns drawn. When they tramped through a shallow puddle, the splashes seemed huge from Marty's perspective.

As they reached him, he said, "It's okay. I live here. This is my house." His speech, already raspy, was further distorted by the shivers that wracked him. He worried that he sounded drunk or demented. "This is my house."

"Just stay down," one of them said sharply. "Keep your hands behind your back and stay down."

The other one asked, "You have any ID?"

Shuddering so badly that his teeth chattered, he said, "Yeah, sure, in my wallet."

Taking no chances, they cuffed him before fishing his wallet out of his hip pocket. The steel bracelets were still warm from the heated air of the patrol car.

He felt exactly as if he were a character in one of his own novels. It was decidedly *not* a good feeling.

The second siren died. Car doors slammed. He heard the crackling static and tinny voices of police-band radios.

"You have any photo ID in here?" asked the cop who had taken his wallet.

Marty rolled his left eye, trying to see something of the man above knee-level. "Yeah, of course, in one of those plastic windows, a driver's license."

In his novels, when innocent characters were suspected of crimes they hadn't committed, they were often worried and afraid. But Marty had never written about the *humiliation* of such an experience. Lying on the frigid blacktop, prone before the police officers, he was mortified as never before in his life, even though he'd done nothing wrong. The situation itself—being in a position of utter submission while regarded with deep suspicion by figures of authority—seemed to trigger some innate guilt, a congenital sense of culpability in some monstrous transgression that couldn't quite be identified, feelings of shame because he was going to be found out, even though he *knew* there was nothing for which he could be blamed.

"How old is this picture on your license?" asked the cop with his wallet.

"Uh, I don't know, two years, three."

"Doesn't look much like you."

"You know what DMV photos are like," Marty said, dismayed to hear more plea than anger in his voice.

"Let him up, it's all right, he's my husband, he's Marty Stillwater," Paige shouted, evidently hurrying toward them from the Delorios' house.

Marty couldn't see her, but her voice gladdened him and restored a sense of reality to the nightmarish moment.

He told himself that everything was going to be all right. The cops would recognize their error, let him up, search the shrubbery around the house and in neighbors' yards, quickly find the look-alike, and arrive at an explanation for all the weirdness of the past hour.

"He's my husband," Paige repeated, much closer now, and Marty could sense the cops staring at her as she approached.

He was blessed with an attractive wife who was well worth staring at even when rain-soaked and distraught; she wasn't merely attractive but smart, charming, amusing, loving, singular. His daughters were great kids. He had a prospering career as a novelist, and he profoundly enjoyed his work. Nothing was going to change any of that. Nothing.

Yet even as the cops removed the handcuffs and helped him to his feet, even as Paige hugged him and as he embraced her gratefully, Marty was acutely and uncomfortably aware that twilight was giving way to nightfall. He looked over her shoulder, searching countless shadowed places along the street, wondering from which nest of darkness the next attack would come. The rain seemed so cold that it ought to have been sleet, the emergency beacons stung his eyes, his throat burned as if he'd gargled with acid, his body ached in a score of places from the battering he had taken, and instinct told him that the worst was yet to come.

No.

No, that wasn't instinct speaking. That was just his overactive imagination at work. The curse of the writer's imagination. Always searching for the next plot twist.

Life wasn't like fiction. Real stories didn't have second and third acts, neat structures, narrative pace, escalating denouements. Crazy things just happened, without the logic of fiction, and then life went on as usual.

The policemen were all watching him hug Paige.

He thought he saw hostility in their faces.

Another siren swelled in the distance.

He was so cold.

THREE

1.

The Oklahoma night made Drew Oslett uneasy. Mile after mile, on both sides of the interstate highway, with rare exception, the darkness was so deep and unrelenting that he seemed to be crossing a bridge over an enormously wide and bottomless abyss. Thousands of stars salted the sky, suggesting an immensity that he preferred not to consider.

He was a creature of the city, his soul in tune with urban bustle. Wide avenues flanked by tall buildings were the largest open spaces with which he was entirely comfortable. He had lived for many years in New York, but he had never visited Central Park; those fields and vales were encircled by the city, yet Oslett found them sufficiently large and bucolic to make him edgy. He was in his element only in sheltering forests of highrises, where sidewalks teemed with people and streets were jammed with noisy traffic. In his midtown Manhattan apartment, he slept with no drapes over the windows, so the ambient light of the metropolis flooded the room. When he woke in the night, he was comforted by periodic sirens, blaring horns, drunken shouts, car-rattled manhole covers, and other more exotic noises that rose from the streets even during the dead hours, though at diminished volume from the glorious clash and jangle of mornings, afternoons, and evenings. The continuous cacophony and infinite distractions of the city were the silk of his cocoon, protecting him, ensuring that he would never find himself in the quiet circumstances that encouraged contemplation and introspection.

Darkness and silence offered no distraction and were, therefore, enemies of contentment. Rural Oklahoma had too damned much of both.

Slightly slumped in the passenger seat of the rented Chevrolet, Drew Oslett shifted his attention from the unnerving landscape to the state-of-the-art electronic map that he was holding on his lap.

The device was as big as an attaché case, though square instead of rectangular, and operated off the car battery through a cigarette-lighter plug. The flat top of it resembled the front of a television set: mostly screen with a narrow frame of brushed steel and a row of control buttons. Against a softly luminous lime-green background, interstate highways were indicated in emerald green, state routes in yellow, and county roads in blue; unpaved dirt and gravel byways were represented by broken black lines. Population centers—precious few in this part of the world—were pink.

Their vehicle was a red dot of light near the middle of the screen. The dot moved steadily along the emerald-green line that was Interstate 40.

"About four miles ahead now," Oslett said.

Karl Clocker, the driver, did not respond. Even in the best of times, Clocker was not much of a conversationalist. The average rock was more talkative.

The square screen of the electronic map was set to a mid-range scale, displaying a hundred square miles of territory in a ten-mile-by-ten-mile grid. Oslett touched one of the buttons, and the map blinked off, replaced almost instantly by a twenty-five-square-mile block, five miles on a side, that enlarged one quadrant of the first picture to fill the screen.

The red dot representing their car was now four times larger than before. It was no longer in the center of the picture but off to the right side.

Near the left end of the display, less than four miles away, a blinking white X remained stationary just a fraction of an inch to the right of Interstate 40. X marked the prize.

Oslett enjoyed working with the map because the screen was so colorful, like the board of a well-designed video game. He liked video games a lot. In fact, although he was thirty-two, some of his favorite places were arcades, where arrays of cool machines tantalized the eye with strobing light in every color and romanced the ear with incessant beeps, tweets, buzzes, hoots, whoops, waw-waws, clangs, booms, riffs of music, and oscillating electronic tones.

Unfortunately, the map had none of the action of a game. And it lacked sound effects altogether.

Still, it excited him because not just anyone could get his hands on the device—which was called a SATU, for Satellite Assisted Tracking Unit. It wasn't sold to the public, partly because the cost was so exorbitant that potential purchasers were too few to justify marketing it broadly. Besides, some of the technology was encumbered by strict national-security prohibitions against dissemination. And because the map was primarily a tool for serious clandestine tracking and surveillance, most of the relatively small number of existing units were currently used by federally controlled law-enforcement and intelligence-gathering agencies or were in the hands of similar organizations in countries allied with the United States.

"Three miles," he told Clocker.

The hulking driver did not even grunt by way of reply.

Wires trailed from the SATU and terminated in a three-inch-diameter suction cup that Oslett had fixed to the highest portion of the curved windshield. A locus of microminiature electronics in the base of the cup was the transmitter and receiver of a satellite up-link package. Through coded bursts of microwaves, the SATU could quickly interface with scores of geosynchronous communication and survey satellites owned by private industry and various military services, override their security systems, insert its program in their logic units, and enlist them in its operations without either disturbing their primary functions or alerting their ground monitors to the invasion.

By using two satellites to search for—and get a lock on—the unique signal of a particular transponder, the SATU could triangulate a precise position for the carrier of that transponder. Usually the target transmitter was an inconspicuous package that had been planted in the undercarriage of the surveillance subject's car—sometimes in his plane or boat—so he could be followed at a distance without ever being aware that someone was tailing him.

In this case, it was a transponder hidden in the rubber heel and sole of a shoe.

Oslett used the SATU controls to halve the area represented on the screen, thereby dramatically enlarging the details on the map. Studying the new but equally colorful display, he said, "He's still not moving. Looks like maybe he's pulled off the side of the road in a rest stop."

The SATU microchips contained detailed maps of every square mile of the continental United States, Canada, and Mexico. If Oslett had been operating in Europe, the Mideast or elsewhere, he could have installed the suitable cartographical library for that territory.

"Two and a half miles," Oslett said.

Driving with one hand, Clocker reached under his sportcoat and withdrew the revolver he carried in a shoulder holster. It was a Colt .357 Magnum, an eccentric choice of weaponry—and somewhat dated—for a man in Karl Clocker's line of work. He also favored tweed jackets with leather-covered buttons, leather patches on the elbows, and on occasion— as now—leather lapels. He had an eccentric collection of sweater vests with bold harlequin patterns, one of which he was currently wearing. His brightly colored socks were usually chosen to clash with everything else, and without fail he wore brown suede Hush Puppies. Considering his size and demeanor, no one was likely to comment negatively on his taste in clothes, let alone make unasked-for observations about his choice of handguns.

"Won't need heavy firepower," Oslett said.

Without saying a word to Oslett, Clocker put the .357 Magnum on the seat beside him, next to his hat, where he could get to it easily.

"I've got the trank gun," Oslett said. "That should do it."

Clocker didn't even look at him.

2.

Before Marty would agree to get out of the rainswept street and tell the authorities what had happened, he insisted that a uniformed officer watch over Charlotte and Emily at the Delorios' house. He trusted Vic and Kathy to do anything necessary to protect the girls. But they would not be a match for the vicious relentlessness of The Other.

He wasn't sanguine that even a well-armed guard was enough protection.

On the Delorios' front porch, rain streamed from the overhang. It looked like holiday tinsel in the glow of the brass hurricane lamp. Sheltering there, Marty tried to make Vic understand the girls were still in danger. "Don't let anyone in except the cops or Paige."

"Sure, Marty." Vic was a physical-education teacher, coach of the local high-school swimming team, Boy Scout troop leader, primary motivator behind their street's Neighborhood Watch program, and organizer of various annual charity fund drives, an earnest and energetic guy who enjoyed helping people and who wore athletic shoes even on occasions when he also wore a coat and tie, as if more formal footwear would not allow him to move as fast and accomplish as much as he wished. "Nobody but the cops or Paige. Leave it to me, the kids will be okay with me and Kathy. Jesus, Marty what happened over there?"

"And for God's sake, don't give the girls to anyone, cops or anyone, unless Paige is with them. Don't even give them to *me* unless Paige is with me."

Vic Delorio looked away from the police activity and blinked in surprise.

In memory, Marty could hear the look-alike's angry voice, see the flecks of spittle flying from his mouth as he raged: *I want my life, my Paige . . . my Charlotte, my Emily . . .*

"You understand, Vic?"

"Not to you?"

"Only if Paige is with me. *Only* then."

"What—"

"I'll explain later," Marty interrupted. "Everybody's waiting for me." He turned and hurried along the front walk toward the street, looking back once to say, "Only Paige."

. . . my Paige . . . my Charlotte, my Emily . . .

At home, in the kitchen, while recounting the assault to the officer who had caught the call and been first on the scene, Marty allowed a police technician to ink his fingers and roll them on a record sheet. They needed to be able to differentiate between his prints and those of the intruder. He wondered if he and The Other would prove to be as identical in that regard as they seemed in every other.

Paige also submitted to the process. It was the first time in their lives that either of them had been fingerprinted. Though Marty understood the need for it, the whole process seemed invasive.

After he got what he required, the technician moistened a paper towel with a glycerol cleanser and said that it would remove all the ink. It didn't. No matter how hard he rubbed, dark stains remained in the whorls of his skin.

Before sitting down to make a more complete statement to the officer in charge, Marty went upstairs to change into dry clothes. He also took four Anacin.

He turned up the thermostat, and the house quickly overheated. But periodic shivers still plagued him—largely because of the unnerving presence of so many police officers.

They were everywhere in the house. Some were in uniforms, others were not, and all of them were strangers whose presence made Marty feel further violated.

He hadn't anticipated how utterly a victim's privacy was peeled away beginning the moment he reported a serious crime. Policemen and technicians were in his office to photograph the room where the violent confrontation had begun, dig a couple of bullets out of the wall, dust for fingerprints, and take blood samples from the carpet. They were also photographing the upstairs hall, stairs, and foyer. In their search for evidence that the intruder might have left behind, they assumed they had an invitation to poke into any room or closet.

Of course they were in his house to help him, and Marty was grateful for their efforts. Yet it was embarrassing to think that strangers might be noting the admittedly obsessive way he organized the clothes in his closet according to color—he and Emily both—the fact that he collected pennies and nickels in a half-gallon jar as might a boy saving for his first bicycle, and other unimportant yet highly personal details of his life.

And he was more unsettled by the plainclothes detective in charge than by the rest of them combined. The guy's name was Cyrus Lowbock, and he elicited a complex response that went beyond mere embarrassment.

The detective could have made a good living as a male model posing for magazine advertisements for Rolls-Royce, tuxedoes, caviar, and stock-brokerage services. He was about fifty, trim, with salt-and-pepper hair, a tan even in November, an aquiline nose, fine cheekbones, and extraordinary gray eyes. In black loafers, gray cords, dark-blue cable-knit sweater, and white shirt—he had taken off a windbreaker—Lowbock managed to appear both distinguished and athletic, although the sports one would associate with him were not football and baseball but tennis, sailing, powerboat racing, and other pursuits of the upper classes. He looked less like any popular image of a cop than like a man who had been born to wealth and knew how to manage and preserve it.

Lowbock sat across the dining-room table from Marty, listening intently to his account of the assault, asking questions largely to clarify the details, and writing in a spiral-bound notebook with an expensive black-and-gold Montblanc pen. Paige sat beside Marty, offering emotional support. They were the only three people in the room, although uniformed officers interrupted periodically to confer with Lowbock, and twice the detective excused himself to examine evidence that had been deemed relevant to the case.

Sipping Pepsi from a ceramic mug, soothing his throat while recounting the life-and-death struggle with the intruder, Marty also experienced a resurgence of the inexplicable guilt that had first troubled him when he'd lain on the wet street with his hands cuffed. The feeling was no less irrational than before, considering that the biggest crime of which he could justifiably be accused was routine contempt for the speed limits on certain roads. But this time he understood that part of his uneasiness resulted from the perception that Lieutenant Cyrus Lowbock regarded him with quiet suspicion.

Lowbock was polite, but he did not say much. His silences were vaguely accusatory. When he wasn't taking notes, his zinc-gray eyes focused unwaveringly, challengingly, on Marty.

Why the detective should suspect him of being less than entirely truthful was not clear. However, Marty supposed that after years of police work, dealing with the worst elements of society day in and day out, the understandable tendency was toward cynicism. Regardless of what the Constitution of the United States promised, a long-time cop probably felt justified in the conviction that all men—and women—were guilty until proven innocent.

Marty finished his story and took another long sip of cola. Cold fluids had done all they could for his sore throat; the greater discomfort was now in the tissues of his neck, where throttling hands had left the skin reddened and where extensive bruising would surely appear by morning. Though the four Anacin were beginning to kick in, a pain akin to whiplash made him wince when he turned his head more than a few degrees in either direction, so he adopted a stiff-necked posture and movement.

For what seemed an excessive length of time, Lowbock paged through his notes, reviewing them in silence, quietly tapping the Montblanc pen against the pages.

The splash and tap of rain still enlivened the night, though the storm had abated somewhat.

Floorboards upstairs creaked now and then with the weight of the policemen still at their assigned tasks.

Under the table, Paige's right hand sought Marty's left, and he gave it a squeeze as if to say that everything was all right now.

But everything wasn't all right. Nothing had been explained or resolved. As far as he knew, their trouble was just beginning.

. . . my Paige . . . my Charlotte, my Emily . . .

At last Lowbock looked at Marty. In a flat tone of voice that was damning precisely because of its complete *lack* of interpretable inflection, the detective said, "Quite a story."

"I know it sounds crazy." Marty stifled the urge to assure Lowbock that he had not exaggerated the degree of resemblance between himself and the look-alike or any other aspect of his account. He had told the truth. He was not required to apologize for the fact that the truth, in this instance, was as astounding as any fantasy.

"And you say you don't have a twin brother?" Lowbock asked.

"No, sir."

"No brother at all?"

"I'm an only child."

"Half brother?"

"My parents were married when they were eighteen. Neither of them was ever married to anyone else. I assure you, Lieutenant, there's no easy explanation for this guy."

"Well, of course, no other marriages would've been necessary for you to have a half brother . . . or a full brother, for that matter," Lowbock said, meeting Marty's eyes so directly that to look away from him would have been an admission of something.

As Marty digested the detective's statement, Paige squeezed his hand under the table, an admonition not to let Lowbock rattle him. He tried to tell himself that the detective was only stating a fact, which he was, but it would have been decent to look at the notebook or at the window when making such implications.

Replying almost as stiffly as he was holding his head, Marty said, "Let me see . . . I guess I have three choices then. Either my father knocked up my mother before they were married, and they put this full brother—this *bastard* brother—up for adoption. Or after my folks were married, Dad screwed around with some other woman, and she gave birth to my half brother. Or my mother got pregnant by some other guy, either before or after she married my father, and that whole pregnancy is a deep, dark family secret."

Maintaining eye contact, Lowbock said, "I'm sorry if I offended you, Mr. Stillwater."

"I'm sorry you did, too."

"Aren't you being a little sensitive about this?"

"Am I?" Marty asked sharply, though he wondered if in fact he *was* over-reacting.

"Some couples *do* have a first child before they're ready to make that commitment," the detective said, "and they often put it up for adoption."

"Not my folks."

"Do you know that for a fact?"

"I know *them.*"

"Maybe you should ask them."

"Maybe I will."

"When?"

"I'll think about it."

A smile, as faint and brief as the passing shadow of a bird in flight, crossed Lowbock's face.

Marty was sure he saw sarcasm in that smile. But, for the life of him, he couldn't understand why the detective would regard him as anything less than an innocent victim.

Lowbock looked down at his notes, letting the silence build for a while. Then he said, "If this look-alike isn't related to you, brother or half brother, then do you have any idea how to explain such a remarkable resemblance?"

Marty started to shake his head, winced as pain shot through his neck. "No. No idea at all."

Paige said, "You want some aspirin?"

"Had some Anacin," Marty said. "I'll be okay."

Meeting Marty's eyes again, Lowbock said, "I just thought you might have a theory."

"No. Sorry."

"You being a writer and all."

Marty didn't get the detective's meaning. "Excuse me?"

"You use your imagination every day, you earn a living with it."

"So?"

"So I thought maybe you'd figure out this little mystery if you put your mind to it."

"I'm no detective. I'm clever enough at constructing mysteries, but I don't unravel them."

"On television," Lowbock said, "the mystery writer—any amateur detective, for that matter—is always smarter than the cops."

"It's not that way in real life," Marty said.

Lowbock let a few seconds of silence drift past, doodling on the bottom of a page of his notes, before he replied: "No, it's not."

"I don't confuse fantasy and reality," Marty said a little too harshly.

"I wouldn't have thought you do," Cyrus Lowbock assured him, concentrating on his doodle.

Marty turned his head cautiously to see if Paige showed any sign of perceiving hostility in the detective's tone and manner. She was frowning thoughtfully at Lowbock, which made Marty feel better; maybe he was not over-reacting, after all, and didn't need to add paranoia to the list of symptoms he had recounted to Paul Guthridge.

Emboldened by Paige's frown, Marty faced Lowbock again and said, "Lieutenant, is something wrong here?"

Raising his eyebrows as if surprised by the question, Lowbock said archly, "It's certainly my impression that something's wrong, or otherwise you wouldn't have called us."

Restraining himself from making the caustic reply that Lowbock deserved, Marty said, "I mean, I sense hostility here, and I don't understand the reason for it. What *is* the reason?"

"Hostility? Do you?" Without looking up from his doodle, Lowbock frowned. "Well, I wouldn't want the victim of a crime to be as intimidated by us as by the creep who assaulted him. That wouldn't be good public relations, would it?" With that, he neatly avoided a direct answer to Marty's question.

The doodle was finished. It was a drawing of a pistol.

"Mr. Stillwater, the gun with which you shot this intruder—was that the same weapon taken from you out in the street?"

"It wasn't taken from me. I voluntarily dropped it when told to do so. And, yes, it was the same gun."

"A Smith and Wesson nine-millimeter pistol?"

"Yes."

"Did you purchase that weapon from a licensed gun dealer?"

"Yes, of course." Marty told him the name of the shop.

"Do you have a receipt from the store and proof of pre-purchase review by the proper law-enforcement agency?"

"What does this have to do with what happened here today?"

"Routine," Lowbock said. "I have to fill out all the little lines on the crime report later. Just routine."

Marty didn't like the way the interview increasingly seemed to be turning into an interrogation, but he didn't know what to do about it. Frustrated, he looked to Paige for the answer to Lowbock's inquiry because she kept their financial records for the accountant.

She said, "All the paperwork from the gun shop would be stapled together and filed with all of our canceled checks for that year."

"We bought it maybe three years ago," Marty said.

"That stuff's packed away in the garage attic," Paige added.

"But you can get it for me?" Lowbock asked.

"Well . . . yes, with a little digging around," Paige said, and she started to get up from her chair.

"Oh, don't trouble yourself right this minute," Lowbock said. "It's not that urgent." He turned to Marty again: "What about the Korth thirty-eight in the glovebox of your Taurus? Did you buy that at the same gun shop?"

Surprised, Marty said, "What were you doing in the Taurus?"

Lowbock feigned surprise at Marty's surprise, but it seemed calculated to look false, to needle Marty by mimicking him. "In the Taurus? Investigating the case. That is what we've been asked to do? I mean, there aren't any places, any subjects, you'd rather we didn't look into? Because, of course, we'd respect your wishes in that regard."

The detective was so subtle in his mockery and so vague in his insinuations that any strong response on Marty's part would appear to be the reaction of a man with something to hide. Clearly, Lowbock thought he *did* have something to hide and was toying with him, trying to rattle him into an inadvertent admission.

Marty almost wished he *did* have an admission to make. As they were currently playing this game, it was enormously frustrating.

"Did you buy the thirty-eight at the same gun shop where you purchased the Smith and Wesson?" Lowbock persisted.

"Yes." Marty sipped his Pepsi.

"Do you have the paperwork on that?"

"Yes, I'm sure we do."

"Do you always carry that gun in your car?"

"No."

"It was in your car today."

Marty was aware that Paige was looking at him with some degree of surprise. He couldn't explain about his panic attack now or tell her about the strange awareness of an onrushing Juggernaut which had preceded it, and which had driven him to take extraordinary precautions. Considering the unexpected and less-than-benign turn the questioning had taken, this was not information he wanted to share with the detective, for fear he'd sound unbalanced and would find himself involuntarily committed for psychiatric evaluation.

Marty sipped some Pepsi, not to soothe his throat but to gain a little time to think before responding to Lowbock. "I didn't know it was there," he said at last.

Lowbock said, "You didn't know the gun was in your glovebox?"

"No."

"Are you aware that it's illegal to carry a loaded weapon in your car?"

And just what the hell were you people doing, poking around in my car?

"Like I said, I didn't know it was there, so of course I didn't know it was loaded, either."

"You didn't load it yourself?"

"Well, I probably did."

"You mean, you don't remember if you loaded it or how it got in the Taurus?"

"What probably happened . . . the last time I went to the shooting range, maybe I loaded it for one more round of target practice and then forgot."

"And brought it home from the shooting range in your glovebox?"

"That's right."

"When was the last time you were at the shooting range?"

"I don't know . . . three, four weeks ago."

"Then you've been carrying a loaded gun around in your car for a month?"

"But I'd forgotten it was in there."

One lie, told to avoid a misdemeanor gun-possession charge, had led to a string of lies. All were minor falsehoods, but Marty had enough grudging respect for Cyrus Lowbock's abilities to know that he perceived them as untruthful. Because the detective already seemed unreasonably convinced that the apparent victim should be regarded instead as a suspect, he would assume that each mendacity was further proof that dark secrets were being concealed from him.

Tilting his head back slightly, staring cooly yet accusingly at Marty, using his patrician looks to intimidate but keeping his voice soft and without inflection, Lowbock said, "Mr. Stillwater, are you always so careless with guns?"

"I don't believe I've been careless."

The raised eyebrow again. "Don't you?"

"No."

The detective picked up his pen and made a cryptic note in his spiral-bound notebook. Then he began to doodle again. "Tell me, Mr. Stillwater, do you have a permit to carry a concealed weapon?"

"No, of course not."

"I see."

Marty sipped his Pepsi.

Under the table, Paige sought his hand again. He was grateful for the contact.

The new doodle was taking shape. A pair of handcuffs.

Lowbock said, "Are you a gun enthusiast, a collector?"

"No, not really."

"But you have a lot of guns."

"Not so many."

Lowbock enumerated them on the fingers of one hand. "Well, the Smith and Wesson, the Korth—the Colt M16 assault rifle in the foyer closet."

Oh, sweet Jesus.

Looking up from his hand, meeting Marty's eyes with that cool, intense gaze, Lowbock said, "Were you aware the M16 was also loaded?"

"I've bought all the guns primarily for research, book research. I don't like to write about a gun without having used it." It was the truth, but even to Marty it sounded like flimflam.

"And you keep them loaded, tucked into drawers and closets all over the house?"

No safe answer occurred to Marty. If he said he knew the rifle was loaded, Lowbock would want to know why anyone would need to keep a military weapon in such a state of readiness in a peaceful, quiet residential neighborhood. An M16 was sure as hell not a suitable home-defense gun except, perhaps, if you lived in Beirut or Kuwait City or South Central Los Angeles. On the other hand, if he said that he hadn't known the rifle was loaded, there would be more snide questions about his carelessness with guns and bolder insinuations that he was lying.

Besides, whatever he said might seem foolish or deceptive in the extreme if they had also found the Mossberg shotgun under the bed in the master bedroom or the Beretta that he had stashed in a kitchen cabinet.

Trying not to lose his temper, he said, "What do my guns have to do with what happened today? It seems to me we've gotten way off the track, Lieutenant."

"Is that how it seems?" Lowbock asked, as if genuinely puzzled by Marty's attitude.

"Yes, that's how it seems," Paige said sharply, obviously realizing she was in a better position than Marty to be harsh with the detective. "You make it seem as if Marty's the one who broke into somebody's home and tried to strangle them to death."

Marty said, "Do you have men searching the neighborhood, have you put out an APB?"

"An APB?"

Marty was irritated by the detective's intentional obtuseness. "An APB for The Other."

Frowning, Lowbock said, "For the what?"

"For the look-alike, the other *me.*"

"Oh, yes, him." That wasn't actually an answer, but Lowbock went on with his agenda before Marty or Paige could insist on a more specific reply: "Is the Heckler and Koch another one of the weapons you purchased for research?"

"Heckler and Koch?"

"The P7. Fires nine-millimeter ammunition."

"I don't own a P7."

"You don't? Well, it was lying on the floor of your office upstairs."

"That was *his* gun," Marty said. "I told you he had a gun."

"Did you know the barrel on that P7 is threaded for a silencer?"

"He had a gun, that's all I knew. I didn't take time to notice if it had a silencer. I didn't exactly have the leisure to catalogue all its features."

"Wasn't a silencer on it, actually, but it's threaded for one. Mr. Stillwater, did you know it's illegal to equip a firearm with a silencer?"

"It's not my gun, Lieutenant."

Marty was beginning to wonder if he should refuse to answer any more questions without an attorney present. But that was crazy. He hadn't done anything. He was innocent. He was the victim, for God's sake. The police wouldn't even have been there if he hadn't told Paige to call them.

"A Heckler and Koch P7 threaded for a silencer—that's very much a professional's weapon, Mr. Stillwater. Hitman, assassin, whatever you want to call him. What *would* you call him?"

"What do you mean?" Marty asked.

"Well, I was wondering, if you were writing about such a man, a professional, what are the various terms you'd use to refer to him?"

Marty sensed an unspoken implication in the question, something that was getting close to the heart of whatever agenda Lowbock was promoting, but he was not quite sure what it was.

Apparently Paige sensed it, too, for she said, "Exactly what are you trying to say, Lieutenant?"

Frustratingly, Cyrus Lowbock edged away from confrontation again. In fact, he lowered his gaze to his notes and pretended as if there had been nothing more to his question than casual curiosity about a writer's choice of synonyms. "Anyway, you're very lucky that a professional like this, a man who would carry a P7 threaded for a silencer, wasn't able to get the best of you."

"I surprised him."

"Evidently."

"By having a gun in my desk drawer."

"It always pays to be prepared," Lowbock said. Then quickly: "But you were lucky to get the best of him in hand-to-hand combat, too. A professional like that would be a good close-in fighter, maybe even know Tae Kwon Do or something, like they always do in books and movies."

"He was slowed a little. Two shots in the chest."

Nodding, the detective said, "Yes, that's right, I remember. Ought to've brought down any ordinary man."

"He was lively enough." Marty tenderly touched his throat.

Changing subjects with a suddenness meant to be disconcerting, Lowbock said, "Mr. Stillwater, were you drinking this afternoon?"

Giving in to his anger, Marty said, "It can't be explained away that easily, Lieutenant."

"You weren't drinking this afternoon?"

"No."

"Not at all?"

"No."

"I don't mean to be argumentative, Mr. Stillwater, really I don't, but when we first met, I smelled alcohol on your breath. Beer, I believe. And there's a can of Coors lying in the living room, beer spilled on the wood floor."

"I drank some beer after."

"After what?"

"After it was over. He was lying on the foyer floor with a broken back. At least I thought it was broken."

"So you figured, after all that shooting and fighting, a cold beer was just the thing."

Paige glared at the detective. "You're trying so hard to make the whole business sound silly—"

"—and I wish to hell you'd just come right out and tell us *why* you don't believe me," Marty added.

"I don't *dis*believe you, Mr. Stillwater. I know this is all very frustrating, you feel put-upon, you're still shaken up, tired. But I'm still absorbing, listening and absorbing. That's what I do. It's my job. And I really haven't formed any theories or opinions yet."

Marty was certain that was not the truth. Lowbock had carried with him a set of fully formed opinions when he'd first sat down at the dining-room table.

After draining the last of the Pepsi in the mug, Marty said, "I almost drank some milk, orange juice, but my throat was so sore, hurt like hell, as if it was on fire. I couldn't swallow without agony. When I opened the refrigerator, the beer just looked a lot better than anything else, the most refreshing."

With his Montblanc pen, Lowbock was again doodling on one corner of a page in his notebook. "So you only had that one can of Coors."

"Not all of it. I drank half, maybe two-thirds. When my throat was feeling a little better, I went back to see how The Other . . . how the look-alike was doing. I was carrying the beer with me. I was so surprised to see the bastard gone, after he'd looked half dead, the can of Coors just sort of slipped out of my hand."

Even though it was upside-down, Marty was able to see what the detective was drawing. A bottle. A long-necked beer bottle.

"So then half a can of Coors," Lowbock said.

"That's right."

"Maybe two-thirds."

"Yes."

"But nothing more."

"No."

Finishing his doodle, Lowbock looked up from the notebook and said, "What about the three empty bottles of Corona in the trash can under the kitchen sink?"

3.

"Rest area, this exit," Drew Oslett read. Then he said to Clocker, "You see that sign?"

Clocker did not reply.

Returning his attention to the SATU screen in his lap, Oslett said, "That's where he is, all right, maybe taking a leak in the men's room, maybe even stretched out on the back seat of whatever car he's driving, catching a few winks."

They were about to go into action against an unpredictable and formidable adversary, but Clocker appeared unperturbed. Even though driving, he seemed to be lost in a meditative state. His bearlike body was as relaxed as that of a Tibetan monk in a transcendental swoon. His enormous hands rested on the steering wheel, the thick fingers only slightly curled, maintaining the minimum grip. Oslett wouldn't have been surprised to learn that the big man was steering the car mostly with some arcane power of the mind. Nothing in Clocker's broad, blunt-featured face indicated that he knew what the word "tension" meant: pale brow as smooth as polished marble; cheeks unlined; sapphire-blue eyes softly radiant in the reflected light of the instrument panel, gazing into the distance, not merely at the road ahead but possibly beyond this world. His wide mouth was open just enough to accept a thin communion wafer. His lips were curved in the faintest of smiles, but it was impossible to know if he was pleased by something he was contemplating in a spiritual reverie or by the prospect of imminent violence.

Karl Clocker had a talent for violence.

For that reason, in spite of his taste in clothes, he was a man of his times.

"Here's the rest area," Oslett said as they neared the end of the access road.

"Where else would it be?" Clocker responded.

"Huh?"

"It is where it is."

The big man wasn't much of a talker, and when he *did* have something to say, half the time it was cryptic. Oslett suspected Clocker of being either a closet existentialist or—at the other end of the spectrum—a New Age mystic. Though the truth might be that he was so totally self-contained, he didn't need much human contact or interaction; his own thoughts and observations adequately engaged and entertained him. One thing was certain: Clocker was not as stupid as he looked; in fact, he had an IQ well above average.

The rest-area parking lot was illuminated by eight tall sodium-vapor lamps. After so many grim miles of unrelieved darkness, which had begun to seem like the blasted black barrens of a post-nuclear landscape, Oslett's spirits were lifted by the glow of the tall lamps, though it was a sickly urine-yellow reminiscent of the sour light in a bad dream. No one would ever mistake the place for any part of Manhattan, but it confirmed that civilization still existed.

A large motorhome was the only vehicle in sight. It was parked near the concrete-block building that housed the comfort stations.

"We're right on top of him now." Oslett switched off the SATU screen and placed the unit on the floor between his feet. Popping the suction cup off the windshield, dropping it on the electronic map, he said, "No doubt about it—our Alfie's snug in that road hog. Probably ripped it off some poor shmuck, now he's on the run with all the comforts of home."

They drove past a grassy area with three picnic tables and parked about twenty feet away from the Road King, on the driver's side.

No lights were on in the motorhome.

"No matter how far off the tracks Alfie's gone," Oslett said, "I still think he'll respond well to us. We're all he has, right? Without us, he's alone in the world. Hell, we're like his family."

Clocker switched off the lights and the engine.

Oslett said, "Regardless of what condition he's in, I don't think he'd hurt us. Not old Alfie. Maybe he'd waste anyone else who got in his way but not us. What do you think?"

Getting out of the Chevy, Clocker plucked both his hat and his Colt .357 Magnum off the front seat.

Oslett took a flashlight and the tranquilizer gun. The bulky pistol had two barrels, over and under, each loaded with a fat hypodermic cartridge. It was designed for use in zoos and wasn't accurate at more than fifty feet, which was good enough for Oslett's purpose, since he wasn't planning to go after any lions on the veldt.

Oslett was grateful that the rest area was not crowded with travelers. He hoped that he and Clocker could finish their business and get away before any cars or trucks pulled in from the highway.

On the other hand, when he got out of the Chevy and eased the door shut behind him, he was disturbed by the emptiness of the night. Except for the singing of tires and the air-cutting *whoosh* of passing traffic on the interstate, the silence was as oppressive as it must be in the vacuum of deep space. A copse of tall pines stood as backdrop to the entire rest area, and, in the windless darkness, their heavy boughs drooped like swags of funeral bunting.

He craved the hum and bustle of urban streets, where ceaseless activity offered continuous distractions. Commotion provided escape from contemplation. In the city, the flash-clatter-spin of daily life allowed his attention to be directed forever outward if he wished, sparing him the dangers inherent in self-examination.

Joining Clocker at the driver's door of the Road King, Oslett considered making as stealthy an entrance as possible. But if Alfie was inside, as the SATU electronic map specifically indicated, he was probably already aware of their arrival.

Besides, on the deepest cognitive levels, Alfie was conditioned to respond to Drew Oslett with absolute obedience. It was almost inconceivable that he would attempt to harm him.

Almost.

They had also been certain that the chances of Alfie going AWOL were so small as to be nonexistent. They had been wrong about that. Time might prove them wrong about other things.

That was why Oslett had the tranquilizer gun.

And that was why he didn't try to dissuade Clocker from bringing the .357 Magnum.

Steeling himself for the unexpected, Oslett knocked on the metal door. Knocking seemed a ludicrous way to announce himself under the circumstances, but he knocked anyway, waited several seconds, and knocked again, louder.

No one answered.

The door was unlocked. He opened it.

Enough yellow light from the parking-lot lamps filtered through the windshield to illuminate the cockpit of the motorhome. Oslett could see that no immediate threat loomed.

He stepped up onto the door sill, leaned in, and looked back through the Road King, which tunneled away into a swarming darkness as deep as the chambers of ancient catacombs.

"Be at peace, Alfie," he said softly.

That spoken command should have resulted in an immediate ritual response, as in a litany: *I am at peace, Father.*

"Be at peace, Alfie," Oslett repeated less hopefully.

Silence.

Although Oslett was neither Alfie's father nor a man of the cloth, and therefore in no way could lay a legitimate claim to the honorific, his heart nevertheless would have been gladdened if he had heard the whispered and obedient reply: *I am at peace, Father.* Those five simple words, in an answering murmur, would have meant that all was essentially well, that Alfie's deviation from his instructions was less a rebellion than a temporary confusion of purpose, and that the killing spree on which he had embarked was something that could be forgiven and put behind them.

Though he knew it was useless, Oslett tried a third time, speaking louder than before: "Be at peace, Alfie."

When nothing in the darkness answered him, he switched on the flashlight and climbed into the Road King.

He couldn't help but think what a waste and humiliation it would be if he got himself shot to death in a strange motorhome along an interstate in the Oklahoma vastness at the tender age of thirty-two. Such a bright young man of such singular promise (the mourners would say), with two degrees—one from Princeton, one from Harvard—and an enviable pedigree.

Moving out of the cockpit as Clocker entered behind him, Oslett swept the beam of the flashlight left and right. Shadows billowed and flapped like black capes, ebony wings, lost souls.

Only a few members of his family—fewer still among that circle of Manhattan artists, writers, and critics who were his friends—would know in what line of duty he had perished. The rest would find the details of his demise baffling, bizarre, possibly sordid, and they would gossip with the feverishness of birds tearing at carrion.

The flashlight revealed Formica-sheathed cabinets. A stove top. A stain-less-steel sink.

The mystery surrounding his peculiar death would ensure that myths would grow like coral reefs, incorporating every color of scandal and vile supposition, but leaving his memory with precious little tint of respect. Respect was one of the few things that mattered to Drew Oslett. He had demanded respect since he was only a boy. It was his birthright, not merely a pleasing accoutrement of the family name but a tribute that must be paid to all of the family's history and accomplishments embodied in him.

"Be at peace, Alfie," he said nervously.

A hand, as white as marble and as solid-looking, had been waiting for the flashlight beam to find it. The alabaster fingers trailed on the carpet beside the padded booth of a dining nook. Higher up: the white-haired body of a man slumped over the bloodstained table.

4.

Paige got up from the dining-room table, went to the nearest window, tilted the shutter slats to make wider gaps, and stared out at the gradually fading storm. She was looking into the backyard, where there were no lights. She could see nothing clearly except the tracks of rain on the other side of the glass, which seemed like gobs of spit, maybe because she wanted to spit at Lowbock, right in his face.

She had more hostility in her than did Marty, not just toward the detective but toward the world. All her adult life, she had been struggling to resolve the conflicts of childhood that were the source of her anger. She had made considerable progress. But in the face of provocation like this, she felt the resentments and bitterness of her childhood rising anew, and her directionless anger found a focus in Lowbock, making it difficult for her to keep her temper in check.

Conscious avoidance—facing the window, keeping the detective out of sight—was a proven technique for maintaining self-control. *Counselor, counsel thyself.* Reducing the level of interaction was supposed to reduce anger as well.

She hoped it worked better for her clients than it worked for her, because she was still *seething.*

At the table with the detective, Marty seemed determined to be reasonable and cooperative. Being Marty, he would cling as long as possible to the hope that Lowbock's mysterious antagonism could be assuaged. Angry as he might be himself—and he was angrier than she had ever seen him—he still had tremendous faith in the power of good intentions and words, especially words, to restore and maintain harmony under any circumstances.

To Lowbock, Marty said, "It had to be him drank the beers."

"Him?" Lowbock asked.

"The look-alike. He must've been in the house a couple of hours while I was out."

"So the intruder drank the three Coronas?"

"I emptied the trash last night, Sunday night, so I know they aren't empties left from the weekend."

"This guy, he broke into your house because . . . how did he say it exactly?"

"He said he needed his life."

"Needed his life?"

"Yes. He asked me why I'd stolen his life, who was I."

"So he breaks in here," Lowbock said, "agitated, talking crazy, well-armed . . . but while he's waiting for you to come home, he decides to kick back and have three bottles of Corona."

Without turning away from the window, Paige said, "My husband didn't have those beers, Lieutenant. He's not a drunk."

Marty said, "I'd certainly be willing to take a Breathalyzer test, if you'd like. If I drank that many beers, one after another, my blood-alcohol level would show it."

"Well," Lowbock said, "if we were going to do that, we should have tested you first thing. But it's not necessary, Mr. Stillwater. I'm certainly not saying you were intoxicated, that you imagined the whole thing under the influence."

"Then what are you saying?" Paige demanded.

"Sometimes," Lowbock observed, "people drink to give themselves the courage to face a difficult task."

Marty sighed. "Maybe I'm dense, Lieutenant. I know there's an unpleasant implication in what you just said, but I can't for the life of me figure out what I'm supposed to infer from it."

"Did I say I meant for you to infer anything?"

"Would you just please stop being cryptic and tell us why you're treating me like this, like a suspect instead of a victim?"

Lowbock was silent.

Marty pressed the issue: "I *know* this situation is incredible, this dead-ringer business, but if you'd just bluntly tell me the reasons you're so skeptical, I'm sure I could eliminate your doubts. At least I could try."

Lowbock was unresponsive for so long that Paige almost turned from the window to have a look at him, wondering if his expression would reveal something about the meaning of his silence.

Finally he said, "We live in a litigious world, Mr. Stillwater. If a cop makes the slightest mistake handling a delicate situation, the department gets sued and sometimes the officer's career gets flushed away. It happens to good men."

"What've lawsuits got to do with this? I'm not going to sue anyone, Lieutenant."

"Say a guy catches a call about an armed robbery in progress, so he answers it, does his duty, finds himself in real jeopardy, getting shot at, blows away the perp in self-defense. And what happens next?"

"I guess you'll tell me."

"Next thing you know, the perp's family and the ACLU are after the department about excessive violence, want a financial settlement. They want the officer dismissed, even put the poor sucker on trial, accuse him of being a fascist."

Marty said, "It stinks. I agree with you. These days it seems like the world's been turned upside-down but—"

"If the same cop *doesn't* respond with force, and some bystander gets hurt 'cause the perp wasn't blown away at the first opportunity, the department gets sued for negligence by the victim's family, and the same activists come down on our necks like a ton of bricks, but for different reasons. People say the cop didn't pull the trigger fast enough because he's insensitive to the minority group the victim was a part of, would've been quicker if the victim was white, or they say he's incompetent, or he's a coward."

"I wouldn't want your job. I know how difficult it is," Marty commiserated. "But no cop has shot or failed to shoot anyone here, and I don't see what this has to do with our situation."

"A cop can get in as much trouble making accusations as he can shooting perps," Lowbock said.

"So your point is, you're skeptical of my story, but you won't say *why* until you've got absolute proof it's bullshit."

"He won't even admit to being skeptical," Paige said sourly. "He won't take any position, one way or the other, because taking a position means taking a risk."

Marty said, "But, Lieutenant, how are we going to get done with this, how am I going to be able to convince you all of this happened just as I said it did, if you *won't* tell me why you doubt it?"

"Mr. Stillwater, I haven't said that I doubt you."

"Jesus," Paige said.

"All I ask," Lowbock said, "is that you do your best to answer my questions."

"And all *we* ask," Paige said, still keeping her back to the man, "is that you find the lunatic who tried to kill Marty."

"This look-alike." Lowbock spoke the word flatly, without any inflection whatsoever, which seemed more sarcastic than if he had said it with a heavy sneer.

"Yes," Paige hissed, "this look-alike."

She didn't doubt Marty's story, as wild as it was, and she knew that somehow the existence of the dead-ringer was tied to—and would ultimately explain—her husband's fugue, bizarre nightmare, and other recent problems.

Now her fury at the detective faded as she began to accept that the police, for whatever reason, were not going to help them. Anger gave way to fear because she realized they were up against something exceedingly strange and were going to have to deal with it entirely on their own.

5.

Clocker returned from the front of the Road King to report that the keys were in the ignition in the ON position, but the fuel tank was evidently empty and the battery dead. The cabin lights could not be turned on.

Worried that the flashlight beam, seen from outside, would look suspicious to anyone pulling into the rest area, Drew Oslett quickly examined the two cadavers in the cramped dining nook. Because the spilled blood was thoroughly dry and caked hard, he knew the man and woman had been dead more than just a few hours. However, although rigor mortis was still present in both bodies, they were no longer entirely stiff; the rigor evidently had peaked and had begun to fade, as it usually did between eighteen and thirty-six hours after death.

The bodies had not begun to decompose noticeably as yet. The only bad smell came from their open mouths—the sour gases produced by the rotting food in their stomachs.

"Best guesstimate—they've been dead since sometime yesterday afternoon," he told Clocker.

The Road King had been sitting in the rest area for more than twenty-four hours, so at least one Oklahoma Highway Patrol officer must have seen it on two separate shifts. State law surely forbade using rest areas as campsites. No electrical connections, water supplies, or sewage-tank pump-outs were provided, which created a potential for health problems. Sometimes cops might be lenient with retirees afraid of driving in weather as inclement as the storm that had assaulted Oklahoma yesterday; the American Association of Retired People bumpersticker on the back of the motorhome might have gained these people some dispensation. But not even a sympathetic cop would let them park *two* nights. At any moment, a patrol car might pull into the rest area and a knock might come at the door.

Averse to complicating their already serious problems by killing a highway patrolman, Oslett turned away from the dead couple and hastily proceeded with the search of the motorhome. He was no longer cautious out of fear that Alfie, dysfunctional and disobedient, would put a bullet in his head. Alfie was long gone from here.

He found the discarded shoes on the kitchen counter. With a large serrated knife, Alfie had sawed at one of the heels until he had exposed the electronic circuitry and the attendant chain of tiny batteries.

Staring at the Rockports and the pile of rubber shavings, Oslett was chilled by a premonition of disaster. "He never knew about the shoes. Why would he get it in his head to cut them open?"

"Well, he knows what he knows," Clocker said.

Oslett interpreted Clocker's statement to mean that part of Alfie's training included state-of-the-art electronic surveillance equipment and techniques. Consequently, though he was not told that he was "tagged," he knew that a microminiature transponder could be made small enough to fit in the heel of a shoe and, upon receipt of a remote microwave activating signal, could draw sufficient power from a series of watch batteries to transmit a trackable signal for at least seventy-two hours. Although he was unable to recall what he was or who controlled him, Alfie was intelligent enough to apply his knowledge of surveillance to his own situation and reach the logical conclusion that his controllers had made prudent provisions for locating and following him in the event he went renegade, even if they had been thoroughly convinced rebellion was not possible.

Oslett dreaded reporting the bad news to the home office in New York. The organization didn't kill the bearer of bad tidings, especially not if his surname happened to be Oslett. However, as Alfie's primary handler, he knew that some of the blame would stick to him even though the operative's rebellion was not his fault to any degree whatsoever. The error must be in Alfie's fundamental conditioning, damn it, not in his handling.

Leaving Clocker in the kitchen to keep a lookout for unwanted visitors, Oslett quickly inspected the rest of the motorhome.

He found nothing else of interest except a pile of discarded clothes on the floor of the main bedroom at the back of the vehicle. In the beam of the flashlight, he needed to disturb the garments only slightly with the toe of his shoe to see that they were what Alfie had been wearing when he had boarded the plane for Kansas City on Saturday morning.

Oslett returned to the kitchen, where Clocker waited in the dark. He turned the flashlight on the dead pensioners one last time. "What a mess. Damn it, this didn't have to happen."

Referring disdainfully to the murdered couple, Clocker said, "Who cares, for God's sake? They were nothing but a couple of fucking Klingons anyway."

Oslett had been referring not to the victims but to the fact that Alfie was more than merely a renegade now, was an *untraceable* renegade, thus jeopardizing the organization and everyone in it. He had no more pity for the dead man and woman than did Clocker, felt no responsibility for what had happened to them, and figured the world, in fact, was better off without two more nonproductive parasites sucking on the substance of society and hindering traffic in their lumbering home on wheels. He had no love for the masses. As he saw it, the basic problem with the average man and woman was precisely that they were so *average* and that there were so many of them, taking far more than they gave to the world, quite incapable of managing their own lives intelligently let alone society, government, the economy, and the environment.

Nevertheless, he was alarmed by the way Clocker had phrased his contempt for the victims. The word "Klingons" made him uneasy because it was the name of the alien race that had been at war with humanity through so many television episodes and movies in the *Star Trek* series before events in that fictional far future had begun to reflect the improvement of relations between the United States and the Soviet Union in the real world. Oslett found *Star Trek* tedious, insufferably boring. He never had understood why so many people had such a passion for it. But Clocker was an ardent fan of the series, unabashedly called himself a "Trekker," could reel off the plots of every movie and episode ever filmed, and knew the personal histories of every character as if they were all his dearest friends. *Star Trek* was the only topic about which he seemed willing or able to conduct a conversation; and as taciturn as he was most of the time, he was to the same degree garrulous when the subject of his favorite fantasy arose.

Oslett tried to make sure that it *never* arose.

Now, in his mind, the dreaded word "Klingons" clanged like a firehouse bell.

With the entire organization at risk because Alfie's trail had been lost, with something new and exquisitely violent loose in the world, the return trip to Oklahoma City through so many miles of lightless and unpeopled land was going to be bleak and depressing. The last thing Oslett needed was to be assaulted by one of Clocker's exhaustingly enthusiastic monologues about Captain Kirk, Mr. Spock, Scotty, the rest of the crew, and their adventures in the far reaches of a universe that was, on film, stuffed with far more meaning and moments of sophomoric enlightenment than was the real universe of hard choices, ugly truths, and mindless cruelty.

"Let's get out of here," Oslett said, pushing past Clocker and heading for the front of the Road King. He didn't believe in God, but he prayed nonetheless ardently that Karl Clocker would subside into his usual self-absorbed silence.

6.

Cyrus Lowbock excused himself temporarily to confer with some colleagues who wanted to talk to him elsewhere in the house.

Marty was relieved by his departure.

When the detective left the dining room, Paige returned from the window and sat once more in the chair beside Marty.

Although the Pepsi was gone, some of the ice cubes had melted in the mug, and he drank the cold water. "All I want now is to put an end to this. We shouldn't be here, not with that guy out there somewhere, loose."

"Do you think we should be worried about the kids?"

. . . need . . . my Charlotte, my Emily . . .

Marty said, "Yeah. I'm worried shitless."

"But you shot the guy twice in the chest."

"I thought I'd left him in the foyer with a broken back, too, but he got up and ran away. Or limped away. Or maybe even vanished into thin air. I don't know what the hell's going on here, Paige, but it's wilder than anything I've ever put in a novel. And it's not over, not by a long shot."

"If it was just Vic and Kathy looking after them, but there's a cop over there too."

"If this bastard knew where the girls were, he'd waste that cop, Vic, and Kathy in about a minute flat."

"You handled him."

"I was lucky, Paige. Just damned lucky. He never imagined I had a gun in the desk drawer or that I'd use one if I had it. I took him by surprise. He won't let that happen again. He'll have all the surprise on *his* side."

He tilted the mug to his lips, let a melting ice cube slide onto his tongue.

"Marty, when did you take the guns out of the garage cabinet and load them?"

Speaking around the ice cube, he said, "I saw how that jolted you. I did it this morning. Before I went to see Paul Guthridge."

"Why?"

As best he could, Marty described the curious feeling he'd had that something was bearing down on him and was going to destroy him before he even got a chance to identify it. He tried to convey how the feeling intensified into a panic attack, until he was certain he would need guns to defend himself and became almost incapacitated by fear.

He would have been embarrassed to tell her, would have sounded unbalanced—if events had not proved the validity of his perceptions and precautions.

"And something *was* coming," she said. "This dead-ringer. You sensed him coming."

"Yeah. I guess so. Somehow."

"Psychic."

He shook his head. "No, I wouldn't call it that. Not if you mean a psychic vision. There wasn't any vision. I didn't see what was coming, didn't have a clear premonition. Just this . . . this awful sense of pressure, gravity . . . like on one of those whip rides at an amusement park, when it swings you around real fast and you're pinned to the seat, feel a weight on your chest. You know, you've been on rides like that, Charlotte always loves them."

"Yeah. I understand . . . I guess."

"This started out like that . . . and got a hundred times worse, until I could hardly breathe. Then suddenly it just stopped as I was leaving for the doctor's office. And later, when I came home, the sonofabitch was here, but I didn't feel anything when I walked into the house."

They were silent for a moment.

Wind flung pellets of rain against the window.

Paige said, "How could he look exactly like you?"

"I don't know."

"Why would he say you stole his life?"

"I don't know, I just don't know."

"I'm scared, Marty. I mean, it's all so weird. What're we going to do?"

"Past tonight, I don't know. But tonight, at least, we're not staying here. We'll go to a hotel."

"But if the police don't find him dead somewhere, then there's tomorrow . . . and the day after tomorrow."

"I'm battered and tired and not thinking straight. For now I can only concentrate on tonight, Paige. I'll just have to worry about tomorrow when tomorrow gets here."

Her lovely face was lined with anxiety. He had not seen her even half this distraught since Charlotte's illness five years ago.

"I love you," he said, laying his hand gently against the side of her head.

Putting her hand over his, she said, "Oh, God, I love you, too, Marty, you and the girls, more than anything, more than life itself. We can't let anything happen to us, to what we all have together. We just *can't.*"

"We won't," he said, but his words sounded as hollow and false as a young boy's braggadocio.

He was aware that neither of them had expressed the slightest hope that the police would protect them. He could not repress his anger over the fact they were not accorded anything resembling the service, courtesy, and consideration that the characters in his novels always received from the authorities.

At the core, mystery novels were about good and evil, about the triumph of the former over the latter, and about the reliability of the justice system in a modern democracy. They were popular because they reassured the reader that the system worked far more often than not, even if the evidence of daily life sometimes pointed toward a more troubling conclusion. Marty had been able to work in the genre with conviction and tremendous pleasure because he liked to believe that law-enforcement agencies and the courts delivered justice most of the time and thwarted it only inadvertently. But now, the first time in his life that he'd turned to the system for help, it was in the process of failing him. Its failure not only jeopardized his life—as well as the lives of his wife and children—but seemed to call into doubt the value of everything that he had written and the worthiness of the purpose to which he had committed so many years of hard work and struggle.

Lieutenant Lowbock returned through the living room, looking and moving as if in the middle of an *Esquire* magazine fashion-photography session. He was carrying a clear plastic evidence bag, which contained a black zippered case about half the size of a shaving kit. He put the bag on the dining-room table as he sat down.

"Mr. Stillwater, was the house securely locked when you left it this morning?"

"Locked?" Marty asked, wondering where they were headed now, trying not to let his anger show. "Yes, locked up tight. I'm careful about that sort of thing."

"Have you given any thought as to how this intruder might have gained entry?"

"Broke a window, I guess. Or forced a lock."

"Do you know what's in this?" he asked, tapping the black leather case through the plastic bag.

"I'm afraid I don't have X-ray vision," Marty said.

"I thought you might recognize it."

"No."

"We found it in your master bedroom."

"I've never seen it before."

"On the dresser."

Paige said, "Get it over with, Lieutenant."

Lowbock's faint shadow of a smile passed across his face again, like a visiting spirit shimmering briefly in the air above a séance table. "It's a complete set of lock picks."

"That's how he got in?" Marty asked.

Lowbock shrugged. "I suppose that's what I'm expected to deduce from it."

"This is tiresome, Lieutenant. We have children we're worried about. I agree with my wife—just get it over with."

Leaning over the table and regarding Marty once more with his patented intense gaze, the detective said, "I've been a cop for twenty-seven years, Mr. Stillwater, and this is the first time I've ever encountered a break-in at a private residence where the intruder used a set of professional lock picks."

"So?"

"They break glass or force a lock, like you said. Sometimes they pry a sliding door or window out of its track. The average burglar has a hundred ways of getting in—all of which are a lot faster than picking a lock."

"This wasn't an average burglar."

"Oh, I can see that," Lowbock said. He leaned away from the table, settled back in his chair. "This guy is a lot more theatrical than the average perp. He contrives to look exactly like you, spouts a lot of strange stuff about wanting his life back, comes armed with an assassin's gun threaded for a silencer, uses burglary tools like a Hollywoodized professional heist artist in a caper movie, takes two bullets in the chest but isn't fazed, loses enough blood to kill an ordinary man but walks away. He's downright flamboyant, this guy, but he's also *muy misterioso,* the kind of character Andy Garcia could play in a movie or, a lot better yet, that Ray Liotta who was in *Goodfellas.*"

Marty suddenly saw where the detective was headed and understood why he was going there. The inevitable terminus of the interrogation should have been obvious sooner, but Marty simply hadn't tumbled to it because it was *too* obvious. As a writer, he had been seeking some more exotic, complex reason for Lowbock's barely concealed disbelief and hostility, when all the while Cyrus Lowbock had been going for the cliché.

Still, the detective had one more unpleasant surprise to reveal. He leaned forward again and made eye contact in what had ceased to be an effective confrontational manner and had become instead a personal tic as annoying and transparent as Peter Falk's disarmingly humble posture and relentless self-deprecation when he played Columbo, Nero Wolfe's thoughtful puckering of the mouth in moments of inspiration, James Bond's knowing smirk, or any of the slew of colorful traits by which Sherlock Holmes was characterized. "Do your daughters have pets, Mr. Stillwater?"

"Charlotte does. Several."

"An odd collection of pets."

Paige said cooly, "Charlotte doesn't think they're odd."

"Do you?"

"No. What does it matter if they're odd or not?"

"Has she had them long?" Lowbock inquired.

"Some longer than others," Marty said, baffled by this new twist in the questioning even as he remained convinced that he understood the theory Lowbock was laboring to prove.

"She loves them, her pets?"

"Yes. Very much. Like any kid. Odd as you might think they are, she loves them."

Nodding, leaning away from the table again, drumming his pen against his notebook, Lowbock said, "It's another flamboyant touch, but also convincing. I mean, if you were a detective and disposed to doubt the whole scenario, you'd have to think twice if the intruder killed all of the daughter's pets."

Marty's heart began sinking in him like a dropped stone seeking the bottom of a pond.

"Oh, no," Paige said miserably. "Not poor little Whiskers, Loretta, Fred . . . not all of them?"

"The gerbil was crushed to death," Lowbock said, his gaze fixed on Marty. "The mouse had its neck broken, the turtle was smashed underfoot, and so was the beetle. I didn't examine the others that carefully."

Marty's anger flared into barely contained fury, and he curled his hands into tight fists under the table, because he knew Lowbock was accusing him of having killed the pets merely to lend credibility to an elaborate lie. No one would believe a loving father would stomp his daughter's pet turtle and break the neck of her cute little mouse for the shabby purpose that Lowbock thought motivated Marty; therefore, perversely, the detective assumed that Marty *had* done it, after all, because it was so outrageous as to exonerate him, the perfect finishing touch.

"Charlotte's going to be heartbroken," Paige said.

Marty knew that he was flushed with rage. He could feel the heat in his face, as if he'd spent the past hour under a sunlamp, and his ears felt almost as if they were on fire. He also knew the cop would interpret his anger as a blush of shame that was a testament of guilt.

When Lowbock revealed that fleeting smile again, Marty wanted to punch him in the mouth.

"Mr. Stillwater, please correct me if I'm wrong, but haven't you recently had a book on the paperback bestseller list, the reprint of a hardcover that was first released last year?"

Marty didn't answer him.

Lowbock didn't require an answer. He was rolling now. "And a new book coming out in a month or so, which some people think might be your first hardcover bestseller? And you're probably working on yet another book even now. There's a portion of a manuscript on the desk in your office, anyway. And I guess, once you get a couple of good career breaks, you've got to keep your foot on the gas, so to speak, take full advantage of the momentum."

Frowning, her whole body tense again, Paige seemed on the verge of precisely grasping the detective's ludicrous interpretation of Marty's crime report, the source of his antagonism. She had the temper in the family; and since Marty was barely able to keep from striking the cop, he wondered what Paige's reaction would be when Lowbock made his idiotic suspicions explicit.

"It must help a career to be profiled in *People* magazine," the detective continued. "And I guess when Mr. Murder himself becomes the target of a *muy misterioso* killer, then you'll get a lot more free publicity in the press, and just at a crucial turning point in your career."

Paige jerked in her chair as if she'd been slapped.

Her reaction drew Lowbock's attention. "Yes, Mrs. Stillwater?"

"You can't actually believe . . ."

"Believe what, Mrs. Stillwater?"

"Marty isn't a liar."

"Have I said he is?"

"He loathes publicity."

"Then they must have been quite persistent at *People.*"

"Look at his neck, for Christ's sake! The redness, swelling, it'll be covered with bruises in a few hours. You can't believe he did that to himself."

Maintaining a maddening pretense of objectivity, Lowbock said, "Is that what you believe, Mrs. Stillwater?"

She spoke between clenched teeth, saying what Marty felt he couldn't allow himself to say: "You stupid ass."

Raising his eyebrows and looking stricken, as if he couldn't imagine what he'd done to earn such enmity, Lowbock said, "Surely, Mrs. Stillwater, you realize there are people out there, a world of cynics, who might say that attempted strangulation is the safest form of assault to fake. I mean, stabbing yourself in the arm or leg would be a convincing touch, but there's always the danger of a slight miscalculation, a nicked artery, then suddenly you find yourself bleeding a lot more seriously than you'd intended. And as for self-inflicted gunshot wounds—well, the risk is even higher, what with the possibility that a bullet might ricochet off a bone and into deeper flesh, and there's always the danger of shock."

Paige bolted to her feet so abruptly that she knocked over her chair. "Get out."

Lowbock blinked at her, feigning innocence long past the point of diminishing returns. "Excuse me?"

"Get out of my house," she demanded. "Now."

Although Marty realized they were throwing away their last slim hope of winning over the detective and gaining police protection, he also got up from his chair, so angry that he was trembling. "My wife is right. I think you and your men better leave, Lieutenant."

Remaining seated because to do so was a challenge to them, Cyrus Lowbock said, "You mean, leave before we finish our investigation?"

"Yes," Marty said. "Finished or not."

"Mr. Stillwater . . . Mrs. Stillwater . . . you *do* realize that it's against the law to file a false crime report?"

"We haven't filed a false report," Marty said.

Paige said, "The only fake in this room is you, Lieutenant. You *do* realize that it's against the law to impersonate a police officer?"

It would have been satisfying to see Lowbock's face color with anger, to see his eyes narrow and his lips tighten at the insult, but his equanimity remained infuriatingly unshaken.

As he got slowly to his feet, the detective said, "If the blood samples taken from the upstairs carpet are, say, only pig's blood or cow's blood or anything like that, the lab will be able to determine the exact species, of course."

"I'm aware of the analytic powers of forensic science," Marty assured him.

"Oh, yes, that's right, you're a mystery writer. According to *People* magazine, you do a great deal of research for your novels."

Lowbock closed his notebook, clipped his pen to it.

Marty waited.

"In your various researches, Mr. Stillwater, have you learned how much blood is in the human body, say in a body approximately the size of your own?"

"Five liters."

"Ah. That's correct." Lowbock put the notebook on top of the plastic bag containing the leather case of lock picks. "At a guess, but an educated guess, I'd say there's somewhere between one and two liters of blood soaked into the upstairs carpet. Between twenty and forty percent of this look-alike's entire supply, and closer to forty unless I miss my guess. You know what I'd expect to find along with that much blood, Mr. Stillwater? I'd expect to find the body it came from, because it really does stretch the imagination to picture such a grievously wounded man being able to flee the scene."

"I've already told you, I don't understand it either."

"Muy misterioso," Paige said, investing those two words with a measure of scorn equal to the mockery with which the detective had spoken them earlier.

Marty decided there was at least one good thing about this mess: the way Paige had not doubted him for an instant, even though reason and logic virtually demanded doubt; the way she stood beside him now, fierce and resolute. In all the years they had been together, he had never loved her more than at that moment.

Picking up the notebook and the evidence bag, Lowbock said, "If the blood upstairs proves to be human blood, that raises all sorts of other questions that would require us to finish the investigation whether or not you'd prefer to be rid of us. Actually, whatever the lab results, you'll be hearing from me again."

"We'd simply adore seeing you again," Paige said, the edge gone from her voice, as if suddenly she ceased to see Lowbock as a threat and could not help but view him as a comic figure.

Marty found her attitude infecting him, and he realized that with him, as with her, this sudden dark hilarity was a reaction to the unbearable tension of the past hour. He said, "By all means, drop by again."

"We'll make a nice pot of tea," Paige said.

"And scones."

"Crumpets."

"Tea cakes."

"And by all means, bring the wife," Paige said. "We're quite broadminded. We'd love to meet her even if she is of another species."

Marty was aware that Paige was perilously close to laughing out loud, because he was close to it himself, and he knew their behavior was childish, but he required all of his self-control not to continue making fun of Lowbock all the way out the front door, driving him backward with jokes the way that Professor Von Helsing might force Count Dracula to retreat by brandishing a crucifix at him.

Strangely, the detective was disconcerted by their frivolity as he had never been by their anger or by their earnest insistence that the intruder had been real. Visible self-doubt took hold of him, and he looked as if he might suggest they sit down and start over again. But self-doubt was a weakness unfamiliar to him, and he could not sustain it for long.

Uncertainty quickly gave way to his familiar smug expression, and he said, "We'll be taking the look-alike's Heckler and Koch, as well as your guns, of course, until you can produce the paperwork that I requested."

For a terrible moment, Marty was sure that they had found the Beretta in the kitchen cupboard and the Mossberg shotgun under the bed upstairs, as well as the other weapons, and were going to leave him defenseless.

But Lowbock listed the guns and mentioned only three: "The Smith and Wesson, the Korth thirty-eight, and the M16."

Marty tried not to let his relief show.

Paige distracted Lowbock by saying, "Lieutenant, are you ever going to get the fuck out of here?"

The detective finally could not prevent his face from tightening with anger. "You can certainly hurry me along, Mrs. Stillwater, if you would repeat your request in the presence of two other officers."

"Always worrying about those lawsuits," Marty said.

Paige said, "Happy to oblige, Lieutenant. Would you like me to phrase the request in the same language I just used?"

Never before had Marty heard her use the F-word except in the most intimate circumstances—which meant, though masked by her light tone of voice and frivolous manner, her anger was as strong as ever. That was good. After the police left, she would need the anger to get her through the night ahead. Anger would help keep fear at bay.

7.

When he closes his eyes and tries to picture the pain, he can see it as a filigree of fire. A beautifully luminous lacework, white-hot with shadings of red and yellow, stretches from the base of his throbbing neck across his back, encircling his sides, looping and knotting intricately across his chest and abdomen as well.

By visualizing the pain, he has a better sense of whether his condition is improving or deteriorating. Actually, his only concern is how *fast* he is improving. He has been wounded on other occasions, though never this grievously, and knows what to expect; continued deterioration would be a wholly new and alarming experience for him.

The pain had been vicious during the minute or two after he'd been shot. He had felt as if a monstrous fetus had come awake within him and was burrowing its way out.

Fortunately, he has a singularly high tolerance for pain. He also draws courage from the knowledge that the agony will swiftly subside to a less crippling level.

By the time he staggers through the rear door of the house and heads for the Honda, the bleeding stops completely, and his hunger pangs become more terrible than the pain of his wounds. His stomach knots, loosens with a spasm, but immediately knots again, violently clenching and unclenching repeatedly, as if it is a grasping fist that can seize the nourishment he so desperately needs.

Driving away from his house through gray torrents at the height of the storm, he becomes so achingly ravenous that he begins to shake with deprivation. They are not mere tremors of need but wracking shudders that clack his teeth together. His twitching hands beat a palsied tattoo upon the steering wheel, and he is barely able to hold it firmly enough to control the vehicle. Fits of dry wheezing convulse him, hot flashes alternate with chills, and the sweat gushing from him is colder than the rain that still soaks his hair and clothes.

His extraordinary metabolism gives him great strength, keeps his energy level high, frees him from the need to sleep every night, allows him to heal with miraculous rapidity, and is in general a cornucopia of physical blessings, but it also makes demands on him. Even on a normal day, he has an appetite formidable enough for two lumberjacks. When he denies himself sleep, when he is injured, or when any other unusual demands are made on his system, mere hunger soon becomes a ravenous craving, and craving escalates almost at once into a dire *need* for sustenance that drives all other thoughts from his mind and forces him into the rapacious consumption of whatever he can find.

Although the interior of the Honda is adrift in empty food containers—wrappers and packages and bags of every description—there is no hidden morsel in the trash. In the final plummet from the San Bernardino Mountains into the lowlands of Orange County, he feverishly consumed every crumb that remained. Now there are only dried smears of chocolate and mustard, thin films of glistening oil, grease, sprinkles of salt, none of it sufficiently fortifying to compensate for the energy needed to rummage for it in the darkness and lick it up.

By the time he locates a fast-food restaurant with a drive-in window, at the center of his gut is an icy void into which he seems to be dissolving, growing hollower and hollower, colder and colder, as if his body is consuming itself to repair itself, catabolizing two cells for every one it creates. He almost bites his own hand in a frantic and despairing attempt to relieve the grueling pangs of starvation. He imagines tearing out chunks of his own flesh with his teeth and greedily swallowing, sucking down his own hot blood, anything to moderate his suffering—*anything,* no matter how repulsive it might be. But he restrains himself because, in the madness of his inhuman hunger, he is half convinced no flesh remains on his bones. He feels utterly hollow, more fragile than the thinnest spun-glass Christmas ornament, and believes he might dissolve into thousands of lifeless fragments the moment his teeth puncture his brittle skin and thereby shatter the illusion of substance.

The restaurant is a McDonald's outlet. The tinny speaker of the intercom at the ordering post has been exposed to enough years of summer sun and winter chill that the greeting of the unseen clerk is quavery and static-riddled. Confident that his own strained and shaky voice won't sound unusual, the killer orders enough food to satisfy the staff of a small office: six cheeseburgers, Big Macs, fries, a couple of fish sandwiches, two chocolate milkshakes—and large Cokes because his racing metabolism, if not fueled, leads as swiftly to dehydration as to starvation.

He is in a long line of cars, and progression toward the pick-up window is aggravatingly slow. He has no choice but to wait, for with his blood-soaked clothes and bullet-torn shirt, he can't walk into a restaurant or convenience store and get what he needs unless he is willing to draw a lot of attention to himself.

In fact, though blood vessels have been repaired, the two bullet wounds in his chest remain largely unhealed due to the shortage of fuel for anabolic processes. Those sucking holes, into which he can insert his thickest finger to a disturbing depth, would cause more comment than his bloody shirt.

One of the slugs passed completely through him, out his back to the left of his spine. He knows the exit wound is larger than either of the holes in his chest. He feels the ragged lips of it spreading apart when he leans back against the car seat.

He is fortunate that neither round pierced his heart. That might have stopped him for good. That and a brain-scrambling shot to the head are the only wounds he fears.

When he reaches the cashier's window, he pays for the order with some of the money he took from Jack and Frannie in Oklahoma more than twenty-four hours ago. The young woman at the cash register can see his arm as he holds the currency toward her, so he strives to repress the severe tremors that might prick her curiosity. He keeps his face averted; in the night and rain, she can't see his ravaged chest or the agony that contorts his pale features.

At the pick-up window, his order comes in several white bags, which he piles on the littered seat beside him, successfully averting his face from this clerk as well. All of his willpower is required to restrain himself from ripping the bags asunder and tearing into the food immediately upon receipt of it. He retains enough clarity of mind to realize he must not cause a scene by blocking the take-out lane.

He parks in the darkest corner of the restaurant lot, switches off the headlights and windshield wipers. His face looks so gaunt when he glimpses it in the rearview mirror that he knows he has lost several pounds in the past hour; his eyes are sunken and appear to be ringed with smudges of soot. He dims the instrument-panel lights as far as possible, but lets the engine run because, in his current debilitated condition, he needs to bask in the warm air from the heater vents. He is swaddled in shadows. The rain streaming down the glass shimmers with reflected light from neon signs, and it bends the night world into mutagenic forms, simultaneously screening him from prying eyes.

In this mechanical cave, he reverts to savagery and is, for a time, something less than human, tearing at his food with animalistic impatience, stuffing it into his mouth faster than he can swallow. Burgers and buns and fries crumble against his lips, his teeth, and leave a growing slope of organic scree across his chest; cola and milkshake dribble down the front of his shirt. He chokes repeatedly, spraying food on the steering wheel and dashboard, but eats no less wolfishly, no less urgently, issuing small wordless greedy sounds and low moans of satisfaction.

His feeding frenzy translates into a period of numb and silent withdrawal much like a trance, from which he eventually arises with three names on his lips, whispered like a prayer: *"Paige . . . Charlotte . . . Emily . . ."*

From experience he knows that, in the hours before dawn, he will suffer new bouts of hunger, though none as devastating and obsessive as the seizure he has just endured. A few bars of chocolate or cans of Vienna sausages or packages of hot dogs—depending on whether it is carbohydrates or proteins that he craves—will ensure abatement of the pangs.

He will be able to focus his attention on other critical issues without worrying about major distractions of a physiological nature. The most serious of those crises is the continued enslavement of his wife and children by the man who has stolen his life.

"Paige . . . Charlotte . . . Emily . . ."

Tears cloud his vision when he thinks of his family in the hands of the hateful imposter. They are so precious to him. They are his only fortune, his reason for existence, his future.

He recalls the wonder and joy with which he explored his house, standing in his daughters' room, later touching the bed in which he and his wife make love. The moment he had seen their faces in the photograph on his desk, he had known they were his destiny and that in their loving embrace he would find surcease from the confusion, loneliness, and quiet desperation that have plagued him.

He remembers, as well, the first surprising confrontation with the imposter, the shock and amazement of their uncanny resemblance, the perfectly matched pitch and timbre of their voices. He had understood at once how the man could have stepped into his life without anyone being the wiser.

Though his exploration of the house provided no clue to explain the imposter's origins, he was reminded of certain films from which answers might be garnered when he had a chance to view them again. Both versions of *Invasion of the Body Snatchers,* the first starring Kevin McCarthy, the second, Donald Sutherland. John Carpenter's remake of *The Thing,* though not the first version. Perhaps even *Invaders from Mars.* Bette Midler and Lily Tomlin in a film whose title he could not recall. *The Prince and the Pauper. Moon Over Parador.* There must be others.

Movies had all the answers to life's problems. From the movies he had learned about romance and love and the joy of family life. In the darkness of theaters, passing time between killings, hungry for meaning, he had learned to need what he didn't have. And from the great lessons of the movies he might eventually unravel the mystery of his stolen life.

But first he must act.

That is another lesson he has learned from the movies. Action must come before thought. People in movies rarely sit around brooding about the predicament in which they find themselves. By God, they *do* something to resolve even their worst problems; they keep moving, ceaselessly moving, resolutely seeking confrontation with those who oppose them, grappling with their enemies in life-or-death struggles that they always win as long as they are sufficiently determined and righteous.

He is determined.

He is righteous.

His life has been stolen.

He is a victim. He has suffered.

He has known despair.

He has endured abuse and anguish and betrayal and loss like Omar Sharif in *Doctor Zhivago,* like William Hurt in *The Accidental Tourist,*

Robin Williams in *The World According to Garp,* Michael Keaton in *Batman,* Sidney Poitier in *In the Heat of the Night,* Tyrone Power in *The Razor's Edge,* Johnny Depp in *Edward Scissorhands.* He is one with all of the brutalized, despised, downtrodden, misunderstood, cheated, outcast, manipulated people who live upon the silver screen and who are heroic in the face of devastating tribulations. His suffering is as important as theirs, his destiny every bit as glorious, his hope of triumph just as great.

This realization moves him deeply. He is wrenched by shuddering sobs, weeping not with sadness but with joy, overwhelmed by a feeling of belonging, brotherhood, a sense of common humanity. He has deep bonds with those whose lives he shares in theaters, and this glorious Epiphany motivates him to get up, move, move, confront, challenge, grapple, and prevail.

"Paige, I'm coming for you," he says through his tears.

He throws open the driver's door and gets out in the rain.

"Emily, Charlotte, I won't fail you. Depend on me. Trust me. I'll die for you if I have to."

Shedding the detritus of his gluttony, he goes around to the back of the Honda and opens the trunk. He finds a tire iron that is a prybar on one end, for popping loose hubcaps, and a lug wrench on the other end. It has satisfying heft and balance.

He returns to the front seat, slides in behind the wheel, and puts the tire iron on top of the fragrant trash that overflows the seat beside him.

As he sees in memory the photograph of his family, he murmurs, "I'll die for you."

He is healing. When he explores the bullet holes in his chest, he can probe little more than half the depth that he was previously able to plumb.

In the second wound, his finger encounters a hard and gnarled lump which might be a wad of dislocated gristle. He quickly realizes it is, instead, the lead slug that didn't pass through him and out of his back. His body is rejecting it. He picks and pries until the misshapen bullet oozes free with a thick wet sound, and he throws it on the floor.

Although he is aware that his metabolism and recuperative powers are extraordinary, he does not see himself as being much different from other men. Movies have taught him that all men are extraordinary in one way or another: some have a powerful magnetism for women, who are unable to resist them; others have courage beyond measure; still others, like those whose lives Arnold Schwarzenegger and Sylvester Stallone have portrayed, can walk through a hail of bullets untouched and prevail in hand-to-hand combat with half a dozen men at one time or in quick succession. Rapid convalescence seems less exceptional, by comparison, than the common ability of on-screen heroes to pass unscathed through Hell itself.

Plucking a cold fish sandwich from the remaining pile of food, bolting it down in six large bites, he leaves McDonald's. He begins searching for a shopping mall.

Because this is southern California, he finds what he's looking for in short order: a sprawling complex of department and specialty stores, its roof composed of more sheets of metal than a battleship, textured concrete walls as formidable as the ramparts of any Medieval fortress, surrounded by acres of lamp-lit blacktop. The ruthless commercial nature of the place is disguised by parklike rows and clusters of carrotwood trees, Indian laurels, willowy melaleucas, and palms.

He cruises endless aisles of parked cars until he spots a man in a raincoat hurrying away from the mall and burdened by two full plastic shopping bags. The shopper stops behind a white Buick, puts down the bags, and fumbles for keys to unlock the trunk.

Three cars from the Buick, an open parking space is available. The Honda, with him all the way from Oklahoma, has outlived its usefulness. It must be abandoned here.

He gets out of the car with the tire iron in his right hand. Gripping the tapered end, he holds it close to his leg to avoid calling attention to it.

The storm is beginning to lose some of its force. The wind is abating. No lightning scores the sky.

Although the rain is no less cold than it was earlier, he finds it refreshing rather than chilling.

As he heads toward the mall—and the white Buick—he surveys the huge parking lot. As far as he can tell, no one is watching him. None of the bracketing vehicles along that aisle is in the process of leaving: no lights, no telltale plumes of exhaust fumes. The nearest moving car is three rows away.

The shopper has found his keys, opened the trunk of the Buick, and stowed away the first of the two plastic bags. Bending to pick up the second bag, the stranger becomes aware that he is no longer alone, turns his head, looks back and up from his bent position in time to see the tire iron sweeping toward his face, on which an expression of alarm barely has time to form.

The second blow is probably unnecessary. The first will have driven fragments of facial bones into the brain. He strikes again, anyway, at the inert and silent shopper.

He throws the tire iron in the open trunk. It hits something with a dull clank.

Move, move, confront, challenge, grapple, and prevail.

Wasting no time looking around to determine if he is still unobserved, he plucks the man off the wet blacktop in the manner of a bodybuilder beginning a clean-and-jerk lift with a barbell. He drops the corpse into the trunk, and the car rocks with the impact of the dead weight.

The night and rain provide what little cover he needs to wrestle the raincoat off the cadaver while it lies hidden in the open trunk. One of the dead eyes stares fixedly while the other rolls loosely in the socket, and the mouth is frozen in a broken-toothed howl of terror that was never made.

When he pulls the coat on over his wet clothes, it is somewhat roomy and an inch long in the sleeves but adequate for the time being. It covers his bloodstained, torn, and food-smeared clothes, making him reasonably presentable, which is all that he cares about. It is still warm from the shopper's body heat.

Later he will dispose of the cadaver, and tomorrow he will buy new clothes. Now he has much to do and precious little time in which to do it.

He takes the dead man's wallet, which has a pleasingly thick sheaf of currency in it.

He tosses the second shopping bag on top of the corpse, slams the trunk lid. The keys are dangling from the lock.

In the Buick, fiddling with the heater controls, he drives away from the mall.

Move, move, confront, challenge, grapple, and prevail.

He starts looking for a service station, not because the Buick needs fuel but because he has to find a pay phone.

He remembers the voices in the kitchen while he had twitched in agony midst the ruins of the stair railing. The imposter had been hustling Paige and the girls out of the house before they could come into the foyer and see their real father struggling to get off his back onto his hands and knees.

". . . take them across the street to Vic and Kathy's . . ."

And seconds later, there had been a name more useful still: *". . . over to the Delorios' place . . ."*

Although they are his neighbors, he can't remember Vic and Kathy

Delorio or which house is theirs. That knowledge was stolen from him with the rest of his life. However, if they have a listed phone, he will be able to find them.

A service station. A blue Pacific Bell sign.

Even as he drives up beside the Plexiglas-walled phone booth, he can dimly see the thick directory secured by a chain.

Leaving the Buick engine running, he sloshes through a puddle into the booth. He closes the door to turn on the overhead light, and flips frantically through the White Pages.

Luck is with him. Victor W. Delorio. The only listing under that name. Mission Viejo. His own street. Bingo. He memorizes the address.

He runs into the service station to buy candy bars. Twenty of them. Hershey's bars with almonds, 3 Musketeers, Mounds, Nestle's white chocolate Crunch. His appetite is sated for the time being; he does not want the candy now—but the need will soon arise.

He pays with some of the cash that belongs to the dead man in the trunk of the Buick.

"You sure have a sweet tooth," says the attendant.

In the Buick again, pulling out of the service station into traffic, he is afraid for his family, which remains unwittingly under the thrall of the imposter. They might be taken away to a far place where he won't be able to find them. They might be harmed. Or even killed. Anything can happen. He has just seen their photograph and has only begun to re-acquaint himself with them, yet he might lose them before he ever has a chance to kiss them again or tell them how much he loves them. So unfair. Cruel. His heart pounds fiercely, re-igniting some of the pain that had been recently extinguished in his steadily knitting wounds.

Oh God, he *needs* his family. He needs to hold them in his arms and be held in return. He needs to comfort them and be comforted and hear them say his name. Hearing them say his name, he once and for all *will be* somebody.

Accelerating through a traffic light as it turns from yellow to red, he speaks aloud to his children in a voice that quavers with emotion: "Charlotte, Emily, I'm coming. Be brave. Daddy's coming. Daddy's coming. Daddy. Is. Coming."

8.

Lieutenant Lowbock was the last cop out of the house.

On the front stoop, as the doors of squad cars slammed in the street behind him and engines started, he turned to Paige and Marty to favor them with one more short-lived and barely perceptible smile. He was evidently loath to be remembered for the tightly controlled anger they had finally stirred in him. "I'll be seeing you as soon as we have the lab results."

"Can't be too soon," Paige said. "We've had such a *charming* visit, we simply can't wait for the next time."

Lowbock said, "Good evening, Mrs. Stillwater." He turned to Marty. "Good evening, Mr. Murder."

Marty knew it was childish to close the door in the detective's face, but it was also satisfying.

Sliding the security chain into place as Marty engaged the dead-bolt lock, Paige said, "Mr. Murder?"

"That's what they call me in the *People* article."

"I haven't seen it yet."

"Right in the headline. Oh, wait'll you read it. It makes me look ridiculous, spooky-old-scary-old Marty Stillwater, book hustler extraordinary. Jesus, if he happened to read that article today, I don't half blame Lowbock for thinking this was all a publicity scam of some kind."

She said, "He's an idiot."

"It *is* an unlikely damn story."

"I believed it."

"I know. And I love you for that."

He kissed her. She clung to him but briefly.

"How's your throat?" she asked.

"I'll live."

"That idiot thinks you choked *yourself.*"

"I didn't. But it's possible, I suppose."

"Stop seeing his side of it. You're making me mad. What now? Shouldn't we get out of here?"

"Fast as we can," he agreed. "And don't come back until we can figure out what the hell this is all about. Can you throw a couple of suitcases together, basics for all of us for a few days?"

"Sure," she said, already heading for the stairs.

"I'll go call Vic and Kathy, make sure everything's all right over there, then I'll come help you. And Paige—the Mossberg is under the bed in our room."

Starting up the stairs, stepping over the splintery debris, she said, "Okay."

"Get it out, put it on top of the bed while you pack."

"I will," she said, already a third of the way up the stairs.

He didn't think he had sufficiently impressed her with the need for uncommon caution. "Take it with you to the girls' room."

"All right."

Speaking sharply enough to halt her, pain encircling his neck when he tilted his head back to stare up at her, he said, "Damn it, I mean it, Paige."

She looked down, surprised because he never used that tone of voice. "Okay. I'll keep it close."

"Good."

He headed for the telephone in the kitchen and made it as far as the dining room when he heard Paige cry out from the second floor. Heart pounding so hard he could draw only shallow staccato breaths, Marty raced back into the foyer, expecting to see her in The Other's grasp.

She was standing at the head of the stairs, horrified by the gruesome stains on the carpet, which she was seeing for the first time. "Hearing about it, I still didn't think . . ." She looked down at Marty. "So *much* blood. How could he just . . . just walk away?"

"He couldn't if he was . . . just a man. That's why I'm sure he'll be back. Maybe not tonight, maybe not tomorrow, maybe not for a month, but he'll be back."

"Marty, this is crazy."

"I know."

"Sweet Jesus," she said, less in any profane sense than as a prayer, and hurried into the master bedroom.

Marty returned to the kitchen and took the Beretta out of the cabinet. Although he had loaded the pistol himself, he popped out the magazine, checked it, slammed it back into place, and jacked a round into the chamber.

He noticed scores of overlapping dirty footprints all across the Mexican-tile floor. Many were still wet. During the past two hours, the police had tramped in and out of the rain, and evidently not all of them had been thoughtful enough to wipe their feet at the door.

Though he knew the cops had been busy and that they had better things to do than worry about tracking up the house, the footprints—and the thoughtlessness they represented—seemed to be nearly as profound a violation as the assault by The Other. A surprisingly intense resentment uncoiled in Marty.

While sociopaths stalked the modern world, the judicial system operated on the premise that evil was spawned primarily by societal injustice. Thugs were considered victims of society as surely as the people they robbed or killed were *their* victims. Recently a man had been released from a California prison after serving six years for raping and murdering an eleven-year-old girl. Six years. The girl, of course, was still as dead as she had ever been. Such outrages were now so common that the story got only minor press coverage. If the courts would not protect eleven-year-old innocents, and if the House and Senate wouldn't write laws to force the courts to do so, then judges and politicians couldn't be counted on to protect anyone, anywhere, at any time.

But, damn it, at least you expected the *cops* to protect you because cops were on the street every day, in the thick of it, and they knew what the world was really like. The grand poobahs in Washington and smug eminences in courtrooms had isolated themselves from reality with high salaries, endless perks, and lush pensions; they lived in gate-guarded neighborhoods with private security, sent their kids to private schools—and lost touch with the damage they perpetrated. But not cops. Cops were blue-collar. Working men and women. In their work they saw evil every day; they knew it was as widespread among the privileged as among the middle-class and the poor, that society was less at fault than the flawed nature of the human species.

The police were supposed to be the last line of defense against barbarity. But if they became cynical about the system they were asked to uphold, if they believed they were the only ones who cared about justice any more, they would cease caring. When you needed them, they would conduct their forensic tests, fill out thick files of paperwork to please the bureaucracy, track dirt across your once-clean floors, and leave you without even sympathy.

Standing in his kitchen, holding the loaded Beretta, Marty knew that he and Paige now constituted their own last line of defense. No one else. No greater authority. No guardian of the public welfare.

He needed courage but also the free-wheeling imagination that he brought to the writing of his books. Suddenly he seemed to be living in a *noir* novel, in that amoral realm where stories by James M. Cain or Elmore Leonard took place. Survival in such a dark world depended upon quick thinking, fast action, utter ruthlessness. Most of all it hinged on the ability to imagine the worst that life could come up with next and, by imagining, be ready for it rather than surprised.

His mind was blank.

He had no idea where to go, what to do. Pack up and get out of the house, yes. But then what?

He just stared at the gun in his hand.

Although he loved the works of Cain and Leonard, his own books were not that dark. They celebrated reason, logic, virtue, and the triumph of social order. His imagination did not lead him toward vigilante solutions, situational ethics, or anarchism.

Blank.

Worried about his ability to cope when so much was riding on him, Marty picked up the kitchen phone and called the Delorios. When Kathy answered on the first ring, he said, "It's Marty."

"Marty, are you okay? We saw all the police leaving, and then the officer over here left, too, but nobody's made the situation clear to us. I mean, is everything all right? What in the world is going on?"

Kathy was a good neighbor and genuinely concerned, but Marty had no intention of wasting time in a full recounting of what he'd been through with either the would-be killer or the police. "Where are Charlotte and Emily?"

"Watching TV."

"Where?"

"Well, in the family room."

"Are your doors locked?"

"Yes, of course, I think so."

"Be sure. Check them. Do you have a gun?"

"A gun? Marty, what is this?"

"Do you have a gun?" he insisted.

"I don't believe in guns. But Vic has one."

"Is he carrying it now?"

"No. He's—"

"Tell him to load it and carry it until Paige and I can get there to pick up the girls."

"Marty, I don't like this. I don't—"

"Ten minutes, Kathy. I'll pick up the girls in ten minutes or less, fast as I can."

He hung up before she was able to respond.

He hurried upstairs to the guest room that doubled as Paige's home office. She did the family bookkeeping, balanced the checkbook, and looked after the rest of their financial affairs.

In the right-hand bottom drawer of the pine desk were files of receipts, invoices, and canceled checks. The drawer also contained their checkbook and savings-account passbook, which Marty retrieved fixed together with a rubberband. He stuffed them into one pocket of his chinos.

His mind wasn't blank any more. He'd thought of some precautions he ought to take, though they were too feeble to be considered a plan of action.

In his office he went to the walk-in storage closet and hastily selected four cardboard cartons from stacks of thirty to forty boxes of the same size and shape. Each held twenty hardcover books. He could only carry two at a time to the garage. He put them in the trunk of the BMW, wincing from the pain in his neck, which the effort exacerbated.

Entering the master bedroom after his second hasty trip to the car, he was brought up short just past the threshold by the sight of Paige snatching up the shotgun and whipping around to confront him.

"Sorry," she said, when she saw who it was.

"You did it right," he said. "Have you gotten the girls' things together?"

"No, I'm just finishing here."

"I'll get started on theirs," he said.

Following the blood trail to Charlotte and Emily's room, passing the broken-out section of gallery railing, Marty glanced at the foyer floor below. He still expected to see a dead man sprawled on the cracked tiles.

9.

Charlotte and Emily were slumped on the Delorios' family-room sofa, heads close together. They were pretending to be deeply involved in a stupid television comedy show about a stupid family with stupid kids and stupid parents doing stupid things to resolve a stupid problem. As long as they appeared to be caught up in the program, Mrs. Delorio stayed in the kitchen, preparing dinner. Mr. Delorio either paced through the house or stood at the front windows watching the cops outside. Ignored, the girls had a chance to whisper to each other and try to figure out what was happening at home.

"Maybe Daddy's been shot," Charlotte worried.

"I told you already a million times he wasn't."

"What do you know? You're only seven."

Emily sighed. "He told us he was okay, in the kitchen, when Mommy thought he was hurt."

"He was covered with blood," Charlotte fretted.

"He said it wasn't his."

"I don't remember that."

"I do," Emily said emphatically.

"If Daddy wasn't shot, then who was?"

"Maybe a burglar," Emily said.

"We're not rich, Em. What would a burglar want in our place? Hey, maybe Daddy had to shoot Mrs. Sanchez."

"Why shoot Mrs. Sanchez? She's just the cleaning lady."

"Maybe she went berserk," Charlotte said, and the possibility appealed enormously to her thirst for drama.

Emily shook her head. "Not Mrs. Sanchez. She's nice."

"Nice people go berserk."

"Do not."

"Do too."

Emily folded her arms on her chest. "Name one."

"Mrs. Sanchez," Charlotte said.

"Besides Mrs. Sanchez."

"Jack Nicholson."

"Who's he?"

"You know, the actor. In *Batman* he was the Joker, and he was totally massively berserk."

"So maybe he's always totally massively berserk."

"No, sometimes he's nice, like in that movie with Shirley MacLaine, he was an astronaut, and Shirley's daughter got real sick and they found out she had cancer, she died, and Jack was just so sweet and nice."

"Besides, this isn't Mrs. Sanchez's day," Emily said.

"What?"

"She only comes on Thursdays."

"Really, Em, if she went berserk, she wouldn't know what *day* it was," Charlotte countered, pleased with her response, which made such perfect sense. "Maybe she's loose from a looney-tune asylum, goes around getting housekeeping jobs, then sometimes when she's berserk she kills the family, roasts them, and eats them for dinner."

"You're weird," Emily said.

"No, listen," Charlotte insisted in an urgent whisper, "like Hannibal Lecter."

"Hannibal the Cannibal!" Emily gasped.

Neither of them had been allowed to see the movie—which Emily insisted on calling *The Sirens of the Lambs*—because Mom and Daddy didn't think they were old enough, but they'd heard about it from other kids in school who'd seen it on video a billion times.

Charlotte could tell that Emily was no longer so sure about Mrs. Sanchez. After all, Hannibal the Cannibal had been a *doctor* who went humongously berserk and bit off people's noses and stuff, so the idea of a berserk cannibal cleaning lady suddenly made a lot of sense.

Mr. Delorio came into the family room to part the drapes over the sliding glass doors and study the backyard, which was pretty much revealed by the patio lights. In his right hand he held a gun. He had not been carrying a gun before.

Letting the drapes fall back into place, turning away from the glass doors, he smiled at Charlotte and Emily. "You kids okay?"

"Yes, sir," Charlotte said. "This is a great show."

"You need anything?"

"No thanks, sir," Emily said. "We just want to watch the show."

"It's a great show," Charlotte repeated.

As Mr. Delorio left the room, both Charlotte and Emily turned to watch him until he was out of sight.

"Why's he have a gun?" Emily wondered.

"Protecting us. And you know what that means? Mrs. Sanchez must still be alive and on the loose, looking for someone to eat."

"But what if Mr. Delorio goes berserk next? He's got a gun, we could never get away from him."

"Be serious," Charlotte said, but then she realized a physical-education teacher was just as likely to go berserk as any cleaning lady. "Listen, Em, you know what to do if he goes berserk?"

"Call nine-one-one."

"You won't have time for that, silly. So what you'll have to do is, you'll have to kick him in the nuts."

Emily frowned. "Huh?"

"Don't you remember the movie Saturday?" Charlotte asked.

Mom had been upset enough about the movie to complain to the theater manager. She'd wanted to know how the picture could have received a PG rating with the language and violence in it, and the manager had said it was PG-13, which was very different.

One of the things that bothered Mom was a scene where the good guy got away from the bad guy by kicking him hard between the legs. Later, when someone asked the good guy what the bad guy wanted, the good guy said, "I don't know what he wanted, but what he *needed* was a good kick in the nuts."

Charlotte had sensed, at once, that the line annoyed her mother. Later, she could have asked for an explanation, and her mother would have given her one. Mom and Daddy believed in answering all of a child's questions honestly. But sometimes, it was more exciting to try to learn the answer on her own, because then it was something she knew that they didn't *know* she knew.

At home, she'd checked the dictionary to see if there was any definition of "nuts" that would explain what the good guy had done to the bad guy and also explain why her mother was so unhappy about it. When she saw that one meaning of the word was obscene slang for "testicles," she checked that mysterious word in the same dictionary, learned what she could, then sneaked into Daddy's office and used his medical encyclopedia to discover more. It was pretty bizarre stuff. But she understood it. Sort of. Maybe more than she wanted to understand. She had explained it as best she could to Em. But Em didn't believe a word of it and, evidently, promptly forgot about it.

"Just like in the movie Saturday," Charlotte reminded her. "If things get real bad and he goes berserk, kick him between the legs."

"Oh, yeah," Em said dubiously, "kick him in his tickles."

"Testicles."

"It was tickles."

"It was testicles," Charlotte insisted firmly.

Emily shrugged. "Whatever."

Mrs. Delorio walked into the family room, drying her hands on a yellow kitchen towel. She was wearing an apron over her skirt and blouse. She smelled of onions, which she had been chopping; she'd been starting to prepare dinner when they'd arrived. "Are you girls ready for more Pepsi?"

"No, ma'am," Charlotte said, "we're fine, thank you. Enjoying the show."

"It's a great show," Emily said.

"One of our favorites," Charlotte said.

Emily said, "It's about a boy with tickles and everyone keeps kicking them."

Charlotte almost thumped the little twerp on the head.

Frowning with confusion, Mrs. Delorio glanced back and forth from the television screen to Emily. "Tickles?"

"Pickles," Charlotte said, making a lame effort at covering.

The doorbell rang before Em could do more damage.

Mrs. Delorio said, "I'll bet that's your folks," and hurried out of the family room.

"Peabrain," Charlotte said to her sister.

Emily looked smug. "You're just mad because I showed it was all a lie. She never heard of boys having tickles."

"Sheesh!"

"So there," Emily said.

"Twerp."

"Snerp."

"That's not even a word."

"It is if I want it to be."

The doorbell rang and rang as if someone was leaning on it.

✳   ✳   ✳

Vic peered through the fish-eye lens at the man on the front stoop. It was Marty Stillwater.

He opened the door, stepping back so his neighbor could enter. "My God, Marty, it looked like a police convention over there. What was that all about?"

Marty stared at him intensely for a moment, especially at the gun in his right hand, then seemed to make some decision and blinked. Wet from the rain, his skin looked glazed and as unnaturally white as the face of a porcelain figurine. He seemed shrunken, shriveled, like a man recovering from a serious illness.

"Are you all right, is Paige all right?" Kathy asked, entering the hall behind Vic.

Hesitantly, Marty stepped across the threshold and stopped just inside the foyer, not entering quite far enough to allow Vic to close the door.

"What," Vic asked, "you're worried about dripping on the floor? You *know* Kathy thinks I'm a hopeless mess, she's had everything in the house Scotchgarded! Come in, come in."

Without entering farther, Marty looked past Vic into the living room, then up toward the head of the stairs. He was wearing a black raincoat buttoned to the neck, and it was too large for him, which was part of the reason he seemed shrunken.

Just when Vic thought the man was stricken mute, Marty said, "Where're the kids?"

"They're okay," Vic assured him, "they're safe."

"I need them," Marty said. His voice was no longer raspy, as it had been earlier, but wooden. "I need them."

"Well, for God's sake, old buddy, can't you at least come in long enough to tell us what—"

"I need them now," Marty said, "they're mine."

Not a wooden voice, after all, Vic Delorio realized, but tightly controlled, as if Marty was biting back anger or terror or some other strong emotion, afraid of losing his grip on himself. He trembled a little. Some of that rain on his face might have been sweat.

Coming forward along the hall, Kathy said, "Marty, what's wrong?"

Vic had been about to ask the same question. Marty Stillwater was usually such an easy-going guy, relaxed, quick to smile, but now he was stiff, awkward. Whatever he'd been through tonight, it had left deep marks on him.

Before Marty could respond, Charlotte and Emily appeared at the end of the hall, where it opened on the family room. They must have slipped into their raincoats the minute they heard their father's voice. They were buttoning up as they came.

Charlotte's voice wavered as she said, "Daddy?"

At the sight of his daughters, Marty's eyes flooded with tears. When Charlotte spoke to him, he took another step inside, so Vic could close the door.

The kids ran past Kathy, and Marty dropped to his knees on the foyer floor, and the kids just about flew into his arms hard enough to knock him over. As the three of them hugged one another, the girls talked at once: "Daddy, are you okay? We were so scared. Are you okay? I love you, Daddy. You were all yucky bloody. I told her it wasn't *your* blood. Was it a burglar, was it Mrs. Sanchez, did she go berserk, did the mailman go berserk, who went berserk, are you all right, is Mommy all right, is it over now, why do nice people just suddenly go berserk anyway?" All three were chattering at once, in fact, because Marty kept talking through all of their questions: "My Charlotte, my Emily, my kids, I love you, I love you so much, I won't let them steal you away again, never again." He kissed their cheeks, their foreheads, hugged them fiercely, smoothed their hair with his shaky hands, and in general made over them as if he hadn't seen them in years.

Kathy was smiling and at the same time crying quietly, daubing at her eyes with a yellow dish towel.

Vic supposed the reunion was touching, but he wasn't as moved by it as his wife was, partly because Marty looked and sounded peculiar to him, not strange in the way he expected a man to be strange after fighting off an intruder in his house—if that was actually what had happened—but just . . . well, just strange. Odd. The things Marty was saying were slightly weird: "My Emily, Charlotte, mine, just as cute as in your picture, mine, we'll be together, it's my destiny." His tone of voice was also unusual, too shaky and urgent if the ordeal was over, which the departure of the police surely indicated, but also too forced. Dramatic. Overly dramatic. He wasn't speaking spontaneously but seemed to be playing a stage role, struggling to remember the right thing to say.

Everyone said creative people were strange, especially writers, and when Vic first met Martin Stillwater, he expected the novelist to be eccentric. But

Marty had disappointed in that regard; he had been the most normal, levelheaded neighbor anyone could hope to have. Until now.

Getting to his feet, holding on to his daughters, Marty said, "We've got to go." He turned toward the front door.

Vic said, "Wait a second, Marty, buddy, you can't just blow out of here like that, with us so damned curious and all."

Marty had let go of Charlotte only long enough to open the door. He grabbed her hand again as the wind whistled into the foyer and rattled the framed embroidery of bluebirds and spring flowers that hung on the wall.

When the writer stepped outside without responding to Vic in any way, Vic glanced at Kathy and saw her expression had changed. Tears still glistened on her cheeks, but her eyes were dry, and she looked puzzled.

So it isn't just me, he thought.

He went outside and saw that the writer was already off the stoop, heading down the walk in the wind-tossed rain, holding the girls' hands. The air was chilly. Frogs were singing, but their songs were unnatural, cold and tinny, like the grinding-racheting of stripped gears in frozen machinery. The sound of them made Vic want to go back inside, sit in front of the fire, and drink a lot of hot coffee with brandy in it.

"Damn it, Marty, wait a minute!"

The writer turned, looked back, with the girls cuddling close to his sides.

Vic said, "We're your friends, we want to help. Whatever's wrong, we want to help."

"Nothing you can do, Victor."

"Victor? Man, you know I hate 'Victor,' nobody calls me that, not even my dear old gray-haired mother if she knows what's good for her."

"Sorry . . . Vic. I'm just . . . I've got a lot on my mind." With the girls in tow, he started down the walkway again.

A car was parked directly at the end of the walk. A new Buick. It looked bejeweled in the rain. Engine running. Lights on. Nobody inside.

Dashing off the stoop into the storm, which was no longer the cloud-burst it had been but still drenching, Vic caught up with them. "This your car?"

"Yeah," Marty said.

"Since when?"

"Bought it today."

"Where's Paige?"

"We're going to meet her." Marty's face was as white as the skull hidden beneath it. He was trembling visibly, and his eyes looked strange in the glow of the street lamp. "Listen, Vic, the kids are going to be soaked to the skin."

"I'm the one getting soaked," Vic said. "They've got raincoats. Paige isn't over at the house?"

"She left already." Marty glanced worriedly at his house across the street, where lights still glowed at both the first- and second-floor windows. "We're going to meet her."

"You remember what you told me—"

"Vic, please—"

"I almost forgot myself, what you told me, and then you were on your way down the walk and I remembered."

"We've got to go, Vic."

"You told me not to give the kids to anyone if Paige wasn't with them. Not anyone. You remember what you said?"

* * *

Marty carried two large suitcases downstairs, into the kitchen.

The Beretta 9mm Parabellum was stuffed under the waistband of his chinos. It pressed uncomfortably against his belly. He wore a reindeer-pattern wool sweater, which concealed the gun. His red-and-black ski jacket was unzipped, so he could reach the pistol easily, just by dropping the bags.

Paige entered the kitchen behind him. She was carrying one suitcase and the Mossberg 12-gauge shotgun.

"Don't open the outer door," Marty told her as he went through the small connecting door between the kitchen and the dark garage.

He didn't want the two-bay door open while they loaded the car because then it would become a point of vulnerability. As far as he knew, The Other might have crept back when the cops had left, might be outside at that very minute.

Following him into the garage, Paige switched on the overhead fluorescent panels. The long bulbs flickered but didn't immediately catch because the starters were bad. Shadows leaped and spun along the walls, between the cars, in the open rafters.

Torturing his injured neck, Marty involuntarily turned his head sharply toward each leaping phantom. None of them had a face at all, let alone a face identical to his.

The fluorescent came on all the way. The hard white light, cold and flat as a winter-morning sun, brought the shadow dancers to a sudden halt.

*   *   *

He is within a few feet of the Buick, holding tightly to his kids' hands, so close to getting away with them. His Charlotte. His Emily. His future, his destiny, so close, so infuriatingly close.

But Vic won't let go. The guy is a leech. Follows them all the way from the house, as if oblivious of the rain, continuously babbling, asking questions, a nosy bastard.

So close to the car. The engine running, headlights on. Emily in one hand, Charlotte in the other, and they love him, they really love him. They were hugging and kissing him back there in the foyer, so happy to see him, his little girls. They know their daddy, their *real* daddy. If he can just get into the car, close the doors, and drive away, they're his forever.

Maybe he can kill Vic, the nosy bastard. Then it would be so easy to escape. But he's not sure he can pull it off.

"You told me not to give the kids to anyone if Paige wasn't with them," Vic says. "Not anyone. You remember what you said?"

He stares at Vic, not thinking about an answer as much as about wasting the son of a bitch. But he's hungry again, shaky and weak in the knees, starting to crave the candy bars on the front seat, sugar, carbohydrates, more energy for the repairs he's still undergoing.

"Marty? You remember what you said?"

He has no gun, either, which wouldn't ordinarily be a problem. He's been well-trained to kill with his hands. He might even have enough strength to do so, in spite of his condition and the fact that Vic appears to be tough enough to put up a fight.

"I thought it was strange," Vic says, "but you told me, you said not even to give them to *you* unless Paige was with you."

The problem is that the bastard *does* have a gun. And he's suspicious.

Second by second, all hope of escape is crumbling, washing away in the rain. The girls are still holding his hand. He's got a firm grip on them, yes, but they're about to start slipping away, and he doesn't know what to do. He gapes at Vic, mind spinning, as stuck for something to say as he was stuck for something to write when he sat in his office earlier in the day and tried to begin a new book.

Move, move, confront, challenge, grapple, and prevail.

Abruptly he realizes that to confront this problem and prevail, he needs to act like a friend, the way friends treat each other and talk with each other in the movies. That will allay all suspicion.

A river of movie memories rushes through his mind, and he flows with them. "Vic, good heavens, Vic, did I . . . did I say that?" He imagines he is Jimmy Stewart because everyone likes and trusts Jimmy Stewart. "I don't know what I meant, musta been outta my head with worry. Gosh, it's just that . . . just that I've been so darned crazy scared with all this stuff that's been happening, this crazy stuff."

"What *has* been happening, Marty?"

Fearful but still gracious, halting but sincere, Jimmy Stewart in a Hitchcock film: "It's complicated, Vic, it's all . . . it's screwy, unbelievable, I half don't believe it myself. It'd take an hour to tell you, and I don't have an hour, don't have an hour, no sir, not now, I sure don't. My kids, these kids, they're in danger, Vic, and God help me if anything happens to them. I wouldn't want to live."

He can see that his new manner is having the desired effect. He hustles the kids the last few steps to the car, confident that the neighbor isn't going to stop them.

But Vic follows, splashing through a puddle. "Can't you tell me *anything?*"

Opening the back door of the Buick, ushering the girls inside, he turns to Vic once more. "I'm ashamed to say this, but it's me put them in danger, me, their father, because of what I do for a living."

Vic looks baffled. "You write books."

"Vic, you know what an obsessive fan is?"

Vic's eyes widen, then narrow as a gust of wind flings raindrops in his face. "Like that woman and Michael J. Fox a few years ago."

"That's it, that's right, like Michael J. Fox." The girls are both in the car. He slams the door. "Only it's a guy bothering us, not some crazy woman, and tonight he goes too far, breaks in the house, he's violent, I had to hurt him. Me. You imagine *me* having to hurt anybody, Vic? Now I'm afraid he'll be back, and I've got to get the girls away from here."

"My God," Vic says, totally suckered by the tale.

"Now that's all I have time to tell you, Vic, *more* than I have time to tell you, so you just . . . you just . . . you go back inside there before you catch your death of pneumonia. I'll call you in a few days, I'll tell you the rest."

Vic hesitates. "If we can do anything to help—"

"Go on now, go on, I appreciate what you've done already, but the only thing more you can do to help is get out of this rain. Look at you, you're drenched, for heaven's sake. Go get out of this rain, so I don't have to worry about you comin' down with pneumonia on account of me."

❋   ❋   ❋

Joining Marty at the back of the BMW, where he had dropped the bags, Paige put down the third suitcase and the Mossberg. When he unlocked and raised the trunk lid, she saw the three boxes inside. "What're those?"

He said, "Stuff we might need."

"Like what?"

"I'll explain later." He heaved the suitcases into the trunk.

When only two of the three would fit, she said, "The stuff I've packed is all bare necessities. At least one box has to go."

"No. I'll put the smallest suitcase in the back seat, on the floor, under Emily's feet. Her feet don't reach the floor anyway."

❋   ❋   ❋

Halfway to the house, Vic looks back toward the Buick.

Still playing Jimmy Stewart: "Go on, Vic, go on now. There's Kathy on the stoop, gonna catch her death, too, if you don't get inside, the both of you."

He turns away, rounds the back of the Buick, and only looks at the house again when he reaches the driver's door.

Vic is on the stoop with Kathy, too far away now to prevent his escape, with or without a gun.

He waves at the Delorios, and they wave back. He gets into the Buick, behind the steering wheel, the oversize raincoat bunching up around him. He pulls the door shut.

Across the street, in his own house, lights are aglow upstairs and down. The imposter is in there with Paige. His beautiful Paige. He can't do anything about that, not yet, not without a gun.

When he turns to look into the back seat, he sees that Charlotte and Emily have already buckled themselves into the safety harnesses. They are good girls. And so cute in their yellow raincoats and matching vinyl hats. Even in their picture, they are not this cute.

They both start talking, Charlotte first: "Where're we going, Daddy, where'd we get this car?"

Emily says, "Where's Mommy?"

Before he can answer them, they launch an unmerciful salvo of questions:

"What happened, who'd you shoot, did you kill anybody?"

"Was it Mrs. Sanchez?"

"Did she go berserk like Hannibal the Cannibal, Daddy, was she really whacko?" Charlotte asked.

Peering through the passenger-side window, he sees the Delorios go into their house together and close the front door.

Emily says, "Daddy, is it true?"

"Yeah, Daddy, is it true, what you told Mr. Delorio, like with Michael J. Fox, is it true? He's cute."

"Just be quiet," he tells them impatiently. He shifts the Buick into gear, tramps the accelerator. The car bucks in place because he's forgotten to release the handbrake, which he does, but then the car jolts forward and stalls.

"Why isn't Mom with you?" Emily asks.

Charlotte's excitement is growing, and the sound of her voice is making him dizzy: "Boy, you had blood all over your shirt, you sure must've shot *somebody,* it was really disgusting, maximum gross."

The craving for food is intense. His hands are shaking so badly that the keys jangle noisily when he tries to restart the engine. Although the hunger won't be nearly as bad this time as previously, he'll be able to go only a few blocks before he'll be overwhelmed with a need for those candy bars.

"Where's Mommy?"

"He must've tried to shoot you first, did he try to shoot you first, did he have a knife, that would've been scary, a knife, what did he have, Daddy?"

The starter grinds, the car chugs, but the engine won't turn over, as if he has flooded it.

"Where's Mommy?"

"Did you actually fight him with your bare hands, take a knife away from him or something, Daddy, how could you do that, do you know karate, do you?"

"Where's Mommy? I want to know where Mommy is."

Rain thumps off the car roof. Pongs off the hood. The flooded engine is maddeningly unresponsive: *ruuurrrrr-ruuurrrrr-ruuurrrrr*. Windshield wipers thudding, thudding. Back and forth. Back and forth. Pounding incessantly. Girlish voices in the back seat, increasingly shrill. Like the strident buzzing of bees. *Buzz-buzz-buzz.* Has to concentrate to keep his trembling hand firmly on the key. Sweaty, spastic fingers keep slipping off. Afraid of overcompensating, maybe snap the key off in the ignition. *Ruuurrrrr-ruuurrrrr.* Starving. Need to eat. Need to get away from here. Thump. Pong. Incessant pounding. Pain revives in his nearly healed wounds. Hurts to breathe. Damn engine. *Ruuurrrrr.* Won't start. *Ruuurrrrr-ruuurrrrr.* Daddy-Daddy-Daddy-Daddy-Daddy, *buzzzzzzzzzzzz.*

Frustration to anger, anger to hatred, hatred to violence. Violence sometimes soothes.

Itching to hit something, anything, he turns in his seat, glares back at the girls, screams at them, *"Shut up, shut, up, shut up!"*

They are stunned. As if he has never spoken to them like this before.

The little one bites her lip, can't bear to look at him, turns her face to the side window.

"Quiet, for Christ's sake, be quiet!"

When he faces forward again and tries to start the car, the older girl bursts into tears as if she's a baby. Wipers thudding, starter grinding, engine wallowing, the steady thump of rain, and now her whiny weeping, so piercing, grating, just too much to bear. He screams wordlessly at her, loud enough to drown out her crying and all the other sounds for a moment. He considers climbing into the back seat with the damn shrieking little thing, make it stop, hit it, shake it, clamp one hand over its nose and mouth until it can't make a sound of any kind, until it finally stops crying, stops struggling, just stops, stops—

—and abruptly the engine chugs, turns over, purrs sweetly.

❋　　❋　　❋

"I'll be right back," Paige said as Marty put the suitcase on the floor behind the driver's seat of the BMW.

He looked up in time to see that she was heading into the house. "Wait, what're you doing?"

"Got to turn off all the lights."

"To hell with that. Don't go back in there."

It was a moment from fiction, straight out of a novel or movie, and Marty recognized it as such. Having packed, having gotten as far as the car, *that* close to escaping unscathed, they would return to the house to complete an inessential task, confident of their safety, and somehow the psychopath would be in there, either because he had returned while they were in the garage or because he had successfully hidden in some cleverly concealed niche throughout the police search of the premises. They would move from room to room, switching off the lights, letting darkness spill through the house—whereupon the look-alike would materialize, a shadow out of shadows, wielding a large butcher's knife taken from the rack of implements in their own kitchen, slashing, stabbing, killing one or both of them.

Marty knew real life was neither as extravagantly colorful as the most eventful fiction nor half as drab as the average academic novel—and less predictable than either. His fear of returning to the house to switch off the lights was irrational, the product of a too-fertile imagination and a novelist's predilection to anticipate drama, malevolence, and tragedy in every turn of human affairs, in every change of weather, plan, dream, hope, or roll of dice.

Nevertheless, they weren't going back into the damn house. No way in hell.

"Leave the lights on," he said. "Lock up, raise the garage door, let's get the kids and get out of here."

Maybe Paige had lived with a novelist long enough for her own imagination to be corrupted, or maybe she remembered all of the blood in the upstairs hall. For whatever reason, she didn't protest that leaving so many lights on would be a waste of electricity. She thumbed the button to activate the Genie lift, and shut the door to the kitchen with her other hand.

As Marty closed and locked the trunk of the BMW, the garage door finished rising. With a final clatter it settled into the full-open position.

He looked out at the rainy night, his right hand straying to the butt of the Beretta at his waistband. His imagination was still churning, and he was prepared to see the indomitable look-alike coming up the driveway.

What he saw, instead, was worse than any image conjured by his imagination. A car was parked across the street in front of the Delorios' house. It wasn't the Delorios' car. Marty had never seen it before. The headlights were on, though the driver was having difficulty getting the engine to turn over; it cranked and cranked. Although the driver was only a dark shape, the small pale oval of a child's face was visible at the rear window, staring out from the back seat. Even at a distance, Marty was sure that the little girl in the Buick was Emily.

At the connecting door to the kitchen, Paige was fumbling for house keys in the pockets of her corduroy jacket.

Marty was in the grip of paralytic shock. He couldn't call out to Paige, couldn't move.

Across the street, the engine of the Buick caught, chugged consumptively, then roared fully to life. Clouds of crystallized fumes billowed from the exhaust pipe.

Marty didn't realize he'd shattered the paralysis and begun to move until he was out of the garage, in the middle of the driveway, sprinting through the cold rain toward the street. He felt as though he had teleported thirty feet in a tiny fraction of a second, but it was just that, operating on instinct and sheer animal terror, his body was ahead of his mind.

The Beretta was in his hand. He didn't recall drawing it out of his waistband.

The Buick pulled away from the curb and Marty turned left to follow it. The car was moving slowly because the driver had not yet realized that he was being pursued.

Emily was still visible. Her frightened face was now pressed tightly to the glass. She was staring directly at her father.

Marty was closing on the car, ten feet from the rear bumper. Then it accelerated smoothly away from him, much faster than he could run. Its tires parted the puddles with a percolative burble and plash.

Like a passenger on Charon's gondola, Emily was being ferried not just along a street but across the river Styx, into the land of the dead.

A black wave of despair washed over Marty, but his heart began to pound even more fiercely than before, and he found a strength he had not imagined he possessed. He ran harder than ever, splashing through puddles, feet hammering the blacktop with what seemed like jackhammer force, pumping his arms, head tucked down, eyes always on the prize.

At the end of the block the Buick slowed. It came to a full stop at the intersection.

Gasping, Marty caught up with it. Back bumper. Rear fender. Rear door.

Emily's face was at the window.

She was looking up at him now.

His senses were as heightened by terror as if he'd taken mind-altering drugs. He was hallucinogenically aware of every detail of the scores of raindrops on the glass between himself and his daughter—their curved and pendulous shapes, the bleak whorls and shards of light from the street lamps reflected in their quivering surfaces—as if each of those droplets was equal in importance to anything else in the world. Likewise, he saw the interior of the car not just as a dark blur but as an elaborate dimensional tapestry of shadows in countless hues of gray, blue, black. Beyond Emily's pale face, in that intricate needlework of dusk and gloom, was another figure, a second child: Charlotte.

Just as he drew even with the driver's door and reached for the handle, the car began to move again. It swung right, through the intersection.

Marty slipped and almost fell on the wet pavement. He regained his balance, held on to the gun, and scrambled after the Buick as it turned into the cross street.

The driver was looking to the right, unaware of Marty on his left. He was wearing a black coat. Only the back of his head was visible through the rain-streaked side window. His hair was darker than Vic Delorio's.

Because the car was still moving slowly as it completed the turn, Marty caught up with it again, breathing strenuously, ears filled with the hard drumming of his heart. He didn't reach for the door this time because maybe it was locked. He would squander the element of surprise by trying it. Raising the Beretta, he aimed at the back of the man's head.

The kids could be hit by a ricochet, flying glass. He had to risk it. Otherwise, they were lost forever.

Though there was little chance the driver was Vic Delorio or another innocent person, Marty couldn't squeeze the trigger without knowing for sure at whom he was shooting. Still moving, paralleling the car, he shouted, *"Hey, hey, hey!"*

The driver snapped his head around to look out the side window.

Along the barrel of the pistol, Marty stared at his own face. The Other. The glass before him seemed like a cursed mirror in which his reflection was not confined to precise mimicry but was free to reveal more vicious emotions than anyone would ever want the world to see: as it confronted him, that looking-glass face clenched with hatred and fury.

Startled, the driver had let his foot slip off the accelerator. For the briefest moment the Buick slowed.

No more than four feet from the window, Marty squeezed off two rounds. In the instant before the resonant thunder of the first gunshot echoed off an infinitude of wet surfaces across the rainswept night, he thought he saw the driver drop to the side and down, still holding the steering wheel with at least one hand but trying to get his head out of the line of fire. The muzzle flashed, and shattering glass obscured the bastard's fate.

Even as the second shot boomed close after the first, the car tires shrieked. The Buick bolted forward, as a mean horse might explode out of a rodeo gate.

He ran after the car, but it blew away from him with a backwash of turbulent air and exhaust fumes. The look-alike was still alive, perhaps injured but still alive and determined to escape.

Rocketing eastward, the Buick began to angle onto the wrong side of the two-lane street. On that trajectory, it was going to jump the curb and crash into someone's front lawn.

In his treacherous mind's eye, Marty imagined the car hitting the curb at high speed, flipping, rolling, slamming into one of the trees or the side of a house, bursting into flames, his daughters trapped in a coffin of blazing steel. In the darkest corner of his mind, he could even hear them screaming as the fire seared the flesh from their bones.

Then, as he pursued it, the Buick swung back across the center line, into its own lane. It was still moving fast, too fast, and he had no hope of catching it.

But he ran as if it was his own life for which he was running, his throat beginning to burn again as he breathed through his open mouth, chest aching, needles of pain lancing the length of his legs. His right hand was clamped so fiercely around the butt of the Beretta that the muscles in his arm throbbed from wrist to shoulder. And with each desperate stride, the names of his daughters echoed through his mind in an unvoiced scream of loss and grief.

❋   ❋   ❋

When their father shouted at them to shut up, Charlotte was as hurt as if he'd slapped her face, for in her nine years, nothing she had said and no stunt she'd pulled had ever before made him so angry. Yet she didn't understand what had infuriated him because all she'd done was ask some questions. His scolding of her was so unfair; and the fact that he had never been unfair in her recollection only added sting to his reprimand. He seemed angry with her for no other reason than that she was herself, as if something about her very nature suddenly repelled and disgusted him, which was an unbearable thought because she couldn't change who she was, what she was, and maybe her own father was never again going to *like* her. He would never be able to take back the look of rage and hatred on his face, and she would never be able to forget it as long as she lived. Everything had changed between them forever. All of this she thought and understood in a second, even before he had finished shouting at them, and she burst into tears.

Dimly aware that the car finally started, pulled away from the curb, and reached the end of the block, Charlotte rose partway out of her misery only when Em turned from the window, grabbed her arm, and shook her. Em whispered fiercely, *"Daddy."*

At first, Charlotte thought Em was unjustly peeved with her for making Daddy angry and was warning her to be quiet. But before she could launch into sisterly combat, she realized there had been joyful excitement in Em's voice.

Something important was happening.

Blinking back tears, she saw that Em was already pressed to the window again. As the car pulled through the intersection and turned right, Charlotte followed the direction of her sister's gaze.

As soon as she spotted Daddy running alongside the car, she knew he was her *real* father. The daddy behind the wheel—the daddy with the hateful look on his face, who screamed at children for no reason—was a fake. Somebody else. Or some *thing* else, maybe like in the movies, grown out of a seed pod from another galaxy, one day just a lot of ugly goop and the next day all formed into Daddy's look-alike. She suffered no confusion at the sight of two identical fathers, had no trouble knowing which was the real one, as an adult might have, because she was a kid and kids knew these things.

Keeping pace with the car as it turned into the next street, pointing the gun at the window of the driver's door, Daddy yelled, *"Hey, hey, hey!"*

As the fake daddy realized who was shouting at him, Charlotte reached out as far as her safety belt would allow, grabbed a handful of Em's coat, and yanked her sister away from the window. "Get down, cover your face, quick!"

They leaned toward each other, cuddled together, shielded each other's heads with their arms.

BAM!

The gunfire was the loudest sound Charlotte had ever heard. Her ears rang.

She almost started to cry again, in fear this time, but she had to be tough for Em. At a time like this a big sister had to think about her responsibilities.

BAM!

Even as the second shot boomed a heartbeat after the first, Charlotte knew the fake daddy had been hit because he squealed with pain and cursed, spitting out the S-word over and over. He was still in good enough shape to drive, and the car leaped forward.

They seemed out of control, swinging to the left, going very fast, then turning sharply back to the right.

Charlotte sensed they were going to crash into something. If they weren't smashed to smithereens in the wreck, she and Em had to be ready to move fast when they came to a stop, get out of the car, and out of the way so Daddy could deal with the fake.

She had no doubt Daddy could handle the other man. Though she wasn't old enough to have read any of his novels, she knew he wrote about killers and guns and car chases, just this sort of thing, so he would know *exactly* what to do. The fake would be real sorry he had messed with Daddy; he would wind up in prison for a long, long time.

The car swerved back to the left, and in the front seat the fake made small bleating sounds of pain that reminded her of the cries of Wayne the Gerbil that time when somehow he'd gotten one small foot stuck in the mechanism of his exercise wheel. But Wayne never cursed, of course, and this man was cursing more angrily than ever, not just using the S-word but God's name in vain, plus all sorts of words she had never heard before but knew were unquestionably bad language of the worst kind.

Keeping a grip on Em, Charlotte felt along her seatbelt with her free hand, seeking the release button, found it, and held her thumb lightly on it.

The car jolted over something, and the driver hit the brakes. They slid sideways on the wet street. The back end of the car swung around to the left, and her tummy turned over as if they were on an amusement-park ride.

The driver's side of the car slammed hard into something, but not hard enough to kill them. She jammed her thumb on the release button, and her safety belt retracted. Fumbling at Em's waist—"Your belt, get your belt off!"—she found her sister's release button in a second or two.

Em's door was jammed against whatever they had hit. They had to go out Charlotte's side.

She pulled Em across her. Pushed open the door. Shoved Em through it.

At the same time, Em was pulling *her,* as if Em herself was the one doing the rescuing, and Charlotte wanted to say, *Hey, who's the big sister here?*

The fake daddy saw or heard them getting out. He lunged for them across the back of the front seat—"Little bitch!"—and grabbed Charlotte's floppy rain hat.

She scooted out from under the hat, through the door, into the night and rain, tumbling onto her hands and knees on the blacktop. Looking up, she saw that Em was already tottering across the street toward the far sidewalk, wobbling like a baby that had just learned to walk. Charlotte scrambled up and ran after her sister.

Somebody was shouting their names.

Daddy.

Their *real* Daddy.

*   *   *

Three-quarters of a block away, the speeding Buick hit a broken tree branch in a huge puddle and slid on a churning foam of water.

Marty was heartened by the chance to close the gap but horrified by the thought of what might happen to his daughters. The mental film clip of a car crash didn't just play through his mind again; it had never *stopped* playing. Now it seemed about to be translated out of his imagination, the way scenes were translated from mental images into words on the page, except that this time he was taking it one large step further, leaping over typescript, translating directly from imagination into reality. He had the crazy idea that the Buick wouldn't have gone out of control if he hadn't pictured it doing so, and that his daughters would burn to death in the car merely because he had imagined it happening.

The Buick came to a sudden and noisy stop against the side of a parked Ford Explorer. Though the clang of the collision jarred the night, the car didn't roll or burn.

To Marty's astonishment, the right-side rear passenger door flew open, and his kids erupted like a pair of joke snakes exploding from a tin can.

As far as he could tell, they weren't seriously hurt, and he shouted at them to get away from the Buick. But they didn't need his advice. They had an agenda of their own, and immediately scrambled across the street, looking for cover.

He kept running. Now that the girls were out of the car, his fury was greater than his fear. He wanted to hurt the driver, kill him. It wasn't a hot rage but cold, a mindless reptilian savagery that scared him even as he surrendered to it.

He was less than a third of a block from the car when its engine shrieked and the spinning tires began to smoke. The Other was trying to get away, but the vehicles were hung up on each other. Tortured metal abruptly screeched, popped, and the Buick started to tear loose of the Explorer.

Marty would have preferred to be closer when he opened fire, so he'd have a better chance of hitting The Other, but he sensed he was as close as he was going to get. He skidded to a halt, raised the Beretta, holding it with both hands, shaking so badly he couldn't hold the sight on target, cursing himself for his weakness, trying to be a rock.

The recoil of the first shot kicked the barrel high, and Marty lowered it before firing another round.

The Buick broke free of the Explorer and lurched forward a few feet. For a moment its tires lost traction on the slick pavement and spun in place again, spewing behind it a silvery spray of water.

He pulled the trigger, grunting in satisfaction as the rear window of the Buick imploded, and squeezed off another round right away, aiming for the driver, trying to visualize the bastard's skull imploding as the window had done, hoping that what he imagined would translate into reality. When its tires got a bite of the pavement, the Buick shot away from him. Marty pumped another round and another, even though the car was already out of range. The girls weren't in the line of fire and no one else seemed to be on the rainy street, but it was irresponsible to continue shooting because he had little chance of hitting The Other. He was more likely to blow away an innocent who happened to pass on some cross street ahead, more likely to shatter a window in one of the nearby houses and waste someone sitting in front of a TV. But he didn't care, couldn't stop himself, wanted blood, vengeance, emptied the magazine, repeatedly pulled the trigger after the last bullet had been expended, making primitive wordless sounds of rage, totally out of control.

* * *

In the BMW, Paige ran the stop sign. The car slid around the corner, almost tipping onto two wheels before she straightened it out, facing east on the cross street.

The first thing she saw after making the corner was Marty in the middle of the street. He was standing with his legs widely spread, his back to her, firing the pistol at the dwindling Buick.

Her breath caught and her heart seized up. The girls must be in the receding car.

She tramped the accelerator to the floor, intending to swing around Marty and catch up with the Buick, ram the back of it, run it off the road, fight the kidnapper with her bare hands, claw the son of a bitch's eyes out, whatever she had to do, anything. Then she saw the girls in their bright yellow rain slickers on the right-hand sidewalk, standing under a street lamp. They were holding each other. They looked so small and fragile in the drizzling rain and bitter yellowish light.

Past Marty, Paige pulled to the curb. She threw open the door and got out of the BMW, leaving the headlights on and the engine running.

As she ran to the kids, she heard herself saying, "Thank God, thank God, thank God, thank God." She couldn't stop saying it even when she crouched and swept both girls into her arms at the same time, as if on some level she believed that the two words had magic power and that her children would suddenly vanish from her embrace if she stopped chanting the mantra.

The girls hugged her fiercely. Charlotte buried her face against her mother's neck. Emily's eyes were huge.

Marty dropped to his knees beside them. He kept touching the kids, especially their faces, as if he was having difficulty believing that their skin was still warm and their eyes lively, astonished to see that breath still steamed from them. He repeatedly said, "Are you all right, are you hurt, are you all right?'' The only injury he could find was a minor abrasion on Charlotte's left palm, incurred when she'd plunged from the Buick and landed on her hands and knees.

The only major and troubling difference in the girls was their unusual constraint. They were so subdued that they seemed meek, as if they had just been severely chastised. The brief experience with the kidnapper had left them frightened and withdrawn. Their usual self-confidence might not return for some time, might never be as strong as it had once been. For that reason alone Paige wanted to make the man in the Buick suffer.

Along the block, a couple of people had come out on their front porches to see what the commotion was about—now that the shooting had stopped. Others were at their windows.

Sirens wailed in the distance.

Rising to his feet, Marty said, "Let's get out of here."

"The police are coming," Paige said.

"That's what I mean."

"But they—"

"They'll be as bad as last time, worse."

He picked up Charlotte and hurried with her to the BMW as the sirens swelled louder.

❋   ❋   ❋

Chips of glass are lodged in his left eye. For the most part, the tempered window had dissolved in a gummy mass. It had not cut his face. But tiny shards are embedded deep in the tender ocular tissues, and the pain is devastating. Every movement of the eye works the glass deeper, does more damage.

Because his eye twitches when the worst needle-sharp pains stitch through it, he keeps blinking involuntarily, although it is torture to do so. To stop the blinking, he holds the fingers of his left hand against his closed eyelid, applying only the gentlest pressure. As much as possible, he drives with just his right hand.

Sometimes he has to let the eye twitch unattended because he needs to use the left hand to drive. With the right, he tears open one of the candy bars and crams it into his mouth as fast as he can chew. His metabolic furnace demands fuel.

A bullet crease marks his forehead above the same eye. The furrow is as wide as his index finger and a little more than an inch long. To the bone. At first it bled freely. Now the clotting blood oozes thickly over his eyebrow and seeps between the fingers that he holds to the eyelid.

If the bullet had been one inch to the left, it would have taken him in the temple and drilled into his brain, jamming splinters of bone in front of it.

He fears head wounds. He is not confident that he can recover from brain damage either as entirely or as swiftly as from other injuries. Maybe he can't recover from it at all.

Half blind, he drives cautiously. With only one eye he has lost depth perception. The rain-pooled streets are treacherous.

The police now have a description of the Buick, perhaps even the license number. They will be looking for it, routinely if not actively, and the damage along the driver's side will make it easier to spot.

He is in no condition to steal another car at this time. He's not only half blind but still shaky from the gunshot wounds that he suffered three hours ago. If he is caught in the act of stealing an unattended car, or if he encounters resistance when trying to kill another motorist such as the one whose raincoat he wears and who is temporarily entombed in the Buick's trunk, he is likely to be apprehended or more seriously wounded.

Driving north and west from Mission Viejo, he quickly crosses the city line into El Toro. Though in a new community, he does not feel safe. If there is an APB out on the Buick, it will probably be county-wide.

The greatest danger arises from staying on the move, increasing the risk of being seen by the cops. If he can find a secluded place to park the Buick, where it will be safe from discovery at least until tomorrow, he can curl up on the back seat and rest.

He needs to sleep and give his body a chance to mend. He has gone two nights without rest since leaving Kansas City. Ordinarily he could remain alert and active for a third night, possibly a fourth, with no diminution of his faculties. But the toll of his injuries, combined with lost sleep and tremendous physical exertion, requires time out for convalescence.

Tomorrow he will get his family back, reclaim his destiny. He has wandered alone and in darkness for so long. One more day will make little difference.

He was *so* close to success. For a brief time his daughters belonged to him again. His Charlotte. His Emily.

He recalls the joy he felt in the foyer of the Delorio house, holding the girls' small bodies against him. They were so sweet. Butterfly-soft kisses on his cheeks. Their musical voices—"Daddy, Daddy"—so full of love for him.

Remembering how close he was to taking permanent possession of them, he is on the brink of tears. He must not cry. The convulsion of the muscles in his damaged eye will amplify his pain unbearably, and tears in his right eye will reduce him to virtual blindness.

Instead, as he cruises residential neighborhoods from El Toro into Laguna Hills, where house lights glow warmly in the rain and taunt him with images of domestic bliss, he thinks about how those same children ultimately defied and abandoned him, for this subject leads him away from tears and toward anger. He does not understand why his sweet little girls would choose the charlatan over their real father, when minutes previously they had showered him with thrilling kisses and adoration. Their betrayal disturbs him. Gnaws at him.

✼　　✼　　✼

While Marty drove, Paige sat in the back seat with Charlotte and Emily, holding their hands. She was emotionally incapable of letting go of them just yet.

Marty followed an indirect route across Mission Viejo, initially stayed off main streets as much as possible, and successfully avoided the police. Block after block, Paige continued to study the traffic around them, expecting the battered Buick to appear and try to force them off the pavement. Twice she turned to look out the rear window, certain that the Buick was following them, but her fears were never realized.

When Marty picked up the Marguerite Parkway and headed south, Paige finally asked, "Where are we going?"

He glanced at her in the rearview mirror. "I don't know. Just away from here. I'm still thinking about where."

"Maybe they would've believed you this time."

"Not a chance."

"People back there must've seen the Buick."

"Maybe. But they didn't see the man driving it. None of them can back up my story."

"Vic and Kathy must've seen him."

"And thought he was me."

"But now they'll realize he wasn't."

"They didn't see us *together,* Paige. That's what matters, damn it! Someone seeing us together, an independent witness."

She said, "Charlotte and Emily. They saw him and you at the same time."

Marty shook his head. "Doesn't count. I wish it did. But Lowbock won't put any stock in the testimony of little kids."

"Not so little," Emily piped up from beside Paige, sounding even younger and tinier than she actually was.

Charlotte remained uncharacteristically quiet. Both girls were still shivering, but Charlotte had a worse case of the shakes than did Emily. She was leaning against her mother for warmth, her head pulled turtlelike into the collar of her coat.

Marty had the heater turned up as high as it would go. The interior of the BMW should have been suffocatingly hot. It wasn't.

Even Paige was cold. She said, "Maybe we should go back and try to talk sense to them anyway."

Marty was adamant. "Honey, no, we can't. Think about it. They'll sure as hell take the Beretta. I shot at the guy with it. From their point of view, one way or another, there's been a crime, and the gun was used in the commission of it. Either somebody really attempted to kidnap the girls, and I tried to kill him. Or it's still all a hoax to sell books, get me higher on the bestseller list. Maybe I hired a friend to drive the Buick, shot a bunch of blanks at him, induced my own kids to lie, now I'm filing *another* false police report."

"After all this, Lowbock won't still be pushing that ridiculous theory."

"Won't he? The hell he won't."

"Marty, he can't."

He sighed. "Okay, all right, maybe he won't, probably he won't."

Paige said, "He'll realize that something a lot more serious is going on—"

"But he won't believe *my* story either, which I've got to admit sounds nuttier than a giant-size can of Planters finest. And if you'd read the piece in *People* . . . Anyway, he'll take the Beretta. What if he discovers the shotgun in the trunk?"

"There's no reason for him to take that."

"He might find an excuse. Listen, Paige, Lowbock's not going to change his mind about me that easily, not just because the kids tell him it's all true.

He'll still be a lot more suspicious of me than of any guy in a Buick he's never seen. If he takes both guns, we're defenseless. Suppose the cops leave, then this bastard, this look-alike, he walks into the house two minutes later, when we don't have anything to protect ourselves."

"If the police still don't believe it, if they won't give us protection, then we won't stay at the house."

"No, Paige, I literally mean what if the bastard walks in *two minutes* after the cops leave, doesn't even give us a chance to clear out?"

"He's not likely to risk—"

"Oh, yes, he is! Yes, he is. He came back almost *immediately* after the cops left the first time—didn't he?—just boldly walked up to the Delorios' front door and rang the damn bell. He seems to *thrive* on risk. I wouldn't put it past the bastard to break in on us while the cops were still there, shoot everyone in sight. He's crazy, this whole situation is crazy, and I don't want to bet my life or yours or the kids' lives on what the creep is going to do next."

Paige knew he was right.

However, it was difficult, even painful, to accept that their situation was so dire as to place them beyond the help of the law. If they couldn't receive official assistance and protection, then the government had failed them in its most basic duty: to provide civil order through the fair but strict enforcement of a criminal code. In spite of the complex machine in which they rode, in spite of the modern highway on which they traveled and the sprawl of suburban lights that covered most of the southern California hills and vales, this failure meant they were not living in a civilized world. The shopping malls, elaborate transit systems, glittering centers for the performing arts, sports arenas, imposing government buildings, multiplex movie theaters, office towers, sophisticated French restaurants, churches, museums, parks, universities, and nuclear power plants amounted to nothing but an elaborate facade of civilization, tissue-thin for all its apparent solidity, and in truth they were living in a high-tech anarchy, sustained by hope and self-delusion.

The steady hum of the car tires gave birth in her to a mounting dread, a mood of impending calamity. It was such a common sound, hard rubber tread spinning at high speed over blacktop, merely a part of the quotidian music of daily life, but suddenly it was as ominous as the drone of approaching bombers.

When Marty turned southwest on the Crown Valley Parkway, toward Laguna Niguel, Charlotte at last broke her silence. "Daddy?"

Paige saw him glance at the rearview mirror and knew by his worried eyes that he, too, had been troubled by the girl's unusual spell of introversion.

He said, "Yes, baby?"

"What was that thing?" Charlotte asked.

"What thing, honey?"

"The thing that looked like you."

"That's the million-dollar question. But whoever he is, he's just a man, not a thing. He's just a man who looks an awful lot like me."

Paige thought about all the blood in the upstairs hall, about how quickly the look-alike had recovered from two chest wounds to make a quick escape and to return, a short time later, strong enough to renew the assault. He didn't seem human. And Marty's statements to the contrary were, she knew, nothing but the obligatory reassurances of a father who knew that children sometimes needed to believe in the omniscience and unshakable equanimity of adults.

After further silence, Charlotte said, "No, it wasn't a man. It was a thing. Mean. Ugly inside. A cold thing." A shudder wracked her, causing her next words to issue tremolo: "I kissed it and said 'I love you' to it, but it was just a *thing.*"

❄   ❄   ❄

The upscale garden-apartment complex encompasses a score or more of large buildings housing ten or twelve apartments each. It sprawls over parklike grounds shaded by a small forest of trees.

The streets within the complex are serpentine. Residents are provided with community carports, redwood structures with only a back wall and roof, eight or ten stalls in each. Bougainvillea climbs the columns that support each roof, lending a note of grace, although at night the vivid blossoms are bleached of most of their color by the detergent-blue light of mercury-vapor security lamps.

Throughout the development are uncovered parking areas where the white curbs are stenciled with black letters: VISITOR PARKING ONLY.

In a deep cul-de-sac, he finds a visitors' zone that provides him with a perfect place to spend the night. None of the six spaces is occupied, and the last is flanked on one side by a five-foot-high oleander hedge. When he backs the car into the slot, tight against the hedge, the oleander conceals the damage along the driver's side.

An acacia tree has been allowed to encroach upon the nearest street lamp. Its leafy limbs block most of the light. The Buick stands largely in darkness.

The police are not likely to cruise the complex more than once or twice between now and dawn. And when they do, they will not be checking license plates but scanning the grounds for indications of burglary or other crimes in progress.

He switches off the headlights and the engine, gathers up what remains of his store of candy, and gets out of the car, shaking off the bits of gummy, tempered glass that cling to him.

Rain is no longer falling.

The air is cool and clean.

The night keeps its own counsel, silent but for the tick and plop of still-dripping trees.

He gets into the back seat and softly closes the door. It is not a comfortable bed. But he has known worse. He settles into the fetal position, curled around candy bars instead of an umbilicus, blanketed only by the roomy raincoat.

As he waits for sleep to overtake him, he thinks again of his daughters and their betrayal.

Inevitably, he wonders if they prefer their other father to him, the false to the real. This is a dreadful possibility to be forced to explore. If it is true, it means that those he loves the most are not victims, as he is, but are active participants in the Byzantine plot against him.

Their false father is probably lenient with them. Allows them to eat what they want. Lets them go to bed as late as they please.

All children are anarchists by nature. They need rules and standards of behavior, or they grow up to be wild and antisocial.

When he kills the hateful false father and retakes control of his family, he will establish rules for everything and will strictly enforce them. Misbehavior will be instantly punished. Pain is one of life's greatest teachers, and he is an expert in the application of pain. Order will be restored within the Stillwater household, and his children will commit no act without first soberly reflecting upon the rules that govern them.

Initially, of course, they will hate him for being so stern and uncompromising. They will not understand that he is acting in their best interests.

However, each tear that his punishments wring from them will be sweet to him. Each cry of pain will be a gladdening music. He will be unrelenting with them because he knows that in time they will realize he imposes guidance upon them only because he cares so profoundly about them. They will love him for his stern fatherly concern. They will adore him for providing the discipline which they need—and secretly desire—but which it is their very nature to resist.

Paige also will need to be disciplined. He knows about women's needs. He remembers a film with Kim Basinger in which sex and a craving for discipline were shown to be inextricably entwined. He anticipates Paige's instructions with particular pleasure.

Since the day that his career, family, and memories were stolen from him—which might be a year or ten years ago, for all he knows—he has lived primarily through the movies. The adventures he has experienced and the poignant lessons he has learned in countless darkened theaters seem as real to him as the car seat on which he now lies and the chocolate dissolving on his tongue. He remembers making love to Sharon Stone, to Glenn Close, from both of whom he learned the potential for sexual mania and treachery inherent in all women. He remembers the exuberant fun of sex with Goldie Hawn, the rapture of Michelle Pfeiffer, the exciting sweaty urgency of Ellen Barkin when he incorrectly suspected her of being a murderess but pinned her to the wall of his apartment and penetrated her anyway. John Wayne, Clint Eastwood, Gregory Peck, and so many other men have taken him under their wings and have taught him courage and determination. He knows that death is a mystery of infinite complication because he has learned so many conflicting lessons about it: Tim Robbins has shown him that the afterlife is only an illusion, while Patrick Swayze has shown him that the afterlife is a joyous place as real as anywhere and that those you love (like Demi Moore) will see you there when they eventually pass from this world, yet Freddy Krueger has shown him that the afterlife is a gruesome nightmare from which you can return for gleeful vengeance. When Debra Winger died of cancer, leaving Shirley MacLaine bereft, he had been inconsolable, but only a few days later he had seen her, alive again, younger and more beautiful than ever, reincarnated in a new life where she enjoyed a new destiny with Richard Gere. Paul Newman has often shared with him bits of wisdom about death, life, pool, poker, love, and honor; therefore, he considers this man one of his most important mentors. Likewise, Wilford Brimley, Gene Hackman, burly old Edward Asner, Robert Redford, Jessica Tandy. Often he absorbs quite contradictory lessons from such friends, but he has heard some of these people say that all beliefs are of equal value and that there is no one truth, so he is comfortable with the contradictions by which he lives.

He learned the most secret of all truths not in a public theater or on a pay-per-view movie service in a hotel room. Instead, that moment of stunning insight had come in the private media chamber of one of the men it was his duty to kill.

His target had been a United States Senator. A requirement of the termination was that it be made to look like a suicide.

He had to enter the Senator's residence on a night when the man was known to be alone. He was provided with a key so there would be no signs of forced entry.

After gaining access to the house, he found the Senator in the eight-seat home media room, which featured THX Sound and a theater-quality projection system capable of displaying television, videotape, or laserdisc images on a five-by-six-foot screen. It was a plush, windowless space. There was even an antique Coke machine which, he learned later, dispensed the soft drink in classic ten-ounce glass bottles, plus a candy-vending machine stocked with Milk Duds, Jujubes, Raisinettes, and other favorite movie-house snacks.

Because of the music in the film, he found it easy to creep up behind the Senator and overpower him with a chloroform-soaked rag, which he pulled out of a plastic bag a second before putting it to use. He carried the politician upstairs to the ornate master bath, undressed him, and gently conveyed him into a Roman tub filled with hot water, periodically employing the chloroform to assure continued unconsciousness. With a razor blade, he made a deep, clean incision across the Senator's right wrist (since the politician was a southpaw and most likely to use his left hand to make his first cut), and let that arm drop into the water, which was quickly discolored by the arterial gush. Before dropping the razor blade in the water, he made a few feeble attempts to slash the left wrist, never scoring deeply, because the Senator wouldn't have been able to grip the blade firmly in his right hand after cutting the tendons and ligaments along with the artery in that wrist.

Sitting on the edge of the tub, administering chloroform every time the politician groaned and seemed about to wake, he gratefully shared the sacred ceremony of death. When he was the only living man in the room, he thanked the departed for the precious opportunity to share that most intimate of experiences.

Ordinarily, he would have left the house then, but what he had witnessed on the movie screen drew him back to the media room on the first floor. He had seen pornography before, in adult theaters in many cities, and from those experiences he had learned all of the possible sexual positions and techniques. But the pornography on that home screen was different from everything he'd seen previously, for it involved chains, handcuffs, leather straps, metal-studded belts, as well as a wide variety of other instruments of punishment and restraint. Incredibly, the beautiful women on the screen seemed to be excited by brutality. The more cruelly they were treated, the more willingly they gave themselves to orgasmic pleasure; in fact, they frequently begged to be dealt with even more harshly, ravished more sadistically.

He settled into the seat from which he had removed the Senator. He stared with fascination at the screen, absorbing, learning.

When that videotape reached a conclusion, a quick search turned up an open walk-in vault—usually cleverly concealed behind the wall paneling—that contained a collection of similar material. There was an even more stunning trove of tapes depicting children involved in carnal acts with adults. Daughters with fathers. Mothers with sons. Sisters with brothers, sisters with sisters. He sat for hours, until almost dawn, transfixed.

Absorbing.

Learning, learning.

To have become a United States Senator, an exalted leader, the dead man in the bathtub must have been extremely wise. Therefore, his personal film library would, of course, contain diverse material of a transcendent nature, reflecting his singular intellectual and moral insights, embodying philosophies far too complex to be within the grasp of the average filmgoer at a public theater. How very fortunate to have discovered the politician lounging in the media room rather than preparing a snack in the kitchen or reading a book in bed. Otherwise, this opportunity to share the wisdom in the great man's hidden vault would never have arisen.

Now, curled fetally on the back seat of the Buick, he may be temporarily blinded in one eye, bullet-creased and bullet-pierced, weak and weary, defeated for the moment, but he is not despairing. He has another advantage in addition to his magically resilient body, unparalleled stamina, and

202 * DEAN KOONTZ

exhaustive knowledge of the killing arts. Equally important, he possesses what he perceives to be great wisdom, acquired from movie screens both public and private, and that wisdom will ensure his ultimate triumph. He knows what he believes to be the great secrets that the wisest people hide in concealed vaults: those things which women really need but which they may not know they subconsciously desire, those things which children want but of which they dare not speak. He understands that his wife and children will welcome and thrive upon utter domination, harsh discipline, physical abuse, sexual subjugation, even humiliation. At first opportunity, he intends to fulfill their deepest and most primitive longings, as the lenient false father apparently will never be able to do, and together they will be a family, living in harmony and love, sharing a destiny, held together forever by his singular wisdom, strength, and demanding heart.

He drifts toward healing sleep, confident of waking with full health and vigor in several hours.

A few feet from him, in the trunk of the car, lies the dead man who once owned the Buick—cold, stiff, and without any appealing prospects of his own.

How good it is to be special, to be needed, to have a destiny.

PART

TWO

Story Hour
in the Madhouse

At the point where hope and reason part,
lies the spot where madness gets a start.
Hope to make the world kinder and free—
but flowers of hope root in reality.

No peaceful bed exists for lamb and lion,
unless on some world out beyond Orion.
Do not instruct the owls to spare the mice.
Owls acting as owls must is not a vice.

Storms do not respond to heartfelt pleas.
All the words of men can't calm the seas.
Nature—always beneficent *and* cruel—
won't change for a wise man or a fool.

Mankind shares all Nature's imperfections,
clearly visible to casual inspections.
Resisting betterment is the human trait.
The ideal of utopia is our tragic fate.

—*The Book of Counted Sorrows*

We sense that life is a dark comedy and maybe we can live with that.
However, because the whole thing is written for the entertainment of
the gods, too many of the jokes go right over our heads.

—*Two Vanished Victims*, **Martin Stillwater**

FOUR

1.

Immediately after leaving the roadside rest area where the dead retirees relaxed forever in the cozy dining nook of their motorhome, heading back along I-40 toward Oklahoma City with the inscrutable Karl Clocker behind the wheel, Drew Oslett used his state-of-the-art cellular phone to call the home office in New York City. He reported developments and requested instructions.

The telephone he used wasn't yet for sale to the general public. To the average citizen, it would *never* be available with all of the features that Oslett's model offered.

It plugged into the cigarette lighter like other cellulars; however, unlike others, it was operable virtually anywhere in the world, not solely within the state or service area in which it was issued. Like the SATU electronic map, the phone incorporated a direct satellite up-link. It could directly access at least ninety percent of the communications satellites currently in orbit, bypassing their land-based control stations, override security-exclusion programs, and connect with any telephone the user wished, leaving absolutely no record that the call had been made. The violated phone company would never issue a bill for Oslett's call to New York because they would never know that it had been placed using their system.

He spoke freely to his New York contact about what he had found at the rest stop, with no fear that he would be overheard by anyone, because his phone also included a scrambling device that he activated with a simple switch. A matching scrambler on the home-office phone rendered his report intelligible again upon receipt, but to anyone who might intercept the signal between Oklahoma and the Big Apple, Oslett's words would sound like gibberish.

New York was concerned about the murdered retirees only to the extent that there might be a way for the Oklahoma authorities to link their killing to Alfie or to the Network, which was the name they used among themselves to describe their organization. "You didn't leave the shoes there?" New York asked.

"Of course not," Oslett said, offended at the suggestion of incompetence.

"All of the electronics in the heel—"

"I have the shoes here."

"That's right-out-of-the-lab stuff. Any knowledgeable person who sees it, he's going to go apeshit and maybe—"

"I have the shoes," Oslett said tightly.

"Good. Okay, then let them find the bodies and bang their heads against the wall trying to solve it. None of our business. Somebody else can haul away the garbage."

"Exactly."

"I'll be back to you soon."

"I'm counting on it," Oslett said.

After disconnecting, while he waited for a response from the home office, he was filled with uneasiness at the prospect of passing more than a hundred black and empty miles with no company but himself and Clocker. Fortunately, he was prepared with noisy and involving entertainment. From the floor behind the driver's seat, he retrieved a Game Boy and slipped the headset over his ears. Soon he was happily distracted from the unnerving rural landscape by the challenges of a rapidly paced computer game.

Suburban lights speckled the night when Oslett next looked up from the miniature screen in response to a tap on the shoulder from Clocker. On the floor between his feet, the cellular phone was ringing.

The New York contact sounded as somber as if he had just come from his own mother's funeral. "How soon can you get to the airport in Oklahoma City?"

Oslett relayed the question to Clocker.

Clocker's impassive face didn't change expressions as he said, "Half an hour, forty minutes—assuming the fabric of reality doesn't warp between here and there."

Oslett relayed to New York only the estimated traveling time and left out the science fiction.

"Get there quick as you can," New York said. "You're going to California."

"Where in California?"

"John Wayne Airport, Orange County."

"You have a lead on Alfie?"

"We don't know what the fuck we've got."

"Please don't make your answers so darn technical," Oslett said. "You're losing me."

"When you get to the airport in Oklahoma City, find a newsstand. Buy the latest issue of *People* magazine. Look on pages sixty-six, sixty-seven, sixty-eight. Then you'll know as much as we do."

"Is this a joke?"

"We just found out about it."

"About what?" Oslett asked. "Look, I don't *care* about the latest scandal in the British royal family or what diet Julia Roberts follows to keep her figure."

"Pages sixty-six, sixty-seven, and sixty-eight. When you've seen it, call me. Looks as if we might be standing hip-deep in gasoline, and someone just struck a match."

New York disconnected before Oslett could respond.

"We're going to California," he told Clocker.

"Why?"

"People magazine thinks we'll like the place," he said, deciding to give the big man a taste of his own cryptic dialogue.

"We probably will," Clocker replied, as if what Oslett had said made perfect sense to him.

As they drove through the outskirts of Oklahoma City, Oslett was relieved to find himself surrounded by signs of civilization—though he would have blown his brains out rather than live there. Even at its busiest hour, Oklahoma City didn't assault all five senses the way Manhattan did. He didn't merely thrive on sensory overload; he found it almost as essential to life as food and water, and more important than sex.

Seattle had been better than Oklahoma City, although it still hadn't measured up to Manhattan. Really, it had far too much sky for a city, too little crowding. The streets were so comparatively quiet, and the people seemed so inexplicably . . . *relaxed.* You would think they didn't know that they, like everyone else, would die sooner or later.

He and Clocker had been waiting at Seattle International at two o'clock yesterday afternoon, Sunday, when Alfie had been scheduled to arrive on a flight from Kansas City, Missouri. The 747 touched down eighteen minutes late, and Alfie wasn't on it.

In the nearly fourteen months that Oslett had been handling Alfie, which was the entire time that Alfie had been in service, nothing like that had ever happened. Alfie faithfully showed up where he was supposed to, traveled wherever he was sent, performed whatever task was assigned to him, and was as punctual as a Japanese train conductor. Until yesterday.

They had not panicked right away. It was possible that a snafu—perhaps a traffic accident—had delayed Alfie on his way to the airport, causing him to miss his flight.

Of course, the moment he went off schedule, a "cellar command," implanted in his deep subconscious, should have been activated, compelling him to call a number in Philadelphia to report his change of plans. But that was the trouble with a cellar command: sometimes it was so deeply buried in the subject's mind that the trigger didn't work and it *stayed* buried.

While Oslett and Clocker waited at the airport in Seattle to see if their boy would show up on a later flight, a Network contact in Kansas City drove to the motel where Alfie had been staying to check it out. The concern was that their boy might have dumped his entire conditioning and training, much the way that information could be lost when a computer hard disk crashed, in which case the poor geek would still be sitting in his room, in a catatonic condition.

But he hadn't been at the motel.

He had not been on the next Kansas City/Seattle flight, either.

Aboard a private Learjet belonging to a Network affiliate, Oslett and Clocker flew out of Seattle. By the time they arrived in Kansas City on Sunday night, Alfie's abandoned rental car had been found in a residential neighborhood in Topeka, an hour or so west. They could no longer avoid facing the truth. They had a bad boy on their hands. Alfie was renegade.

Of course, it was impossible for Alfie to become a renegade. Catatonic, yes. AWOL, no. Everyone intimately involved with the program was convinced of that. They were as confident as the crew of the *Titanic* prior to the kiss of the iceberg.

Because it monitored the police communications in Kansas City, as elsewhere, the Network knew that Alfie had killed his two assigned targets in their sleep sometime in the hour between Saturday midnight and one o'clock Sunday morning. Up to that point, he had been right on schedule.

Thereafter, they could not account for his whereabouts. They had to assume that he'd snapped and gone on the run as early as one A.M. Sunday, Central Standard Time, which meant that in three hours he would have been renegade for two full days.

Could he have driven all the way to California in forty-eight hours? Oslett wondered as Clocker turned into the approach road to the Oklahoma City airport.

They believed Alfie was in a car because a Honda had been stolen off a residential street not far from where the rental car had been abandoned.

Kansas City to Los Angeles was seventeen or eighteen hundred miles. He could have driven that far in a lot less than forty-eight hours, assuming he had been single-minded about it and hadn't slept. Alfie could go three or four days without sleep. And he was as single-minded as a politician pursuing a crooked dollar.

Sunday night, Oslett and Clocker had gone to Topeka to examine the abandoned rental car. They had hoped to turn up a lead on their wayward assassin.

Because Alfie was smart enough not to use the fake credit cards with which they had supplied him—and by which he could be tracked—and because he had all of the skills needed to make a splendid success of armed robbery, they used Network contacts to access and review computerized files of the Topeka Police Department. They discovered that a convenience store had been held up by persons unknown at approximately four o'clock Sunday morning; the clerk had been shot once in the head, fatally, and from the ejected cartridge found at the scene, it had been ascertained that the murder weapon fired 9mm ammunition. The gun with which Alfie had been supplied for the Kansas City job was a Heckler & Koch P7 9mm Parabellum pistol.

The clincher was the nature of the last sale the clerk had made minutes before being killed, which the police had ascertained from an examination of the computerized cash register records. It was an inordinately large purchase for a convenience store: multiple units of Slim Jims, cheese crackers, peanuts, miniature doughnuts, candy bars, and other high-calorie items. With his racing metabolism, Alfie would have stocked up on items like those if he had been on the run with the intention of forgoing sleep for a while.

And at that point they had lost him for too long.

From Topeka he could have gone west on Interstate 70 all the way into Colorado. North on Federal Highway 75. South by diverse routes to Chanute, Fredonia, Coffeyville. Southwest to Wichita. Anywhere.

Theoretically, minutes after he had been judged a renegade, it should have been possible to activate the transponder in his shoe by means of a coded microwave signal broadcast via satellite to the entire continental United States. Then they should have been able to use a series of geosynchronous tracking satellites to pinpoint his location, hunt him down, and bring him home within a few hours.

But there had been problems. There were always problems. The kiss of the iceberg.

Not until Monday afternoon had they located the transponder signal in Oklahoma, east of the Texas border. Oslett and Clocker, on standby in Topeka, had flown to Oklahoma City and taken a rental car west on Interstate 40, equipped with the electronic map, which had led them to the dead senior citizens and the pair of Rockport shoes with one heel shaved to expose the electronics.

Now they were at the Oklahoma City airport again, rolling back and forth like two pinballs inside the slowest game machine in the known universe. By the time they drove into the rental agency lot to leave the car, Oslett was ready to scream. The only reason he *didn't* scream was because there was no one to hear him except Karl Clocker. Might as well scream at the moon.

In the terminal he found a newsstand and purchased the latest issue of *People* magazine.

Clocker bought a pack of Juicy Fruit chewing gum, a lapel button that said I'VE BEEN TO OKLAHOMA—NOW I CAN DIE, and the paperback edition of the gazillionth *Star Trek* novelization.

Outside in the promenade, where pedestrian traffic was neither as heavy nor as interestingly bizarre as it was at either JFK or La Guardia in New

York, Oslett sat on a bench framed by sickly greenery in large planters. He riffled through the magazine to pages sixty-six and sixty-seven.

MR. MURDER

IN SOUTHERN CALIFORNIA, MYSTERY NOVELIST
MARTIN STILLWATER SEES DARKNESS AND EVIL
WHERE OTHERS SEE ONLY SUNSHINE.

The two-page spread that opened the three-page piece was largely occupied by a photograph of the writer. Twilight. Ominous clouds. Spooky trees as a backdrop. A weird angle. Stillwater was sort of lunging at the camera, his features distorted, eyes shining with reflected light, making like a zombie or crazed killer.

The guy was obviously a jackass, an obnoxious self-promoter who would be happy to dress up in Agatha Christie's old clothes if it would sell his books. Or license his name for a breakfast cereal: Martin Stillwater's Mystery Puffs, made of oats and enigmatic milling by-products; a free action figure included in each box, one in a series of eleven murder victims, each wasted in a different fashion, all wounds detailed in "Day-Glo" red; start your collection today and, at the same time, let our milling by-products do your bowels a favor.

Oslett read the text on the first page, but he still didn't see why the article had put the New York contact's blood pressure in the stroke-risk zone. Reading about Stillwater, he thought the headline ought to be "Mr. Tedium." If the guy ever did license his name for a cereal, it wouldn't need high fiber content because it would be guaranteed to *bore* the crap out of you.

Drew Oslett disliked books as intensely as some people disliked dentists, and he thought that the people who wrote them—especially novelists—had been born into the wrong half of the century and ought to get *real* jobs in computer design, cybernetic management, the space sciences, or applied fiber optics, industries that had something to contribute to the quality of life here on the cusp of the millennium. As entertainment, books were so *slow*. Writers insisted on taking you into the minds of characters, showing you what they were thinking. You didn't have to put up with that in the movies. Movies never took you inside characters' minds. Even if movies *could* show you what the people in them were thinking, who would want to go inside the mind of Sylvester Stallone or Eddie Murphy or Susan

Sarandon, anyway, for God's sake? Books were just too *intimate*. It didn't matter what people thought, only what they did. Action and speed. Here on the brink of a new high-tech century, there were only two watchwords: action and speed.

He turned to the third page of the article and saw another picture of Martin Stillwater.

"Holy shit."

In this second photograph, the writer was sitting at his desk, facing the camera. The quality of light was strange, since it seemed to come mainly from a stained-glass lamp behind and to one side of him, but he looked entirely different from the blazing-eyed zombie on the previous pages.

Clocker was sitting on the other end of the bench, like a huge trained bear dressed in human clothes and patiently waiting for the circus orchestra to strike up his theme music. He was engrossed in the first chapter of the *Star Trek* novelization *Spock Gets the Clap* or whatever the hell it was called.

Holding out the magazine so Clocker could see the photo, Oslett said, "Look at this."

After taking the time to finish the paragraph he was reading, Clocker glanced at *People*. "That's Alfie."

"No, it isn't."

Gnawing on his wad of Juicy Fruit, Clocker said, "Sure looks like him."

"Something's very wrong here."

"Looks exactly like him."

"The kiss of the iceberg," Oslett said ominously.

Frowning, Clocker said, "Huh?"

❋   ❋   ❋

In the comfortable cabin of the twelve-passenger private jet, which was warmly and tastefully decorated in soft camel-brown suede and contrasting crackle-finish leather with accents in forest green, Clocker sat toward the front and read *The Alien Proctology Menace* or whatever the damned paperback was titled. Oslett sat toward the middle of the plane.

As they were still ascending out of Oklahoma City, he phoned his contact in New York. "Okay, I've seen *People*."

"Like a kick in the face, isn't it?" New York said.

"What's going on here?"

"We don't know yet."

"You think the resemblance is just a coincidence?"

"No. Jesus, they're like identical twins."

"Why am I going to California—to get a look at this writer jerk?"

"And maybe to find Alfie."

"You think Alfie's in California?"

New York said, "Well, he had to go *somewhere*. Besides, the minute this *People* thing fell on us, we started trying to learn everything we could about Martin Stillwater, and right away we find out there was some trouble at his house in Mission Viejo late this afternoon, early this evening."

"What kind of trouble?"

"The police report's been written up, but it isn't logged into their computer yet, so we can't just access it. We need to get our hands on a hard copy. We're working on that. So far, we know there was an intruder in the house. Stillwater apparently shot somebody, but the guy got away."

"You think it has something to do with Alfie?"

"Nobody here's a big believer in coincidence."

The pitch of the Lear engines changed. The jet had come out of its climb, leveled off, and settled down to cruising speed.

Oslett said, "But how would Alfie know about Stillwater?"

"Maybe he reads *People*," New York said, and laughed nervously.

"If you're thinking the intruder was Alfie—why would he go after this guy?"

"We don't have a theory yet."

Oslett sighed. "I feel as if I'm standing in a cosmic toilet, and God just flushed it."

"Maybe you should've taken more care with the way you were handling him."

"This wasn't a handling screwup," Oslett bristled.

"Hey, I'm making no accusations. I'm only telling you one of the things that's being said back here."

"Seems to me the big screwup was in satellite surveillance."

"Can't expect them to locate him after he took off the shoes."

"But how come they needed a day and a half to find the damned shoes? Bad weather over the Midwest. Sunspot activity, magnetic disturbances. Too many hundreds of square miles in the initial search zone. Excuses, excuses, excuses."

"At least they *have* some," New York said smugly.

Oslett fumed in silence. He hated being away from Manhattan. The moment the shadow of his plane crossed the city line, the knives came out, and the ambitious pygmies started trying to whittle his reputation down to their size.

"You'll be met by an advance man in California," New York said. "He'll give you an update."

"Terrific."

Oslett frowned at the phone and pressed END, terminating the call.

He needed a drink.

In addition to the pilot and co-pilot, the flight crew included a stewardess. With a button on the arm of his chair, he could summon her from the small galley at the back of the plane. In seconds she arrived, and he ordered a double Scotch on the rocks.

She was an attractive blonde in a burgundy blouse, gray skirt, and matching gray jacket. He turned in his seat to watch her walk back to the galley.

He wondered how easy she was. If he charmed her, maybe she'd let him take her into the john and do it to her standing up.

For all of a minute, he indulged that fantasy, but then faced reality and put her out of his mind. Even if she was easy, there would be unpleasant consequences. Afterward, she would want to sit beside him, probably all the way to California, and share with him her thoughts and feelings about everything from love and fate to death and the significance of Cheez Whiz. He didn't care what she thought and felt, only what she could do, and he was in no mood to pretend to be a sensitive nineties kind of guy.

When she brought the Scotch, he asked what videotapes were available. She gave him a list of forty titles. The best movie of all time was in the plane's library: *Lethal Weapon 3*. He had lost track of how many times he'd seen it, and the pleasure he took from it did not diminish with repetition. It was the ideal film because it had no story line that made enough sense to bother following, did not expect the viewer to watch the characters change and grow, was composed entirely of a series of violent action sequences, and was louder than a stockcar race and a Megadeath concert combined.

Four separately positioned monitors made it possible for four films to be shown simultaneously to different passengers. The stewardess ran *Le-*

thal Weapon 3 on the monitor nearest to Oslett and gave him a set of headphones.

He put on the headset, turned the volume high, and settled back in his seat with a grin.

Later, after he finished the Scotch, he dozed off while Danny Glover and Mel Gibson screamed unintelligible dialogue at each other, fires raged, machine guns chattered, explosives detonated, and music thundered.

2.

Monday night they stayed in a pair of connecting units in a motel in Laguna Beach. The accommodations didn't qualify as five- or even four-star lodging, but the rooms were clean and the bathrooms had plenty of towels. With the holiday weekend gone and the summer tourist season months in the future, at least half of the motel was unoccupied, and though they were right off Pacific Coast Highway, quiet ruled.

The events of the day had taken their toll. Paige felt as if she had been awake for a week. Even the too-soft and slightly lumpy motel mattress was as enticing as a bed of clouds on which gods and goddesses might sleep.

For dinner they ate pizza in the motel. Marty went out to fetch it—also salads and cannoli with deliciously thick ricotta custard—from a restaurant a couple of blocks away.

When he returned with the food, he pounded insistently on the door, and he was pale and hollow-eyed when he rushed inside, arms laden with take-out boxes. At first Paige thought he had seen the look-alike cruising the area, but then she realized he expected to return and find them gone—or dead.

The outer doors of both rooms featured sturdy dead-bolt locks and security chains. They engaged these and also wedged straight-backed desk chairs under the knobs.

Neither Paige nor Marty could imagine any means by which The Other could possibly find them. They wedged the chairs under the knobs anyway. Tight.

Incredibly, in spite of the terror they had been through, the kids were willing to let Marty convince them that the night away from home was a special treat. They were not accustomed to staying in motels, so everything from the coin-operated vibrating mattress to the free stationery to the miniature bars of fragrant soap was sufficiently exotic to fascinate them when Marty drew their attention to it.

They were especially intrigued that the toilet seats in both rooms were wrapped by crisp white paper bands on which were printed assurances in three languages that the facilities had been sanitized. From this, Emily deduced that some motel guests must be "real pigs" who didn't know enough to clean up after themselves, and Charlotte speculated about whether such a special notice indicated that more than soap or Lysol had been used to sterilize the surfaces, perhaps flamethrowers or nuclear radiation.

Marty was clever enough to realize that the more exotic flavors of soft drinks in the motel vending machines, which the girls did not get at home, would also delight them and lift their spirits. He bought chocolate Yoo-Hoo, Mountain Dew, Sparkling Grape, Cherry Crush, Tangerine Treat, and Pineapple Fizz. The four of them sat on the two queen-size beds in one of the rooms, containers of food spread around them on the mattresses, bottles of colorful sodas on the nightstands. Charlotte and Emily had to taste some of each beverage before the end of dinner, which made Paige queasy.

Through her family-counseling practice, Paige had long ago learned that children were potentially more resilient than adults when it came to coping with trauma. That potential was best realized when they enjoyed a stable family structure, received large doses of affection, and believed themselves to be respected and loved. She felt a rush of pride that her own kids were proving so emotionally elastic and strong—then superstitiously and surreptitiously knocked one knuckle softly against the wooden headboard, silently asking God not to punish either her or the children for her hubris.

Most surprisingly, once Charlotte and Emily had bathed, put on pajamas, and been tucked into the beds in the connecting room, they wanted Marty to conduct his usual story hour and continue the verses about Santa's evil twin. Paige recognized an uncomfortable—in fact, uncanny—similarity between the fanciful poem and recent frightening events in their own lives. She was sure Marty and the girls were also aware of the connection. Yet Marty seemed as pleased by the opportunity to share more verses as the kids were eager to hear them.

He positioned a chair at the foot of—and exactly between—the two beds. In their rush to get packed and out of the house, he had even remembered to bring the notebook that was labeled *Stories for Charlotte and Emily,* with its clip-on, battery-powered reading lamp. He sat down and held the notebook at reading distance.

The shotgun lay on the floor beside him.

The Beretta was on the dresser, where Paige could reach it in two seconds flat.

Marty waited for the silence to develop the proper quality of expectation.

The scene was remarkably like the one Paige had witnessed so often in the girls' room at home, except for two differences. The queen-size beds dwarfed Charlotte and Emily, making them seem like children in a fairy tale, homeless waifs who had sneaked into a giant's castle to steal some of his porridge and enjoy his guest rooms. And the miniature reading lamp clipped to the notebook was not the sole source of light; one of the nightstand lamps was aglow as well, and would remain so all night—the girls' only apparent concession to fear.

Surprised to discover that she, too, was looking forward with pleasure to the continuation of the poem, Paige sat on the foot of Emily's bed.

She wondered what it was about storytelling that made people want it almost as much as food and water, even more so in bad times than good. Movies had never drawn more patrons than during the Great Depression. Book sales often improved in a recession. The need went beyond a mere desire for entertainment and distraction from one's troubles. It was more profound and mysterious than that.

When a hush had fallen on the room and the moment seemed just right, Marty began to read. Because Charlotte and Emily had insisted he start at the beginning, he recited the verses they had already heard on Saturday and Sunday nights, arriving at that moment when Santa's evil twin stood at the kitchen door of the Stillwater house, intent upon breaking inside.

> *"With picks, loids, gwizzels, and zocks,*
> *he quickly and silently opens both locks.*
> *He enters the kitchen without a sound.*
> *Now chances for devilment truly abound.*
> *He opens the fridge and eats all the cake,*
> *pondering what sort of mess he can make.*
> *He pours the milk all over the floor,*

> *pickles, pudding, ketchup, and Coors.*
> *He scatters the bread—white and rye—*
> *and finally he spits right in the pie."*

"Oh, gross," Charlotte said.

Emily grinned. "Hocked a greenie."

"What kind of pie was it?" Charlotte wondered.

Paige said, "Mincemeat."

"Yuck. Then I don't blame him for spitting in it."

> *"At the corkboard by the phone and stool,*
> *he sees drawings the kids did at school.*
> *Emily has painted a kind, smiling face.*
> *Charlotte has drawn elephants in space.*
> *The villain takes out a red felt-tip pen,*
> *taps it, uncaps it, chuckles, and then,*
> *on both pictures, scrawls the word 'Poo!'*
> *He always knows the worst things to do."*

"He's a critic!" Charlotte gasped, making fists of her small hands and punching vigorously at the air above her bed.

"Critics," Emily said exasperatedly and rolled her eyes the way she had seen her father do a few times.

"My God," Charlotte said, covering her face with her hands, "we have a critic in our house."

"You *knew* this was going to be a scary story," Marty said.

> *"Mad giggles from him continue to bubble,*
> *while he gets into far greater trouble.*
> *He's hugely more evil than he is brave,*
> *so then after he loads up the microwave*
> *with ten whole pounds of popping corn*
> *(oh, we should rue the day he was born),*
> *he turns and runs right out of the room,*
> *because that old oven is gonna go BOOM!"*

"Ten pounds!" Charlotte's imagination swept her away. She rose up on her elbows, head off the pillows, and babbled excitedly: "Wow, you'd need a forklift and a dump truck to carry it all away, once it was popped, 'cause it'd be like snowdrifts only popcorn, *mountains* of popcorn. We'd need a vat of caramel and maybe a zillion pounds of pecans just to make it all into popcorn balls. We'd be up to our asses in it."

"What did you say?" Paige asked.

"I said you'd need a forklift—"

"No, that word you used."

"What word?"

"Asses," Paige said patiently.

Charlotte said, "That's not a bad word."

"Oh?"

"They say it on TV all the time."

"Not everything on TV is intelligent and tasteful," Paige said.

Marty lowered the story notebook. "Hardly anything, in fact."

To Charlotte, Paige said, "On TV, I've seen people driving cars off cliffs, poisoning their fathers to get the family inheritance, fighting with swords, robbing banks—all sorts of things I better not catch *either* of you doing."

"Especially the father-poisoning thing," Marty said.

Charlotte said, "Okay, I won't say 'ass.' "

"Good."

"What should I say instead? Is 'butt' okay?"

"How does 'bottom' strike you?" Paige asked.

"I guess I can live with that."

Trying not to burst out laughing, not daring to glance at Marty, Paige said: "You say 'bottom' for a while, and then as you get older you can slowly work your way up to 'butt,' and when you're really mature you can say 'ass.' "

"Fair enough," Charlotte agreed, settling back on her pillows.

Emily, who had been thoughtful and silent through all of this, changed the subject. "Ten pounds of unpopped corn wouldn't fit in the microwave."

"Of course it would," Marty assured her.

"I don't think so."

"I researched this before I started writing," he said firmly.

Emily's face was puckered with skepticism.

"You *know* how I research everything," he insisted.

"Maybe not this time," she said doubtfully.

Marty said, "Ten pounds."

"That's a lot of corn."

Turning to Charlotte, Marty said, "We have *another* critic in the house."

"Okay," Emily said, "go on, read some more."

Marty raised one eyebrow. "You really want to hear more of this poorly researched, unconvincing claptrap?"

"A little more, anyway," Emily acknowledged.

With an exaggerated, long-suffering sigh, Marty glanced slyly at Paige, raised the notebook again, and continued to read:

> *"He prowls the downstairs—wicked, mean—*
> *looking to cause yet one more bad scene.*
> *When he spies the presents under the tree,*
> *he says, 'I'll go on a gift-swapping spree!*
> *I'll take out all of the really good stuff,*
> *then box up dead fish, cat poop, and fluff.*
> *In the morning, the Stillwaters will find*
> *coffee grounds, peach pits, orange rinds.*
> *Instead of nice sweaters, games, and toys,*
> *they'll get slimy, stinky stuff that annoys.'"*

"He won't get away with this," Charlotte said.

Emily said, "He might."

"He won't."

"Who's gonna stop him?"

> *"Charlotte and Emmy are up in their beds,*
> *dreams of Christmas filling their heads.*
> *Suddenly a sound startles these sleepers.*
> *They sit up in bed and open their peepers.*
> *Nothing should be stirring, not one mouse,*
> *but the girls sense a villain in the house.*
> *You can call it psychic, a hunch, osmosis—*
> *or maybe they smell the troll's halitosis.*
> *They leap out of bed, forgetting slippers,*
> *two brave and foolhardy little nippers.*
> *'Something's amiss,' young Emily whispers.*
> *But they can handle it—they're sisters!"*

This development—Charlotte and Emily as the heroines of the story—delighted the girls. They turned their heads to face each other across the gap between beds, and grinned.

Charlotte repeated Emily's question: "Who's gonna stop him?"

"We are!" Emily said.

Marty said, "Well . . . maybe."

"Uh-oh," Charlotte said.

Emily was hip. "Don't worry. Daddy's just trying to keep us in suspense. We'll stop the old troll, all right."

> *"Down in the living room, under the tree*
> *Santa's evil twin is chortling with glee.*
> *He's got a collection of gift replacements*
> *taken from dumps, sewers, and basements.*
> *He replaces a nice watch meant for Lottie*
> *with a nasty gift for a girl who's naughty,*
> *which is one thing Lottie has never been.*
> *Forgetting her vitamins is her biggest sin.*
> *In place of the watch, he wraps up a clot*
> *of horrid, glistening, greenish toad snot.*
> *From a package for Emily, he steals a doll*
> *and gives her a new gift sure to appall.*
> *It's oozing, rancid, and starting to fizz.*
> *Not even the villain knows what it is."*

"What do you think it is, Mom?" Charlotte asked.

"Probably those dirty kneesocks you misplaced six months ago."

Emily giggled, and Charlotte said, "I'll *find* those socks sooner or later."

"If that's what's in the box, then for sure I ain't opening it," Emily said.

"I'm *not* opening it," Paige corrected.

"Nobody's opening it," Emily agreed, missing the point. "Phew!"

> *"In jammies, slipperless, now on the prowl,*
> *the girls go looking for whatever's foul.*
> *Right to the top of the stairs they zoom,*
> *making less noise than moths in a tomb.*
> *They're both so delicate, slim, and petite,*
> *and both of them have such tiny pink feet.*

How can these small girls hope to fight
a Santa who's liable to kick and to bite?
Are they trained in karate or Tae Kwon Do?
No, no, I'm afraid that the answer is no.
Grenades tucked in their jammie pockets?
Lasers implanted inside their eye sockets?
No, no, I'm afraid that the answer is no.
Yet down, down the shadowy stairs they go.
The danger below, they can't comprehend.
This Santa has gone far 'round the bend.
He's meaner than flu, toothaches, blisters.
But they're tough too—they're sisters!"

Charlotte defiantly thrust one small fist into the air and said, "Sisters!"

"Sisters!" Emily said, thrusting her fist into the air as well.

When they discovered that they had reached the stopping point for the night, they insisted Marty read the new verses again, and Paige found that she, too, wanted to hear the lines a second time.

Though he pretended to be tired and needed some coaxing to oblige them, Marty would have been disappointed if he hadn't been importuned to do another reading.

By the time her father reached the end of the last verse, Emily was only able to murmur sleepily, "Sisters." Charlotte was already snoring softly.

Marty quietly returned the reading chair to the corner from which he had gotten it. He checked the locks on the door and the windows, then made sure there were no gaps in the drapes through which someone could look into the room from outside.

As Paige tucked the blankets around Emily's shoulders, then around Charlotte's, she kissed each of them goodnight. The love she felt for them was so intense, like a weight on her chest, that she could not draw a deep breath.

When she and Marty retired to the adjoining room, taking the guns with them, they didn't turn off the nightstand lamp, and they left the connecting door wide open. Nevertheless, her daughters seemed dangerously far from her.

By unspoken agreement, she and Marty stretched out side by side on the same queen-size bed. The thought of being separated by even a few feet was intolerable.

One bedside lamp was lit, but he switched it off. Enough light came through the door from the adjoining unit to reveal the larger part of their own room. Shadows attended every corner, but deeper darkness was kept at bay.

They held hands and stared at the ceiling as if their fate could be read in the curiously portentous patterns of light and shadow on the plaster. It wasn't only the ceiling; during the past few hours, virtually everything Paige looked at seemed to be filled with omens, menacingly significant.

Neither she nor Marty undressed for the night. Although it was difficult to believe they could have been followed without being aware of it, they wanted to be able to move fast.

The rain had stopped a couple of hours ago, but aqueous rhythms still lulled them. The motel was on a bluff above the Pacific, and the cadenced crashing of the surf was, in its metronomic certainty, a soothing and peaceful sound.

"Tell me something," she said, speaking softly to prevent her voice from carrying into the other room.

He sounded tired. "Whatever the question is, I probably don't have the answer."

"What happened over there?"

"Just now? In the other room?"

"Yeah."

"Magic."

"I'm serious."

"So am I," Marty said. "You can't analyze the deeper effects that storytelling has on us, can't figure out the why and how, any more than King Arthur could understand how Merlin could do and know the things he did."

"We came here shattered, frightened. The kids were so silent, half numb with fear. You and I were snapping at each other—"

"Not snapping."

"Yes, we were."

"Okay," he admitted, "we were, just a little."

"Which, for us, is a lot. All of us were . . . uneasy with one another. In knots."

"I don't think it was that bad."

She said, "Listen to a family counselor with some experience—it was that bad. Then you tell a story, a lovely nonsense poem but nonsense nonetheless . . . and everyone's more relaxed. It helps us knit together somehow. We have fun, we laugh. The girls wind down, and before you know it, they're able to sleep."

For a while neither of them spoke.

The metrical susurration of the night surf was like the slow and steady beating of a great heart.

When Paige closed her eyes, she imagined she was a little girl again, curled in her mother's lap as she had so seldom been allowed to do, her head against her mother's breast, one ear attuned to the woman's hidden heart, listening intently for some small sound that was not solely biological, a special whisper that she might recognize as the precious sound of love. She'd never heard anything but the *lub-dub* of atrium and ventricle, hollow, mechanical.

Yet she'd been soothed. Perhaps on a deep subconscious level, listening to her mother's heart, she had recalled her nine months in the womb, during which that same iambic beat had surrounded her twenty-four hours a day. In the womb there is a perfect peace never to be found again; as long as we remain unborn, we know nothing of love and cannot know the misery that arises from being deprived of it.

She was grateful that she had Marty, Charlotte, Emily. But, as long as she lived, moments like this would occur, when something as simple as the surf would remind her of the deep well of sadness and isolation in which she'd dwelt throughout her childhood.

She always strived to ensure that her daughters never for an instant doubted they were loved. Now she was equally determined that the intrusion of this madness and violence into their lives would not steal any fraction of Charlotte's or Emily's childhood as her own had been stolen in its entirety. Because her own parents' estrangement from each other had been exceeded by their estrangement from their only child, Paige had been forced to grow up fast for her own emotional survival; even as a grammar-school girl, she was aware of the cold indifference of the world, and understood that strong self-reliance was imperative if she was to cope with the cruelties life sometimes could inflict. But, damn it, her own daughters were not going to be required to learn such hard lessons overnight. Not at the tender ages of seven and nine. No way. She wanted desperately to shelter them for a few more years from the harsher realities of human existence, and allow them the chance to grow up gradually, happily, without bitterness.

Marty was the first to break the comfortable silence between them. "When Vera Conner had the stroke and we spent so much time that week in the lounge outside the intensive care unit, there were a lot of other people, came and went, waiting to learn whether their friends and relatives would live or die."

"Hard to believe it's almost two years Vera's been gone."

Vera Conner had been a professor of psychology at UCLA, a mentor to Paige when she had been a student, and then an exemplary friend in the years that followed. She still missed Vera. She always would.

Marty said, "Some of the people waiting in that lounge just sat and stared. Some paced, looked out windows, fidgeted. Listened to a Walkman with headphones. Played a Game Boy. They passed the time all kinds of ways. But—did you notice?—those who seemed to deal best with their fear or grief, the people most at peace, were the ones reading novels."

Except for Marty, and in spite of a forty-year age difference, Vera had been Paige's dearest friend and the first person who ever cared about her. The week Vera was hospitalized—first disoriented and suffering, then comatose—had been the worst week of Paige's life; nearly two years later, her vision still blurred when she recalled the last day, the final hour, as she'd stood beside Vera's bed, holding her friend's warm but unresponsive hand. Sensing the end was near, Paige had said things she hoped God allowed the dying woman to hear: *I love you, I'll miss you forever, you're the mother to me that my own mother never could be.*

The long hours of that week were engraved indelibly in Paige's memory, in more excruciating detail than she would have liked, for tragedy was the sharpest engraving instrument of all. She not only remembered the layout and furnishings of the ICU visitors' lounge in dreary specificity, but could still recall the faces of many of the strangers who, for a time, shared that room with her and Marty.

He said, "You and I were passing the time with novels, so were some other people, not just to escape but because . . . because, at its best, fiction is medicine."

"Medicine?"

"Life is so damned disorderly, things just happen, and there doesn't seem any point to so much of what we go through. Sometimes it seems the world's a madhouse. Storytelling condenses life, gives it order. Stories have beginnings, middles, ends. And when a story's over, it *meant* something, by God, maybe not something complex, maybe what it had to say was simple, even naive, but there was meaning. And that gives us hope, it's a medicine."

"The medicine of hope," she said thoughtfully.

"Or maybe I'm just full of shit."

"No, you're not."

"Well, I *am,* yes, probably at least half full of shit—but maybe not about this."

She smiled and gently squeezed his hand.

"I don't know," he said, "but I think if some university did a long-term study, they'd discover that people who read fiction don't suffer from depression as much, don't commit suicide as often, are just happier with their lives. Not all fiction, for sure. Not the human-beings-are-garbage-life-stinks-there-is-no-God novels filled with fashionable despair."

"Dr. Marty Stillwater, dispensing the medicine of hope."

"You *do* think I'm full of shit."

"No, baby, no," she said. "I think you're wonderful."

"I'm not, though. *You're* wonderful. I'm just a neurotic writer. By nature, writers are too smug, selfish, insecure and at the same time too full of themselves ever to be wonderful."

"You're not neurotic, smug, selfish, insecure, or conceited."

"That just proves you haven't been listening to me all these years."

"Okay, I'll give you the neurotic part."

"Thank you, dear," he said. "It's nice to know you've been listening at least *some* of the time."

"But you're also wonderful. A wonderfully neurotic writer. I wish I was a wonderfully neurotic writer, too, dispensing medicine."

"Bite your tongue."

She said, "I mean it."

"Maybe *you* can live with a writer, but I don't think I'd have the stomach for it."

She rolled onto her right side to face him, and he turned onto his left side, so they could kiss. Tender kisses. Gentle. For a while they just held each other, listening to the surf.

Without resorting to words, they had agreed not to discuss any further their worries or what might need to be done in the morning. Sometimes a touch, a kiss, or an embrace said more than all the words a writer could marshal, more than all the carefully reasoned advice and therapy that a counselor could provide.

In the body of the night, the great heart of the ocean beat slowly, reliably. From a human perspective, the tide was an eternal force; but from a divine view, transitory.

On the downslope of consciousness, Paige was surprised to realize that she was sliding into sleep. Like the sudden agitation of a blackbird's wings, alarm fluttered through her at the prospect of lying unaware—therefore vulnerable—in a strange place. But her weariness was greater than her fear, and the solace of the sea wrapped her and carried her, on tides of dreams, into childhood, where she rested her head against her mother's breast and listened with one ear for the special, secret whisper of love somewhere in the reverberant heartbeats.

3.

Still wearing a set of headphones, Drew Oslett woke to gunfire, explosions, screams, and music loud enough and strident enough to be God's background theme for doomsday. On the TV screen, Glover and Gibson were running, jumping, punching, shooting, dodging, spinning, leaping through burning buildings in a thrilling ballet of violence.

Smiling and yawning, Oslett checked his wristwatch and saw that he had been asleep for over two and a half hours. Evidently, after the movie had played once, the stewardess, seeing how like a lullaby it was to him, had rewound and rerun it.

They must be close to their destination, surely much less than an hour out of John Wayne Airport in Orange County. He took off the headset, got up, and went forward in the cabin to tell Clocker what he had learned earlier in his telephone conversation with New York.

Clocker was asleep in his seat. He had taken off the tweed jacket with the leather patches and lapels, but he was still wearing the brown porkpie hat with the small brown and black duck feather in the band. He wasn't snoring, but his lips were parted, and a thread of drool escaped the corner of his mouth; half his chin glistened disgustingly.

Sometimes Oslett was half convinced that the Network was playing a colossal joke on him by pairing him with Karl Clocker.

His own father was a mover and shaker in the organization, and Oslett wondered if the old man would hitch him to a ludicrous figure like Clocker as a way of humiliating him. He loathed his father and knew the feeling was mutual. Finally, however, he could not believe that the old man, in spite of deep and seething antagonism, would play such games—largely because, by doing so, he would be exposing an Oslett to ridicule. Protecting the honor and integrity of the family name always took precedence over personal feelings and the settling of grudges between family members.

In the Oslett family, certain lessons were learned so young that Drew almost felt as if he'd been born with that knowledge, and a profound understanding of the value of the Oslett name seemed rooted in his genes. Nothing—except a vast fortune—was as precious as a good name, maintained through generations; from a good name sprang as much power as from tremendous wealth, because politicians and judges found it easier to accept briefcases full of cash, by way of bribery, when the offerings came from people whose bloodline had produced senators, secretaries of state, leaders of industry, noted champions of the environment, and much-lauded patrons of the arts.

His pairing with Clocker was simply a mistake. Eventually he would have the situation rectified. If the Network bureaucracy was slow to rearrange assignments, and if their renegade was recovered in a condition that still allowed him to be handled as before, Oslett would take Alfie aside and instruct *him* to terminate Clocker.

The paperback *Star Trek* novel, spine broken, lay open on Karl Clocker's chest, pages down. Careful not to wake the big man, Oslett picked up the book.

He turned to the first page, not bothering to mark Clocker's stopping place, and began to read, thinking that perhaps he would get a clue as to why so many people were fascinated by the starship *Enterprise* and its crew. Within a few paragraphs, the damned author was taking him inside the mind of Captain Kirk, mental territory that Oslett was willing to explore only if his alternatives were otherwise limited to the stultifying minds of all the presidential candidates in the last election. He skipped ahead a couple of chapters, dipped in, found himself in Spock's prissily rational mind, skipped more pages and discovered he was in the mind of "Bones" McCoy.

Annoyed, he closed *Journey to the Rectum of the Universe,* or whatever the hell the book was called, and slapped Clocker's chest with it to wake him.

The big man sat straight up so suddenly that his porkpie hat popped off and landed in his lap. Sleepily, he said, "Wha? Wha?"

"We'll be landing soon."

"Of course we will," Clocker said.

"There's a contact meeting us."

"Life is contact."

Oslett was in a foul mood. Chasing a renegade assassin, thinking about his father, pondering the possible catastrophe represented by Martin Still-water, reading several pages of a *Star Trek* novel, and now being peppered with more of Clocker's cryptograms was too much for any man to bear and still be expected to keep his good humor. He said, "Either you've been drooling in your sleep, or a herd of snails just crawled over your chin and into your mouth."

Clocker raised one burly arm and wiped the lower part of his face with his shirt sleeve.

"This contact," Oslett said, "might have a lead on Alfie by now. We have to be sharp, ready to move. Are you fully awake?"

Clocker's eyes were rheumy. "None of us is ever fully awake."

"Oh, please, will you cut that half-baked mystical crap? I just don't have any patience for that right now."

Clocker stared at him a long moment and then said, "You've got a turbulent heart, Drew."

"Wrong. It's my stomach that's turbulent from having to listen to this crap."

"An inner tempest of blind hostility."

"Fuck you," Oslett said.

The pitch of the jet engines changed subtly. A moment later the steward-ess approached to announce that the plane had entered its approach to the Orange County airport and to ask them to put on their seatbelts.

According to Oslett's Rolex, it was 1:52 in the morning, but that was back in Oklahoma City. As the Lear descended, he reset his watch until it showed eight minutes to midnight.

By the time they landed, Monday had ticked into Tuesday like a bomb clock counting down toward detonation.

*   *   *

The advance man—who appeared to be in his late twenties, not much younger than Drew Oslett—was waiting in the lounge at the private-aircraft terminal. He told them his name was Jim Lomax, which it most likely was not.

Oslett told him that their names were Charlie Brown and Dagwood Bumstead.

The contact didn't seem to get the joke. He helped them carry their luggage out to the parking lot, where he loaded it in the trunk of a green Oldsmobile.

Lomax was one of those Californians who had made a temple of his body and then had proceeded to more elaborate architecture. The exercise-and-health-food ethic had long ago spread into every corner of the country, and for years Americans had been striving for hard buns and healthy hearts to the farthest outposts of snowy Maine. However, the Golden State was where the first carrot-juice cocktail had been poured, where the first granola bar had been made, and was still the only place where a significant number of people believed that sticks of raw jicama were a satisfactory substitute for french fries, so only certain fanatically dedicated Californians had enough determination to exceed the structural requirements of a temple. Jim Lomax had a neck like a granite column, shoulders like limestone door lintels, a chest that could buttress a nave wall, a stomach as flat as an altar stone, and had pretty much made a great *cathedral* out of his body.

Although a storm front had passed through earlier in the night and the air was still damp and chilly, Lomax was wearing just jeans and a T-shirt on which was a photo of Madonna with her breasts bared (the rock singer, not the mother of God), as if the elements affected him as little as they did the quarried walls of any mighty fortress. He virtually strutted instead of walking, performing every task with calculated grace and evident self-consciousness, obviously aware and pleased that people were prone to watch and envy him.

Oslett suspected Lomax was not merely a proud man but profoundly vain, even narcissistic. The only god worshipped in the cathedral of his body was the ego that inhabited it.

Nevertheless Oslett liked the guy. The most appealing thing about Lomax was that, in his company, Karl Clocker appeared to be the smaller of the two. In fact it was the *only* appealing thing about the guy, but it was enough. Actually, Lomax was probably only slightly—if at all—larger than Clocker, but he was harder and better honed. By comparison, Clocker seemed slow, shambling, old, and soft. Because he was sometimes intimidated by Clocker's size, Oslett delighted at the thought of Clocker intimidated by Lomax—though, frustratingly, if the Trekker was at all impressed, he didn't show it.

Lomax drove. Oslett sat up front, and Clocker slumped in the back seat.

Leaving the airport, they turned right onto MacArthur Boulevard. They were in an area of expensive office towers and complexes, many of which seemed to be the regional or national headquarters of major corporations, set back from the street behind large and meticulously maintained lawns, flowerbeds, swards of shrubbery, and lots of trees, all illuminated by artfully placed landscape lighting.

"Under your seat," Lomax told Oslett, "you'll find a Xerox of the Mission Viejo Police report on the incident at the Stillwater house. Wasn't easy to get hold of. Read it now, 'cause I have to take it with me and destroy it."

Clipped to the report was a penlight by which to read it. As they followed MacArthur Boulevard south and west into Newport Beach, Oslett studied the document with growing astonishment and dismay. They reached the Pacific Coast Highway and turned south, traveling all the way through Corona Del Mar before he finished.

"This cop, this Lowbock," Oslett said, looking up from the report, "he thinks it's all a publicity stunt, thinks there wasn't even an intruder."

"That's a break for us," Lomax said. He grinned, which was a mistake, because it made him look like the poster boy for some charity formed to help the willfully stupid.

Oslett said, "Considering the whole damn Network is maybe being sucked down a drain here, I think we need more than a break. We need a miracle."

"Let me see," Clocker said.

Oslett passed the report and penlight into the back seat, and then said to Lomax, "How did our bad boy know Stillwater was even out here, how did he find him?"

Lomax shrugged his limestone-lintel shoulders. "Nobody knows."

Oslett made a wordless sound of disgust.

To the right of the highway, they passed a pricey gate-guarded golf-course community, after which the lightless Pacific lay so vast and black to the west that they seemed to be driving along the edge of eternity.

Lomax said, "We figure if we keep tabs on Stillwater, sooner or later our man will turn up, and we'll recover him."

"Where's Stillwater now?"

"We don't know."

"Terrific."

"Well, see, not half an hour after the cops left, there was this other thing happened to the Stillwaters, before we got to them, and after that they seemed to . . . go into hiding, I guess you'd say."

"What other thing?"

Lomax frowned. "Nobody's sure. It happened right around the corner from their house. Different neighbors saw different pieces, but a guy fitting Stillwater's description fired a lot of shots at another guy in a Buick. The Buick slams into a parked Explorer, see, gets hung up on it for a second. Two kids fitting the description of the Stillwater girls tumble out the back seat of the Buick and run, the Buick takes off, Stillwater empties his gun at it, and then this BMW—which fits the description of one of the cars registered to the Stillwaters—it comes around the corner like a bat out of hell, driven by Stillwater's wife, and all of them get in it and take off."

"After the Buick?"

"No. It's long gone. It's like they're trying to get out of there before the cops arrive."

"Any neighbors see the guy in the Buick?"

"No. Too dark."

"It was our bad boy."

Lomax said, "You really think so?"

"Well, if it wasn't him, it must've been the Pope."

Lomax gave him an odd look, then stared thoughtfully at the highway ahead.

Before the dimwit could ask how the Pope was involved in all of this, Oslett said, "Why don't we have the police report on the second incident?"

"Wasn't one. No complaint. No crime victim. Just a report of the hit-and-run damage to the Explorer."

"According to what Stillwater told the cops, our Alfie thinks *he* is Stillwater, or ought to be. Thinks his life was stolen from him. The poor boy's totally over the edge, whacko, so to him it makes sense to go right back and steal the Stillwater kids because somehow he thinks they're *his* kids. Jesus, what a mess."

A highway sign indicated they would soon reach the city limits of Laguna Beach.

Oslett said, "Where are we going?"

"Ritz-Carlton Hotel in Dana Point," Lomax replied. "You've got a suite there. I took the long way so you'd both have a chance to read the police report."

"We napped on the plane. I sort of thought, once we landed, we'd get right into action."

Lomax looked surprised. "Doing what?"

"Go to the Stillwater house for starters, have a look around, see what we can see."

"Nothing to see. Anyway, I'm supposed to take you to the Ritz. You're to get some sleep, be ready to go by eight in the morning."

"Go where?"

"They expect to have a lead on Stillwater or your boy or both by morning. Someone will come to the hotel to give you a briefing at eight o'clock, and you've gotta be rested, ready to move. Which you should be, since it's the Ritz. I mean, it's a terrific hotel. Great food too. Even from room service. You can get a good, healthy breakfast, not typical greasy hotel crap. Egg-white omelets, seven-grain bread, all kinds of fresh fruit, non-fat yogurt—"

Oslett said, "I sure hope I can get a breakfast like I have in Manhattan every morning. Alligator embryos and chicken-fried eel heads on a bed of seaweed sautéed in a garlic butter, with a double side order of calves' brains. Ahhh, man, you never in your life feel half as *pumped* as you do after that breakfast."

So astonished that he let the speed of the Oldsmobile fall to half of what it had been, Lomax stared at Oslett. "Well, they have great food at the Ritz but maybe not as exotic as what you can get in New York." He looked at the street again, and the car picked up speed. "Anyway, you sure that's healthy food? Sounds packed with cholesterol to me."

Not a hint of irony, not a trace of humor informed Lomax's voice. It was clear that he actually believed Oslett ate eel heads, alligator embryos, and calves' brains for breakfast.

Reluctantly, Oslett had to face the fact that there were worse potential partners than the one he already had. Karl Clocker only *looked* stupid.

In Laguna Beach, December was the off season, and the streets were nearly deserted at a quarter to one on a Tuesday morning. At the three-way intersection in the heart of town, with the public beach on the right, they stopped for the red traffic signal, even though no other moving car was in sight.

Oslett thought the town was as unnervingly dead as any place in Oklahoma, and he longed for the bustle of Manhattan: the all-night rush of police vehicles and ambulances, the noir music of sirens, the endless honking of horns. Laughter, drunken voices, arguments, and the mad gibbering of the drug-blasted schizophrenic street dwellers that echoed up to his apartment even in the deepest hours of the night were sorely lacking in this somnolent burg on the edge of the winter sea.

As they continued out of Laguna, Clocker passed the Mission Viejo Police report forward from the back seat.

Oslett waited for a comment from the Trekker. When none was forthcoming, and when he could no longer tolerate the silence that filled the car and seemed to blanket the world outside, he half-turned to Clocker and said, "Well?"

"Well what?"

"What do you think?"

"Not good," Clocker pronounced from his nest of shadows in the back seat.

"Not good? That's all you can say? Looks like one colossal mess to me."

"Well," Clocker said philosophically, "into every crypto-fascist organization, a little rain must fall."

Oslett laughed. He turned forward, glanced at the solemn Lomax, and laughed harder. "Karl, sometimes I actually think maybe you're not a bad guy."

"Good or bad," Clocker said, "everything resonates with the same movement of subatomic particles."

"Now don't go ruining a beautiful moment," Oslett warned him.

4.

In the deepest swale of the night, he rises from vivid dreams of slashed throats, bullet-shattered heads, pale wrists carved by razor blades, and strangled prostitutes, but he does not sit up or gasp or cry out like a man waking from a nightmare, for he is always soothed by his dreams. He lies in the fetal position upon the back seat of the car, half in and half out of convalescent sleep.

One side of his face is wet with a thick, sticky substance. He raises one hand to his cheek and cautiously, sleepily works the viscous material between his fingers, trying to understand what it is. Discovering prickly bits of glass in the congealing slime, he realizes that his healing eye has rejected the splinters of the car window along with the damaged ocular matter, which has been replaced by healthy tissue.

He blinks, opens his eyes, and can again see as well through the left as through the right. Even in the shadow-filled Buick, he clearly perceives shapes, variations of texture, and the lesser darkness of the night that presses at the windows.

Hours hence, by the time the palm trees are casting the long west-falling shadows of dawn and tree rats have squirmed into their secret refuges among the lush fronds to wait out the day, he will be completely healed. He will be ready once more to claim his destiny.

He whispers, *"Charlotte . . ."*

Outside, a haunting light gradually arises. The clouds trailing the storm are thin and torn. Between some of the ragged streamers, the cold face of the moon peers down.

". . . Emily . . ."

Beyond the car windows, the night glimmers softly like slightly tarnished silver in the glow of a single candle flame.

". . . Daddy is going to be all right . . . all right . . . don't worry . . . Daddy is going to be all right. . . ."

He now understands that he was drawn to his double by a magnetism which arose because of their essential oneness and which he perceived through a sixth sense. He'd had no awareness that another self existed, but he'd been pulled toward him as if the attraction was an autonomic function of his body to the same extent that the beating of his heart, the production and maintenance of his blood supply, and the functioning of internal organs were autonomic functions proceeding entirely without need of conscious volition.

Still half embraced by sleep, he wonders if he can apply that sixth sense with conscious intention and reach out to find the false father any time he wishes.

Dreamily, he imagines himself to be a figure sculpted from iron and magnetized. The other self, hiding somewhere out there in the night, is a similar figure. Each magnet has a negative and positive pole. He imagines his positive is aligned with the false father's negative. Opposites attract.

He seeks attraction, and almost at once he finds it. Invisible waves of force tug lightly at him, then less lightly.

West. West and south.

As during his frantic and compulsive drive across more than half the country, he feels the power of the attractant grow until it is like the ponderous gravity of a planet pulling a minor asteroid into the fiery promise of its atmosphere.

West and south. Not far. A few miles.

The pull is exigent, strangely pleasant at first but then almost painful. He feels as if, were he to get out of the car, he would instantly levitate off the ground and be drawn through the air at high speed directly into the orbit of the hateful false father who has taken his life.

Suddenly he senses that his enemy is aware of being sought and perceives the lines of power connecting them.

He stops imagining the magnetic attraction. Immediately he retreats into himself, shuts down. He isn't quite ready to re-engage the enemy in combat and doesn't want to alert him to the fact that another encounter is only hours away.

He closes his eyes.

Smiling, he drifts into sleep.

Healing sleep.

At first his dreams are of the past, peopled by those he has assassinated and by the women with whom he has had sex and on whom he has bestowed post-coital death. Then he is enraptured by scenes that are surely prophetic, involving those whom he loves—his sweet wife, his beautiful daughters, in moments of surpassing tenderness and gratifying submission, bathed in golden light, so lovely, all in a lovely golden light, flares of silver, ruby, amethyst, jade, and indigo.

❊   ❊   ❊

Marty woke from a nightmare with the feeling that he was being crushed. Even when the dream shattered and blew away, though he knew that he was awake and in the motel room, he could not breathe or move so much as a finger. He felt small, insignificant, and was strangely certain he was about to be hammered into billions of disassociated atoms by some cosmic force beyond his comprehension.

Breath came to him suddenly, implosively. The paralysis broke with a spasm that shook him from head to foot.

He looked at Paige on the bed beside him, afraid that he had disturbed her sleep. She murmured to herself but didn't wake.

He got up as quietly as possible, stepped to the front window, cautiously separated the drapery panels, and looked out at the motel parking lot and Pacific Coast Highway beyond. No one moved to or from any of the parked cars. As far as he remembered, all of the shadows that were out there now had been out there earlier. He saw no one lurking in any corner. The storm had taken all the wind with it into the east, and Laguna was so still that the trees might have been painted on a stage canvas. A truck passed, heading north on the highway, but that was the only movement in the night.

In the wall opposite the front window, draperies covered a pair of sliding glass doors beyond which lay a balcony overlooking the sea. Through the doors and past the deck railing, down at the foot of the bluff, lay a width of pale beach onto which waves broke in garlands of silver foam. No one could easily climb to the balcony, and the sward was deserted.

Maybe it had been only a nightmare.

He turned away from the glass, letting the draperies fall back into place, and he looked at the luminous dial of his wristwatch. Three o'clock in the morning.

He had been asleep about five hours. Not long enough, but it would have to do.

His neck ached intolerably, and his throat was mildly sore.

He went into the bathroom, eased the door shut, and snapped on the light. From his travel kit he took a bottle of Extra-Strength Excedrin. The label advised a dosage of no more than two tablets at a time and no more than eight in twenty-four hours. The moment seemed made for living dangerously, however, so he washed down four of them with a glass of water drawn from the sink tap, then popped a sore-throat lozenge in his mouth and sucked on it.

After returning to the bedroom and picking up the short-barreled shot-gun from beside the bed, he went through the open connecting door to the girls' room. They were asleep, burrowed in their covers like turtles in shells to avoid the annoying light of the nightstand lamp.

He looked out their windows. Nothing.

Earlier, he had returned the reading chair to the corner, but now he moved it farther out into the room, where light would reach it. He didn't want to alarm Charlotte and Emily if they woke before dawn and saw an unidentifiable man in the shadows.

He sat with his knees apart, the shotgun across his thighs.

Although he owned five weapons—three of them now in the hands of the police—although he was a good shot with all of them, although he had written many stories in which policemen and other characters handled weapons with the ease of familiarity, Marty was surprised by how un-hesitatingly he had resorted to guns when trouble arose. After all, he was neither a man of action nor experienced in killing.

His own life and then his family had been in jeopardy, but he would have thought, before learning differently, that he'd have reservations when his finger first curled around the trigger. He would have expected to experience at least a flicker of regret after shooting a man in the chest even if the bastard deserved shooting.

He clearly remembered the dark glee with which he had emptied the Beretta at the fleeing Buick. The savage lurking in the human genetic heritage was as accessible to him as to any man, regardless of how edu-cated, well-read, and civilized he was.

What he had discovered about himself did not displease him as much as perhaps it should. Hell, it didn't displease him at all.

He knew that he was capable of killing any number of men to save his own life, Paige's life, or the lives of his children. And although he swam in a society where it was intellectually correct to embrace pacifism as the only hope of civilization's survival, he didn't see himself as a hopeless reactionary or an evolutionary throwback or a degenerate but merely as a man acting precisely as nature intended.

Civilization began with the family, with children protected by mothers and fathers willing to sacrifice and even die for them.

If the family wasn't safe any more, if the government couldn't or wouldn't protect the family from the depredations of rapists and child molesters and killers, if homicidal sociopaths were released from prison after serving less time than fraudulent evangelists who embezzled from their churches and greedy hotel-rich millionairesses who underpaid their taxes, then civilization had ceased to exist. If children were fair game—as any issue of a daily paper would confirm they were—then the world had devolved into savagery. Civilization existed only in tiny units, within the walls of those houses where the members of a family shared a love strong enough to make them willing to put their lives on the line in the defense of one another.

What a day they'd been through. A terrible day. The only good thing about it was—he had discovered that his fugue, nightmares, and other symptoms didn't result from either physical or mental illness. The trouble was *not* within him, after all. The boogeyman was real.

But he could take minimal satisfaction from that diagnosis. Although he had regained his self-confidence, he had lost so much else.

Everything had changed.

Forever.

He knew that he didn't even yet grasp just how dreadfully their lives had been altered. In the hours remaining before dawn, as he tried to think what steps they must take to protect themselves, and as he dared to consider the few possible origins of The Other that logic dictated, their situation inevitably would seem increasingly difficult and their options narrower than he could yet envision or admit.

For one thing, he suspected that they would never be able to go home again.

*   *   *

He wakes half an hour before dawn, healed and rested.

He returns to the front seat, switches on the interior light, and examines his forehead and left eye in the rearview mirror. The bullet furrow in his brow has knit without leaving any scar that he can detect. His eye is no longer damaged—or even bloodshot.

However, half his face is crusted with dried blood and the grisly biological waste products of the accelerated healing process. A portion of his countenance looks like something out of *The Abominable Dr. Phibes* or *Darkman.*

Rummaging in the glove compartment, he finds a small packet of Kleenex. Under the tissues is a travel-size box of Handi Wipes, moistened towelettes sealed in foil packets. They have a lemony scent. Very nice. He uses the Kleenex and towelettes to scrub the muck off his face, and he smooths out his sleep-matted hair with his hands.

He won't frighten anyone now, but he is still not presentable enough to be inconspicuous, which is what he desires to be. Though the bulky raincoat, buttoned to the neck, covers his bullet-torn shirt, the shirt reeks of blood and the variety of foods that he spilled on it during his feeding frenzy in McDonald's rainswept parking lot last evening, in the now-abandoned Honda, before he'd ever met the unlucky owner of the Buick. His pants aren't pristine, either.

On the off chance he'll find something useful, he takes the keys from the ignition, gets out of the car, goes around to the back, and opens the trunk. From the dark interior, lit only partially by an errant beam from the nearby tree-shrouded security lamp, the dead man stares at him with wide-eyed astonishment, as if surprised to see him again.

The two plastic shopping bags lie atop the body. He empties the contents of both on the corpse. The owner of the Buick had been shopping for a variety of items. The thing that looks most useful at the moment is a bulky crew-neck sweater.

Clutching the sweater in his left hand, he gently closes the trunk lid with his right to make as little noise as possible. People will be getting up soon, but sleep still grips most if not all of the apartment residents. He locks the trunk and pockets the keys.

The sky is dark, but the stars have faded. Dawn is no more than fifteen minutes away.

Such a large garden-apartment complex must have at least two or three community laundry rooms, and he sets out in search of one. In a minute he finds a signpost that directs him to the recreation building, pool, rental office, and nearest laundry room.

The walkways connecting the buildings wind through large and attractively landscaped courtyards under spreading laurels and quaint iron carriage lamps with verdigris patina. The development is well-planned and attractive. He would not mind living here himself. Of course his own house, in Mission Viejo, is even more appealing, and he is sure the girls and Paige are so attached to it that they will never want to leave.

The laundry-room door is locked, but it doesn't pose a great obstacle. Management has installed a cheap lockset, a latch-bolt not a dead-bolt. Having anticipated the need, he has a credit card from the cadaver's wallet, which he slips between the faceplate and the striker plate. He slides it upward, encounters the latch-bolt, applies pressure, and pops the lock.

Inside, he finds six coin-operated washing machines, four gas dryers, a vending machine filled with small boxes of detergents and fabric softeners, a large table on which clean clothes can be folded, and a pair of deep sinks. Everything is clean and pleasant under the fluorescent lights.

He takes off the raincoat and the grossly soiled flannel shirt. He wads up both the shirt and the coat and stuffs them into a large trash can that stands in one corner.

His chest is unmarked by bullet wounds. He doesn't need to look at his back to know that the single exit wound is also healed.

He washes his armpits at one of the laundry sinks and dries with paper towels taken from a wall dispenser.

He looks forward to taking a long hot shower before the day is done, in his own bathroom, in his own home. Once he has located the false father and killed him, once he has recovered his family, he will have time for simple pleasures. Paige will shower with him. She will enjoy that.

If necessary, he could take off his jeans and wash them in one of the laundry-room machines, using coins taken from the owner of the Buick. But when he scrapes the crusted food off the denim with his fingernails and works at the few stains with damp paper towels, the result is satisfactory.

The sweater is a pleasant surprise. He expects it to be too large for him, as the raincoat was, but the dead man evidently did not buy it for himself. It fits perfectly. The color—cranberry red—goes well with the blue jeans and is also a good color for him. If the room had a mirror, he is sure it would show that he is not only inconspicuous but quite respectable and even attractive.

Outside, dawn is just a ghost light in the east.

Morning birds are chirruping in the trees.

The air is sweet.

Tossing the Buick keys into some shrubbery, abandoning the car and the dead man in it, he proceeds briskly to the nearest multiple-stall carport and systematically tries the doors of the vehicles parked under the bougainvillea-covered roof. Just when he thinks all of them are going to be locked, a Toyota Camry proves to be open.

He slips in behind the wheel. Checks behind the sun visor for keys. Under the seat. No such luck.

It doesn't matter. He's nothing if not resourceful. Before the sky has brightened appreciably, he hot-wires the car and is on the road again.

Most likely, the owner of the Camry will discover it's missing in a couple of hours, when he's ready to go to work, and will quickly report it stolen. No problem. By then the license plates will be on another car, and the Camry will be sporting a different set of tags that will make it all but invisible to the police.

He feels invigorated, driving through the hills of Laguna Niguel in the rose light of dawn. The early sky is as yet only a faded blue, but the high formations of striated clouds are runneled with bright pink.

It is the first day of December. Day one. He is making a fresh start. From now on, everything will go his way because he will no longer underestimate his enemy.

Before he kills the false father, he will put out the bastard's eyes in retribution for the wound that he himself suffered. He will require his daughters to watch, for this will be an important lesson to them, proof that false fathers cannot triumph in the long run and that their real father is a man to be disobeyed only at the risk of severe punishment.

FIVE

1.

Shortly after dawn, Marty woke Charlotte and Emily. "Got to get show-ered and hit the road, ladies. Lots to do this morning."

Emily was fully awake in an instant. She scrambled out from under the covers and stood on the bed in her daffodil-yellow pajamas, which brought her almost to eye-level with him. She demanded a hug and a good-morning kiss. "I had a super dream last night."

"Let me guess. You dreamed you were old enough to date Tom Cruise, drive a sports car, smoke cigars, get drunk, and puke your guts out."

"Silly," she said. "I dreamed, for breakfast, you went out to the vending machines and got us Mountain Dew and candy bars."

"Sorry, but it wasn't prophetic."

"Daddy, don't be a writer using big words."

"I meant, your dream isn't going to come true."

"Well, I know *that,"* she said. "You and Mommy would blow a basket if we had candy for breakfast."

"Gasket. Not basket."

She wrinkled her face. "Does it really matter?"

"No, I guess not. Basket, gasket, whatever you say."

Emily squirmed out of his arms and jumped down from the bed. "I'm going to the potty," she announced.

"That's a start. Then take a shower, brush your teeth, and get dressed."

Charlotte was, as usual, slower to come fully awake. By the time Emily was closing the bathroom door, Charlotte had only managed to push back the blankets and sit on the edge of her bed. She was scowling down at her bare feet.

Marty sat beside her. "They're called 'toes.' "

"Mmmm," she said.

"You need them to fill out the ends of your socks."

She yawned.

Marty said, "You'll need them a lot more if you're going to be a ballet dancer. But for most other professions, however, they're not essential. So if you *aren't* going to be a ballet dancer, then you could have them surgically removed, just the biggest ones or all ten, that's entirely up to you."

She cocked her head and gave him a Daddy's-being-cute-so-let's-humor-him look. "I think I'll keep them."

"Whatever you want," he said, and kissed her forehead.

"My teeth feel furry," she complained. "So does my tongue."

"Maybe during the night you ate a cat."

She was awake enough to giggle.

In the bathroom the toilet flushed, and a second later the door opened. Emily said, "Charlotte, you want privacy for the potty, or can I shower now?"

"Go ahead and shower," Charlotte said. "You smell."

"Yeah? Well, you stink."

"You reek."

"That's because I *want* to," Emily said, probably because she couldn't think of a comeback word for "reek."

"My gracious young daughters, such little ladies."

As Emily disappeared back into the bathroom and began to fiddle with the shower controls, Charlotte said, "Gotta get this fuzz off my teeth." She got up and went to the open door. At the threshold she turned to Marty. "Daddy, do we have to go to school today?"

"Not today."

"I didn't think so." She hesitated. "Tomorrow?"

"I don't know, honey. Probably not."

Another hesitation. "Will we be going to school again ever?"

"Well, sure, of course."

She stared at him for too long, then nodded and went into the bathroom.

Her question rattled Marty. He wasn't sure if she was merely fantasizing about a life without school, as most kids did now and then, or whether she was expressing a more genuine concern about the depth of the trouble that had rolled over them.

He had heard the television come on in the other room while he had been sitting on the edge of the bed with Charlotte, so he knew Paige was awake. He got up to go say good morning to her.

As he was approaching the connecting door, Paige called to him. "Marty, quick, look at this."

When he hurried into the other room, he saw her standing in front of the TV. She was watching an early-morning news program.

"It's about us," she said.

He recognized their own home on the screen. A woman reporter was standing in the street, her back to the house, facing the camera.

Marty squatted in front of the television and turned up the sound.

". . . so the mystery remains, and the police would very much like to talk to Martin Stillwater this morning . . ."

"Oh, this *morning* they want to talk," he said disgustedly.

Paige shushed him.

". . . an irresponsible hoax by a writer too eager to advance his career, or something far more sinister? Now that the police laboratory has confirmed the large amount of blood in the Stillwater house is indeed of human origin, the need for the authorities to answer that question has overnight become more urgent."

That was the end of the piece. As the reporter gave her name and location, Marty registered the word "LIVE" in the upper left-hand corner of the screen. Although the four letters had been there all along, the importance of them hadn't registered immediately.

"Live?" Marty said. "They don't send reporters out live unless the story's ongoing."

"It is ongoing," Paige said. She was standing with her arms folded across her chest, frowning down at the television. "The lunatic is still out there somewhere."

"I mean, like a robbery in progress or a hostage situation with a SWAT team waiting to storm the place. By TV standards, this is boring, no action, no one on scene to shove a microphone at, just an empty house for visuals. It's not the kind of story they use for a live spot, too expensive and no excitement."

The broadcast had gone back to the studio. To his surprise, the anchorman wasn't one of the second-string newsreaders from a Los Angeles station, who would ordinarily have pulled duty on an early-morning program, but a well-known network face.

Astonished, Marty said, "This is *national.* Since when does a breaking-and-entry report rate national news?"

"You were assaulted too," Paige said.

"So what? These days, there's a worse crime than this every ten seconds somewhere in the country."

"But you're a celebrity."

"The hell I am."

"You may not like it, but you are."

"I'm not *that* much of a celebrity, not with only two paperback bestsellers. You know how hard it is to get on this program for one of their chat segments, as an invited guest?" He rapped a knuckle against the face of the anchorman on the screen. "Harder than getting an invitation to a state dinner at the White House! Even if I hired a publicist who'd sold his soul to the devil, he couldn't get me on this program, Paige. I'm just not big enough. I'm a nobody to them."

"So . . . what're you saying?"

He went to the window that provided a view of the parking lot, and parted the draperies. Pale sunlight. Steady traffic out on Pacific Coast Highway. The trees stirred lazily in the mildest of on-shore breezes.

Nothing in the scene was threatening or unusual, yet it seemed ominous to him. He felt that he was looking out at a world that was no longer familiar, a world changed for the worse. The differences were indefinable, subjective rather than objective, perceptible to the spirit more than to the senses but nonetheless real. And the pace of that dark change was accelerating. Soon the view from this room or any other would be, to him, like something seen through the porthole of a spacecraft on a far alien planet which superficially resembled his own world but which was, below its deceptive surface, infinitely strange and inimical to human life.

"I don't think," he said, "that the police would ordinarily have completed their tests on those blood samples so quickly, and I *know* it's not standard practice to release crime-lab results so casually to the media." He let the draperies fall into place and turned to Paige, whose brow was furrowed with worry. "National news? Live, on the scene? I don't know what the hell is happening, Paige, but it's even stranger than I thought it was last night."

* * *

While Paige showered, Marty pulled up a chair in front of the television and channel-hopped, searching for other news programs. He caught the end of a second story about himself on a local channel—and then a third piece, complete, on a national show.

He was trying to guard against paranoia, but he had the distinct impression that both stories suggested, without making accusations, that the falsity of his statement to the Mission Viejo Police was a foregone conclusion and that his real motive was either to sell more books or something darker and weirder than mere career-pumping. Both programs made use of the photograph from the current issue of *People,* in which he resembled a movie zombie with glowing eyes, lurching out of shadows, violent and demented. And both pointedly mentioned the three guns of which he'd been relieved by the police, as if he might be a suburban survivalist living atop a bunker packed solid with arms and ammunition. Toward the end of the third report, he thought an implication was made to the effect that he might even be dangerous, although it was so smooth and so subtly inserted that it was more a matter of the reporter's tone of voice and expressions than any words in the script.

Rattled, he switched off the television.

For a while he stared at the blank screen. The gray of the dead monitor matched his mood.

* * *

After everyone was showered and dressed, the girls got in the back seat of the BMW and dutifully put on their seatbelts while their parents stowed the luggage in the trunk.

When Marty slammed the trunk lid and locked it, Paige spoke to him quietly, so Charlotte and Emily couldn't hear. "You really think we have to go this far, do these things, it's really that bad?"

"I don't know. Like I told you, I've been brooding about this ever since I woke up, since three o'clock this morning, and I still don't know if I'm over-reacting."

"These are serious steps to take, even risky."

"It's just that . . . as strange as this already is, with The Other and everything he said to me, whatever underlies it all is stranger still. More dangerous than one lunatic with a gun. Deadlier and a lot bigger than that. Something so big it'll crush us if we try to stand up to it. That's how I felt in the middle of the night, afraid, more scared even than when he had the kids in his car. And after what I saw on TV this morning, I'm more—not less—inclined to go with my gut feelings."

He realized that his expression of dread was extreme, with an unmistakable flavor of paranoia. But he was no alarmist, and he was confident that his instincts could be trusted. Events had dissolved all of his doubts about his mental well-being.

He wished he could identify an enemy other than the improbable deadringer, for he knew intuitively that there *was* another enemy, and it would be comforting to have it defined. The Mafia, Ku Klux Klan, neo-Nazis, consortiums of evil bankers, the board of directors of some ferociously greedy international conglomerate, right-wing generals intent on establishing a military dictatorship, a cabal of insane Mideastern zealots, mad scientists intent on blowing the world to smithereens for the sheer hell of it, or Satan himself in all his horned splendor—any of the standard villains of television dramas and countless novels, regardless of how unlikely and clichéd, would be preferable to an adversary without face or form or name.

Chewing her lower lip, lost in thought, Paige let her gaze travel across the breeze-ruffled trees, other parked cars, and the front of the motel, before tilting her head back and looking up at three shrieking sea gulls that wheeled across the mostly blue and uncaring azure sky.

"You sense it too," he said.

"Yes."

"Oppressive. We're not being watched, but the feeling is almost the same."

"More than that," she said. "Different. The world has changed—or the way I look at it."

"Me too."

"Something's been . . . lost."

And we'll never find it again, he thought.

2.

The Ritz-Carlton was a remarkable hotel, exquisitely tasteful, with generous applications of marble, limestone, granite, quality art, and antiques throughout its public areas. The enormous flower arrangements, on display wherever one turned, were the most artfully fashioned that Oslett had ever seen. Attired in subdued uniforms, courteous, omnipresent, the staff seemed to outnumber the guests. All in all, it reminded Oslett of home, the Connecticut estate on which he had been raised, although the family mansion was larger than the Ritz-Carlton, was furnished with antiques only of museum quality, had a staff-to-family ratio of six to one, and featured a landing pad large enough to accommodate the military helicopters in which the President of the United States and his retinue sometimes traveled.

The two-bedroom suite with spacious living room, in which Drew Oslett and Clocker were quartered, offered every amenity from a fully stocked bar to marble shower stalls so spacious that it would have been possible for a visiting ballet dancer to practice entrechats during his morning ablutions. The towels were not by Pratesi, as were those he had used all his life, but they were good Egyptian cotton, soft and absorbent.

By 7:50 Tuesday morning, Oslett had dressed in a white cotton shirt with whalebone buttons by Theophilus Shirtmakers of London, a navy-blue cashmere blazer crafted with sublime attention to detail by his personal tailor in Rome, gray wool slacks, black oxfords (an eccentric touch) handmade by an Italian cobbler living in Paris, and a club tie in stripes of navy, maroon, and gold. The color of his silk pocket handkerchief precisely matched the gold in his tie.

Thus attired, his mood elevated by his sartorial perfection, he went looking for Clocker. He didn't desire the big man's company, of course; he just preferred, for his own peace of mind, to know what Clocker was up to at all times. And he nurtured the hope that one blessed day he would discover Karl Clocker dead, felled by a massive cardiac infarction, cerebral hemorrhage, or an alien death ray like those about which the big man was always reading.

Clocker was in a patio chair on the balcony off the living room, ignoring a breathtaking view of the Pacific, his nose stuck in the last chapter of

Shape-Changing Gynecologists of the Dark Galaxy, or whatever the hell it was called. He was wearing the same hat with the duck feather, tweed sportcoat, and Hush Puppies, although he had on new purple socks, fresh slacks, and a clean white shirt. He'd changed into a different harlequin-pattern sweater-vest, as well, this one in blue, pink, yellow, and gray. Though he was not sporting a tie, so much black hair bristled from the open neck of his shirt that, at a glance, he appeared to be wearing a cravat.

After failing to respond to Oslett's first "good morning," Clocker replied to the repetition of those words with the improbable split-finger greeting that characters gave each other on *Star Trek,* his attention still riveted to the paperback. If Oslett had possessed a chainsaw or cleaver, he would have severed Clocker's hand at the wrist and tossed it into the ocean. He wondered if room service would send up a suitably sharp instrument from the chef's collection of kitchen cutlery.

The day was warmish, already seventy. Blue skies and balmy breezes were a welcome change from the chill of the previous night.

Promptly at eight o'clock—barely in time to prevent Oslett from being driven mad by the lulling cries of sea gulls, the tranquilizing rumble of the incoming combers, and the faint laughter of the early surfers paddling their boards out to sea—the Network representative arrived to brief them on developments. He was a far different item from the hulking advance man who'd driven them from the airport to the Ritz-Carlton several hours earlier. Savile Row suit. Club tie. Good Bally wingtips. One look at him was all Oslett needed to be certain that he owned no article of clothing on which was printed a photo of Madonna with her breasts bared.

He said his name was Peter Waxhill, and he was probably telling the truth. He was high enough in the organization to know Oslett's and Clocker's real names—although he had booked them into the hotel as John Galbraith and John Maynard Keynes—so there was no reason for him to conceal his own.

Waxhill appeared to be in his early forties, ten years older than Oslett, but the razor-cut hair at his temples was feathered with gray. At six feet, he was tall but not overbearing; he was slim but fit, handsome but not dauntingly so, charming but not familiar. He handled himself not merely as if he had been a diplomat for decades but as if he had been genetically engineered for that career.

After introducing himself and commenting on the weather, Waxhill said, "I took the liberty of inquiring with room service if you'd had breakfast, and as they said you hadn't, I'm afraid I took the further liberty of ordering for the three of us, so we can breakfast and discuss business simultaneously. I hope you don't mind."

"Not at all," Oslett said, impressed by the man's suaveness and efficiency.

No sooner had he responded than the suite doorbell rang, and Waxhill ushered in two waiters pushing a serving cart covered with a white tablecloth and stacked with dishes. In the center of the living room, the waiters raised hidden leaves on the cart, converting it into a round table, and distributed chargers-plates-napkins-cups-saucers-glassware-flatware with the grace and speed of magicians manipulating playing cards. Together they caused to appear a variety of serving dishes from bottomless compartments under the table, until suddenly breakfast appeared as if from thin air: scrambled eggs with red peppers, bacon, sausages, kippers, toast, croissants, hot-house strawberries accompanied by brown sugar and small pitchers of heavy cream, fresh orange juice, and a silver-plated thermospot of coffee.

Waxhill complimented the waiters, thanked them, tipped them, and signed for the bill, remaining in motion the whole time, so that he was returning the room-service ticket and hotel pen to them as they were crossing the threshold into the corridor.

When Waxhill closed the door and returned to the table, Oslett said, "Harvard or Yale?"

"Yale. And you?"

"Princeton. Then Harvard."

"In my case, Yale and then Oxford."

"The President went to Oxford," Oslett noted.

"Did he indeed," Waxhill said, raising his eyebrows, pretending this was news. "Well, Oxford endures, you know."

Apparently having finished the final chapter of *Planet of the Gastrointestinal Parasites,* Karl Clocker entered from the balcony, a walking embarrassment as far as Oslett was concerned. Waxhill allowed himself to be introduced to the Trekker, shook hands, and gave every impression he was not choking on revulsion or hilarity.

They pulled up three straight-backed occasional chairs and sat down to breakfast. Clocker didn't take off his hat.

As they transferred food from the serving dishes to their plates, Waxhill said, "Overnight, we've picked up a few interesting bits of background on

Martin Stillwater, the most important of which relates to his oldest daughter's hospitalization five years ago."

"What was wrong with her?" Oslett asked.

"They didn't have a clue at first. Based on the symptoms, they suspected cancer. Charlotte—that's the daughter, she was four years old at the time—was in rather desperate shape for a while, but it eventually proved to be an unusual blood-chemistry imbalance, quite treatable."

"Good for her," Oslett said, though he didn't care whether the Stillwater girl had lived or died.

"Yes, it was," Waxhill said, "but at her lowest point, when the doctors were edging toward a more terminal diagnosis, her father and mother underwent bone-marrow aspiration. Extraction of bone marrow with a special aspirating needle."

"Sounds painful."

"No doubt. Doctors required samples to determine which parent would be the best donor in case a marrow transplant was required. Charlotte's marrow was producing little new blood, and indications were that malignancy was inhibiting blood-cell formation."

Oslett took a bite of the eggs. There was basil in them, and they were marvelous. "I fail to see where Charlotte's illness could have any relationship to our current problem."

After pausing for effect, Waxhill said, "She was hospitalized at Cedars-Sinai in Los Angeles."

Oslett froze with a second forkful of eggs halfway to his mouth.

"Five years ago," Waxhill repeated for emphasis.

"What month?"

"December."

"What day did Stillwater give the marrow sample?"

"The sixteenth. December sixteenth."

"Damn. But we had a blood sample as well, a backup—"

"Stillwater also gave blood samples. One of them would have been packaged with each marrow sample for lab work."

Oslett conveyed the forkful of eggs to his mouth. He chewed, swallowed, and said, "How could our people screw up like this?"

"We'll probably never know. Anyway, the 'how' doesn't matter as much as the fact they *did* screw up, and we have to live with it."

"So we never started where we thought we did."

"Or with whom we thought we started," Waxhill rephrased.

Clocker was eating like a horse without a feed bag. Oslett wanted to throw a towel over the big man's head to spare Waxhill the unpleasant sight of such vigorous mastication. At least the Trekker had not yet punctuated the conversation with inscrutable commentary.

"Exceptional kippers," Waxhill said.

Oslett said, "I'll have to try one."

After sipping orange juice and patting his mouth with his napkin, Waxhill said, "As to how your Alfie knew Stillwater existed and was able to find him . . . there are two theories at the moment."

Oslett noticed the "your Alfie" instead of "our Alfie," which might mean nothing—or might indicate an effort was already under way to shift the blame to him in spite of the incontrovertible fact that the disaster was directly the result of sloppy scientific procedures and had nothing whatsoever to do with how the boy had been handled during his fourteen months of service.

"First," Waxhill said, "there's a faction that thinks Alfie must have come across a book with Stillwater's picture on the jacket."

"It can't be anything that simple."

"I agree. Though, of course, the about-the-author paragraph on the flap of his last two books says he lives in Mission Viejo, which would have given Alfie a good lead."

Oslett said, "Anybody, seeing a picture of an identical twin he never knew he had, would be curious enough to look into it—except Alfie. Whereas an ordinary person has the freedom to pursue a thing like that, Alfie doesn't. He's tightly focused."

"Aimed like a bullet."

"Exactly. He broke training here, which required a monumental trauma. Hell, it's more than training. That's a euphemism. It's indoctrination, brainwashing—"

"He's programmed."

"Yes. Programmed. He's the next thing to a machine, and just seeing a photograph of Stillwater wouldn't send him spinning out of control any more than the personal computer in your office would start producing sperm and grow hair on its back just because you scanned a photograph of Marilyn Monroe onto its hard disk."

Waxhill laughed softly. "I like the analogy. I think I'll use it to change some minds, though of course I'll credit it to you."

Oslett was pleased by Waxhill's approval.

"Excellent bacon," said Waxhill.

"Yes, isn't it."

Clocker just kept eating.

"The second and smaller faction," Waxhill continued, "proposes a more exotic—but, at least to me, more credible—hypothesis to the effect that Alfie has a secret ability of which we're not aware and which he may not fully understand or control himself."

"Secret ability?"

"Rudimentary psychic perception perhaps. Very primitive . . . but strong enough to make a connection between him and Stillwater, draw them together because of . . . well, because of all they share."

"Isn't that a bit far out?"

Waxhill smiled and nodded. "I'll admit it sounds like something out of a *Star Trek* movie—"

Oslett cringed and glanced at Clocker, but the big man's eyes didn't shift from the food heaped on his plate.

"—though the whole project smacks of science fiction, doesn't it?" Waxhill concluded.

"I guess so," Oslett conceded.

"The fact is, the genetic engineers have given Alfie some truly exceptional abilities. Intentionally. So doesn't it seem possible they've unintentionally, inadvertently given him other superhuman qualities?"

"Even *in*human qualities," Clocker said.

"Well, now, you've just shown me a more unpleasant way to look at it," Waxhill said, regarding Karl Clocker soberly, "and all too possibly a more accurate view." Turning to Oslett: "Some psychic link, some strange mental connection, might have shattered Alfie's conditioning, erased his program or caused him to override it."

"Our boy was in Kansas City, and Stillwater was in southern California, for God's sake."

Waxhill shrugged. "A TV broadcast goes on forever, to the end of the universe. Beam a laser from Chicago toward the far end of the galaxy, and that light will get there someday, thousands of years from now, after Chicago is dust—and it'll keep on going. So maybe distance is meaningless when you're dealing with thought waves, too, or whatever it was that connected Alfie to this writer."

Oslett had lost his appetite.

Clocker seemed to have found it and added it to his own.

Pointing to the basket of croissants, Waxhill said, "These are excellent—and in case you didn't realize, there are two kinds here, some plain and some with almond paste inside."

"Almond croissants are my favorite," Oslett said, but didn't reach for one.

Waxhill said, "The best croissants in the world—"

"—are in Paris," Oslett interjected, "in a quaint café less than a block off—"

"—the Champs Elysées," Waxhill finished, surprising Oslett.

"The proprietor, Alfonse—"

"—and his wife, Mirielle—"

"—are culinary geniuses and hosts without equal."

"Charming people," Waxhill agreed.

They smiled at each other.

Clocker served himself more sausages, and Oslett wanted to knock that stupid hat off his head.

"If there's any chance that our boy has extraordinary powers, however feeble, which we never intended to give him," Waxhill said, "then we must consider the possibility that some qualities we *did* intend to give him didn't turn out quite as we thought they did."

"I'm afraid I don't follow," Oslett said.

"Essentially, I'm talking about sex."

Oslett was surprised. "He has no interest in it."

"We're sure of that, are we?"

"He's apparently male, of course, but he's impotent."

Waxhill said nothing.

"He was *engineered* to be impotent," Oslett stressed.

"A man can be impotent yet have a keen interest in sex. Indeed, one might make a good argument for the case that his very inability to attain an erection frustrates him, and that his frustration leads him to be *obsessed* with sex, with what he cannot have."

Oslett had been shaking his head the entire time Waxhill had been speaking. "No. Again, it's not that simple. He's not only impotent. He's received hundreds of hours of intense psychological conditioning to eliminate sexual interest, some of it when he's been in deep hypnosis, some under the influence of drugs that make the subconscious susceptible to *any* suggestion, some through virtual-reality subliminal feeds during sedative-induced sleep. To this boy, the primary difference between men and women is the way they dress."

Unimpressed with Oslett's argument, spreading orange marmalade on a slice of toast, Waxhill said, "Brainwashing, even at its most sophisticated, can fail. Would you agree with that?"

"Yes, but with an ordinary subject, you have problems because you've got to counter a lifetime of experience to install a new attitude or false memory. But Alfie was different. He was a blank slate, a beautiful blank slate, so there wasn't any resistance to whatever attitudes, memories, or feelings we wanted to stuff in his nice empty head. There was nothing in his brain to wash *out* first."

"Maybe mind-control failed with Alfie precisely because we were so confident that he was an easy mark."

"The mind is its own control," Clocker said.

Waxhill gave him an odd look.

"I don't think it failed," Oslett insisted. "Anyway, there's still the little matter of his engineered impotence to get around."

Waxhill took time to chew and swallow a bite of toast, and then washed it down with coffee. "Maybe his body got around it for him."

"Say again?"

"His incredible body with its superhuman recuperative powers."

Oslett twitched as if the idea had pierced like a pin. "Wait a minute, now. His wounds heal exceptionally fast, yes. Punctures, gashes, broken bones. Once damaged, his body can restore itself to its original engineered condition in miraculously short order. But that's the key. *To its original engineered condition.* It can't start to *remake* itself on any fundamental level, can't mutate, for God's sake."

"We're sure of that, are we?"

"Yes!"

"Why?"

"Well . . . because . . . otherwise . . . it's unthinkable."

"Imagine," Waxhill said, "if Alfie is potent. And interested in sex. The boy's been engineered to have a tremendous potential for violence, a biological killing machine, without compunctions or remorse, capable of any savagery. Imagine that bestiality coupled with a sex drive, and consider how sexual compulsions and violent impulses can feed on each other and amplify each other when they're not tempered by a civilized and moral spirit."

Oslett pushed his plate aside. The sight of food was beginning to sicken him. "It *has* been considered. That's why so damned many precautions were taken."

"As with the *Hindenburg.*"

As with the Titanic, Oslett thought grimly.

Waxhill pushed his plate aside, too, and folded his hands around his coffee cup. "So now Alfie has found Stillwater, and he wants the writer's family. He's a complete man now, at least physically, and thoughts of sex lead eventually to thoughts of procreation. A wife. Children. God knows what strange, twisted understanding he has of the meaning and purpose of a family. But here's a ready-made family. He wants it. Wants it badly. Evidently he feels it belongs to him."

3.

The bank offered extensive hours as part of its competitive edge. Marty and Paige intended to be at the doors, with Charlotte and Emily, when the manager unlocked for business at eight o'clock Tuesday morning.

He disliked returning to Mission Viejo, but he felt they would be able to effect their transactions with the least difficulty at the particular branch where they maintained their accounts. It was only eight or nine blocks from their house. Many of the tellers would recognize him and Paige.

The bank was in a free-standing brick building in the northwest corner of a shopping-center parking lot, nicely landscaped and shaded by pine trees, flanked on two sides by streets and on the other two sides by acres of blacktop. At the far end of the parking lot, to the south and east, was an L-shaped series of connected buildings that housed thirty to forty businesses, including a supermarket.

Marty parked on the south side. The short walk from the BMW to the bank door, with the kids between him and Paige, was unnerving because they had to leave their guns in the car. He felt vulnerable.

He could imagine no way in which they might secretly bring a shotgun inside with them, even a compact pistol-grip model like the Mossberg. He didn't want to risk carrying the Beretta under his ski jacket because he wasn't sure whether some bank-security systems included the ability to detect a hidden handgun on anyone who walked through the door. If a bank employee mistook him for a holdup man and the police were summoned by a silent alarm, the cops would never give him the benefit of the doubt—not considering the reputation he had with them after last night.

While Marty went directly to one of the teller's windows, Paige took Charlotte and Emily to an arrangement of two short sofas and two armchairs at one end of the long room, where patrons waited when they had appointments with loan officers. The bank was not a cavernous marble-lined monument to money with massive Doric columns and vaulted ceiling, but a comparatively small place with an acoustic-tile ceiling and all-weather green carpet. Though Paige and the kids were only sixty feet from him, clearly visible any time he chose to glance their way, he didn't like being separated from them by even that much distance.

The teller was a young woman—Lorraine Arakadian, according to the nameplate at her window—whose round tortoise-shell glasses gave her an owlish look. When Marty told her that he wanted to make a withdrawal of seventy thousand dollars from their savings account—which had a balance of more than seventy-four—she misunderstood, thinking he meant to transfer that amount to checking. When she put the applicable form in front of him to effect the transaction, he corrected her misapprehension and asked for the entire amount in hundred-dollar bills if possible.

She said, "Oh. I see. Well . . . that's a larger transaction than I can make on my own authority, sir. I'll have to get permission from the head teller or assistant manager."

"Of course," he said unconcernedly, as if he made large cash withdrawals every week. "I understand."

She went to the far end of the long teller's cage to speak to an older woman who was examining documents in one drawer of a large bank of files. Marty recognized her—Elaine Higgens, assistant manager. Mrs. Higgens and Lorraine Arakadian glanced at Marty, then put their heads together to confer again.

While he waited for them, Marty monitored both the south and east entrances to the lobby, trying to look nonchalant even though he expected The Other to walk through one door or another at any moment, this time armed with an Uzi.

A writer's imagination. Maybe it wasn't a curse, after all. At least not entirely. Maybe sometimes it was a survival tool. One thing for sure: even the most fanciful writer's imagination had trouble keeping up with reality these days.

* * *

He needs more time than he expected to find plates to swap for those on the stolen Toyota Camry. He slept too late and took far too long to make himself presentable. Now the world is coming awake, and he hasn't the advantage of the dead-of-night privacy that would make the switch easy. Large garden-apartment complexes, with shadowy carports and a plenitude of vehicles, offer the ideal shopping for what he requires, but as he tries one after another of these, he discovers too many residents out and about, on their way to work.

Eventually his diligent search is rewarded in the parking lot behind a church. A morning service is in progress. He can hear organ music. Parishioners have left fourteen cars from which he can select, not a large turnout for the Lord but adequate for his own purposes.

He leaves the engine of the Camry running while he looks for a car in which the owner has left the keys. In the third one, a green Pontiac, a full set dangles from the ignition.

He unlocks the trunk of the Pontiac, hoping it will contain at least an emergency tool kit with a screwdriver. Because he hot-wired the Camry, he doesn't have keys to its trunk. Again, he is in luck: a complete road-emergency kit with flares, first-aid items, and a tool packet that includes four screwdrivers of different types.

God is with him.

In a few minutes he exchanges the Camry's plates for those on the Pontiac. He returns the tool kit to the trunk of the Pontiac and the keys to the ignition.

As he's walking to the Camry, the church organ launches into a hymn with which he is not familiar. That he doesn't know the name of the hymn is not surprising, since he has only been to church three times that he can recall. In two instances, he had gone to church to kill time until movie theaters opened. On the third occasion he had been following a woman he'd seen on the street and with whom he would have liked to share sex and the special intimacy of death.

The music stirs him. He stands in the mild morning breeze, swaying dreamily, eyes closed. He is moved by the hymn. Perhaps he has musical talent. He should find out. Maybe playing an instrument of some kind and composing songs would be easier than writing novels.

When the song ends, he gets in the Camry and leaves.

✳   ✳   ✳

Marty exchanged pleasantries with Mrs. Higgens when she returned with the teller. Evidently no one at the bank had seen the news about him, as neither woman mentioned the assault. His crew-neck sweater and button-down shirt concealed livid bruises around his neck. His voice was mildly hoarse but not sufficiently so to cause comment.

Mrs. Higgens observed that the cash withdrawal he wished to make was unusually large, phrasing her comment to induce him to explain why he would risk carrying so much money around. He merely agreed it was, indeed, unusually large and expressed the hope that he wasn't putting them to much trouble. Unflagging affability was probably essential to completing the transaction as swiftly as possible.

"I'm not sure we can pay it entirely in hundreds," Mrs. Higgens said. She spoke softly, discreetly, though there were only two other customers in the bank and neither of them nearby. "I'll have to check our supply of bills in that denomination."

"Some twenties, fifties are okay," Marty assured her. "I'm just trying to prevent it from getting too bulky."

Though both the assistant manager and the teller were smiling and polite, Marty was aware of their curiosity and concern. They were in the money business, after all, and they knew there weren't many legitimate— and fewer sensible—reasons for anyone to carry seventy thousand in cash.

Even if he had felt comfortable leaving Paige and the kids in the car, Marty would not have done so. The first suspicion to cross a banker's mind would be that the cash was needed to meet a ransom payment, and prudence would require a call to the police. With the entire family present, kidnapping could be ruled out.

Marty's teller began to consult with other tellers, tabulating the number of hundreds contained in all their drawers, while Mrs. Higgens disappeared through the open door of the vault at the back of the cage.

He glanced at Paige and the girls. East entrance. South. His watch. Smiling, smiling all the while, smiling like an idiot.

We'll be out of here in fifteen minutes, he told himself. Maybe as few as ten. Out of here and on our way and safe.

The dark wave hit him.

* * *

At a Denny's, he uses the men's room, then selects a booth by the windows and orders an enormous breakfast.

His waitress is a cute brunette named Gayle. She makes jokes about his appetite. She is coming on to him. He considers trying to make a date with her. She has a lovely body, slender legs.

Having sex with Gayle would be adultery because he is married to Paige. He wonders if it would still be adultery if, after having sex with Gayle, he killed her.

He leaves her a good tip and decides to return within a week or two and ask her for a date. She has a pert nose, sensuous lips.

In the Camry again, before he starts the engine, he closes his eyes, clears his mind, and imagines he is magnetized, likewise the false father, opposite poles toward each other. He seeks attraction.

This time he is pulled into the orbit of the other man quicker than he was when he tried to make a connection in the middle of the night, and the adducent power is immeasurably greater than before. Indeed, the pull is so strong, so instantly, he grunts in surprise and locks his hands around the steering wheel, as if he is in real danger of being yanked out of the Toyota through the windshield and shooting like a bullet straight to the heart of the false father.

His enemy is immediately aware of the contact. The man is frightened, threatened.

East.

And south.

That will lead him back in the general direction of Mission Viejo, though he doubts the imposter feels safe enough to have returned home already.

* * *

A pressure wave, as from an enormous explosion, smashed into Marty and nearly rocked him off his feet. With both hands he clutched the countertop in front of the teller's window to keep his balance. He leaned into the counter, bracing himself against it.

The sensation was entirely subjective. The air seemed compressed to the point of liquefaction, but nothing disintegrated, cracked, or fell over. He appeared to be the only person affected.

After the initial shock of the wave, Marty felt as if he'd been buried under an avalanche. Weighed down by immeasurable megatons of snow. Breathless. Paralyzed. Cold.

He suspected that his face had turned pale, waxy. He knew for certain that he would be unable to speak if spoken to. Were anyone to return to the teller's window while the seizure gripped him, the fear beneath his casual pose would be revealed. He would be exposed as a man in desperate trouble, and they would be reluctant to hand so much cash to someone who was so clearly either ill or deranged.

He grew dramatically colder when he experienced a mental caress from the same malignant, ghostly presence that he'd sensed yesterday in the garage as he'd been trying to leave for the doctor's office. The icy "hand" of the spirit pressed against the raw surface of his brain, as if reading his location by fingering data that was Brailled into the convoluted tissues of his cerebral cortex. He now understood that the spirit was actually the look-alike, whose uncanny powers were not limited to spontaneous recovery from mortal chest wounds.

❋   ❋   ❋

He breaks the magnetic connection.

He drives out of the restaurant parking lot.

He turns on the radio. Michael Bolton is singing about love.

The song is touching. He is deeply moved by it, almost to tears. Now that he finally is somebody, now that a wife waits for him and two young children need his guidance, he knows the meaning and value of love. He wonders how he could have lived this long without it.

He heads south. And east.

Destiny calls.

❋   ❋   ❋

Abruptly, the spectral hand lifted from Marty.

The crushing pressure was released, and the world snapped back to normal—if there was such a thing as normality any more.

He was relieved that the attack had lasted only five or ten seconds. None of the bank employees had been aware anything was wrong with him.

However, the need to obtain the cash and get out of there was urgent. He looked at Paige and the kids in the open lounge at the far end of the room. He shifted his gaze worriedly to the east entrance, the south entrance, east again.

The Other knew where they were. In minutes, at most, their mysterious and implacable enemy would be upon them.

4.

The scrambled eggs on Oslett's abandoned plate acquired a faint grayish cast as they cooled and congealed. The salty aroma of bacon, previously so appealing, induced in him a vague nausea.

Stunned by the consideration that Alfie might have developed into a creature with sexual urges and with the ability to satisfy them, Oslett was nonetheless determined not to appear concerned, at least not in front of Peter Waxhill. "Well, all of this still amounts to nothing but conjecture."

"Yes," said Waxhill, "but we're checking the past to see if the theory holds water."

"What past?"

"Police records in every city where Alfie has been on assignment in the past fourteen months. Rapes and rape-murders during the hours he wasn't actually working."

Oslett's mouth was dry. His heart was thudding.

He didn't care what happened to the Stillwater family. Hell, they were only Klingons.

He didn't care, either, if the Network collapsed and all of its grand ambitions went unfulfilled. Eventually an organization similar to it would be formed, and the dream would be renewed.

But if their bad boy proved impossible to recapture or stop, the potential was here for a stain to spread deep into the Oslett family, jeopardizing its wealth and seriously diminishing its political power for decades to come. Above all, Drew Oslett demanded respect. The ultimate guarantor of respect had always been family, bloodline. The prospect of the Oslett name becoming an object of ridicule and scorn, target of public outrage, brunt of every TV comedian's puerile jokes, and the subject of embarrassing stories in papers as diverse as the *New York Times* and the *National Enquirer* was soul-shaking.

"Didn't you ever wonder," Waxhill asked, "what your boy did with his free time, between assignments?"

"We monitored him closely, of course, for the first six weeks. He went to movies, restaurants, parks, watched television, did all the things that people do to kill time—just as we wanted him to act outside a controlled environment. Nothing strange. Nothing at all out of the ordinary. Certainly nothing to do with women."

"He would have been on his best behavior, naturally, if he was aware that he was being watched."

"He wasn't aware. Couldn't be. He never made our surveillance men. No way. They're the best." Oslett realized he was protesting too much. Nevertheless, he couldn't keep from adding, "No way."

"Maybe he was aware of them the same way he became aware of this Martin Stillwater. Some low-key psychic perception."

Oslett was beginning to dislike Waxhill. The man was a hopeless pessimist.

Picking up the thermos-pot and pouring more coffee for all of them, Waxhill said, "Even if he was only going to movies, watching television—didn't that worry you?"

"Look, he's supposed to be the perfect assassin. Programmed. No remorse, no second thoughts. Hard to catch, harder to kill. And if something *does* go wrong, he can never be traced to his handlers. He doesn't know who we are or why we want these people terminated, so he can't turn state's evidence. He's nothing, a shell, a totally hollow man. *But* he's got to function in society, be inconspicuous, act like an ordinary Joe, *do things real people do in their spare time.* If we had him sitting around hotel rooms staring at walls, maids would comment to one another, think he's weird, remember him. Besides, what's the harm in a movie, some television?"

"Cultural influences. They could change him somehow."

"It's nature that matters, how he was engineered, not what he did with his Saturday afternoon." Oslett leaned back in his chair, feeling guardedly better, having convinced himself to some degree, if not Waxhill. "Check into the past. But you won't find anything."

"Maybe we already have. A prostitute in Kansas City. Strangled in a cheap motel across the street from a bar called the Blue Life Lounge. Two different bartenders at the lounge gave the Kansas City Police a description of the man she left with. Sounds like Alfie."

Oslett had perceived a bond of class and experience between himself and Peter Waxhill. He had even entertained the prospect of friendship. Now he had the uneasy feeling that Waxhill was taking pleasure from being the bearer of all this bad news.

Waxhill said, "One of our contacts managed to get us a sample of the sperm that the Kansas City Police Scientific Investigation Division recovered from the prostitute's vagina. It's being flown to our New York lab now. If it's Alfie's sperm, we'll know."

"He can't produce sperm. He was engineered—"

"Well, if it's his, we'll know. We have his genetic structure mapped, we know it better than Rand McNally knows the world. And it's unique. More individual than fingerprints."

Yale men. They were all alike. Smug, self-satisfied bastards.

Clocker picked up a plump hot-house strawberry between thumb and forefinger. Examining it closely, as if he had excruciatingly high standards for comestibles and would not eat anything that failed to pass his demanding inspection, he said, "If Alfie's drawn to Martin Stillwater, then what we need to know is where we can find Stillwater now." He popped the entire berry, half as large as a lemon, onto his tongue and into his mouth, in the manner of a toad taking a fly.

"Last night we sent a man into their house for a look around," Waxhill said. "Indications are, they packed in a hurry. Bureau drawers left open, clothes scattered around, a few empty suitcases left out after they decided not to use them. Judging by appearances, they don't intend to return home within the next few days, but we're having the place watched just in case."

"And you have no idea in hell where to find them," Oslett said, taking perverse pleasure in putting Waxhill on the defensive.

Unruffled, Waxhill said, "We can't say where they are at this moment, no—"

"Ah."

"—but we think we can predict one place we can get a lead on them. Stillwater's parents live in Mammoth Lakes. He has no other relatives on the West Coast, and unless there's a close friend we don't know about, he's almost certain to call his father and mother, if not go there.''

"What about the wife's parents?"

"When she was sixteen, her father shot her mother in the face and then killed himself."

"Interesting." What Oslett meant was that the tawdriness of the average person's life never ceased to amaze him.

"It is interesting, actually," Waxhill said, perhaps meaning something different from what Oslett meant. "Paige came home from school and found their bodies. For a few months, she was under the guardianship of an aunt. But she didn't like the woman, and she filed a petition with the court to have herself declared a legal adult."

"At sixteen?"

"The judge was sufficiently impressed with her to rule in her favor. It's rare but it does happen."

"She must've had one hell of an attorney."

"I suppose she did. She studied the applicable statutes and precedents, then represented herself."

The situation was bleaker all the time. Even if he'd been lucky, Martin Stillwater had gotten the better of Alfie, which meant he was a more formidable man than the jerk in *People*. Now it was beginning to seem as if his wife had more than a common measure of fortitude, as well, and would make a worthy adversary.

Oslett said, "To push Stillwater to get in touch with his folks, we should use Network affiliates in the media to hype the incidents at his house last night onto the front page."

"We are," Peter Waxhill said infuriatingly. He framed imaginary headlines with his hands: " 'Bestselling Author Shoots Intruder. Hoax or Real Threat? Author and Family Missing. Hiding from Killer or Avoiding Police Scrutiny?' That sort of thing. When Stillwater sees a newspaper or TV news program, he's going to call his parents right then because he'll know they've seen the news and they're worried."

"We've tapped their phone?"

"Yes. We have caller-ID equipment on the line. The moment the connection is made, we'll have a number where Stillwater's staying."

"What do we do in the meantime?" Oslett asked. "Just sit around here having manicures, eating strawberries?"

At the rate Clocker was eating strawberries, the hotel supply would be gone shortly, and soon thereafter the entire hot-house crop in California and adjacent states would also be exhausted.

Waxhill looked at his gold Rolex.

Drew Oslett tried to detect some indication of ostentation in the way Waxhill consulted the expensive timepiece. He would have been pleased to note any revelatory action that might expose a gauche pretender under the veneer of grace and sophistication.

But Waxhill seemed to regard the wristwatch as Oslett did his own gold Rolex: as though it was no different from a Timex purchased at K-Mart. "In fact, you'll be flying up to Mammoth Lakes later this morning."

"But we can't be certain Stillwater's going to show up there."

"It's a reasonable expectation," Waxhill said. "If he does, then there's a good chance Alfie will follow. You'll be in position to collect our boy. And if Stillwater doesn't go there, just calls his dear *mater* and *pater,* you can fly out or drive out at once to wherever he called from."

Reluctant to sit a moment longer, for fear that Waxhill would use the time to deliver more bad news, Oslett put his napkin on the table and pushed his chair back. "Then let's get moving. The longer our boy's on the loose, the greater the chance someone's going to see him and Stillwater at the same time. When that happens, the police are going to start believing his story."

Remaining in his chair, picking up his coffee cup, Waxhill said, "One more thing."

Oslett had risen. He was loath to sit again because it would appear as if Waxhill controlled the moment. Waxhill *did* control the moment, in fact, but only because he possessed needed information, not because he was Oslett's superior in rank or in any other sense. At worst, they held equal power in the organization; and more likely, Oslett was the heavyweight of the two. He remained standing beside the table, gazing down at the Yale man.

Although he was finally finished eating, Clocker stayed in his chair. Oslett didn't know whether his partner's behavior was a minor betrayal or only evidence that the Trekker's mind was off with Spock and the gang in some distant corner of the universe.

After a sip of coffee, Waxhill said, "If you have to terminate our boy, that's regrettable but acceptable. If you can bring him back into the fold, at least until he can be gotten into a secure facility and restrained, even better. However it goes . . . Stillwater, his wife, and his kids have to be eliminated."

"No problem."

5.

The branch manager, Mrs. Takuda, visited Marty while he waited at the teller's window, shortly after the dark wave slammed into him and washed away. If he had been confronted by his reflection, he would have expected to see that he was still tight-lipped and pale, with an animal wildness in his eyes; however, if Mrs. Takuda noticed anything strange in his appearance, she was too polite to mention it. Primarily she was concerned that he might be withdrawing the majority of his savings because something about the bank displeased him.

He was surprised he could summon a convincing smile and enough charm to assure her that he had no quarrel with the bank and to set her mind at rest. He was chilled and shaking deep inside, but none of the tremors reached the surface or affected his voice.

When Mrs. Takuda went to assist Elaine Higgens in the vault, Marty looked at Paige and the kids, the east door, the south door, and his Timex. The sight of the red sweep hand cleaning the seconds off the dial made sweat break out on his brow. The Other was coming. How long? Ten minutes, two minutes, five seconds?

Another wave hit him.

❋　　❋　　❋

Cruising a wide boulevard. Morning sun flaring off the chrome of passing cars. Phil Collins on the radio, singing about betrayal.

Sympathizing with Collins, he again imagines magnetism. Click. Contact. He feels an irresistible pull farther east and south, so he is still heading in the right direction.

He breaks contact seconds after establishing it, hoping to get another fix on the false father without revealing himself. But even during that brief linkage, the enemy senses the intrusion.

*   *   *

Though the second wave was of shorter duration than the first, it was no less powerful. Marty felt as if he had been hit in the chest with a hammer.

With Mrs. Higgens, the teller returned to the window. She had loose cash and banded packets of both hundred- and twenty-dollar bills. It amounted to two stacks of approximately three inches each.

The teller started to count out the seventy thousand.

"That's all right," Marty said. "Just put it in a couple of manila envelopes."

Surprised, Mrs. Higgens said, "Oh, but Mr. Stillwater, you've signed the withdrawal order, we ought to count it in front of you."

"No, I'm sure you've already counted correctly."

"But bank procedure—"

"I trust you, Mrs. Higgens."

"Well, thank you, but I really think—"

"Please."

6.

Merely by remaining seated at the room-service table while Drew Oslett stood impatiently beside it, Waxhill exerted control. Oslett disliked him and grudgingly admired him simultaneously.

"It's almost certain," Waxhill said, "that the wife and children saw Alfie in that second incident last night. They know very little about what's going on, but if they know Stillwater was telling the truth when he talked about a look-alike, then they know too much."

"I said, no problem," Oslett reminded him impatiently.

Waxhill nodded. "Yes, all right, but the home office wants it done in a certain way."

Sighing, Oslett gave up and sat down. "Which is?"

"Make it look as if Stillwater went off the deep end."

"Murder-suicide?"

"Yes, but not just any murder-suicide. The home office would be pleased if it could be made to appear as if Stillwater was acting out a particular psychopathic delusion."

"Whatever."

"The wife must be shot in each breast and in the mouth."

"And the daughters?"

"First, make them undress. Tie their wrists behind them. Tie their ankles together. Nice and tight. There's a particular brand of braided wire we'd like you to use. It'll be provided. Then shoot each girl twice. Once in her . . . private parts, then between the eyes. Stillwater must appear to have shot himself once through the roof of his mouth. Will you remember all of that?"

"Of course."

"It's important that you do everything precisely that way, no deviations from the script."

"What's the story we're trying to tell?" Oslett asked.

"Didn't you read the article in *People?*"

"Not all the way through," Oslett admitted. "Stillwater seemed like such a jerk—and a boring jerk, at that."

Waxhill said, "A few years ago, in Maryland, a man killed his wife and two daughters in exactly this fashion. He was a pillar of the community, so it shocked everybody. Tragic story. Everyone was left wondering why. It seemed so meaningless, so out of character. Stillwater was intrigued by the crime and considered writing a novel based on it, to explore the possible motivation behind it. But after he'd done a lot of research, he dropped the project. In *People*, he says it just depressed him too much. Says that fiction, his kind of fiction, needs to make sense of things, bring order to chaos, but he just couldn't find any meaning in what happened in Maryland."

Oslett sat in silence for a moment, trying to hate Waxhill but finding that his dislike for the man was fading rapidly. "I must say . . . this is very nice."

Waxhill smiled almost shyly and shrugged.

"This was your idea?" Oslett asked.

"Mine, yes. I proposed it to the home office, and they went for it right away."

"It's ingenious," Oslett said with genuine admiration.

"Thank you."

"Very neat. Martin Stillwater kills his family the same way the guy did in Maryland, and it looks as if the *real* reason he couldn't write a novel about the original case was because it struck too close to home, because it was what he secretly wanted to do to *his* family."

"Exactly."

"And it's been preying on his mind ever since."

"Haunts his dreams."

"This psychotic urge to symbolically rape—"

"—and literally kill—"

"—his daughters—"

"—kill his wife, too, the woman who—"

"—nurtured them," Oslett finished.

They were smiling at each other again, as they had smiled when discussing that lovely café off the Champs Elysées.

Waxhill said, "No one will ever be able to figure out what killing his family had to do with his crazy report of a look-alike intruder, but they'll figure the look-alike was somehow part of his delusion, too."

"I just realized, samples of Alfie's blood taken from the house in Mission Viejo are going to appear to be Stillwater's blood."

"Yes. Was he periodically exsanguinating himself, saving his own blood for the hoax? And why? A great many theories are sure to be put forth, and in the end it'll be a mystery of less interest than what he did to his family. No one will ever untangle the truth from all that."

Oslett was beginning to hope they might recover Alfie, salvage the Network, and keep their reputations intact after all.

Turning to Clocker, Waxhill said, "What about you, Karl? Do you have a problem with any of this?"

Though he was sitting at the table, Clocker appeared distant in spirit. He pulled his attention back to them as if his thoughts had been with the *Enterprise* crew on a hostile planet in the Crab nebula. "There are five billion people on earth," he said, "so we think it's crowded, but for every one of us, the universe contains countless thousands of stars, an *infinity* of stars for each of us."

Waxhill stared at Clocker, waiting for elucidation. When he realized that Clocker had nothing more to say, he turned to Oslett.

"I believe what Karl means," Oslett said, "is that . . . Well, in the vast scheme of things, what does it matter if a few people die a little sooner than they would have in the natural course of events?"

7.

The sun is high over the distant mountains, where the loftiest peaks are capped with snow. It seems odd to have a view of winter from this springlike December morning full of palm trees and flowers.

He drives south and east into Mission Viejo. He is vengeance on wheels. Justice on wheels. Rolling, rolling.

He considers locating a gun shop and buying a shotgun or hunting rifle, some weapon for which there is no waiting period prior to the right of purchase. His adversary is armed, but he is not.

However, he doesn't want to delay his pursuit of the kidnapper who has stolen his family. If the enemy is kept off balance and on the move, he is more likely to make mistakes. Unrelenting pressure is a better weapon than any gun.

Besides, he is vengeance, justice, and virtue. He is the hero of this movie, and heroes do not die. They can be shot, clubbed, run off the road in high-speed car chases, slashed with a knife, pushed from a cliff, locked in a dungeon filled with poisonous snakes, and endure an endlessly imaginative series of abuses without perishing. With Harrison Ford, Sylvester Stallone, Steven Seagal, Bruce Willis, Wesley Snipes, and so many other heroes, he shares the invincibility of virtue and high noble purpose.

He realizes why his initial assault on the false father, in his house yesterday, was doomed to fail in spite of his being a hero. He'd been drawn westward by the powerful attraction between him and his double; to the same degree that he had been aware of something pulling him, the double had been aware of something approaching all day Sunday and Monday. By the time they encountered each other in the upstairs study, the false father had been alerted and had prepared for battle.

Now he understands that he can initiate and terminate the connection between them at will. Like the electrical current in any household circuit, it can be controlled by an ON-OFF switch. Instead of leaving the switch in the ON position all the time, he can open the pathway for brief moments, just long enough to feel the pull of the false father and take a fix on him.

Logic suggests he also can modify the power flowing along the psychic wire. By imagining the psychic control is a dimmer switch—a rheostat—he should be able to adjust downward the amperage of the current in the circuit, making the contact more subtle than it has been to date. After all, by using a rheostatic switch, the light of a chandelier can be reduced smoothly by degrees until there is barely a visible glow. Likewise, imagining the psychic switch as another rheostat, he might be able to open the connection at such a low amperage that he can track the false father without that adversary being alerted to the fact he's being sought.

Stopping at a red traffic light in the heart of Mission Viejo, he imagines a dial-type dimmer switch with a three-hundred-sixty-degree brightness range. He turns it only ninety degrees, and at once feels the pull of the false father, slightly farther east and now somewhat to the north.

❊ ❊ ❊

Outside of the bank, halfway to the BMW, Marty suddenly felt another wave of pressure—and behind it, the crushing Juggernaut of his dreams. The sensation was not as strong as the experiences in the bank, but it caught him in mid-step and threw him off balance. He staggered, stumbled, and fell. The two manila envelopes full of cash flew out of his hands and slid across the blacktop.

Charlotte and Emily scampered after the envelopes, and Paige helped Marty to his feet.

As the wave passed and Marty stood shakily, he said, "Here, take my keys, you better drive. He's hunting me. He's coming."

She looked around the bank lot in panic.

Marty said, "No, he's not here yet. It's like before. This sense of being in the path of something very powerful and fast."

❊ ❊ ❊

Two blocks. Maybe not that far.

Driving slowly. Scanning the street ahead, left and right. Looking for them.

A car horn toots behind him. The driver is impatient.

Slow, slow, squinting left and right, checking people on the sidewalks as well as in passing cars.

The horn behind him. He gestures obscenely, which seems to spook the guy into silence.

Slow, slow.

No sight of them.

Try the mental rheostat again. A sixty-degree turn this time. Still a strong contact, an urgent and irresistible *pull*.

Ahead. On the left. Shopping center.

❋   ❋   ❋

As Marty got into the front passenger seat and shut the door, holding the envelopes of cash that the kids had retrieved for him, he was shaken again by contact with The Other. Although the impact of the probe was less disturbing than ever before, he took no solace from the diminishment of its power.

"Get us the hell out of here," he urged Paige, as he retrieved the loaded Beretta from under the seat.

Paige started the engine, and Marty turned to the kids. They were buckling their seatbelts.

As Paige slammed the BMW into reverse and backed out of the parking space, the girls met Marty's eyes. They were scared.

He had too much respect for their perceptiveness to lie to them. Rather than pretend everything was going to be all right, he said, "Hang on. Your Mom's gonna try to drive like I do."

Popping the car out of reverse, Paige asked, "Where's he coming from?"

"I don't know. Just don't go out the same way we came in. I feel uneasy about that. Use the other street."

❋   ❋   ❋

He is drawn to the bank rather than the shopping center itself, and he parks near the east entrance.

As he switches the engine off, he hears a brief shriek of tires. From the corner of his eye, he is aware of a car driving away fast from the south end of the building. Turning, he sees a white BMW eighty to a hundred feet away. It streaks toward the shopping center, past him in a flash.

He catches sight of only a portion of the driver's face—one cheekbone, jaw line, curve of chin. And a shimmer of golden hair.

Sometimes it's possible to identify a favorite song by only three notes, because the melody has left an indelible impression on the mind. Likewise, from that partial profile, glimpsed in a flicker of shadow and light, in a blur of motion, he recognizes his precious wife. Unknown people have eradicated his memories of her, but the photograph he discovered yesterday is imprinted on his heart.

He whispers, "Paige."

He starts the Camry, backs out of the parking space, and turns toward the shopping center.

Acres of blacktop are empty at that early hour, for only the supermarket, a doughnut shop, and an office-supply store are open for business. The BMW races across the parking lot, swinging wide of the few clusters of cars, to the service road that fronts the stores. It turns left and heads toward the north end of the center.

He follows but not aggressively. If he loses them, locating them again is an easy matter because of the mysterious but reliable link between him and the hateful man who has usurped his life.

The BMW reaches the north exit and turns right into the street. By the time he arrives at that same intersection, the BMW is already two blocks away, stopped at a red traffic signal and barely in sight.

For more than an hour, he follows them discreetly along surface streets, north on the Santa Ana and Costa Mesa freeways, then east on the Riverside Freeway, staying well back from them. Tucked in among the heavy morning commuter traffic, his small Camry is as good as invisible.

On the Riverside Freeway, west of Corona, he imagines switching on the psychic current between himself and the false father. He pictures the rheostat and turns it five degrees out of a possible three hundred and sixty. That is sufficient for him to sense the presence of the false father ahead in traffic, although it gives him no precise fix. Six degrees, seven, eight. Eight is too much. Seven. Seven is ideal. With the switch open only seven degrees, the attraction is powerful enough to serve as a beacon to him without alerting the enemy that the link has been re-established. In the BMW, the imposter rides east toward Riverside, tense and watchful but unaware of being monitored.

Yet, in the hunter's mind, the signal of the prey registers like a blinking red light on an electronic map.

Having mastered control of this strange adducent power, he may be able to strike at the false father with some degree of surprise.

Though the man in the BMW is expecting an attack and is on the run to avoid it, he's also accustomed to being forewarned of assault. When enough time passes without a disturbance in the ether, when he feels no unnerving probes, he'll regain confidence. With a return of confidence, his caution will diminish, and he'll become vulnerable.

The hunter needs only to stay on the trail, follow the spoor, bide his time, and wait for the ideal moment to strike.

As they pass through Riverside, morning traffic thins out around them. He drops back farther, until the BMW is a distant, colorless dot that sometimes vanishes temporarily, miragelike, in a shimmer of sunlight or swirl of dust.

Onward and north. Through San Bernardino. Onto Interstate 15. Into the northern end of the San Bernardino Mountains. Through the El Cajon Pass at forty-three hundred feet.

Soon thereafter, south of the town of Hesperia, the BMW departs the interstate and heads directly north on U.S. Highway 395, into the westernmost reaches of the forbidding Mojave Desert. He follows, continuing to remain at such a distance that they can't possibly realize the dark speck in their rearview mirror is the same car that has trailed them now through three counties.

Within a couple of miles, he passes a road sign indicating the mileage to Ridgecrest, Lone Pine, Bishop, and Mammoth Lakes. Mammoth is the farthest—two hundred and eighty-two miles.

The name of the town has an instant association for him. He has an eidetic memory. He can see the words on the dedication page of one of the mystery novels he has written and which he keeps on the shelves in his home office in Mission Viejo:

This opus is for my mother and father, Jim and Alice Stillwater, who taught me to be an honest man—and who can't be blamed if I am able to think like a criminal.

He recalls, as well, the Rolodex card with their names and address. They live in Mammoth Lakes.

Again, he is poignantly aware of what he has lost. Even if he can reclaim his life from the imposter who wears his name, perhaps he will never regain the memories that have been stolen from him. His childhood. His adolescence. His first date. His high school experiences. He has no recollection of his mother's or his father's love, and it seems outrageous, *monstrous,* that he could be robbed of those most essential and enduringly supportive memories.

For more than sixty miles, he alternates between despair at the estrangement which is the primary quality of his existence and joy at the prospect of reclaiming his destiny.

He desperately longs to be with his father, his mother, to see their dear faces (which have been erased from the tablets of his memory), to embrace them and re-establish the profound bond between himself and the two people to whom he owes his existence. From the movies he has seen, he knows parents can be a curse—the maniacal mother who was dead before the opening scene of *Psycho,* the selfish mother and father who warped poor Nick Nolte in *The Prince of Tides*—but he believes his parents to be of a finer variety, compassionate and true, like Jimmy Stewart and Donna Reed in *It's a Wonderful Life.*

The highway is flanked by dry lakes as white as salt, sudden battlements of red rock, wind-sculpted oceans of sand, scrub, boron flats, distant escarpments of dark stone. Everywhere lies evidence of geological upheavals and lava flows from distant millennia.

At the town of Red Mountain, the BMW leaves the highway. It stops at a service station to refuel.

He follows until he is certain of their intention, but passes the service station without stopping. They have guns. He does not. A better moment will be found to kill the impersonator.

Re-entering Highway 395, he drives north a short distance to Johannesburg, which sits west of the Lava Mountains. He exits again and tanks up the Camry at another service station. He buys crackers, candy bars, and peanuts from the vending machines to sustain him during the long drive ahead.

Perhaps because Charlotte and Emily had to use the restrooms back at the Red Mountain stop, he is on the highway ahead of the BMW, but that doesn't matter because he no longer needs to follow them. He knows where they are going.

Mammoth Lakes, California.

Jim and Alice Stillwater. Who taught him to be an honest man. Who can't be blamed if he is able to think like a criminal. To whom he dedicated a novel. Beloved. Cherished. Stolen from him but soon to be reclaimed.

He is eager to enlist them in his crusade to regain his family and his destiny. Perhaps the false father can deceive his children, and perhaps even Paige can be fooled into accepting the imposter as the real Martin Stillwater. But his parents will recognize their true son, blood of their blood, and will not be misled by the cunning mimicry of that family-stealing fraud.

Since turning onto Highway 395, where traffic is light, the BMW had maintained a steady sixty to sixty-five miles an hour, though the road made greater speed possible in many areas. Now, he pushes the Camry north at seventy-five and eighty. He should be able to reach Mammoth Lakes between two o'clock and two-fifteen, half an hour to forty-five minutes ahead of the imposter, which will give him time to alert his mother and father to the evil intentions of the creature that masquerades as their son.

The highway angles northwest across Indian Wells Valley, with the El Paso Mountains to the south. Mile by mile, his heart swells with emotion at the prospect of being reunited with his mom and dad, from whom he has been cruelly separated. He aches with the need to embrace them and bask in their love, their unquestioning love, their undying and perfect love.

8.

The Bell JetRanger executive helicopter that conveyed Oslett and Clocker to Mammoth Lakes belonged to a motion-picture studio that was a Network affiliate. With black calfskin seats, brass fixtures, and cabin walls plushly upholstered in emerald-green lizard skin, the ambiance was even more luxurious than in the passenger compartment of the Lear. The chopper also offered a more entertaining collection of reading matter than had been available in the jet, including that day's editions of *The Hollywood Reporter* and *Daily Variety* plus the most recent issues of *Premier, Rolling Stone, Mother Jones, Forbes, Fortune, GQ, Spy, The Ecological Watch Society Journal,* and *Bon Appétit.*

To occupy his time during the flight, Clocker produced another *Star Trek* novel, which he had purchased in the gift shop at the Ritz-Carlton Hotel before they checked out. Oslett was convinced that the spread of such fantastical literature into the tastefully appointed and elegantly managed shops of a five-star resort—formerly the kind of place that catered to the cultured and powerful, not merely the rich—was as alarming a sign of society's imminent collapse as could be found, on a par with heavily armed crack-cocaine dealers selling their wares in schoolyards.

As the JetRanger cruised north through Sequoia National Park, King's Canyon National Park, along the western flank of the Sierra Nevadas, and eventually directly into those magnificent mountains, Oslett kept moving from one side of the helicopter to the other, determined not to miss any of the stunning scenery. The vastnesses beneath him were so sparsely populated, they might have been expected to trigger his nearly agoraphobic aversion to open spaces and rural landscapes. But the terrain changed by the minute, presenting new marvels and ever-more-splendid vistas at a sufficiently swift pace to entertain him.

Furthermore, the JetRanger flew at a much lower altitude than the Lear, giving Oslett a sense of headlong forward motion. The interior of the helicopter was noisier and shaken by more vibrations than the passenger compartment of the jet, which he also liked.

Twice he called Clocker's attention to the natural wonders just beyond the windows. Both times the big man merely glanced at the scenery for a second or two, and then without comment returned his attention to *Six-Breasted Amazon Women of the Slime Planet.*

"What's so damned interesting in that book?" Oslett finally demanded, dropping into the seat directly opposite Clocker.

Finishing the paragraph he was reading before looking up, Clocker said, "I couldn't tell you."

"Why not?"

"Because even after I told you what I find interesting in this book, it wouldn't be interesting to you."

"What's that supposed to mean?"

Clocker shrugged. "I don't think you'd like it."

"I hate novels, always have, especially science fiction and crap like that."

"There you go."

"What's *that* supposed to mean?"

"Just that you've confirmed what I said—you don't like this sort of thing."

"Of course I don't."

Clocker shrugged again. "There you go."

Oslett glared at him. Gesturing at the book, he said, "How can you like that trash?"

"We exist in parallel universes," Clocker said.

"What?"

"In yours, Johannes Gutenberg invented the pinball machine."

"Who?"

"In yours, perhaps the most famous guy named Faulkner was a virtuoso on the banjo."

Scowling, Oslett said, "None of this crap is making any sense to me."

"There you go," Clocker said, and returned his attention to *Kirk and Spock in Love,* or whatever the epic was titled.

Oslett wanted to kill him. This time, in Karl Clocker's cryptic patter, he detected a subtly expressed but deeply felt disrespect. He wanted to snatch off the big man's stupid hat and set fire to it, duck feather and all, grab the paperback out of his hands and tear it to pieces, and pump maybe a thousand rounds of hollow-point 9mm ammo into him at extreme close range.

Instead, he turned to the window to be soothed by the majesty of mountain peaks and forests seen at a hundred and fifty miles an hour.

Above them, clouds were moving in from the northwest. Plump and gray, they settled like fleets of dirigibles toward the mountaintops.

❋   ❋   ❋

At 1:10 Tuesday afternoon, at an airfield outside of Mammoth Lakes, they were met by a Network representative named Alec Spicer. He was waiting on the blacktop near the concrete-block and corrugated-steel hangar where they set down.

Though he knew their real names and was, therefore, at least of a rank equal to Peter Waxhill's, he was not as impeccably attired, suave, or well-spoken as that gentleman who had briefed them over breakfast. And unlike the muscular Jim Lomax at John Wayne Airport in Orange County last night, he let them carry their own luggage to the green Ford Explorer that stood at their disposal in the parking area behind the hangar.

Spicer was about fifty years old, five feet ten, a hundred and sixty pounds, with brush-cut iron-gray hair. His face was all hard planes, and his eyes were hidden behind sunglasses even though the sky was overcast. He wore combat boots, khaki slacks, khaki shirt, and a battered leather flight jacket with numerous zippered pockets. His erect posture, disciplined manner, and clipped speech pegged him for a retired—perhaps cashiered—army officer who was unwilling to change the attitudes, habits, or wardrobe of a military careerist.

"You're not dressed properly for Mammoth," Spicer said sharply as

they walked to the Explorer, his breath streaming from his mouth in white plumes.

"I didn't realize it would be quite so cold here," Oslett said, shuddering uncontrollably.

"Sierra Nevadas," Spicer said. "Almost eight thousand feet above sea level where we stand. December. Can't expect palm trees, hula skirts, and piña coladas."

"I knew it would be cold, just not this cold."

"You'll freeze your ass off," Spicer said curtly.

"This jacket's warm," Oslett said defensively. "It's cashmere."

"Good for you," Spicer said.

He raised the hatch on the back of the Explorer and stood aside to let them load their luggage into the cargo space.

Spicer got behind the wheel. Oslett sat up front. In the back seat, Clocker resumed reading *The Flatulent Ferocity from Ganymede*.

Driving away from the airfield into town, Spicer was silent for a while. Then: "Expecting our first snow of the season later today."

"Winter's my favorite time of the year," Oslett said.

"Might not like it so much with snow up to your ass and those nice oxfords turning hard as a Dutchman's wooden shoes."

"Do you know who I am?" Oslett asked impatiently.

"Yes, sir," Spicer said, clipping his words even more than usual but inclining his head slightly in a subtle acknowledgment of his inferior position.

"Good," Oslett said.

In places, tall evergreens crowded both sides of the roadway. Many of the motels, restaurants, and roadside bars boasted ersatz alpine architecture, and in some cases their names incorporated words that called to mind images from movies as diverse as *The Sound of Music* and Clint Eastwood vehicles: Bavarian this, Swiss that, Eiger, Matterhorn, Geneva, Hofbrau.

Oslett said, "Where's the Stillwater house?"

"We're going to your motel."

"I understood there was a surveillance unit staking out the Stillwater house," Oslett persisted.

"Yes, sir. Across the street in a van with tinted windows."

"I want to join them."

"Not a good idea. This is a small town. Not even five thousand people,

when you don't count tourists. Lot of people going in and out of a parked van on a residential street—that's going to draw unwanted attention."

"Then what do you suggest?"

"Phone the surveillance team, let them know where to reach you. Then wait at the motel. The minute Martin Stillwater calls his folks or shows up at their door—you'll be notified."

"He hasn't called them yet?"

"Their phone's rung several times in the past few hours, but they aren't home to answer it, so we don't know if it's their son or not."

Oslett was incredulous. "They don't have an answering machine?"

"Pace of life up here doesn't exactly require one."

"Amazing. Well, if they're not at home, where are they?"

"They went shopping this morning, and not long ago they stopped for a late lunch at a restaurant out on Route 203. They should be home in another hour or so."

"They're being followed?"

"Of course."

In anticipation of the predicted storm, skiers were already arriving in town with loaded ski racks on their cars. Oslett saw a bumper sticker that read MY LIFE IS ALL DOWNHILL—AND I LOVE IT!

As they stopped at a red traffic light behind a station wagon that seemed to be stuffed full of enough young blond women in ski sweaters to populate half a dozen beer or lip-balm commercials, Spicer said, "Hear about the hooker in Kansas City?"

"Strangled," Oslett said. "But there's no proof our boy did it, even if someone resembling him did leave that lounge with her."

"Then you don't know the latest. Sperm sample arrived in New York. Been studied. It's our boy."

"They're sure?"

"Positive."

The tops of the mountains were disappearing into the lowering sky. The color of the clouds had deepened from the shade of abraded steel to a mottled ash-gray and cinder-black.

Oslett's mood grew darker as well.

The traffic signal changed to green.

Following the carful of blondes through the intersection, Alec Spicer said, "So he's fully capable of having sex."

"But he was engineered to be . . ." Oslett couldn't even finish the

sentence. He no longer had any faith in the work of the genetic engineers.

"So far," Spicer said, "through police contacts, the home office has compiled a list of fifteen homicides involving sexual assault that might be attributable to our boy. Unsolved cases. Young and attractive women. In cities he visited, at the times he was there. Similar M.O. in every case, including extreme violence *after* the victim was knocked unconscious, sometimes with a blow to the head but generally with a punch in the face . . . evidently to ensure silence during the actual killing."

"Fifteen," Oslett said numbly.

"Maybe more. Maybe a lot more." Spicer glanced away from the road and looked at Oslett. His eyes were not only unreadable but entirely hidden behind the heavily tinted sunglasses. "And we better hope to God he killed every woman he screwed."

"What do you mean?"

Looking at the road again, Spicer said, "He's got a high sperm count. And the sperm are active. He's fertile."

Though he couldn't have admitted it to himself until Spicer had said it aloud, Oslett had been aware this bad news was coming.

"You know what this means?" Spicer asked.

From the back seat, Clocker said, "The first operative Alpha-generation human clone is a renegade, mutating in ways we might not understand, and capable of infecting the human gene pool with genetic material that could spawn a new and thoroughly hostile race of nearly invulnerable super beings."

For a moment Oslett thought Clocker had read a line from his current *Star Trek* novel, then realized that he had succinctly summed up the nature of the crisis.

Spicer said, "If our boy didn't waste every bimbo he took a tumble with, if he made a few babies and for some reason they weren't aborted—even *one* baby—we're in deep shit. Not just the three of us, not just the Network, but the entire human race."

9.

Heading north through the Owens Valley, with the Inyo Mountains to the east and the towering Sierra Nevadas to the west, Marty found that the cellular phone would not always function as intended because the dramatic topography interfered with microwave transmissions. And on those occasions when he was able to place a call to his parents' house in Mammoth, their phone rang and rang without being answered.

After sixteen rings, he pushed the END button, terminating the call, and said, "Still not home."

His dad was sixty-six, his mom sixty-five. They had been schoolteachers, and both had retired last year. They were still young by modern standards, healthy and vigorous, in love with life, so it was no surprise they were out and about rather than spending the day at home in a couple of armchairs, watching television game shows and soap operas.

"How long are we staying with Grandma and Grandpa?" Charlotte asked from the back seat. "Long enough for her to teach me to play the guitar as good as she does? I'm getting pretty good on the piano, but I think I'd like the guitar, too, and if I'm going to be a famous musician, which I think I might be interested in being—I'm still keeping my options open—then it would be a lot easier to take my music with me everywhere, since you can't exactly carry a piano around on your back."

"We aren't staying with Grandma and Grandpa," Marty said. "In fact, we aren't even stopping there."

Charlotte and Emily groaned with disappointment.

Paige said, "We might visit them later, in a few days. We'll see. Right now we're going to the cabin."

"Yeah!" Emily said, and "All right!" Charlotte said.

Marty heard them smack their hands together in a high-five.

The cabin, which his mom and dad had owned since Marty was a boy, was nestled in the mountains a few miles outside of Mammoth Lakes, between the town and the lakes themselves, not far from the even smaller settlement of Lake Mary. It was a charming place, on which his father had done extensive work over the years, sheltered by hundred-foot pines and firs. To the girls, who had been raised in the suburban maze of Orange County, the cabin was as special as any enchanted cottage in a fairy tale.

Marty needed a few days to think before making any decisions about what to do next. He wanted to study the news and see how the story about him continued to be played; in the media's handling of it, he might be able to assess the power if not the identity of his true enemies, who certainly were not limited to the eerie and deranged look-alike who had invaded their home.

They could not stay at his parents' house. It was too accessible to reporters if the story continued to snowball. It was accessible, as well, to the unknown conspirators behind the look-alike, who had seen to it that a small news item about an assault had gotten major media coverage, painting him as a man of doubtful stability.

Besides, he didn't want to put his mom and dad at risk by taking shelter with them. In fact, when he managed to get a call through, he was going to insist they immediately pack up their motorhome and get out of Mammoth Lakes for a few weeks, a month, maybe longer. While they were traveling, changing campgrounds every night or two, no one could try to get at him through them.

Since the attempted contact at the bank in Mission Viejo, Marty had been subjected to no more of The Other's probes. He was hopeful that the haste and decisiveness with which they'd fled north had bought them safety. Even clairvoyance or telepathy—or whatever the hell it was—must have its limits. Otherwise, they were not merely up against a fantastic mental power but flat-out magic; while Marty could be driven, by experience, to credit the possibility of psychic ability, he simply could not believe in magic. Having put hundreds of miles between themselves and The Other, they were most likely beyond the range of his questing sixth sense. The mountains, which periodically interfered with the operation of the cellular telephone, might further insulate them from telepathic detection.

Perhaps it would have been safer to stay away from Mammoth Lakes and hide out in a town to which he had no connections. However, he opted for the cabin because even those who might target his parents' house as a possible refuge for him would not be aware of the mountain retreat and would be unlikely to learn of it casually. Besides, two of his former high school buddies had been Mammoth County deputy sheriffs for a decade, and the cabin was close to the town in which he had been raised and where he was still well known. As a hometown boy who had never been a hell-raiser in his youth, he could expect to be taken seriously by the authorities and given greater protection if The Other *did* try to contact him again. In a strange place, however, he would be an outsider and regarded with more suspicion even than Detective Cyrus Lowbock had exhibited. Around Mammoth Lakes, if worse came to worst, he would not feel so isolated and alienated as he was certain to be virtually anywhere else.

"Might be bad weather ahead," Paige said.

The sky was largely blue to the east, but masses of dark clouds were surging across the peaks and through the passes of the Sierra Nevadas to the west.

"Better stop at a service station in Bishop," Marty said, "find out if the Highway Patrol's requiring chains to go up into Mammoth."

Maybe he should have welcomed a heavy snowfall. It would further isolate the cabin and make them less accessible to whatever enemies were hunting them. But he felt only uneasiness at the prospect of a storm. If luck was not with them, the moment might come when they needed to get out of Mammoth Lakes in a hurry. Roads drifted shut by a blizzard could cause a delay long enough to be the death of them.

Charlotte and Emily wanted to play Look Who's the Monkey Now, a word game Marty had invented a couple of years ago to entertain them on long car trips. They had already played twice since leaving Mission Viejo. Paige declined to join them, pleading the need to focus her attention on driving, and Marty ended up being the monkey more frequently than usual because he was distracted by worry.

The higher reaches of the Sierras disappeared in mist. The clouds blackened steadily, as if the fires of the hidden sun were burning to extinction and leaving only charry ruin in the heavens.

10.

The motel owners referred to their establishment as a lodge. The buildings were embraced by the boughs of hundred-foot Douglas firs, smaller pines, and tamaracks. The design was studiedly rustic.

The rooms couldn't compare with those at the Ritz-Carlton, of course, and the interior designer's attempt to call to mind Bavaria with knotty-pine paneling and chunky wood-frame furniture was jejune, but Drew Oslett found the accommodations pleasant nonetheless. A sizable stone fireplace, in which logs and starter material already had been arranged, was especially appealing; within minutes of their arrival, a fire was blazing.

Alec Spicer telephoned the surveillance team stationed in a van across the street from the Stillwater house. In language every bit as cryptic as some of Clocker's statements, he informed them that Alfie's handlers were now in town and could be reached at the motel.

"Nothing new," Spicer said when he hung up the phone. "Jim and Alice

Stillwater aren't home yet. The son and his family haven't shown up, either, and there's no sign of our boy, of course."

Spicer turned on every light in the room and opened the drapes because he was still wearing his sunglasses, though he had taken off his leather flight jacket. Oslett suspected that Alec Spicer didn't remove his shades to have sex—and perhaps not even when he went to bed at night.

The three of them settled into swiveling barrel chairs around a herring-bone-pine dinette table off the compact kitchenette. The nearby mullioned window offered a view of the wooded slope behind the motel.

From a black leather briefcase, Spicer produced several items Oslett and Clocker would need to stage the murders of the Stillwater family in the fashion that the home office desired.

"Two coils of braided wire," he said, putting a pair of plastic-wrapped spools on the table. "Bind the daughters' wrists and ankles with it. Not loosely. Tight enough to hurt. That's how it was in the Maryland case."

"All right," Oslett said.

"Don't cut the wire," Spicer instructed. "After binding the wrists, run the same strand to the ankles. One spool for each girl. That's also like Maryland."

The next article produced from the briefcase was a pistol.

"It's a SIG nine-millimeter," Spicer said. "Designed by the Swiss maker but actually manufactured by Sauer in Germany. A very good piece."

Accepting the SIG, Oslett said, "This is what we do the wife and kids with?"

Spicer nodded. "Then Stillwater himself."

Oslett familiarized himself with the gun while Spicer withdrew a box of 9mm ammunition from the briefcase. "Is this the same weapon the father used in Maryland?"

"Exactly," Spicer said. "Records will show it was bought by Martin Stillwater three weeks ago at the same gun shop where he's purchased other weapons. There's a clerk who's been paid to remember selling it to him."

"Very nice."

"The box this gun came in and the sales receipt have already been planted in the back of one of the desk drawers in Stillwater's home office, down in the house in Mission Viejo."

Smiling, filled with genuine admiration, beginning to believe they were going to salvage the Network, Oslett said, "Superb attention to detail."

"Always," Spicer said.

The Machiavellian complexity of the plan delighted Oslett the way Wile E. Coyote's elaborate schemes in Road Runner cartoons had thrilled him as a child—except that, in *this* case, the coyotes were the inevitable winners. He glanced at Karl Clocker, expecting him to be likewise enthralled.

The Trekker was cleaning under his fingernails with the blade of a penknife. His expression was somber. From every indication, his mind was at least four parsecs and two dimensions from Mammoth Lakes, California.

From the briefcase, Spicer produced a Ziploc plastic bag that contained a folded sheet of paper. "This is a suicide note. Forged. But so well done, any graphologist would be convinced it was written by Stillwater's own hand."

"What's it say?" Oslett asked.

Quoting from memory, Spicer said, " 'There's a worm. Burrowing inside. All of us contaminated. Enslaved. Parasites within. Can't live this way. Can't live.' "

"That's from the Maryland case?" Oslett asked.

"Word for word."

"The guy was creepy."

"Won't argue with you on that."

"We leave it by the body?"

"Yeah. Handle it only with gloves. And press Stillwater's fingers all over it after you've killed him. The paper's got a hard, smooth finish. Should take prints well."

Spicer reached into the briefcase once more and withdrew another Ziploc bag containing a black pen.

"Pentel Rolling Writer," Spicer said. "Taken from a box of them in a drawer of Stillwater's desk."

"This is what the suicide note was written with?"

"Yeah. Leave it somewhere in the vicinity of his body, with the cap off."

Smiling, Oslett reviewed the array of items on the table. "This is really going to be fun."

❊   ❊   ❊

While they waited for an alert from the surveillance team that was staking out the elder Stillwater's house, Oslett risked a walk to a ski shop in a cluster of stores and restaurants across the street from the motel. The air seemed to have grown more bitter in the short time they had been in the room, and the sky looked bruised.

The merchandise in the shop was first-rate. He was quickly able to outfit himself in well-made thermal underwear imported from Sweden and a black Hard Corps Gore-Tex/Thermolite storm suit. The suit had a reflective silver lining, foldaway hood, anatomically shaped knees, ballistic nylon scuff guards, insulated snowcuffs with rubberized strippers, and enough pockets to satisfy a magician. Over this he wore a purple U.S. Freestyle Team vest with Thermoloft insulation, reflective lining, elasticized gussets, and reinforced shoulders. He bought gloves too—Italian leather and nylon, almost as flexible as a second skin. He considered buying high-quality goggles but decided to settle for a good pair of sunglasses, since he wasn't actually intending to hit the slopes. His awesome ski boots looked like something a robot Terminator would wear to kick his way through concrete-block walls.

He felt incredibly tough.

As it was necessary to try on every item of clothing, he used the opportunity to change out of the clothes in which he'd entered the shop. The clerk obligingly folded the garments into a shopping bag, which Oslett carried with him when he set out on the return walk to the motel in his new gear.

By the minute, he was more optimistic about their prospects. Nothing lifted the spirits like a shopping spree.

When he returned to the room, though he had been gone half an hour, there had been no news.

Spicer was sitting in an armchair, still wearing sunglasses, watching a talk show. A heavyset black woman with big hair was interviewing four male cross-dressers who had attempted to enlist, as women, in the United States Marine Corps, and had been rejected, though they seemed to believe the President intended to intervene on their behalf.

Clocker, of course, was sitting at the table by the window, in the fall of silvery pre-storm light, reading *Huckleberry Kirk and the Oozing Whores of Alpha Centauri,* or whatever the damn book was called. His only concession to the Sierra weather had been to change from a harlequin-pattern sweater-vest into a fully sleeved cashmere sweater in a stomach-curdling shade of orange.

Oslett carried the black briefcase into one of the two bedrooms that flanked the living room. He emptied the contents on one of the queen-size beds, sat cross-legged on the mattress, took off his new sunglasses, and examined the clever props that would ensure Martin Stillwater's postmortem conviction of multiple murder and suicide.

He had a number of problems to work out, including how to kill all these people with the least amount of noise. He wasn't concerned about the gunfire, which could be muffled one way or another. It was the screaming that worried him. Depending on where the hit went down, there might be neighbors. If alerted, neighbors would call the police.

After a couple of minutes, he put on his sunglasses and went out to the living room. He interrupted Spicer's television viewing: "We waste them, then what police agency's going to be dealing with it?"

"If it happens here," Spicer said, "probably the Mammoth County Sheriff's Department."

"Do we have a friend there?"

"Not now, but I'm sure we could have."

"Coroner?"

"Out here in the boondocks—probably just a local mortician."

"No special forensic skills?"

Spicer said, "He'll know a bullet hole from an asshole, but that's about it."

"So if we terminated the wife and Stillwater first, nobody's going to be sophisticated enough to detect the order of homicides?"

"Big-city forensic lab would have a hard time doing that if the difference was, say, less than an hour."

Oslett said, "What I'm thinking is . . . if we try to deal with the kids first, we'll have a problem with Stillwater and his wife."

"How so?"

"Either Clocker or I can cover the parents while the other one takes the kids into a different room. But stripping the girls, wiring their hands and ankles—it'll take ten, fifteen minutes to do right, like in Maryland. Even with one of us covering Stillwater and his wife with a gun, they aren't going to sit still for that. They'll both rush me or Clocker, whoever's guarding them, and together they might get the upper hand."

"I doubt it," Spicer said.

"How can you be sure?"

"People are gutless these days."

"Stillwater fought off Alfie."

"True," Spicer admitted.

"When she was sixteen, the wife found her father and mother dead. The old man killed the mother, then himself—"

Spicer smiled. "Nice tie-in with our scenario."

Oslett hadn't thought about that. "Good point. Might also explain why Stillwater couldn't write the novel based on the case in Maryland. Anyway, three months later she petitioned the court to free her from her guardian and declare her a legal adult."

"Tough bitch."

"The court agreed. It granted her petition."

"So blow away the parents first," Spicer advised, shifting in the armchair as if his butt had begun to go numb.

"That's what we'll do," Oslett agreed.

Spicer said, "This is fucking crazy."

For a moment Oslett thought Spicer was commenting on their plans for the Stillwaters. But he was referring to the television program, to which his attention drifted again.

On the talk show, the host with big hair had ushered off the crossdressers and introduced a new group of guests. There were four angry-looking women seated on the stage. All of them were wearing strange hats.

As Oslett left the room, he saw Clocker out of the corner of his eye. The Trekker was still at the table by the window, riveted by the book, but Oslett refused to let the big man spoil his mood.

In the bedroom he sat on the bed again, amidst his toys, took off his sunglasses, and happily enacted and re-enacted the homicides in his mind, planning for every contingency.

Outside, the wind picked up. It sounded like wolves.

11.

He stops at a service station to ask directions to the address he remembers from the Rolodex card. The young attendant is able to help him.

By 2:10 he enters the neighborhood in which he was evidently raised. The lots are large with numerous winter-bare birches and a wide variety of evergreens.

His mom and dad's house is in the middle of the block. It's a modest, two-story, white clapboard structure with forest-green shutters. The deep front porch has heavy white balusters, a green handrail, and decoratively scalloped fasciae along the eaves.

The place looks warm and welcoming. It is like a house in an old movie. Jimmy Stewart might live here. You know at a glance that a loving family resides within, decent people with much to share, much to give.

He cannot remember anything in the block, least of all the house in which he apparently spent his childhood and adolescence. It might as well be the residence of utter strangers in a town which he has never seen until this very day.

He is infuriated by the extent to which he has been brainwashed and relieved of precious memories. The lost years haunt him. The total separation from those he loves is so cruel and devastating that he finds himself on the verge of tears.

However, he suppresses his anger and grief. He cannot afford to be emotional while his situation remains precarious.

The only thing he *does* recognize in the neighborhood is a van parked across the street from his parents' house. He has never seen this particular van, but he knows the type. The sight of it alarms him.

It is a recreational vehicle. Candy-apple red. An extended wheel-base provides a roomier interior. Oval camper dome on the roof. Large mud flaps with chrome letters: FUN TRUCK. The rear bumper is papered with overlapping rectangular, round, and triangular stickers memorializing visits to Yosemite National Park, Yellowstone, the annual Calgary Rodeo, Las Vegas, Boulder Dam, and other tourist attractions. Decorative, parallel green and black stripes undulate along the side, interrupted by a pair of mirrored view windows.

Perhaps the van is only what it appears to be, but at first sight he's convinced it's a surveillance post. For one thing, it seems too *aggressively* recreational, flamboyant. With his training in surveillance techniques, he knows that sometimes such vans seek to declare their harmlessness by calling attention to themselves, because potential subjects of surveillance expect a stakeout vehicle to be discreet and would never imagine they were being watched from, say, a circus wagon. Then there's the matter of the mirrored windows on the side, which allow the people within to see without being seen, providing privacy that any vacationer might prefer but that is also ideal for undercover operatives.

He does not slow as he approaches his parents' house, and he strives to show no interest in either the residence or the candy-apple red van. Scratching his forehead with his right hand, he also manages to cover his face as he passes those reflective view windows.

The occupants of the van, if any, must be employed by the unknown people who manipulated him so ruthlessly until Kansas City. They are a link to his mysterious superiors. He is as interested in them as in re-establishing contact with his beloved mother and father.

Two blocks later, he turns right at the corner and heads back toward a shopping area near the center of town, where earlier he passed a sporting-goods store. Lacking a firearm and, in any event, unable to buy one with a silencer, he needs to obtain a couple of simple weapons.

❆   ❆   ❆

At 2:20, the motel-room telephone rang.

Oslett put on his sunglasses, hopped off the bed, and went to the living-room doorway.

Spicer answered the phone, listened, mumbled a word that might have been "good," and hung up. Turning to Oslett, he said, "Jim and Alice Stillwater just came home from lunch."

"Let's hope Marty gives them a ring now."

"He will," Spicer said confidently.

Looking up from his book at last, Clocker said, "Speaking of lunch, we're overdue."

"The refrigerator in the kitchenette is loaded with stuff from the deli," Spicer said. "Cold cuts, potato salad, macaroni salad, cheesecake. We won't starve."

"Nothing for me," Oslett said. He was too excited to eat.

❆   ❆   ❆

By the time he returns to the neighborhood where his parents live, it is 2:45, half an hour after he left. He is acutely aware of the minutes ticking away. The false father, Paige, and the kids could arrive at any time. Even if they made another bathroom stop after Red Mountain or haven't maintained quite as high a speed as when he'd been following them, they are virtually certain to arrive in no more than fifteen or twenty minutes.

He desperately wants to see his parents before the treacherous imposter gets to them. He needs to prepare them for what has happened and enlist their aid in his battle to reclaim his wife and daughters. He is uneasy about the pretender getting to them first. If that creature could insinuate itself so thoroughly with Paige, Charlotte, and Emily, perhaps there is a risk, however small, that it will win over Mom and Dad as well.

When he turns the corner onto the block where he spent his unremembered childhood, he is no longer driving the Camry that he stole in Laguna Hills at dawn. He is in a florist's delivery van, a lucky acquisition he made by force after leaving the sporting-goods store.

He has accomplished a great deal in half an hour. Nevertheless, time is running out.

Though the day is increasingly dreary, he drives with the sun visor down. He is wearing a baseball cap pulled low on his forehead and a fleece-lined varsity jacket that belong to the young man who actually delivers for Murchison's Flowers. Masked by the sun visor and the cap, he will be unidentifiable to anyone observing him behind the wheel.

He pulls to the curb and parks directly behind the recreational van in which he suspects a stakeout team is ensconced. He gets out of his own vehicle and walks quickly to the back of it, giving them no time to observe him.

It has a single rear door. The hinges need lubrication; they squeak.

The dead deliveryman is lying on his back on the floor of the cargo hold. His hands are folded on his chest, and he is surrounded by flowers, as if he is already embalmed and available for viewing by mourners.

From a plastic bag beside the cadaver, he removes the ice axe that he purchased from an extensive display of climbing gear in the sporting-goods store. The one-piece steel tool has a rubber grip around the handle. One head on the business end is the shape and the size of a tack hammer, while the other head is wickedly pointed. He tucks the handle under the waistband of his jeans.

From the same plastic bag he removes an aerosol can of deicing chemical. If sprayed on existing ice, it will melt through in swift order. If applied to car glass, locks, and windshield wipers prior to a freeze, it is guaranteed to prevent an ice build-up. At least that is what the label promises. He doesn't really care whether it works for its intended purpose or not.

He removes the cap from this pressurized can, exposing the nozzle. There are two settings: SPRAY and STREAM. He sets it on STREAM, then slips it into one pocket of his varsity jacket.

Between the legs of the corpse is a huge arrangement of roses, carnations, delicate baby's breath, and ferns in a celadon container. He slides it out of the van and, holding it in both hands, pushes the door shut with one shoulder.

Carrying the arrangement in an entirely natural fashion that nonetheless shields his face from the observers in the red van, he walks to the door of the house in front of which both vehicles are parked. The flowers are not meant for anyone at this address. He hopes no one is home. If someone answers the door, he will pretend to discover that he has the wrong house, so he can return to the street with the arrangement still held in front of him.

He is in luck. No one responds to the doorbell. He rings it several times and, through body language, exhibits impatience.

He turns away from the door. He follows the front walk to the street.

Looking through the spray of flowers and greenery that he holds in front of himself, he sees this side of the red van also sports two mirrored windows on the rear compartment. Considering how deserted and quiet the street is, he knows they are watching him, for want of anything better to do.

That's okay. He's just a florist's frustrated deliveryman. They will see no reason to fear him. Better that they watch him, dismiss him, and turn their attention again to the white clapboard house.

He angles past the side of the surveillance vehicle. However, instead of following the cracked and hoved sidewalk to the back of the florist's van, he steps off the curb in front of it and behind the red "fun truck."

There is a smaller mirrored porthole in the back door of the surveillance vehicle, and in case they are still watching, he fakes an accident. He stumbles, lets the arrangement slip out of his hands, and sputters in anger as it smashes to ruin on the blacktop. "Oh, shit! Son of a bitch. Nice, real nice. Damn it, damn it, damn it."

Even as the expletives are flying from him, he's dropping below the rear porthole and pulling the can of deicing chemical out of his jacket pocket. With his left hand, he grasps the door handle.

If the door is locked, he will have revealed his intentions by the attempt to open it. Failing, he will be in deep trouble because they will probably have guns.

They have no reason to expect an attack, however, and he assumes the door will be unlocked. He assumes correctly. The lever handle moves smoothly.

He does not check to see if anyone has come out on the street and is watching him. Looking over his shoulder would only make him appear more suspicious.

He jerks the door open. Clambering up into the comparatively dark interior of the van, before he is sure anyone's inside, he jams his index finger down on the nozzle of the aerosol can, sweeping it back and forth.

A lot of electronic equipment fills the vehicle. Dimly lit control boards. Two swivel chairs bolted to the floor. Two men on the surveillance team.

The nearest man appears to have gotten out of his chair and turned to the rear door a split second ago, intending to look through the porthole. He is startled as it flies open.

The thick stream of deicing chemical splashes across his face, blinding him. He inhales it, burning his throat, lungs. His breath is choked off before he can cry out.

Blur of motion now. Like a machine. Programmed. In high gear.

Ice axe. Freed from his waistband. Smooth, powerful arc. Swung with great force. To the right temple. A crunch. The guy drops hard. Jerk the weapon loose.

Second man. Second chair. Wearing earphones. Sitting at a bank of equipment behind the cab, his back to the door. Headset muffles his partner's wheezing. Senses commotion. Feels the van rock when first operative goes down. Swivels around. Surprised, reaching too late for gun in shoulder holster. Makeshift Mace showers his face.

Move, move, confront, challenge, grapple, and prevail.

First man on the floor, spasming helplessly. Step on him, over him, keep moving, moving, a blur, straight at the second man.

Axe. Again. Axe. Axe.

Silence. Stillness.

The body on the floor is no longer spasming.

That went nicely. No screams, no shouts, no gunfire.

He knows he is a hero, and the hero always wins. Nevertheless, it's a relief when triumph is achieved rather than just anticipated.

He is more relaxed than he has been all day.

Returning to the rear door, he leans out and looks around the street. No one is in sight. Everything is quiet.

He pulls the door shut, drops the ice axe on the floor, and regards the dead men with gratitude. He feels so close to them because of what they have shared. "Thank you," he says tenderly.

He searches both bodies. Although they have identification in their wallets, he assumes it's phony. He finds nothing of interest except seventy-six dollars in cash, which he takes.

A quick examination of the van turns up no files, notebooks, memo pads, or other papers that might identify the organization that owns the vehicle. They run a tight, clean operation.

A shoulder holster and revolver hang from the back of the chair in which the first operative had been sitting. It's a Smith & Wesson .38 Chief's Special.

He strips out of his varsity jacket, puts on the holster over his cranberry sweater, adjusts it until he is comfortable, and dons the jacket once more. He draws the revolver and breaks open the cylinder. Case heads gleam. Fully loaded. He snaps the cylinder shut and holsters the weapon again.

The dead man on the floor has a leather pouch on his belt. It contains two speedloaders.

He takes this and affixes it to his own belt, which gives him more ammunition than he should need merely to deal with the false father. However, his faceless superiors seem to have caught up with him, and he cannot guess what troubles he may encounter before he has regained his name, his family, and the life stolen from him.

The second dead man, slumped in his chair, chin on his chest, never managed to draw the gun he was reaching for. It remains in the holster.

He removes it. Another Chief's Special. Because of the short barrel, it fits in the relatively roomy pocket of the varsity jacket.

Acutely aware that he is running out of time, he leaves the van and closes the door behind him.

The first snowflakes of the storm spiral out of the northwest sky on a chill breeze. They are few in number, at first, but large and lacy.

As he crosses the street toward the white clapboard house with green shutters, he sticks out his tongue to catch some of the flakes. He probably had done the same thing when, as a boy living on this street, he had delighted in the first snow of the season.

He has no memories of snowmen, snowball battles with other kids, or sledding. Though he must have done those things, they have been expunged along with so much else, and he has been denied the sweet joy of nostalgic recollection.

A flagstone walkway traverses the winter-brown front lawn.

He climbs three steps and crosses the deep porch.

At the door, he is paralyzed by fear. His past lies on the other side of this threshold. The future as well. Since his sudden self-awareness and desperate break for freedom, he has come so far. This may be the most important moment of his campaign for justice. The turning point. Parents can be staunch allies in times of trouble. Their faith. Their trust. Their undying love. He is afraid he will do something, on the brink of success, to alienate them and destroy his chances for regaining his life. So much is at stake if he dares to ring the bell.

Daunted, he turns to look at the street and is enchanted by the scene, for snow is falling much faster than when he approached the house. The flakes are still huge and fluffy, millions of them, whirling in the mild northwest wind. They are so intensely white that they seem luminous, each lacy crystalline form filled with a soft inner light, and the day is no longer dreary. The world is so silent and serene—two qualities rare in his experience—that it no longer seems quite real, either, as if he has been transported by some magic spell into one of those glass globes that contain a diorama of a quaint winter scene and that will fill with an eternal flaky torrent as long as it is periodically shaken.

That fantasy is appealing. A part of him yearns for the stasis of a world under glass, a benign prison, timeless and unchanging, at peace, clean, without fear and struggle, without loss, where the heart is never troubled.

Beautiful, beautiful, the falling snow, whitening the sky before the land below, an effervescence in the air. It's so lovely, touches him so profoundly, that tears brim in his eyes.

He is keenly sensitive. Sometimes the most mundane experiences are so poignant. Sensitivity can be a curse in an abrasive world.

Summoning all his courage, he turns again to the house. He rings the bell, waits only a few seconds, and rings it again.

His mother opens the door.

He has no memory of her, but he knows intuitively that this is the woman who gave him life. Her face is slightly plump, relatively unlined for her age, and the very essence of kindness. His features are an echo of hers. She has the same shade of blue eyes that he sees when he looks into a mirror, though her eyes seem, to him, to be windows on a soul far purer than his own.

"Marty!" she says with surprise and a quick warm smile, opening her arms to him.

Touched by her instant acceptance, he crosses the threshold, into her embrace, and holds fast to her as if to let go would be to drown.

"Honey, what is it? What's wrong?" she asks.

Only then does he realize that he is sobbing. He is so moved by her love, so *grateful* to have found a place where he belongs and is welcome, that he cannot control his emotions.

He presses his face into her white hair, which smells faintly of shampoo. She seems so warm, warmer than other people, and he wonders if that is how a mother always feels.

She calls to his father: "Jim! Jim, come here quick!"

He tries to speak, tries to tell her that he loves her, but his voice breaks before he can form a single word.

Then his father appears in the hallway, hurrying toward them.

Distorting tears can't prevent his recognition of his dad. They resemble each other to a greater extent than do he and his mother.

"Marty, son, what's happened?"

He trades one embrace for the other, inexpressibly thankful for his father's open arms, lonely no more, living now in a world under glass, appreciated and loved, loved.

"Where's Paige?" his mother asks, looking through the open door into the snow-filled day. "Where are the girls?"

"We were having lunch at the diner," his father says, "and Janey Torreson said you were on the news, something about you shot someone but maybe it's a hoax. Didn't make any sense."

He is still choked with emotion, unable to reply.

His father says, "We tried to call you as soon as we walked in the door, but we got the answering machine, so I left a message."

Again his mother asks about Paige, Charlotte, Emily.

He must gain control of himself because the false father might arrive at any minute. "Mom, Dad, we're in bad trouble," he tells them. "You've got to help us, please, my God, you've got to help."

His mother closes the door on the cold December air, and they lead him into the living room, one on each side of him, surrounding him with their love, touching him, their faces filled with concern and compassion. He is home. He is finally home.

He does not remember the living room any more than he remembers his mother, his father, or the snows of his youth. The pegged-oak floor is more than half covered by a Persian-style carpet in shades of peach and green. The furniture is upholstered in a teal fabric, and visible wood is a dark red-brown cherry. On the mantel, flanked by a pair of vases on which are depicted Chinese temple scenes, a clock ticks solemnly.

As she leads him to the sofa, his mother says, "Honey, whose jacket are you wearing?"

"Mine," he says.

"But that's the *new* style varsity jacket."

"Are Paige and the kids all right?" Dad asks.

"Yes, they're okay, they haven't been hurt," he says.

Fingering the jacket, his mother says, "The school only adopted this style two years ago."

"It's mine," he repeats. He takes off the baseball cap before she can notice that it is slightly too large for him.

On one wall is an arrangement of photographs of him, Paige, Charlotte, and Emily at different ages. He averts his eyes from that gallery, for it affects him too deeply and threatens to wring more tears from him.

He must recover and maintain control of his emotions in order to convey the essentials of this complex and mysterious situation to his parents. The three of them have little time to devise a plan of action before the imposter arrives.

His mother sits beside him on the sofa. She holds his right hand in both of hers, squeezing gently, encouragingly.

To his left, his father perches on the edge of an armchair, leaning forward, attentive, frowning with worry.

He has so much to tell them and does not know where to begin. He hesitates. For a moment he is afraid he'll never find the right first word, fall mute, oppressed by a psychological block even worse than the one that afflicted him when he sat at the computer in his office and attempted to write the first sentence of a new novel.

When he suddenly begins to talk, however, the words gush from him as storm waters might explode through a bursting barricade. "A man, there's a man, he looks like me, *exactly* like me, even I can't see any difference, and he's stolen my life. Paige and the girls think he's me, but he's not me, I don't know who he is or how he fools Paige. He took my memories, left me with nothing, and I just don't know how, don't know how, how he managed to steal so much from me and leave me so empty."

His father appears startled, and well might he *be* startled by these terrifying revelations. But there's something wrong with Dad's startlement, some subtle quality that eludes definition.

Mom's hands tighten on his right hand in a way that seems more reflexive than conscious. He dares not look at her.

He hurries on, aware that they are confused, eager to make them understand. "Talks like me, moves and stands like me, seems to *be* me, so I've thought hard about it, trying to understand who he could be, where he could've come from, and I keep going back to the same explanation, even if it seems incredible, but it must be like in the movies, you know, like with Kevin McCarthy, or Donald Sutherland in the remake, *Invasion of the Body Snatchers,* something not human, not of this world, something that can *imitate* us perfectly and bleed away our memories, *become* us, except somehow he failed to kill me and get rid of my body after he took what was in my mind."

Breathless, he pauses.

For a moment, neither of his parents speak.

A look passes between them. He does not like that look. He does not like it at all.

"Marty," Dad says, "maybe you better go back to the beginning, slow down, tell us exactly what's happened, step by step."

"I'm trying to tell you," he says exasperatedly. "I know it's incredible, hard to believe, but I *am* telling you, Dad."

"I want to help you, Marty. I want to believe. So just calm down, tell me everything from the beginning, give me a chance to understand."

"We don't have much time. Don't you understand? Paige and the girls are coming here with this . . . this creature, this inhuman thing. I've got to get them away from it. With your help I've got to kill it somehow and get my family back before it's too late."

His mother is pale, biting her lip. Her eyes blur with nascent tears. Her hands have closed so tightly over his that she is almost hurting him. He dares to hope that she grasps the urgency and dire nature of the threat.

He says, "It'll be all right, Mom. Somehow we'll handle it. Together, we have a chance."

He glances at the front windows. He expects to see the BMW arriving in the snowy street, pulling into the driveway. Not yet. They still have time, perhaps only minutes, seconds, but time.

Dad clears his throat and says, "Marty, I don't know what's happening here—"

"I *told* you what's happening!" he shouts. "Damn it, Dad, you don't know what I've been going through." Tears well up again, and he struggles to repress them. "I've been in such pain, I've been so afraid, for as long as I can remember, so afraid and alone and trying to understand."

His father reaches out, puts a hand on his knee. Dad is troubled but not in a way that he should be. He isn't visibly angry that some alien entity has stolen his son's life, isn't as frightened as he ought to be by the news that an inhuman presence now walks the earth, passing for human. Rather, he seems merely worried and . . . sad. There is an unmistakable and inappropriate sadness in his face and voice. "You're not alone, son. We're always here for you. Surely you know that."

"We'll stand beside you," Mom says. "We'll get you whatever help you need."

"If Paige is coming, like you say," his father adds, "we'll sit down together when she gets here, talk this out, try to understand what's happening."

Their voices are vaguely patronizing, as if they are talking to an intelligent and perceptive child but a child nonetheless.

"Shut up! Just shut up!" He pulls his hand free of his mother's grasp and leaps up from the sofa, shaking with frustration.

The window. Falling snow. The street. No BMW. But soon.

He turns away from the window, faces his parents.

His mother sits on the edge of the sofa, her face buried in her hands, shoulders hunched, in a posture of grief or despair.

He needs to make them understand. He is *consumed* by that need and frustrated by his inability to get even the fundamentals of the situation across to them.

His father rises from the chair. Stands indecisively. Arms at his sides. "Marty, you came to us for help, and we want to help, God knows we do, but we can't help if you won't let us."

Lowering her hands from her face, with tears on her cheeks now, his mother says, "Please, Marty. *Please.*"

"Everyone makes mistakes now and then," his father says.

"If it's drugs," his mother says, through tears, speaking as much to his father as to him, "we can cope with that, honey, we can handle that, we can find treatment for that."

His glass-encased world—beautiful, peaceful, timeless—in which he's been living during the precious minutes since his mother opened her arms to him at the front door, now abruptly fractures. An ugly, jagged crack scars the smooth curve of crystal. The sweet, clean atmosphere of that brief paradise escapes with a *whoosh,* admitting the poisonous air of the hateful world in which existence requires an unending struggle against hopelessness, loneliness, rejection.

"Don't do this to me," he pleads. "Don't betray me. How can you do this to me? How can you turn against me? I am your child." Frustration turns to anger. "Your only child." Anger turns to hatred. "I need. I *need.* Can't you see?" He is trembling with rage. "Don't you care? Are you heartless? How can you be so awful to me, so cruel? How could you let it come to this?"

12.

At a service station in Bishop, they stopped long enough to buy snow chains and to pay extra to have them buckled to the wheels of the BMW. The California Highway Patrol was recommending but not yet requiring that all vehicles heading into the Sierra Nevadas be equipped with chains.

Route 395 became a divided highway west of Bishop, and in spite of the dramatically rising elevation, they made good time past Rovanna and Crowley Lake, past McGee Creek and Convict Lake, exiting 395 onto Route 203 slightly south of Casa Diablo Hot Springs.

Casa Diablo. House of the Devil.

The meaning of the name had never impinged upon Marty before.

Now everything was an omen.

Snow began falling before they reached Mammoth Lakes.

The fat flakes were almost as loosely woven as cheap lace. They fell in such plenitude that it seemed more than half the volume of the air between land and sky was occupied by snow. It immediately began to stick, trimming the landscape in faux ermine.

Paige drove through Mammoth Lakes without stopping and turned south toward Lake Mary. In the back seat, Charlotte and Emily were so entranced by the snowfall that, for the time being, they did not need to be entertained.

East of the mountains, the sky had been gray-black and churning. Here, in the wintry heart of the Sierras, it was like a Cyclopean eye sheathed in a milky cataract.

The turn-off from Route 203 was marked by a copse of pines in which the tallest specimen bore scars from a decade-old lightning strike. The bolt had not merely damaged the pine but had encouraged it into mutant patterns of growth, until it had become a gnarled and malignant tower.

The snowflakes were smaller than before, falling harder, driven by the northwest wind. After a playful debut, the storm was turning serious.

Cutting through mountain meadows and forests—increasingly more of the latter and fewer of the former—the upsloping road eventually passed a chain-link encircled property of over a hundred acres on the right. This plot had been purchased eleven years ago by the Prophetic Church of the Rapture, a cult that had followed the teachings of the Reverend Jonathan Caine and had believed that the faithful would soon be levitated from the earth, leaving only the unbaptized and truly wicked to endure a thousand years of grueling war and hell on earth before final Judgment came to pass.

As it turned out, Caine had been a child molester who videotaped his abuse of cult members' children. He had gone to prison, his two thousand followers had dispersed on the winds of disillusionment and betrayal, and the property with all its buildings had been tied up by litigation for almost five years.

Some fantasies were destructive.

The chain-link fence, topped with coils of dangerous razor wire, was broken down in places. In the distance the spire of their church soared high above the trees. Beneath it were the sloped roofs of a warren of buildings in which the faithful had slept, taken their meals, and waited to be lifted heavenward by the right hand of the Lord Almighty. The spire stood untouched. But the buildings under it were missing many doors and windows, home to rats and possums and raccoons, shorn of glory and hairy with decay. Sometimes the vandals had been human. But wind and ice and snow had done the better part of the damage, as if God, through weather warped to His whim, had passed a judgment on the Church of the Rapture that He had not yet been ready to pass on the rest of humankind.

The cabin was also to the right of the narrow county road, the next property after the huge tract owned by the defunct cult. Set back a hundred yards from the pavement, at the end of a dirt lane, it was one of many similar retreats spread through the surrounding hills, most of them on an acre of land or more.

It was a one-story structure with weather-silvered cedar siding, slate roof, screened front porch, and river-rock foundation. Over the years his father and mother had expanded the original building until it contained two bedrooms, kitchen, living room, and two baths.

They parked in front of the cabin and got out of the BMW. The surrounding firs, sugar pines, and ponderosa pines were ancient and huge, and the crisp air was sweet with the scent of them. Drifts of dead needles and scores of pinecones littered the property. Snow reached the ground only between the trees and through the occasional interstices of their thatched boughs.

Marty went to the woodshed behind the cabin. The door was held shut with a hasp and peg. Inside, to the right of the entrance, against the wall, a spare key was wrapped tightly in plastic and buried half an inch under the dirt floor.

When Marty returned to the front of the cabin, Emily was circling one of the larger trees in a crouch, closely examining the cones that had fallen from it. Charlotte was performing a wildly exaggerated ballet in an open space between trees, where a wide shaft of snow fell like a spotlight on a stage.

"I am the Snow Queen!" Charlotte announced breathlessly as she twirled and leaped. "I have dominion over winter! I can command the snow to fall! I can make the world shiny and white and beautiful!"

As Emily began to gather up an armload of cones, Paige said, "Honey, you're not bringing those in the house."

"I'm going to make some art."

"They're dirty."

"They're beautiful."

"They're beautiful *and* dirty," Paige said.

"I'll make art out here."

"Snow fall! Snow blow! Snow swirl and whirl and caper!" commanded the dancing Snow Queen as Marty climbed the wooden steps and opened the screen door on the porch.

That morning the girls had dressed in jeans and wool sweaters, to be ready for the Sierras, and they were wearing heavily insulated nylon jackets as well as cloth gloves. They wanted to stay outside and play. Even if they'd had boots, however, the outdoors would have been off limits.

This time, the cabin was not simply a vacation getaway but a cloistered retreat which they might have to transform into a fortress, and the surrounding woods might eventually harbor something far more dangerous than wolves.

Inside, the place had a faint musty smell. It actually seemed colder than the snowy day beyond its walls.

Logs were stacked in the fireplace, and additional wood was piled high on one side of the broad, deep hearth. Later they would light a fire. To warm the cabin quickly, Paige went room to room, switching on the electric space heaters set in the walls.

Standing by one of the front windows, looking through the screened porch and down the dirt lane toward the county road, Marty used the cellular phone, which he'd brought in from the car, to try yet again to reach his folks back in Mammoth Lakes.

"Daddy," Charlotte said as he punched in the number, "I just thought—who's going to feed Sheldon and Bob and Fred and the other guys back home while we're not there?"

"I already arranged with Mrs. Sanchez to take care of that," he lied, for he hadn't yet found the courage to tell her that all of her pets had been killed.

"Oh, okay. Then it's a good thing it wasn't Mrs. Sanchez who went totally berserk."

"Who you calling, Daddy?" Emily asked as the first ring sounded at the far end of the line.

"Grandma and Grandpa."

"Tell them I'm gonna make a cone sculpture for them."

"Boy," Charlotte said, "that'll thrill the puke out of 'em."

The phone rang a third time.

"They like my art," Emily insisted.

Charlotte said, "They have to—they're your grandparents."

Four rings.

"Yeah, well, you're not the Snow Queen, either," Emily said.

"I am too."

Five.

"No, you're the Snow Troll."

"You're the Snow Toad," Charlotte countered.

Six.

"Snow Worm."

"Snow Maggot."

"Snow Snot."

"Snow Puke."

Marty gave them a warning look, which put a stop to the name-calling competition, though they stuck their tongues out at each other.

After the seventh ring, he put his finger on the END button. Before he could push it, however, the connection was made.

Whoever picked up the receiver didn't say anything.

"Hello?" Marty said. "Mom? Dad?"

Managing to sound both angry and sad, the man on the other end of the line said, "How did you win them over?"

Marty felt as if ice had formed in his veins and marrow, not because of the penetrating cold in the cabin but because the voice that responded to him was a perfect imitation of his own.

"Why would they love you more than me?" The Other demanded, his voice tremulous with emotion.

A mantle of dread settled on Marty, and a sense of unreality as disorienting as any nightmare. He seemed to be dreaming while awake.

He said, "Don't touch them, you son of a bitch. Don't you lay one finger on them."

"They betrayed me."

"I want to talk to my mother and father," Marty demanded.

"My mother and father," The Other said.

"Put them on the phone."

"So you can tell them more lies?"

"Put them on the phone now," Marty said between clenched teeth.

"They can't listen to any more of your lies."

"What have you done?"

"They're finished listening to you."

"What have you done?"

"They wouldn't give me what I needed."

With understanding, dread became grief. For a moment Marty could not find his voice.

The Other said, "All I needed was to be loved."

"What have you done?" He was shouting. "Who are you, what are you, damn it, what are you, *what have you done?"*

Ignoring the questions, answering them with questions of its own, The Other said, "Have you turned Paige against me? My Paige, my Charlotte, my sweet little Emily? Do I have any hope of getting them back or will I have to kill them too?" The voice cracked with emotion. "Oh God, is there even blood in their veins any more, are they human any more, or have you made them into something else?"

Marty realized they could not conduct a conversation. It was madness to try. However much they might look and sound alike, they were without any common grounds. In fundamental ways, they were as unlike each other as if they had been members of different species.

Marty pushed the END button.

His hands were shaking so badly that he dropped the phone.

When he turned from the window, he saw the girls were standing together, holding hands. They were staring, pale and frightened.

His shouting into the telephone had brought Paige out of one of the bedrooms where she had been adjusting the electric heater.

Images of his parents' faces and treasured memories of a life of love crowded into his mind, but he resolutely repressed them. If he gave in to grief now, wasted precious time in tears, he would be condemning Paige and the girls to certain death.

"He's here," Marty said, "he's coming, and we don't have much time."

PART

THREE

New Maps
of Hell

Those who would banish the sin of greed
embrace the sin of envy as their creed.
Those who seek to banish envy as well,
only draw elaborate new maps of hell.

Those with passion to change the world,
look on themselves as saints, as pearls,
and by the launching of noble endeavor,
flee dreaded introspection forever.

—The Book of Counted Sorrows

Laugh at tyrants and the tragedy they inflict. Such men welcome our
tears as evidence of subservience, but our laughter condemns them
to ignominy.

—Endless River, **Laura Shane**

SIX

1.

He stands in his parents' kitchen, watching the falling snow through the window above the sink, shaking with hunger, and wolfing down leftover meatloaf.

This is one of those decisive moments that separate real heroes from pretenders. When all is darkest, when tragedy piles on tragedy, when hope seems to be a game only for idiots and fools, does Harrison Ford or Kevin Costner or Tom Cruise or Wesley Snipes or Kurt Russell quit? No. Never. Unthinkable. They are heroes. They persevere. Rise to the occasion. They not only deal with adversity but *thrive* on it. From sharing the worst moments of those great men's lives, he knows how to cope with emotional devastation, mental depression, physical abuse in enormous quantities, and even the threat of alien domination of the earth.

Move, move, confront, challenge, grapple, and prevail.

He must not dwell on the tragedy of his parents' deaths. The creatures he destroyed were surely not his mother and father, anyway, but mimics like the one that has stolen his own life. He might never learn when his real parents were murdered and replaced, and in any event he must delay grieving for them.

Thinking too much about his parents—or about anything—is not merely a waste of precious time but anti-heroic. Heroes don't think. Heroes *act*.

Move, move, confront, challenge, grapple, and prevail.

Finished eating, he goes to the garage by way of a laundry room off the kitchen. Switching on fluorescent lights as he crosses the threshold, he discovers two vehicles are available for his use—an old blue Dodge and an apparently new Jeep Wagoneer. He will use the Jeep because of its four-wheel drive.

The keys to the vehicle hang on a pegboard in the laundry room. In a cabinet, he also finds a large box of detergent. He reads the list of chemicals on the box, satisfied with what he discovers.

He returns to the kitchen.

The end of one row of lower cabinets is finished with a wine rack. After locating a corkscrew in a drawer, he opens four bottles and empties the wine into the sink.

In another kitchen drawer he finds a plastic funnel among other odds and ends of cooking implements. A third drawer is filled with clean white dish towels, and a fourth is the source for a pair of scissors and a book of matches.

He carries the bottles and the other items into the laundry room and puts them on the tiled counter beside the deep sink.

In the garage again, he takes a red five-gallon gasoline can from a shelf to the left of the workbench. When he unscrews the cap, high-octane fumes waft out of the container. Spring through autumn, Dad probably keeps gasoline in the can to use in the lawn mower, but it is empty now.

Rummaging through the drawers and cabinets around the workbench, he finds a coil of flexible plastic tubing in a box of repair parts for the drinking-water filtration system in the kitchen. With this he siphons gasoline out of the Dodge into the five-gallon can.

At the sink in the laundry room, he uses the funnel to pour an inch of detergent into the bottom of each empty wine bottle. He adds gasoline. He cuts the dishcloths into useable strips.

Although he has two revolvers and twenty rounds of ammunition, he wants to add gasoline bombs to his arsenal. His experiences of the past twenty-four hours, since first confronting the false father, have taught him not to underestimate his adversary.

He still hopes to save Paige, Charlotte, and little Emily. He continues to desire reunion and the renewal of their life together.

However, he must face reality and prepare for the possibility that his wife and children are no longer who they once were. They may simply have been mentally enslaved. On the other hand, they might also have been infected by parasites not of this world, their brains now hollow and filled with writhing monstrosities. Or they might not be themselves at all, merely replicants of the real Paige, Charlotte, and Emily, just as the false father is a replicant of him, arising out of a seed pod from some distant star.

The varieties of alien infestation are limitless and strange, but one weapon has saved the world more often than any other: fire. Kurt Russell, when he was a member of an Antarctic scientific-research outpost, had been confronted by an extraterrestrial shape-changer of infinite forms and great cunning, perhaps the most frightening and powerful alien ever to attempt colonization of the earth, and fire had been by far the most effective weapon against that formidable enemy.

He wonders if four incendiary devices are enough. He probably won't have time to use more of them, anyway. If something bursts out of the false father, Paige, or the girls, and if it's as hostile as the things that had burst out of people in Kurt Russell's research station, he would no doubt be overwhelmed before he could use more than four gasoline bombs, considering that he must take the time to light each one separately. He wishes he had a flamethrower.

2.

Standing by one of the front windows, watching heavy snow filter through the trees and onto the lane that led out to the county route, Marty plucked handfuls of 9mm ammunition out of the boxes of ammo they'd brought from Mission Viejo. He distributed cartridges in the numerous zippered pockets of his red-and-black ski jacket and in the pockets of his jeans as well.

Paige loaded the magazine of the Mossberg. She'd had less time than Marty to practice with the pistol on the firing range, and she felt more comfortable with the 12-gauge.

They had eighty shells for the shotgun and approximately two hundred 9mm rounds for the Beretta.

Marty felt defenseless.

No amount of weaponry would have made him feel better.

After hanging up on The Other, he had considered getting out of the cabin, going on the run. But if they had been followed this far so easily, they would be followed anywhere they went. It was better to make a stand in a defendable location than to be accosted on a lonely highway or be taken by surprise in a place more vulnerable than the cabin.

He almost called the local police to send them to his parents' house. But The Other would surely be gone before they got there, and the evidence they collected—fingerprints and God knew what else—would only make it appear that he had murdered his own mother and father. The media had already painted him as an unstable character. The scene at the house in Mammoth Lakes would play into the fantasy they were selling. If he were arrested today or tomorrow or next week—or even just detained for a few hours without being booked—Paige and the girls would be left on their own, a situation that he found intolerable.

They had no choice but to dig in and fight. Which wasn't a choice so much as a death sentence.

Side by side on the sofa, Charlotte and Emily were still wearing their jackets and gloves. They held hands, taking strength from each other. Although they were scared, they weren't crying or demanding reassurance as many kids might have been doing in the same situation. They had always been real troopers, each in her own way.

Marty was not sure how to counsel his daughters. Usually, like Paige, he was not at a loss for the guidance they needed to get them through the problems of life. Paige joked that they were the Fabulous Stillwater Parenting Machine, a phrase that contained as much self-mockery as genuine pride. But he was at a loss for words this time because he tried never to lie to them, did not intend to start lying now, yet dared not share with them his own bleak assessment of their chances.

"Kids, come here, do something for me," he said.

Eager for distraction, they scrambled off the sofa and joined him at the window.

"Stand here," he said, "watch the paved road out there. If a car turns into the driveway or even goes by too slow, does anything suspicious, you holler. Got that?"

They nodded solemnly.

To Paige, Marty said, "Let's check all the other windows, make sure they're locked, and close the drapes over them."

If The Other managed to creep up on the cabin without alerting them, Marty didn't want the bastard to be able to watch them—or shoot at them—through a window.

Every window he checked was locked.

In the kitchen, as he covered a window that looked out onto the deep woods behind the cabin, he remembered that his mother had made the drapes on her sewing machine in the spare bedroom of the house in Mammoth Lakes. He had a mental image of her, sitting at the Singer, her foot on the treadle, intently watching the needle as it chattered up and down.

His chest clogged with pain. He took a deep breath, let it shudder out of him, then again, trying not only to expel the pain but also the memory that engendered it.

There would be time for grief later, if they survived.

Right now he had to think only about Paige and the kids. His mother was dead. They were alive. The cold truth: mourning was a luxury.

He caught up with Paige in the second of the two small bedrooms just as she finished adjusting the draperies. She had switched on a nightstand lamp, so she wouldn't be in darkness when she closed off the windows, and now she moved to extinguish it.

"Leave it on," Marty said. "With the storm, it'll be a long and early twilight. From outside, he'll probably be able to tell which rooms are lit, which aren't. No sense making it easier for him to figure exactly where we are."

She was quiet. Staring at the amber cloth of the lampshade. As if their future could be prophesied from the vague patterns in that illuminated fabric.

At last she looked at him. "How long have we got?"

"Maybe ten minutes, maybe two hours. It's up to him."

"What's going to happen, Marty?"

It was his turn to be silent a moment. He didn't want to lie to her, either.

When he finally spoke, Marty was surprised to hear what he told her, because it sprang from subconscious depths, was genuine, and indicated greater optimism than he was aware of on a conscious level. "We're going to kill the fucker." Optimism or fatal self-delusion.

She came to him around the foot of the bed, and they held each other. She felt so right in his arms. For a moment, the world didn't seem crazy any more.

"We still don't even know who he is, what he is, where he comes from," she said.

"And maybe we'll never find out. Maybe, even after we kill the son of a bitch, we'll never know what this was all about."

"If we never find out, then we can't pick up the pieces."

"No."

She put her head on his shoulder and gently kissed the exposed penumbra of the bruises on his throat. "We can never feel safe."

"Not in our old life. But as long as we're together, the four of us," he said, "I can leave everything behind."

"The house, everything in it, my career, yours—"

"None of that's what really matters."

"A new life, new names . . . What future will the girls have?"

"The best we can give them. There were never any guarantees. There never are in this life."

She raised her head from his shoulder and looked into his eyes. "Can I really handle it when he shows up here?"

"Of course you can."

"I'm just a family counselor specializing in the behavioral problems of children, parent-child relations. I'm not the heroine of an adventure story."

"And I'm just a mystery novelist. But we can do it."

"I'm scared."

"So am I."

"But if I'm so scared now, where am I going to find the courage to pick up a shotgun and defend my kids from something . . . something like this?"

"Imagine you *are* the heroine of an adventure story."

"If only it were that easy."

"In some ways . . . maybe it is," he said. "You know I'm not much for Freudian explanations. More often than not, I think we decide to be what we are. You're a living example, after what you went through as a kid."

She closed her eyes. "Somehow, it's easier to imagine myself as a family counselor than as Kathleen Turner in *Romancing the Stone.*"

"When we first met," he said, "you couldn't imagine yourself as a wife and mother, either. A family was nothing but a prison to you, prison and torture chamber. You never wanted to be part of a family again."

She opened her eyes. "You taught me how."

"I didn't teach you anything. I only showed you how to imagine a good family, a healthy family. Once you were able to imagine it, you could learn to believe in the possibility. From there on, you taught yourself."

She said, "So life's a form of fiction, huh?"

"Every life's a story. We make it up as we go along."

"Okay. I'll try to be Kathleen Turner."

"Even better."

"What?"

"Sigourney Weaver."

She smiled. "Wish I had one of those big damned futuristic guns like she got to use when she played Ripley."

"Come on, we better go see if our sentries are still at their post."

In the living room, he relieved the girls of their duty at the only undraped window and suggested they heat some water to make mugs of hot chocolate. The cabin was always stocked with basic canned goods, including a tin of cocoa-flavored milk powder. The electric heaters still hadn't taken the chill off the air, so they could all use a little internal warming. Besides, making hot chocolate was such a *normal* task that it might defuse some of the tension and calm their nerves.

He looked through the window, across the screened porch, past the back end of the BMW. So many trees stood between the cabin and the county road that the hundred-yard-long driveway was pooled with deep shadows, but he could still see that no one was approaching either in a vehicle or on foot.

Marty was reasonably confident that The Other would come at them directly rather than from behind the cabin. For one thing, their property backed up to the hundred acres of church land downhill and to a larger parcel uphill, which made an indirect approach relatively arduous and time-consuming.

Judging by his past behavior, The Other always favored headlong action and blunt approaches. He seemed to lack the knack or patience for strategy. He was a doer more than a thinker, which almost ensured a furious—rather than sneak—attack.

That trait might be the enemy's fatal weakness. It was a hope worth nurturing, anyway.

Snow fell. The shadows deepened.

3.

From the motel room, Spicer called the surveillance van for an update. He let the phone ring a dozen times, hung up, and tried again, but still the call went unanswered.

"Something's happened," he said. "They wouldn't have left the van."

"Maybe something's wrong with their phone," Oslett suggested.

"It's ringing."

"Maybe not on their end."

Spicer tried again with no different result. "Come on," he said, grabbing his leather flight jacket and heading for the door.

"You're not going over there?" Oslett said. "Aren't you still worried about blowing their cover?"

"It's already been blown. Something's wrong."

Clocker had pulled on his tweed coat over his clashing orange cashmere sweater. He didn't bother to put on his hat because he had never bothered to take it off. Tucking the *Star Trek* paperback in a pocket, he also headed for the door.

Following them with the black briefcase, Oslett said, "But what could've gone wrong? Everything was moving along so smoothly again."

Already, the storm had put down half an inch of snow. The flakes were fine and comparatively dry now, and the streets white. Evergreen boughs had begun to acquire Christmasy trimmings.

Spicer drove the Explorer, and in a few minutes they reached the street where Stillwater's parents lived. He pointed out the house when they were still half a block from it.

Across the street from the Stillwater place, two vehicles were parked at the curb. Oslett pegged the red recreational van as the surveillance post because of the mirrored side windows in its rear section.

"What's that florist's van doing here?" Spicer wondered.

"Delivering flowers," Oslett guessed.

"Fat chance."

Spicer pulled past the van and parked the Explorer in front of it.

"Is this really smart?" Oslett wondered.

Using the cellular phone, Spicer called the surveillance team one more time. They didn't answer.

"We don't have a choice," Spicer said as he opened his door and got out into the snow.

The three of them walked to the back of the red van.

On the blacktop between that vehicle and the delivery van, a large floral arrangement lay in ruins. The ceramic container was shattered. The stems of the flowers and ferns were still embedded in the spongy green material that florists used to fix arrangements, so the mild wind had not blown any of them away, though they looked as if they had been stepped on more than once. The colors of some flowers were masked by snow, which meant they hadn't been disturbed in the past thirty to forty-five minutes.

The ruined blossoms and frost-paled ferns had a curious beauty. Snap a photo, hang it in an art gallery, title it something like "Romance" or "Loss," and people would probably stand before it for long minutes, musing.

As Spicer rapped on the back door of the surveillance vehicle, Clocker said, "I'll check the delivery van."

No one answered the knock, so Spicer boldly opened the door and climbed inside.

As he followed, Oslett heard Spicer say softly, "Oh, shit."

The interior of the van was dark. Little light penetrated the two-way mirrors that served as windows. Only the scopes and screens of the electronic equipment illuminated the space.

Oslett took off his sunglasses, saw the dead men, and pulled the rear door shut.

Spicer had taken off his sunglasses too. His eyes were an odd, baleful yellow. Or maybe that was just a color they reflected from the scopes and gauges.

"Alfie must've been coming to the Stillwater place, spotted the van, recognized it for what it was," Spicer said. "Before he went over there, he stopped here, took care of business, so he wouldn't be interrupted across the street."

The electronic gear operated off banks of solar batteries wired to flat solar cells on the roof. When surveillance was conducted at night, the batteries could be charged in the conventional fashion, if necessary, by starting the van's engine for short periods. Even on overcast days, however, the cells collected enough sunlight to keep the system operative.

Without the engine running, the interior temperature of the van was nonetheless comfortable, if slightly cool. The vehicle was unusually well insulated, and the solar cells also operated a small heater.

Stepping over the corpse on the floor, looking through one of the view windows, Oslett said, "If Alfie was drawn to that house, it had to be because Martin Stillwater was already there."

"I guess."

"Yet this team never saw him go in or out."

"Evidently not," Spicer agreed.

"Wouldn't they have let us know if they'd seen Stillwater, his wife, or kids?"

"Absolutely."

"So . . . is he over there now? Maybe they're all over there, the whole family and Alfie."

Peering through the other window, Spicer added, "And maybe not. Somebody left there not long ago. See the tracks in the driveway?"

A vehicle with wide tires had backed out of the garage that was attached to the white clapboard house. It had reversed to the left as it entered the street, then had shifted into forward and had driven away to the right. The snow had barely begun to fill in the multiple arcs of the tracks.

Clocker opened the rear door, startling them. He climbed inside and pulled the door shut after him, with no comment about the bloody ice axe on the floor or the two murdered operatives. "Looks like Alfie must've stolen the florist's van for cover. The deliveryman's in the back with the flowers, dead as the moon."

In spite of the extended wheelbase that added extra room to the interior of the van, the space unoccupied by surveillance equipment and corpses was not large enough to accommodate the three of them comfortably. Oslett felt claustrophobic.

Spicer pulled the seated dead man out of the swivel chair in which he'd died. The corpse tumbled to the floor. Spicer checked the chair for blood before sitting down and turning to the array of monitors and switches, with which he appeared to be familiar.

Uncomfortably aware of Clocker looming over him, Oslett said, "Is it possible there was a phone call to the house that these guys never got a chance to report to us before Alfie wasted them?"

Spicer said, "That's what I'm going to find out."

As Spicer's fingers flew over the programming keyboard, brightly colored graphs and other displays popped onto the half dozen video monitors.

Contriving, in those tight quarters, to ram his elbow into Clocker's gut, Oslett turned again to the first of the side-by-side view windows. He watched the house across the street.

Clocker stooped to look out the other window. Oslett figured the Trekker was pretending to be at a starship portal, squinting through foot-thick glass at an alien world.

A couple of cars passed. A pickup truck. A black dog ran along the sidewalk; with snow on his paws, he looked as if he was wearing four white socks. The Stillwater house stood silent, serene.

"Got it," Spicer said, taking off a set of headphones he had put on when Oslett had been staring out the window.

What he had, as it turned out, was a telephone call monitored, traced, and recorded by the automated equipment perhaps as long as thirty minutes *after* Alfie killed the surveillance team. In fact, Alfie had been in the Stillwater house when the call came through and had answered it after seven rings. Spicer played it back on a speaker instead of through headphones, so the three of them could listen at the same time.

"The first voice you hear is the caller," Spicer said, "because the man who picks up the receiver in the Stillwater house doesn't initially say anything."

"Hello? Mom? Dad?"
"How did you win them over?"

Stopping the tape, Spicer said, "That second voice is the receiving phone—and it's Alfie."

"They both sound like Alfie."

"The other one's Stillwater. Alfie also speaks next."

"Why would they love you more than me?"
"Don't touch them, you son of a bitch. Don't you lay one finger on them."
"They betrayed me."
"I want to talk to my mother and father."
"MY mother and father."
"Put them on the phone."
"So you can tell them more lies?"

They listened to the entire conversation. It was over-the-top creepy because it sounded as if one man was talking to himself, a radically split personality. Worse, their bad boy was obviously not just a renegade but flat-out psychotic.

When the tape ended, Oslett said, "So Stillwater never stopped at his parents' house."

"Evidently not."

"Then how did Alfie find it? And why did he go there? Why was he interested in Stillwater's parents, not just Stillwater himself?"

Spicer shrugged. "Maybe you'll get a chance to ask the boy if you manage to recover him."

Oslett didn't like having so many unanswered questions. It made him feel as if he wasn't in control.

He glanced out the window at the house and at the tire tracks in the snow-covered driveway. "Alfie's probably not over there any more."

"Went after Stillwater," Spicer agreed.

"Where was that call placed?"

"Cellular phone."

Oslett said, "We can still trace that, can't we?"

Pointing to three lines of numbers on a display terminal, Spicer said, "We've got a satellite triangulation."

"That's meaningless to me, just numbers."

"This computer can plot it on a map. To within a hundred feet of the signal source."

"How long will that take?"

"Five minutes tops," Spicer said.

"Good. You work on it. We'll check the house."

Oslett stepped out of the red van with Clocker close behind.

As they crossed the street through the snow, Oslett didn't care if a dozen nosy neighbors were at their windows. The situation was already blown wide open and couldn't be salvaged. He, Clocker, and Spicer would clear out, with their dead, in less than ten minutes, and after that no one would ever be able to prove they'd been there.

They walked boldly onto the elder Stillwaters' porch. Oslett rang the bell. No one answered. He rang it again and tried the door, which proved to be unlocked. From across the street it would appear as if Jim or Alice Stillwater had opened up and invited them inside.

In the foyer, Clocker closed the front door behind them and drew his

Colt .357 Magnum from his shoulder holster. They stood for a few seconds, listening to the silent house.

"Be at peace, Alfie," Oslett said, even though he doubted that their bad boy was still hanging around the premises. When there was no ritual response to that command, he repeated the four words louder than before.

Silence prevailed.

Cautiously they moved deeper into the house—and found the dead couple in the first room they checked. Stillwater's parents. Each of them somewhat resembled the writer—and Alfie, too, of course.

During a swift search of the house, repeating the command phrase before they went through each new doorway, the only thing of interest they found was in the laundry. The small room reeked of gasoline. What Alfie had been up to was made apparent by the scraps of cloth, funnel, and partly empty box of detergent that littered the counter beside the sink.

"He's taking no chances this time," Oslett said. "Going after Stillwater as if it's war."

They had to stop the boy—and fast. If he killed the Stillwater family or even just the writer himself, he would make it impossible to implement the murder-suicide scenario which would so neatly tie up so many loose ends. And depending on what insane, fiery spectacle he had in mind, he might draw so much attention to himself that keeping his existence a secret and returning him to the fold would become impossible.

"Damn," Oslett said, shaking his head.

"Sociopathic clones," Clocker said, almost as if *trying* to be irritating, "are always big trouble."

4.

Sipping hot chocolate, Paige took her turn at guard duty by the front window.

Marty was sitting cross-legged on the living room floor with Charlotte and Emily, playing with a deck of cards they'd gotten from the game chest. It was the least animated game of Go Fish that Paige had ever seen, conducted without comment or argument. Their faces were grim, as if they weren't playing Go Fish at all but consulting a Tarot deck that had nothing but bad news for them.

Studying the snowswept day outside, Paige suddenly knew that both she and Marty shouldn't be waiting in the cabin. Turning away from the window, she said, "This is wrong."

"What?" he asked, looking up from the cards.

"I'm going outside."

"For what?"

"That rock formation over there, under the trees, halfway out toward the county road. I can lie down in there and still see the driveway."

Marty dropped his hand of cards. "What sense does that make?"

"Perfect sense. If he comes in the front way, like we both think he will—like he *has* to—he'll go right past me, straight to the cabin. I'll be behind him. I can pump a couple of rounds into the back of the bastard's head before he knows what's happening."

Getting to his feet, shaking his head, Marty said, "No, it's too risky."

"If we both stay inside here, it'll be like trying to defend a fort."

"A fort sounds good to me."

"Don't you remember all those movies about the cavalry in the Old West, defending the fort? Sooner or later, no matter how strong the place was, the Indians overran it and got inside."

"That's just in the movies."

"Yeah, but maybe he's seen them too. Come here," she insisted. When he joined her at the window, she pointed to the rocks, which were barely visible in the sable shadows under the pines. "It's perfect."

"I don't like it."

"It'll work."

"I don't like it."

"You know it's right."

"Okay, so maybe it's right, but I still don't have to like it," he said sharply.

"I'm going out."

He searched her eyes, perhaps looking for signs of fear that he could exploit to change her mind. "You think you're an adventure-story heroine, don't you?"

"You got my imagination working."

"I wish I'd kept my mouth shut." He stared for a long moment at the shadow-blanketed jumble of rocks, then sighed and said, "All right, but I'm the one who'll go out there. You'll stay in here with the girls."

She shook her head. "It doesn't work that way, baby."

"Don't pull a feminist number on me."

"I'm not. It's just that . . . you're the one he's got a psychic bead on."

"So?"

"He can sense where you are, and depending on how refined that talent is, he might sense you're in the rocks. You have to stay in the cabin so he'll feel you in here, come straight for you—and right past me."

"Maybe he can sense you too."

"Evidence so far indicates it's only you."

He was in an agony of fear for her, his feelings carved in every hollow of his face. "I don't like this."

"You already said. I'm going out."

5.

By the time Oslett and Clocker left the Stillwater house and crossed the street, Spicer was getting behind the wheel of the red surveillance van.

The wind accelerated. Snow was driven out of the sky at a severe angle and harried along the street.

Oslett walked to the driver's door of the surveillance van.

Spicer had his sunglasses on again even though the last hour or so of daylight was upon them. His eyes, yellow or otherwise, were hidden.

He looked down at Oslett and said, "I'm going to drive this heap away from here, clear across the county line and out of local jurisdiction before I call the home office and get some help with body disposal."

"What about the delivery man in the florist's van?"

"Let them haul their own garbage," Spicer said.

He handed Oslett a standard-size sheet of typing paper on which the computer had printed a map, plotting the point from which Martin Stillwater had telephoned his parents' house. Only a few roads were depicted on it. Oslett tucked it inside his ski jacket before either the wind could snatch it out of his hand or the paper could become damp from the snow.

"He's only a few miles away," Spicer said. "You take the Explorer." He started the engine, pulled the door shut, and drove off into the storm.

Clocker was already behind the wheel of the Explorer. Clouds of exhaust billowed from its tailpipe.

Oslett hurried to the passenger side, got in, slammed the door, and fished the computer map out of his jacket. "Let's go. We're running out of time."

"Only on the human scale," Clocker said. Pulling away from the curb and switching on the wipers to deal with the wind-driven snow, he added, "From a cosmic point of view, time may be the one thing of which there's an inexhaustible supply."

6.

Paige kissed the girls and made them promise to be brave and to do exactly what their father told them to do. Leaving them for the uncertainty of what lay ahead was one of the hardest things she had ever done. Pretending not to be afraid, in order to help them with their own quest for courage, was even harder.

When Paige stepped out the front door, Marty went with her onto the porch. Blustery wind hissed through the screen walls and rattled the porch door at the head of the steps.

"There's one other way," he said, leaning close to her to be heard above the storm without shouting. "If it's me that he's drawn to, maybe I should get the hell out of here, on my own, lead him as far away from you as I can."

"Forget it."

"But without you and the girls to worry about, maybe I can deal with him."

"And if he kills you instead?"

"At least we wouldn't all go down."

"You think he won't come looking for us again? He wants your life, remember. Your life, your wife, your children."

"So if he finishes me off and comes after you, you'd still have a chance to blow his brains out."

"Oh, yeah? And when he shows up, during that little window of opportunity I'll have before he gets close to me, how would I know whether it was him or you?"

"You wouldn't," he admitted.

"So we'll play it this way."

"You're so damned strong," he said.

He couldn't know that her bowels were like jelly, her heart was knocking violently, and the faint metallic taste of terror filled her dry mouth.

They hugged but briefly.

Carrying the Mossberg, she went through the porch door, down the steps, across the shallow yard, past the BMW, and into the woods without looking back, worried that he would become aware of the depth of her fear and insist on dragging her back into the cabin.

Under the Quonset curve of sheltering evergreen boughs, the wind sounded hollow and distant except when she passed beneath a couple of flue-like openings that soared all the way up to the blind sky. Pummeling drafts shrieked down those passages, as cold as ectoplasm and as shrill as banshees.

Although the property sloped, the ground beneath the trees was easy to traverse. Underbrush was sparse due to a lack of direct sunlight. Many trees were so old that the lowest branches were above her head, and the view between the thick trunks was unobstructed all the way out to the county road.

The soil was stony. Tables and formations of granite broke the surface here and there, all ancient and smooth.

The formation she had pointed out to Marty was halfway between the cabin and the county road, only twenty feet upslope from the driveway. It resembled a crescent of teeth, blunt molars two to three feet high, like the fossilized dental structure of a gentle herbivorous dinosaur much larger than any ever before suspected or imagined.

Approaching the granite outcropping, in which shadows as dark as condensed pine tar pooled behind the "molars," Paige suddenly had the feeling that the look-alike was already there, watching the cabin from that hiding place. Ten feet from her destination, she halted, skidding slightly on the carpet of loose pine needles.

If he was actually there, he would have seen her coming and could have killed her any time he wished. The fact that she was still alive argued against his presence. Nevertheless, as she tried to get moving again, she felt as if she had plunged to the bottom of a deep ocean trench and was struggling to make progress against the resisting mass of an entire sea.

Heart pounding, she circled the crescent formation and slipped into its shadowed convexity from behind. The look-alike wasn't waiting for her.

She stretched out on her stomach. In her dark-blue ski jacket with the hood covering her blond hair, she knew that she was as good as invisible among the shadows and against the dark stone.

Through gaps in the stone, she could monitor the entire length of the driveway without raising her head high enough to be seen.

Beyond the shelter of the trees, the storm swiftly escalated into a full-scale blizzard. The volume of snow coming down into the driveway between flanking stands of trees was so great that it almost seemed as if she was looking into the foaming face of a waterfall.

Her ski jacket kept her upper body warm, but her jeans couldn't ward off the penetrating cold of the stone on which she lay. As body heat leached away, her hip and knee joints began to ache. She wished she were wearing insulated ski pants, and she realized she should have at least brought a blanket to put between herself and the granite.

Under the influence of the building gale, the highest branches of the firs and pines creaked like scores of doors easing open on rusty hinges. Not even the muffling boughs of the evergreens could soften the rising voice of the wind.

The gradually dimming light of the day's last hour was the steely shade of ice on a winter pond.

Every sight and sound was cold and seemed to exacerbate the chill that pressed into her from the granite. She began to worry about how long she could hold out before she would need to return to the cabin to get warm.

Then a deep-blue Jeep station wagon came uphill on the county road and made a hard, sharp turn into the driveway. It looked like the Jeep that belonged to Marty's parents.

❈　　❈　　❈

Rheostat at seven degrees. South from Mammoth Lakes, through billowing curtains of snow, through whirling snowdevils, through torrents and lashes and blasts and cataracts and airborne walls of snow, along a highway barely defined beneath the deepening mantle, passing slow-moving traffic at high speed, flashing his headlights to encourage obstructionists to pull over and let him go by, even passing a county snowplow and a cinder-spreading truck crowned with yellow and red emergency beacons that briefly transform the millions of white flakes into glowing embers. A left turn. Narrower road. Uphill. Into forested slopes. Long chain-link fence on the right, capped with spiral razor wire, broken down in places. Not there yet. A little farther. Close. Soon.

The four gasoline bombs stand in a cardboard box on the floor in front of the passenger seat, wedged into the knee space. The gaps between them are packed with folded newspapers, so the bottles will not clatter against one another.

Pungent fumes arise from the saturated cloth wicks. The perfume of destruction.

Guided by the magnetic attraction of the false father, he makes an abrupt right turn into a single-lane driveway already half hidden by snow. He brakes as little as possible, cornering in a slide, and moving his foot to the accelerator again even as the Jeep is still finding purchase and both rear tires are spinning-squealing fiercely.

Directly ahead, at least a hundred yards into the woods, stands a cabin. Soft light at the windows. Roof capped with snow.

Even if the BMW was not parked to the left of the place, he'd know he'd found his quarry. The imposter's hateful magnetic presence pulls him forward.

At first sight of the cabin, he decides to make a full frontal assault, regardless of the wisdom or consequences. His mother and father are dead, wife and children probably long dead, too, forms and faces mockingly imitated by the vicious alien species that has stolen his own name and memories. He seethes with rage, hatred so intense it's physically painful, anguish like a fire in his heart, and only swift justice will bring desperately needed relief.

The churning tires bite through the snow into dirt.

He rams his foot down on the accelerator.

The Jeep bolts forward.

A cry of savage fury and vengeance escapes him, and the mental rheostat spins from seven degrees to three hundred and sixty.

* * *

Marty was at the front window when headlight beams pierced the falling snow out on the county road, but at first he couldn't see the source. Coming uphill, the vehicle was hidden by trees and roadside brush. Then it burst into sight—a Jeep—turning hard into the driveway at high speed, the back end fishtailing, plumes of snow and slush erupting behind its spinning rear tires.

An instant later, as he was still reacting to the arrival of the Jeep, he was stricken by a brutal psychic tidal wave as strong as anything he had previously experienced but of a different quality. This was not merely the urgent, questing power that had hammered him on other occasions, but a blast of black and bitter emotion, raw and uncensored, which put him inside the mind of his enemy as no human being ever before could have been inside the mind of another. It was a surrealistic realm of psychotic rage, desperation, infantile self-absorption, terror, confusion, envy, lust, and urgent hungers so vile that a flood of sewage and rotting corpses could not have been as repulsive.

For the duration of that telepathic contact, Marty felt as if he had been pitched into one of the deeper regions of Hell. Though the connection lasted no more than three or four seconds, it seemed interminable. When it was broken, he found himself standing with his hands clamped against his temples, mouth open in a silent scream.

He gasped for breath and shuddered violently.

The roar of an engine brought his eyes back into focus and drew his attention to the day beyond the window. The Jeep station wagon was accelerating up the driveway, toward the cabin.

Maybe he was misjudging the degree of The Other's recklessness and insanity, but he had been *in* that mind, and he thought he knew what was coming. He spun away from the window, toward the girls.

"Run, get out the back, *go!*"

Having already scrambled up from the living-room floor and the two-hand card game in which they'd been pretending to be engrossed, Charlotte and Emily were sprinting toward the kitchen before Marty had finished shouting the warning.

He ran after them.

All in a second, spinning through his mind, an alternate strategy: stay in the living room, hope the Jeep got hung up in the porch and never made it to the front wall of the cabin, then rush outside, after the impact, and shoot the bastard before he climbed out from behind the steering wheel.

And in another second, the dark potential of that strategy: maybe the Jeep *would* make it all the way—cedar siding, shattered two-by-fours, electrical wiring, chunks of plaster, broken glass exploding into the living room with it, rafters buckling, ceiling collapsing, murderous slate roof tiles thundering down on him—and he would be killed by flying debris, or survive but be trapped in the rubble, legs pinned.

The kids would be on their own. Couldn't risk it.

Outside, the roar of the engine swelled nearer.

He caught up with the girls as Charlotte grasped the thumb-turn of the dead-bolt lock on the kitchen door. He reached over her head, slapped open the latch-bolt as she disengaged the lower lock.

The scream of the engine filled the world, curiously less like the sound of a machine than like the savage cry of something huge and Jurassic.

The Beretta. Rattled by the telepathic contact and the hurtling Jeep, he had forgotten the Beretta. It was on the living-room coffee table.

No time to go back for it.

Charlotte twisted the knob. The howling wind tore the door out of her hand and shoved it into her. She was knocked off her feet.

Then *wham,* from the front of the house, like a bomb going off.

✽   ✽   ✽

The big station wagon shot past Paige's hiding place so fast she knew she wasn't going to have a chance to wait for the son of a bitch to park, then creep up on him stealthily from tree to tree and shadow to shadow in the manner of the good adventure heroine that she envisioned herself. He was playing by his own rules, which meant no rules at all, and his every action would be unpredictable.

By the time she scrambled to her feet, the Jeep was within seventy or eighty feet of the cabin. Still accelerating.

Praying her cold-stiffened legs wouldn't cramp, she clambered over the low rock formation. She raced toward the cabin, parallel to the driveway, staying in the gloom of the woods, weaving between tree trunks.

Because the BMW was not parked squarely in front of the cabin but to the left, the Jeep had a clear shot at the porch steps. Less than an inch of snow was insufficient to slow it down. The ground under that white blanket wasn't frozen rock-solid as it would be later in the winter, so the tires cut into bare earth, finding all the traction they needed.

The driver seemed to be standing on the accelerator. He was suicidal. Or convinced of his invulnerability. The engine screamed.

Paige was still a hundred feet from the cabin when the left front tire of the Jeep hit the low concrete porch steps and climbed them as if they were a ramp. The right front tire spun through empty air for an instant, then grabbed the porch floor as the bumper tore through the wall of screen.

She expected the porch to give way under the weight. But the Jeep seemed airborne as the rear left tire launched it off the top of the three steps.

❋   ❋   ❋

Flying. Taking out panels of screen and the frames that hold them in place, as if they're spider webs, gossamer.

Straight at the door. Like an incoming round of mortar fire. A two-ton shell.

Closes his eyes. Windshield might implode.

Bone-jarring impact. Thrown forward. Safety harness jerks him back, he exhales explosively, currents of pain briefly scintillate through his chest.

A percussive symphony of boards splintering, jack studs cracking in half, door jamb disintegrating, lintel fracturing. Then forward motion ceases, the Jeep crashes down.

He opens his eyes.

The windshield is still intact.

The Jeep is in the living room of the cabin, facing a sofa and an overturned armchair. It's tipped forward because the front wheels broke through the flooring into the air space below.

The Jeep doors are above the cabin floor and unobstructed. He disengages the seatbelt and gets out of the station wagon with one of the .38 pistols in his right hand.

Move, move, confront, challenge, grapple, and prevail.

He hears creaking overhead and looks up. The ceiling is broken and sagging but will probably hold together. Powdery snow and dead brown pine needles sift down through the cracks.

The floor is littered with broken glass. The windows flanking the cabin door have shattered.

He is thrilled by the destruction. It inflames his fury.

The living room is deserted. Through the archway he can see most of the kitchen, and no one's in there, either.

Two closed doors are featured in the wide pass-through between living room and kitchen, one to the left and one to the right. He moves to the right.

If the false father is waiting on the other side, the very act of opening the door will trigger a fusillade.

He wants to avoid being shot if at all possible because he does not want to have to crawl away to heal again. He wants to finish this now, here, today.

If his wife and children have not already been replicated and replaced by alien forms, they will surely not be permitted to remain human much longer. Night is coming. Less than an hour away. From movies, he knows these things always happen at night—alien assault, parasite injection, attacks by shape-changers and soul-stealers and things that drink blood, all at night, either when the moon is full or there is no moon at all, but at night.

Instead of throwing the door open even from a safe position to one side, he steps in front of it, raises the .38, and opens fire. The door is not solid wood but a Masonite model with a foam core, and the hollow-point rounds punch big holes at point-blank range.

Jolting through his arms, the recoil of the Chief's Special is enormously satisfying, almost a sexual experience, bringing a small measure of relief from his intense frustration and anger. He keeps squeezing the trigger until the hammer clicks on empty chambers.

No screams from the room beyond. No sounds at all as the roar of the last gunshot fades.

He throws the gun on the floor and draws the second .38 from the shoulder holster under his varsity jacket.

He kicks open the door and goes inside fast, the gun thrust out in front of him.

It's a bedroom. Deserted.

Soaring frustration fans the flames of rage.

Returning to the pass-through, he faces the other closed door.

❊   ❊   ❊

For a moment the sight of the Jeep flying across the porch and slamming through the front wall of the cabin brought Paige to a halt.

Although it was happening in front of her and though she had no doubt that it was real, the crash had the unreal quality of a dream. The station wagon seemed to hang in the air an impossibly long time, virtually floating across the porch, wheels spinning. It appeared almost to *dissolve* through the wall into the cabin, vanishing as if it had never been. The destruction was accompanied by a great deal of noise, yet somehow it was not cacophonous enough, not half as loud as it would have been if the crash had taken place in a movie. Immediately in the wake of it, the comparative quiet of the storm reclaimed the day, with only the moaning of the wind; snow fell in a soundless deluge.

The kids.

In her mind's eye, she saw the wall bursting in on them, the hurtling Jeep right behind it.

She was running again before she realized it. Straight toward the cabin.

She held the shotgun with both hands—left hand on the fore-end slide handle, right hand around the grip and finger on the trigger guard. All she would have to do was halt, swing the bore toward the target, slip her finger to the trigger, and fire. Earlier, loading the Mossberg, she had pumped a round into the breech, so she could fit an extra shell into the magazine tube.

As she sprinted out of the woods and into the driveway, when she was no more than thirty feet from the porch steps, gunfire erupted in the house. Five rounds in quick succession. Instead of giving her pause, the shots spurred her across the driveway and shallow front yard as fast as she could move.

She slipped in the snow and fell to one knee just as she reached the foot of the porch steps. The pain wrung a soft, involuntary curse from her.

If she hadn't stumbled, however, she would have been on the porch or all the way into the living room when Charlotte rounded the corner of the cabin. Marty and Emily appeared close behind Charlotte, running hand in hand.

❄ ❄ ❄

He fires three times into the door on the left side of the pass-through, kicks it open, scuttles across the threshold fast and low, and finds another deserted bedroom.

Outside, a car door slams.

❄ ❄ ❄

Marty left the driver's door open while he got in behind the steering wheel, fumbling under the seat with one hand in search of the keys, and he didn't even think to warn Charlotte and Emily not to slam their door until the act was done and the echo of it reverberated through the surrounding trees.

Paige hadn't gotten into the BMW yet. She was standing at her open door, watching the house, the Mossberg raised and ready.

Where were the damn keys?

He leaned forward, crunching down, trying to feel farther back under the seat.

As Marty's fingers closed over the keys, the Mossberg boomed. He snapped his head up as an answering shot missed Paige, passed through the open car door, and smashed into the dashboard inches from his face. A gauge shattered, showering him with shards of plastic.

"Down!" he shouted to the girls in the back seat.

Paige fired the shotgun and again drew return fire.

The Other stood in the gaping hole where the front door of the cabin had been, framed by jagged ruins, his right arm extended as he squeezed off the shot. Then he ducked back into the living room, perhaps to reload.

Though the shotgun would keep him from coming any closer, he was too far away to be greatly hurt by it, especially considering his unusual recuperative abilities. His handgun, however, packed a solid punch at that distance.

Marty jammed the key in the ignition. The engine turned over without a protest. He released the hand brake, put the BMW in gear.

Paige got in the car, pulled her door shut.

He looked over his shoulder through the rear window, reversed past the front of the cabin, and then turned into the tire tracks left by the Jeep on its kamikaze run.

"Here he comes!" Paige cried.

Still backing up, Marty glanced through the windshield and saw The Other bounding off the porch, down the steps, across the yard, a wine bottle in each hand, rag wicks in the necks, flames leaping off both. Jesus. They were burning furiously, might explode in his hands at any second, but he seemed to have no concern for his own safety, a savage and almost gleeful look on his face, as if he was *born* for this, nothing but this. He skidded to a stop and cocked his right arm like a quarterback ready to pass the ball to his receiver.

"Go!" Paige shouted.

Marty was already going, and he didn't need encouragement to go faster.

Instead of turning to look through the back window, he used the rearview mirror to be sure he stayed on the driveway and didn't angle off into any trees or ditches or jutting rocks, so he was aware of the first bottle arcing through the snow and shattering against the BMW's front bumper. Most of the contents splashed harmlessly onto the driveway, where a patch of snow seemed to burst into flames.

The second bottle slammed into the hood, six inches from the windshield, directly in front of Paige. It shattered, the contents exploded, burning fluid washed the glass, and for a moment the only forward view they had was of seething fire.

In the back, seatbelts engaged, staying down, holding tightly to each other, the girls shrieked in terror.

Marty couldn't do anything to reassure them except to keep backing up, as fast as he dared, hoping the fire on the hood would burn out and the heat wouldn't cause the windshield to implode.

Halfway to the county road. Two-thirds. Accelerating. A hundred yards to go.

The blaze on the windshield was extinguished almost at once, as the thin film of gasoline on the glass was consumed, but flames continued to leap off the hood and off the fender on the passenger side. The paint had ignited.

Through fire and billowing black smoke, Marty saw The Other running toward them again, not as fast as the car but not a whole lot slower, either.

Paige fished two shotgun shells out of a pocket of her ski jacket and stuffed them into the magazine tube, replacing the rounds she had expended.

Sixty yards to the county road.

Fifty.

Forty.

Because of intervening trees and vegetation, Marty could not see downhill, and he was afraid he'd reverse into the path of an oncoming vehicle. Yet he didn't dare slow down.

The roar of the BMW prevented him from hearing the shot. A bullet hole appeared, with a sharp snap, in the windshield below the rearview mirror, between him and Paige. An instant later a second round drilled the windshield, three inches to the right of the first, so close to Paige it was a miracle she wasn't hit. With the second violation, a chain-reaction of millions of tiny cracks webbed across the tempered glass, rendering it milky-opaque.

The transition between the end of the dirt lane and the pavement wasn't smooth. They slammed backward onto the county road hard enough to make them bounce in their seats, and the crazed safety glass collapsed inward in gummy chunks.

Marty pulled the wheel to the right, reversing uphill, and braked to a full stop when they were facing straight down the road. He could feel the heat of the flames that were eating the paint off the hood, but they didn't lick into the car.

A bullet ricocheted off metal.

He shifted out of reverse.

Through his side window, he could see The Other standing spread-legged fifteen yards from the end of the driveway, gun in both hands.

As Marty tramped on the accelerator, another round thudded into his door, below the window, but didn't penetrate to the interior of the car.

The Other broke into a run again as the BMW shot downhill and away from him.

Although the wind carried most of the smoke off to the right, there was suddenly a lot more of it, blacker than ever, and enough churned into the car to make them miserable. Paige started coughing, the girls were wheezing in the back seat, and Marty couldn't clearly see the road ahead.

"Tire's burning!" Paige shouted above the howling wind.

Two hundred yards farther downhill, the burning tire blew, and the BMW spun out of control on the snow-skinned blacktop. Marty turned the wheel into the slide, but applied physics didn't prove reliable this time. The car swung around a hundred and eighty degrees, simultaneously moving sideways, and they only stopped when they careened off the road and fetched up against the chain-link fence that marked the perimeter of the property owned by the defunct Prophetic Church of the Rapture.

Marty climbed out of the car. He yanked open the back door, leaned in, and helped the frightened girls disentangle themselves from their seatbelts.

He didn't even look to see if The Other was still coming because he *knew* the bastard was coming. This guy would never stop, never, not until they killed him, maybe not even then.

As Marty extracted Emily from the back seat, Paige scrambled out of the driver's door because her side of the car was jammed into the chain-link. Having withdrawn the manila envelopes of cash from under her seat, she stuffed them inside her ski jacket. As she zipped shut, she looked uphill.

"Shit," she said, and the shotgun boomed.

Marty helped Charlotte out of the car as the Mossberg thundered again. He thought he heard the hard crack of small-arms fire, too, but the bullet must have gone wide of them.

Shielding the girls, pushing them behind him and away from the burning car, he glanced uphill.

The Other stood arrogantly in the center of the road, about a hundred yards away, convinced he was protected from the shotgun fire by distance, the deflecting power of the wailing wind, and perhaps his own supernatural ability to bounce back from serious damage. He was *exactly* Marty's size, yet even at a distance he seemed to tower over them, a dark and ominous figure. Maybe it was the perspective. Almost nonchalantly, he broke open the cylinder of his revolver and tipped expended cartridges into the snow.

"He's reloading," Paige said, taking the opportunity to jam additional shells into the magazine of her shotgun, "let's get out of here."

"Where?" Marty wondered, looking around frantically at the snow-whipped landscape.

He wished a car would appear from one direction or another.

Then he canceled his own wish because he knew The Other would kill any passersby who tried to interfere.

They moved downhill, into the biting wind, using the time to put some distance between themselves and their pursuer while they figured what to do next.

He ruled out trying to reach one of the other cabins scattered through the high woods. Most were vacation homes. No one would be in residence on a Tuesday in December unless, by morning, the new snow brought them in for the skiing. And if they stumbled into a cabin where someone was at home, with The Other trailing after them, Marty didn't want the deaths of innocent strangers on his conscience.

Route 203 lay at the bottom of the county road. Even in the early hours of a blizzard, steady traffic would be passing between the lakes and Mammoth Lakes itself. If there were a lot of witnesses, The Other couldn't kill them all. He'd have to retreat.

But the bottom of the county road was too distant. They'd never make it before they ran out of shotgun shells to keep their enemy at bay—or before the greater accuracy and range of the revolver allowed him to pick them off one by one.

They came to a gap in the battered chain-link fence.

"Here, come on," Marty said.

"Isn't that place abandoned?" Paige objected.

"There's nowhere else," he said, taking Charlotte and Emily by the hand and leading them onto the church property.

His hope was that someone would come along soon, see the half-burned BMW, and report it to the sheriff's department. Instead of fanning the fire that had been feeding on the paint, the wind had snuffed it, but the tire was still burning, and the battered car was hard to ignore. If a couple of well-armed deputies showed up to check out the area and could be enlisted in the struggle, they wouldn't understand how formidable The Other was, but they wouldn't be as naive and helpless as ordinary citizens, either.

After a brief hesitation, during which she glanced worriedly uphill at their nemesis, Paige followed him and the girls through the hole in the fence.

* * *

The speedloader slips from his fingers and drops into the snow as he removes it from the pouch on his belt. It is the last of the two he took from the dead man in the surveillance van.

He stoops, plucks it out of the snow, and brushes it off against the cranberry-red sweater under his varsity jacket. He brings it to the open revolver, slips it in, twists it, drops it, and snaps the cylinder shut.

He will have to use his last rounds carefully. The replicants are not going to be easy to kill.

He now knows that the woman is a replicant just like the false father. Alien flesh. Inhuman. She cannot be his Paige, for she is too aggressive. His Paige would be submissive, eager for domination, like the women in the Senator's film collection. His Paige is surely dead. He must accept that, difficult as it is. This thing is only masquerading as Paige, and not well. Worse, if Paige is gone forever, so are his loving daughters. The girls, cute and convincingly human, are also replicants—demonic, extraterrestrial, and dangerous.

His former life is irretrievable.

His family is gone forever.

A black abyss of despair yawns under him, but he must not fall into it. He must find the strength to go on and fight either until he achieves victory in the name of all humankind—or is destroyed. He must be as courageous as Kurt Russell and Donald Sutherland were when they found themselves in similar dire straits, for he is a hero, and a hero must persevere.

Downhill, the four creatures disappear through a hole in the chain-link fence. All he wants now is to see them dead, scramble their brains, dismember and decapitate them, eviscerate them, set them afire, take every precaution against their resurrection, for they are not merely the killers of his real family but a threat to the world.

The thought occurs to him that, if he survives, these terrifying experiences will provide him with material for a novel. He surely will be able to get past the opening sentence, an accomplishment of which he was incapable yesterday. Though his wife and children are lost to him forever, he might be able to salvage his career from the ruins of his life.

Slipping and sliding, he hurries toward the gap in the fence.

❋   ❋   ❋

The windshield wipers were caked with snow that was hardening into ice. They stuttered and thumped across the glass.

Oslett consulted the computer-generated map, then pointed to a turn-off ahead. "There, on the right."

Clocker put on the turn signal.

❋   ❋   ❋

Like the ghost ship *Mary Celeste* silently materializing from a strange fog with tattered sails unfurled and decks empty of crew, the abandoned church loomed out of the driving snow.

At first, in the obscuring storm and fading gray light of late afternoon, Marty thought the building was in good repair, but that impression was transient. As they drew nearer, he saw that a lot of roof tiles were missing. Sections of the copper rain gutter were gone, while other pieces dangled precariously, swaying and creaking in the wind. Most of the windows were broken out, and vandals had spray-painted obscenities on the once-hand-some brick walls.

Rambling complexes of buildings—offices, workshops, a nursery, dormitories, a dining hall—stood immediately behind and to both sides of the steepled main structure. The Prophetic Church of the Rapture had been a cult that required its members to contribute all of their worldly belongings upon admittance and to live in a tightly governed commune.

They raced through the inch-deep snow, as fast as the girls could manage, toward the entrance to the church, rather than to one of the other buildings, because the church was closest. They needed to get out of sight as quickly as possible. Though The Other could track them through his connection with Marty no matter where they went, at least he couldn't *shoot* at them if he couldn't see them.

Twelve broad steps led up to a double set of ten-foot-high oak doors with six-foot-high fanlights above each pair. All but a few ruby and yellow shards of glass had been broken out of the fanlights, leaving dark gaps between the thick ribs of leading. The doors were recessed in a twenty-foot-high cinquefoil arch, above which was an enormous and elaborately patterned wheel window that still contained twenty percent of its original glass, most likely because it was a harder target for stones.

The four carved-oak doors were weather-beaten, scarred, cracked, and spray-painted with more obscenities that glowed softly in the ashen light of the premature dusk. On one, a vandal had crudely drawn the white hourglass shape of a female form complete with breasts and a crotch defined by the letter Y, and beside it was a representation of a phallus as large as a man. Beveled letters, cut by a master stone carver, made the same promise in the granite lintel above each set of doors, HE LIFTETH US UNTO HEAVEN; however, over those words, the spoilers had sprayed BULL-SHIT in red paint.

The cult had been creepy, and its founder—Jonathan Caine—had been a fraud and pederast, but Marty was more chilled by the vandals than by the misguided people who had followed Caine. At least the faithful cultists had *believed* in something, no matter how misguided, had yearned to be worthy of God's grace, and had sacrificed for their beliefs, even if the sacrifices ultimately proved to be stupid; they had dared to dream even if their dreams had ended in tragedy. The mindless hatred that informed the scrawlings of the graffitists was the work of empty people who believed in nothing, were incapable of dreaming, and thrived on the pain of others.

One of the doors stood ajar six inches. Marty grabbed the edge of it and pulled. The hinges were corroded, the oak was warped, but the door grated outward another twelve or fourteen inches.

Paige went inside first. Charlotte and Emily trailed close behind her.

Marty never heard the shot that hit him.

As he started to follow the girls, a lance of ice impaled him, entering the upper-left quadrant of his back, exiting through the muscles and tendons below the collar bone on the same side. The piercing chill was so cold that the blizzard hammering the church seemed like a tropical disturbance by comparison, and he shuddered violently.

The next thing he knew, he was lying on the snow-covered brick stoop in front of the door, wondering how he had gotten there. He was half convinced he had just stretched out for a nap, but the pain in his bones indicated he'd dropped hard onto his unlikely bed.

He stared up through the descending snow and wintry light at letters in granite, letters on granite.

HE LIFTETH US UNTO HEAVEN.

BULLSHIT.

He only realized he'd been shot when Paige rushed out of the church and dropped to one knee at his side, shouting, "Marty, oh God, my God, you've been shot, the son of a bitch shot you," and he thought, *Oh, yes, of course, that's it, I've been shot, not stabbed by a lance of ice.*

Paige rose from beside him, raised the Mossberg. He heard two shots. They were exceedingly loud, unlike the stealthy bullet that had knocked him to the bricks.

Curious, he turned his head to see how close their indefatigable enemy had come. He expected to discover the look-alike charging at him, only a few yards away, unfazed by shotgun pellets.

Instead, The Other remained at a distance from the church, out of range of the two rounds Paige had fired. He was a black figure on a field of white, the details of his too-familiar face unrevealed by the waning gray light. Ranging back and forth through the snow, back and forth, lanky and quick, he seemed to be a wolf stalking a herd of sheep, watchful and patient, biding his time until the moment of ultimate vulnerability arrived.

The poniard of ice that transfixed Marty became, from one second to the next, a stiletto of fire. With the heat came excruciating pain that made him gasp. At last the abstract concept of a bullet wound was translated into the language of reality.

Paige lifted the Mossberg again.

Regaining clarity of mind with the pain, Marty said, "Don't waste the ammo. Let him go for now. Help me up."

With her assistance, he was able to get to his feet.

"How bad?" she asked worriedly.

"I'm not dying. Let's get inside before he decides to take another shot at us."

He followed her through the door into the narthex, where the darkness was relieved only by faint rays penetrating the partly open door and glassless fanlights.

The girls were crying, Charlotte louder than Emily, and Marty tried to reassure them. "It's okay, I'm all right, just a little nick. All I need is a Band-Aid, one with a picture of Snoopy on it, and I'll feel all better."

In truth, his left arm was half numb. He only had partial use of it. When he flexed his hand, he couldn't curl it into a tight fist.

Paige eased to the eighteen-inch gap between the big door and the jamb, where the wind whistled and gibbered. She peered out at The Other.

Trying to get a better sense of the damage the bullet had done, Marty slipped his right hand inside his ski jacket and gingerly explored the front of his left shoulder. Even a light touch ignited a flare of pain that made him grit his teeth. His wool sweater was saturated with blood.

"Take the girls farther back into the church," Paige whispered urgently, though their enemy could not possibly have heard her out there in the storm. "All the way to the other end."

"What're you talking about?"

"I'll wait here for him."

The girls protested. "Mommy, don't." "Mom, come with us, you gotta." "Mommy, please."

"I'll be fine," Paige said, "I'll be safe. Really. It'll be perfect. Don't you see? Marty, when the creep senses you moving away, he'll come into the church. He'll expect us to be together." As she talked, she put two more shells into the Mossberg magazine to replace the most recent rounds she'd expended. "He won't expect me to be waiting right here for him."

Marty remembered having this same discussion before, back at the cabin, when she wanted to go outside and hide in the rocks. Her plan hadn't worked then, although not because it was flawed. The Other had driven past her in the Jeep, evidently unaware that she was lying in wait. If he hadn't pulled such an unpredictable stunt, ramming the station wagon right into the house, she might have slipped up on him and dropped him from behind.

Nevertheless, Marty didn't want to leave her alone by the door. But there was no time for debate because he suspected his wound was soon going to begin sapping what strength he still had. Besides, he didn't have a better plan to suggest.

In the gloom, he could barely recognize Paige's face.

He hoped this wouldn't be the last time he saw it.

He shepherded Charlotte and Emily out of the narthex and into the nave. It smelled of dust and dampness and the wild things that nested there in the years since the cultists had left to resume their shattered lives instead of rising to sit at the right hand of the Lord.

On the north side, the restless wind harried snow through the broken windows. If winter had a heart, inanimate and carved of ice, it would have been no more frigid than that place, nor could death have been more arctic.

"My feet are cold," Emily said.

He said, "Sssshhh. I know."

"Mine too," Charlotte said in a whisper.

"I know."

Having something so ordinary to complain about helped to make their situation seem less bizarre, less frightening.

"Really cold," Charlotte elaborated.

"Keep going. All the way to the front."

None of them had boots, only athletic shoes. Snow had saturated the fabric, caked in every crease, and turned to ice. Marty figured they didn't need to worry about frostbite just yet. That took a while to develop. They might not live long enough to suffer from it.

Shadows hung like bunting throughout the nave, but that large chamber was brighter than the narthex. Arched double-lancet windows, long ago relieved of the burden of glass, were featured along both side walls and soared two-thirds of the distance to the vaulted ceiling. They admitted sufficient light to reveal the rows of pews, the long center aisle leading to the chancel rail, the great choir, and even some of the high altar at the front.

The brightest things in the church were the desecrations by the vandals, who had sprayed their obscenities across the interior walls in greater profusion than they had done outside. He'd suspected the paint was luminous when he'd seen it on the exterior of the building; indeed, in dimmer precincts, the serpentine scrawls glowed orange and blue and green and yellow, overlapping, coiling, intertwining, until it almost seemed as if they were real snakes writhing on the walls.

Marty was tense with the expectation of gunfire.

At the chancel rail, the gate was missing.

"Keep going," he urged the girls.

The three of them continued on to the altar platform, from which all of the ceremonial objects had been removed. On the back wall hung a thirty-foot-high cross of wood festooned with cobwebs.

His left arm was numb, yet it felt grossly swollen. The pain was like that of an abscessed tooth misplaced in his shoulder. He was nauseous—though whether from loss of blood or fear for Paige or because of the disorienting weirdness of the church, he didn't know.

*　　*　　*

Paige shrank from the front entrance into an area of the narthex that would remain dark even if the door opened farther.

Staring at the gap between the door and jamb, she saw phantom movements in the fuzzy gray light and churning snow. She repeatedly raised and lowered the gun. Each time the confrontation seemed to have arrived, her breath caught in her throat.

She didn't have to wait long. He came within three or four minutes, and he was not as circumspect as she expected him to be. Apparently sensing Marty's movement toward the far end of the building, The Other entered confidently, boldly.

As he was stepping across the threshold, silhouetted in the waning daylight, she aimed for mid-chest. The gun was shaking in her hands even before she squeezed the trigger, and it jumped with the recoil. She immediately chambered another round, fired again.

The first blast hit him solidly, but the second probably ruined the jamb more thoroughly than it ruined him, because he pitched backward, out of the doorway, out of sight.

She *knew* she'd inflicted a lot of damage, but there were no screams or cries of pain, so she went through the door with as much hope as caution, ready for the sight of a corpse on the steps. He was gone, and somehow that wasn't a surprise, either, although the manner of his swift disappearance was so puzzling that she actually turned and squinted up at the front of the church, as if he might be climbing that sheer facade with the alacrity of a spider.

She could search for tracks in the snow and try to hunt him down. She suspected he might want her to do that very thing.

Unnerved, she re-entered the church at a run.

* * *

Kill them, kill them all, kill them now.

Buckshot. In the throat, working abrasively deep in the meat of him. Along one side of the neck. Hard lumps embedded in his left temple. Left ear ragged and dripping. Lead acne pimples the flesh down the left cheek, across the chin. Lower lip torn. Teeth cracked and chipped. Spitting pellets. A blaze of pain but no eye damage, vision unimpaired.

He scuttles in a crouch along the south side of the church, through a twilight so flat and gray, so wrapped in gauzes of snow, that he casts no shadow. No shadow. No wife, no children, no mother, no father, gone, no life, stolen, used up and thrown away, no mirror in which to look, no reflection to confirm his substance, no shadow, only footprints in the new snow to support his claim to existence, footprints and his hatred, like Claude Rains in *The Invisible Man*, defined by footprints and fury.

He frenziedly seeks an entrance, hastily inspecting each window as he passes it.

Virtually all of the glass is gone from the tall stained-glass panels, but the steel mullions remain. Much of the lead came that defined the original patterns remains between the mullions, though in many places it is bent and twisted and drooping, tortured by weather or by the hands of vandals, rendering the outlines of the original religious symbols and figures unrecognizable, and in their place leaving teratogenic forms as meaningless as the shapes in melted candles.

The next to the last nave window is missing its steel frame, mullions, and came. The granite stool marking the base of the window is five feet off the ground. He boosts himself up with the nimbleness of a gymnast and squats on his haunches on the deep sill. He peers into numberless shadows interleaved with strange sinuous streams of radiant orange, yellow, green, and blue.

A child screams.

❊   ❊   ❊

Racing down the center aisle of the graffiti-smeared church, Paige had the peculiar feeling that she was underwater in tropical climes, beneath a Caribbean cove, in caverns of gaudily luminescent coral, equatorial seaweed waving its feathery and radiant fronds on all sides of her.

Charlotte screamed.

Having reached the chancel rail, Paige spun to face the nave. Swinging the Mossberg left and right, searching in panic for the threat, she saw The Other as Emily shouted, "In the window, get him!"

He was, indeed, squatting in one of the south-wall windows, a dark shape that seemed only half human against the fading light and the whitening showers of snow. Shoulders hunched, head low, arms dangling, he had an apelike aspect.

Her reflexes were quick. She fired the Mossberg without hesitation.

Even if the distance hadn't been in his favor, however, he would have escaped untouched because he was moving even as she pulled the trigger. With the fluid grace of a wolf, he seemed to *pour* off the sill and onto the floor. The buckshot passed harmlessly through the space that he had occupied and clattered off the window jambs that had framed him.

Evidently on all fours, he vanished among the rows of pews, where the deepest shadows in the church were humbled. If she went hunting for him there, he would drag her down and kill her.

She backed through the chancel rail and across the sanctuary to Marty and the girls, keeping the shotgun ready.

The four of them retreated into an adjoining room that might have been the sacristy. A pair of casement windows admitted barely enough light to reveal three doors in addition to the one through which they'd entered.

Paige closed the door to the sanctuary and attempted to lock it. But it wasn't equipped with a lock. No furniture was available to brace or blockade it, either.

Marty tried one of the other doors. "Closet."

Shrill wind and snow erupted through the door that Charlotte opened, so she slammed it shut.

Checking the third possibility, Emily said, "Stairs."

❋   ❋   ❋

Among the pews. Creeping. Cautious.

He hears a door slam shut.

He waits.

Listens.

Hunger. Hot pain fades quickly to a low heat. Bleeding slows to a trickle, an ooze. Now hunger overwhelms him as his body demands enormous amounts of fuel to facilitate the reconstruction of damaged tissues.

Already he's metabolizing body fat and protein to make urgent repairs to torn and severed blood vessels. His metabolism accelerates unmercifully, an entirely autonomic function over which he has no power.

This gift that makes him so much less vulnerable than other men will soon begin to exact a toll. His weight will decline. Hunger will intensify until it is nearly as excruciating as the agony of mortal wounds. The hunger will become a craving. The craving will become a desperate need.

He considers retreating, but he is so close. So close. They are on the run. Increasingly isolated. They cannot hold out against him. If he perseveres, in minutes they will all be dead.

Besides, his hatred and rage are as great as his hunger. He is frantic for the sweet satisfaction that only extreme violence can assure.

On the movie screen of his mind, homicidal images flicker enticingly: bullet-shattered skulls, brutally hammered faces, gouged eyes, torn throats, slashed torsos, flashing knives, hatchets, axes, severed limbs, women on fire, screaming children, the bruised throats of young prostitutes, flesh dissolving under a spray of acid. . . .

He crawls out from among the pews, into the center aisle, rising into a crouch.

The walls swarm with glowing extraterrestrial hieroglyphics.

He is in the nest of the enemy.

Alien and strange. Hostile and inhuman.

His fear is great. But it only feeds his rage.

He hurries to the front of the room, through a gap in a railing, toward the door beyond which they retreated.

❋   ❋   ❋

Light as thin as fish broth seeped down from unseen windows above and around the turns in the spiral staircase.

The buildings to which the church was attached were two stories high. There might be a connecting passage between these stairs and another structure, but Marty had no idea where they were headed. For that reason he almost wished they had taken the door that led outside.

However, the numbness in his arm hampered him severely, and the pain in his shoulder, which grew worse by the minute, was a serious drain on his energy. The building was unheated, as cold as the world outside, but at least it offered shelter from the wind. Between his wound and the storm, he didn't think he would last long beyond the walls of the church.

The girls climbed ahead of him.

Paige came last, worrying aloud because the door at the foot of the stairs, like the sacristy door, did not have a lock. She edged up backward, step by step, covering the territory behind them.

They soon reached a deep-set multifoil window in the outer wall, which had been the source of the meager illumination below. Most of the clear glass was intact. The light on the twisting stairs above was of an equally dreary quality and most likely came from another window of the same size and style.

Marty moved slower and his breathing grew more labored the higher they ascended, as if they were reaching altitudes at which the oxygen content of the air was drastically declining. The pain in his left shoulder intensified, and his nausea thickened.

The stained plaster walls, gray wooden steps, and dishwater light reminded him of depressing Swedish movies from the fifties and sixties, films about hopelessness, despair, and grim fate.

Initially, the handrail along the outer wall was not essential to his progress. However, it swiftly became a necessary crutch. In dismayingly short order, he found that he could not rely entirely on the strength of his increasingly shaky legs and also needed to pull himself upward with his good right arm.

By the time they came to the second multifoil window, with still more steps and gray luminosity ahead, he knew where they were. In a bell tower.

The stairwell was not going to lead to a passageway that would connect them to the second floor of another building, because they were already higher than two floors. Each additional step upward was an irreversible commitment to this single option.

Gripping the rail with his good right hand, beginning to feel lightheaded and afraid of losing his balance, Marty stopped to warn Paige that they better consider going back. Perhaps her reverse perspective on the stairwell had prevented her from realizing the nature of the trap.

Before he could speak, the door clattered open below, out of sight beyond the first few turns.

❋   ❋   ❋

His last clear thought is the sudden realization that he does not have the .38 Chief's Special any longer, must have lost it after being shot at the front entrance to the church, dropped it in the snow, and has not noticed the loss until this moment. He has no time to retrieve it, even if he knew where to search. Now his primary weapon is his body, his hands, his murderous skills, and his exceptional strength. His ferocious hatred is a weapon, as well, because it motivates him to take any risk, confront extreme danger, and endure cruel suffering that would incapacitate an ordinary man. But he is not ordinary, he is a hero, he is judgment and vengeance, he is the rending fury of justice, avenger of his murdered family, nemesis of all creatures that are not of this earth but would try to claim it as their own, savior of humanity. That is his reason for existence. His life has meaning and purpose at last: to save the world from this inhuman scourge.

❋   ❋   ❋

Just before the door opened below Paige, the narrow winding stairs called to mind lighthouses she had seen in movies. From the image of a lighthouse, she leapt to the realization that they were in the church bell tower. Then the lower door opened, out of sight beyond the curving walls of the spiral stairwell, and they had no choice but to continue to the top.

She briefly considered charging downward, opening fire when she was about to come upon him. But hearing her descend, he might retreat into the sacristy, where already the heavy yarn of dusk was knitting into darkness, where he could stalk her in the gloom and attack when her attention was diverted to the wrong skein of shadows.

She could also wait where she was, let him come to her, and blow his head off as soon as he rose into sight. If he sensed her waiting, however, and if he opened fire as he rounded the bend, he couldn't miss her in those tight confines. She might be dead before she could pull the trigger, or might at best get off a shot into the ceiling of the stairwell as she fell, harming nothing but plaster.

Remembering the black silhouette on the sill of the nave window and the uncanny fluidity with which it had moved, she suspected that The Other's senses were sharper than her own. Lying in wait with the hope of surprising it was probably a fool's game.

She continued upward, trying to convince herself that they were in the best of all possible positions: defending high ground against an enemy that was allowed only one narrow approach. It seemed as if the bell-tower platform ought to be an unassailable redoubt.

*　　*　　*

Awash in agonies of hunger, sweating with need and rage, lead pellets popping from his flesh, he heals step by rising step but at a cost. Body fat dwindles and even some muscle tissue and bone mass are sacrificed to the wildly accelerated mending of buckshot wounds. He gnashes his teeth with the compulsive need to chew, chew and swallow, rend and tear, feed, feed, even though there is no food to satisfy the terrible pangs that rack him.

*　　*　　*

At the top of the tower, one half of the space was completely walled, providing a landing for the stairs. An ordinary door gave access from that vestibule to another portion of the platform that was exposed to the elements on three sides. Charlotte and Emily opened the door without difficulty and hurried out of the stairwell.

Marty followed them. He was dismayingly weak but even dizzier than feeble. He gripped the door jamb and then the cast-concrete cap of the waist-high wall—the parapet—that enclosed the other three sides of the outer bell-tower platform.

With the wind-chill factor, the temperature must have been five or ten degrees below zero. He winced as the bitter gale lashed his face—and didn't dare think about how much colder it would seem ten minutes or an hour later.

Though Paige might have enough shotgun shells to prevent The Other from reaching them, they wouldn't all survive the night.

If the weather reports proved correct and the storm lasted until well past dawn, they wouldn't be able to use the Mossberg to try to draw attention to their plight until morning. The wailing wind would disperse the crash of gunfire before that telltale sound could reach beyond church property.

The exposed platform was twelve feet across with a tile floor and scuppers to let out rainwater. Two corner posts, about six feet high, stood atop the perimeter wall and, with the assistance of the full wall on the east side, supported a peaked belfry roof.

No bell hung in the belfry. When Marty squinted up into the dim recesses of that conical space, he saw the black shapes of what might have been loudspeaker horns from which the taped tolling of bells had once been broadcast.

Appearing to grow ever whiter as the day steadily darkened, snow slanted into the belfry on the northwest wind. A small drift was forming along the base of the south wall.

The girls had fled directly across the deck to the west side, as far as they could get from the door, but Marty felt too wobbly to traverse even that short distance without support. As he circled the platform to join them, leaning with his right hand against the waist-high parapet, the floor tiles seemed slippery though they were textured to be less treacherous when wet.

He made the mistake of glancing over the edge of the parapet at the phosphorescent mantle of snow on the ground six or seven stories below. The view prompted an attack of vertigo so strong that he almost passed out before averting his eyes from the long fall.

When he reached his daughters, Marty was more nauseous than ever and shivering so badly that any attempt to speak would have resulted in shuddery chains of sounds only vaguely resembling words. As frigid as he was, perspiration nonetheless trickled the length of his spine. Wind howled, snow whirled, night descended, and the bell tower seemed to be turning like a carrousel.

The pain from the wound in his shoulder had spread through his upper body, until the fiery point of injury was only the center of a more generalized ache that throbbed with every thud of his rapidly pounding heart. He felt helpless, ineffective, and cursed himself for being so useless at that very moment when his family needed him most.

Paige hadn't joined Marty and the girls on the platform. She stood on the far side of the open door, on the enclosed landing, peering down the curved stairs.

Flames spouted from the bore of the gun, making shadows dance. The boom of the shot—and echoes of it—tolled across the bell-tower platform, and from the stairwell came a shriek of pain and rage that was less than human, followed immediately by a second shot and an even more shrill and alien screech.

Marty's hopes soared—and collapsed an instant later when the agonized cry of The Other was followed by Paige's scream.

*　　*　　*

Along the curved wall, step by step, burning with hunger, filled with fire, the body's furnace stoked to a white-hot blaze, tortured by need, alert for a sound, higher, higher, higher in the darkness, churning within, seething, desperate and driven, driven by need, then the looming thing, the Paige-thing on the landing above, a silhouette wrapped in shadows but recognizably the Paige-thing, repulsive and deadly, an alien seed. He crosses his arms over his face, protecting his eyes, absorbing the first hard blast, a thousand spikes of pain, hammered deep, almost knocked backward down the stairs, rocking on his heels, arms paralyzed for an instant, bleeding and torn, afire with need, need, inner pain worse than the outer, *move-move-confront-challenge-grapple-and-prevail,* lunging forward, upward, screaming involuntarily, the second blast a sledgehammer to the chest, heart stutters, stutters, blackness swoops, heart stutters, left lung pops like a balloon, no breath, blood in his mouth. Flesh rips, blood spurts, flesh knits, blood seeps. He inhales, inhales and is still moving upward, upward into the woman, never having endured such agony, a world of pain, cauldron of fire, lava in his veins, a nightmare of all-consuming hunger, testing his miraculous body's limits, teetering on the edge of death, smashes into her, drives her backward, claws at the weapon, tears it away from her, pitches it aside, going for her throat, her face, snapping at her face, biting at her face, she's holding him back, but he needs her face, face, her smooth pale face, alien meat, sustenance to slake the need, the need, the terrible burning endless *need.*

*　　*　　*

The Other tore the shotgun out of Paige's grasp, threw it aside, slammed into her, and knocked her backward through the doorway.

The area under the belfry seemed to be illuminated more by the natural phosphorescence of the falling snow than by the fast-fading light of the dying day. Marty saw The Other had been gruesomely wounded and had undergone strange changes—was *still* undergoing them—although the ashen twilight shrouded details of its metamorphosis.

Paige fell onto the bell-tower platform. The Other dropped atop her like a predator upon its prey, tearing at her ski jacket, issuing a dry hiss of excitement, gnashing its teeth with the ferocity of a wild creature from out of the mountain woods.

It *was* a thing now. Not a man. Something dreadful if not quite identifiable was happening to it.

Driven by desperation, Marty found within himself one last well of strength. He overcame dizziness bordering on total disorientation, and he took a running kick at the hateful thing that wanted his life. He caught it squarely in the head. Although he was wearing sneakers, the kick had tremendous impact, shattering all the ice that had formed on the shoe.

The Other howled, tumbled off Paige, rolled against the south wall, but at once came onto its knees, then into a standing position, cat-quick and unpredictable.

As the thing was still tumbling, Paige scrambled to the kids, crowding them behind her.

Marty lunged for the discarded gun on the landing, inches beyond the other side of the open door. He crouched and, with his right hand, grabbed the Mossberg by the barrel.

Paige and one of the girls yelled a warning.

He didn't have time to reverse his grip on the weapon and pump a round into the chamber. He rose and turned in one movement, issuing a savage scream not unlike the sounds his adversary had been making, and swung the shotgun by the barrel.

The Mossberg stock hammered into The Other's left side, but not hard enough to shatter any ribs. Marty had been forced to wield it with one hand, unable to use his left, and the jolt of the blow rang back on him, sent pain through his chest, hurting him worse than it hurt The Other.

Wrenching the Mossberg from Marty, the look-alike didn't turn the gun to its own use, as if it had devolved into a subhuman state in which it no longer recognized the weapon as anything more than a club. Instead, it pitched the Mossberg away, whirled it over the waist-high wall into the snowy night.

"Look-alike" no longer applied. Marty could still see aspects of himself in that warped countenance, but, even in the murky dusk, no one would mistake them for brothers. The shotgun damage wasn't primarily what made the difference. The pale face was strangely thin and pointed, bone structure too prominent, eyes sunken deep in dark circles: cadaverous.

The Mossberg was still spinning into the falling snow when the thing rushed Marty and drove him into the north wall. The waist-high concrete cap caught him across the kidneys so hard it knocked out of him what little strength he had managed to dredge up.

The Other had him by the throat. Replay of the upstairs hall, yesterday, Mission Viejo. Bending him backward as he'd been bent over the gallery railing. Farther to fall this time, into a darkness blacker than night, into a coldness deeper than winter storms.

The hands around his neck felt not like hands at all. Hard as the metal jaws of a bear trap. Hot in spite of the bitter night, so hot they almost scorched him.

It wasn't just strangling him but trying to bite him as it had tried to bite Paige, striking snakelike, hissing. Growling in the back of its throat. Teeth snapped shut on empty air an inch from Marty's face. Breath sour and thick. The stench of decay. He had the feeling it would devour him if it could, rip out his throat and take his blood.

Reality outstripped imagination.

All reason fled.

Nightmares were real. Monsters existed.

With his good hand, he got a fistful of its hair and pulled hard, jerking its head back, frantic to keep its flashing teeth away from him.

Its eyes glittered and rolled. Foaming spittle flew when it shrieked.

Heat poured off its body, and it was as hot to the touch as the sun-warmed vinyl of a car seat in summer.

Letting go of Marty's throat but still pinning him against the parapet, The Other reached back and seized the hand with which he had clutched its hair. Bony fingers. Inhuman. Hard talons. It seemed fleshless, brittle, yet increasingly fierce and strong, and it almost crushed his hand before he let go of its hair. Then it whipped its head to the side and bit his forearm, ripped the sleeve of his jacket but not his flesh. Tore at him again, sank teeth into his hand, he screamed. It grabbed his ski jacket, pulling him off the parapet as he tried to lean into the void to escape it, snapped at his face, teeth clashing a fraction of an inch short of his cheek, rasped out a single tortured word, *"Need,"* and snapped at his eyes, snapped, snapped at his eyes.

"Be at peace, Alfie."

Marty registered the words but initially wasn't clear-headed enough either to realize what they meant or to grasp that the voice was one he had never heard before.

The Other reared its head back, as if about to make its final lunge for his face. But it held that posture, eyes wild, skeletal face as softly luminous as the snow, teeth bared, rolling its head from side to side, issuing a thin wordless sound as if it wasn't sure why it was hesitating.

Marty knew that he should use the moment to ram a knee into the thing's crotch, try to rush it backward across the platform, to the opposite parapet, up, out, and over. He could imagine what to do, see it in his writer's eye, a fully realized moment of action in a novel or movie, but he had no strength left. The pain in his gunshot wound, throat, and bitten hand swelled anew, dizziness and nausea overwhelmed him, and he knew he was on the verge of a blackout.

"Be at peace, Alfie," the voice repeated more firmly.

Still holding Marty, who was helpless in its ferocious grip, The Other turned its head toward the speaker.

A flashlight winked on, directed at the creature's face.

Blinking toward the light source, Marty saw a bearlike man, tall and barrel-chested, and a smaller man in a black ski suit. They were strangers.

They showed a little surprise but not the shock and horror that Marty would have expected.

"Jesus," the smaller man said, "what's happening to him?"

"Metabolic meltdown," said the larger man.

"Jesus."

Marty glanced toward the west wall of the belfry, where Paige was crouched with the kids, sheltering them, holding their heads against her breast to prevent them from seeing too much of the creature.

"Be at peace, Alfie," the smaller man repeated.

In a voice tortured by rage, pain, and confusion, The Other rasped, "Father. Father. Father?"

Marty was still tightly held, and his attention was again drawn to the thing that had once looked like him.

The flashlight-illuminated face was more hideous than it had appeared in the gloom. Wisps of steam *were* rising off it in some places, confirming his sense that it was hot. Scores of shotgun wounds pocked one side of its head, but they were not bleeding and, in fact, seemed more than half healed. As Marty stared, a black lead pellet squeezed out of the creature's temple and oozed down its cheek in a thin trail of yellowish fluid.

The wounds were its least repulsive features. In spite of the physical strength it still possessed, it was as meagerly padded with flesh as something that had crawled out of a coffin after a year underground. Skin was stretched tightly over its facial bones. Its ears were shriveled into hard knots of cartilage and lay flat against the head. Desiccated lips had shrunk back from the gums, giving the teeth greater prominence, creating the illusion of a nascent muzzle and the wicked bite of a predator.

It was Death personified, the Grim Reaper without his voluminous black robes and scythe, on his way to a masquerade ball in a costume of flesh so thin and cheap that it was not for a moment convincing.

"Father?" it said again, gazing at the stranger in the black ski suit. "Father?"

Insistently: "Be at peace, Alfie."

The name "Alfie" was so unsuited to the grotesque apparition still clutching Marty that he suspected he was hallucinating the arrival of the two men.

The Other turned away from the flashlight beam and glared at Marty once more. It seemed uncertain of what to do next.

Then it lowered its graveyard face to his, cocking its head as if with curiosity. "My life? My life?"

Marty didn't know what it was asking him, and he was so weak from loss of blood or shock or both that he could only push at it feebly with his right hand. "Let me go."

"Need," it said. "Need, need, *need, need, NEED, NEEEEEEEEED.*"

The voice spiraled into a shrill squeal. Its mouth cracked wide in a humorless grin, and it struck at Marty's face.

A gunshot boomed, The Other's head jerked back, Marty sagged against the parapet as the creature let go of him, and its scream of demonic fury drew muffled cries of terror from Emily and Charlotte.

The Other clamped its skeletal hands to its shattered skull, as if trying to hold itself together.

The flashlight beam wavered, found it.

The fissures in the bone healed, and the bullet hole began to close up, forcing the lead slug out of the skull. But the cost of this miraculous healing became obvious as The Other's skull began to change more dramatically, growing smaller and narrower and more lupine, as if bone was melting and reforming under the tight sheath of skin, borrowing mass from one place to rebuild damage in another.

"Cannibalizing itself to close the wound," said the big man.

More ghostly wisps of vapor were rising from the creature, and it began to tear at the clothes it wore as if it could not tolerate the heat.

The smaller man shot it again. In the face.

Still holding its head, The Other reeled across the bell-tower platform and collided with the south parapet. It almost tipped over and out into the void.

It crumpled to its knees, shedding its torn clothing as if the garments were the tatters of a cocoon, squirming forth in a darker and utterly inhuman form, twitching, jittering.

It was no longer shrieking or hissing. It sobbed. In spite of its increasingly monstrous appearance, the sobbing rendered it less threatening and even pitiable.

Relentless, the gunman stepped toward it and fired a third shot.

The sobbing chilled Marty, perhaps because there was something human and pathetic about it. Too weak to stand, he slid down to the floor, his back against the waist-high parapet, and had to look away from the thrashing creature.

An eternity passed before The Other was entirely motionless and quiet.

Marty heard his daughters weeping.

Reluctantly he turned his eyes to the body which lay directly across the platform from him and which was bathed in the mercilessly revealing beam of the flashlight. The corpse was a puzzle of black bones and glistening flesh, the greater part of its substance having been consumed in its frantic attempts to heal itself and stay alive. The twisted and jagged remains more resembled those of an alien life form than those of a man.

Wind blew.

Snow fell.

A greater cold came down.

After a while, the man in the black ski suit turned away from the remains and spoke to the bearish man. "A very bad boy indeed."

The larger man said nothing.

Marty wanted to ask who they were. His grip on consciousness was so tenuous, however, that he thought the effort of speaking might cause him to pass out.

To his partner, the smaller man said, "What'd you think of the church? As weird as anything Kirk and the crew have turned up, isn't it? All those obscenities Day-Gloing on the walls. It'll make our little scenario all the more convincing, don't you think?"

Though he felt as lightheaded as if he had been drinking, and though he was having difficulty keeping his thoughts focused, Marty now had confirmed what he'd suspected when the two men first arrived: they were not saviors, merely new executioners, and only marginally less mysterious than The Other.

"You're going to do it?" the larger of the two asked.

"Too much trouble to haul them back to the cabin. You don't think this weird church is an even better setting?"

"Drew," the big man said, "there are a number of things about you I like."

The smaller man seemed confused. He wiped at the snow that the wind stuck to his eyelashes. "What'd you say?"

"You're damned smart, even if you did go to Princeton and Harvard. You've got a good sense of humor, you really do, you make me laugh, even when it's at my expense. Hell, especially when it's at my expense."

"What're you talking about?"

"But you're a crazy, sick son of a bitch," the big man said, raised his own handgun, and shot his partner.

Drew, if that was his name, hit the tile floor as hard as if he had been made of stone. He landed on his side, facing Marty. His mouth was open, as were his eyes, though he had a blind man's gaze and seemed to have nothing to say.

In the center of Drew's forehead was an ugly bullet hole. For as long as he could hold fast to consciousness, Marty stared at the wound, but it didn't appear to be healing.

Wind blew.

Snow fell.

A greater cold came down—along with a greater darkness.

7.

Marty woke with his forehead pressed to cold glass. Heavy snow churned against the other side of the pane.

They were parked next to service station pumps. Between the pumps and through the falling snow, he saw a well-lighted convenience store with large windows.

He rolled his head away from the glass and sat up straighter. He was in the back seat of a truck-type station wagon, an Explorer or Cherokee.

Behind the steering wheel sat the big man from the bell tower. He was turned around in his seat, looking back. "How you doing?"

Marty tried to answer. His mouth was dry, his tongue stuck to his palate, and his throat was sore. The croak that escaped him was not a word.

"I think you'll be all right," the stranger said.

Marty's ski jacket was open, and he raised one trembling hand to his left shoulder. Under the blood-damp wool sweater, he felt an odd bulky mass.

"Field dressing," the man said. "Best I could do in a hurry. We get out of these mountains, across the county line, I'll clean the wound and rebandage it."

"Hurts."

"Don't doubt it."

Marty felt not merely weak but frail. He lived by words and never failed to have the right ones when he needed them, so it was frustrating to find himself with barely enough energy to speak. "Paige?" he asked.

"In there with the kids," the stranger said, indicating the combination service station and convenience store. "Girls are using the bathroom. Mrs. Stillwater's paying the cashier, getting some hot coffee. I just filled the tank."

"You're . . . ?"

"Clocker. Karl Clocker."

"Shot him."

"Sure did."

"Who . . . who . . . was he?"

"Drew Oslett. Bigger question is—*what* was he?"

"Huh?"

Clocker smiled. "Born of man and woman, but he wasn't much more human than poor Alfie. If there's an evil alien species out there somewhere, marauding through the galaxy, they'll never mess with us if they know we can produce specimens like Drew."

*　　*　　*

Clocker drove, and Charlotte occupied the front passenger seat. He referred to her as "First Officer Stillwater" and assigned her the duty of "handing the captain his coffee when he needs another sip of it and, otherwise, guarding against catastrophic spillage that might irreparably contaminate the ship."

Charlotte was uncharacteristically restrained and unwilling to play.

Marty worried about what psychological scars their ordeal might have left in her—and what additional trouble and trauma might be ahead of them.

In the back seat, Emily sat behind Karl Clocker, Marty behind Charlotte, and Paige between them. Emily was not merely quiet but totally silent, and Marty worried about her too.

Out of Mammoth Lakes on Route 203 and south on 395, progress was slow. Two or three inches of snow were on the ground, and the blizzard was in full howl.

Clocker and Paige drank coffee, and the girls had hot chocolate. The aromas should have been appealing, but they increased Marty's queasiness.

He was allowed apple juice. From the convenience store, Paige had purchased a six-pack of juice in cans.

"It's the only thing you might be able to hold in your stomach," Clocker said. "And even if it makes you gag, you've got to take as much of it as you can because, with that wound, you're sure as hell dehydrating dangerously."

Marty was so shaky that, even with his right hand, he couldn't hold the juice without spilling it. Paige put a straw in it, held it for him, and blotted his chin when he dribbled.

He felt helpless. He wondered if he was more seriously wounded than they had told him or than they realized.

Intuitively, he sensed he was dying—but he didn't know if that was an accurate perception or the curse of a writer's imagination.

❋   ❋   ❋

The night was filled with white flakes, as if the day had not merely faded but shattered into an infinitude of pieces that would drift down forever through an unending darkness.

Over the chittering of the tire chains and the grumble of the engine, as they descended from the Sierras in a train of cars behind a snowplow and cinder truck, Clocker told them about the Network.

It was an alliance of powerful people in government, business, law-enforcement, and the media, who were brought together by a shared perception that traditional Western democracy was an inefficient and inevitably catastrophic system by which to order society. They were convinced that the vast majority of citizens were self-indulgent, sensation-seeking, void of spiritual values, greedy, lazy, envious, racist, and woefully ignorant on virtually all issues of importance.

"They believe," Clocker said, "that recorded history proves the masses have always been irresponsible and civilization has progressed only by luck and by the diligent efforts of a few visionaries."

"Do they think this idea's new?" Paige asked scornfully. "Have they heard of Hitler, Stalin, Mao Tse-tung?"

"What they think's new," Clocker said, "is that we've reached an age when the technological underpinnings of society are so complex and so vulnerable because of this complexity that civilization—in fact, the planet itself—can't survive if government makes decisions based on the whims and selfish motivations of the masses that pull the levers in the voting booths."

"Crap," Paige said.

Marty would have seconded her opinion if he'd felt strong enough to join the discussion. But he had only enough energy to suck at the apple juice and swallow it.

"What they're really about," Clocker said, "is brute power. The only thing new about them, regardless of what they think, is they're working together from different extremes of the political spectrum. The people who want to ban *Huckleberry Finn* from libraries and the people who want to ban books by Anne Rice may seem to be motivated by different concerns but they're spiritual brothers and sisters."

"Sure," Paige said. "They share the same motivation—the desire not merely to control what other people do but what they *think.*"

"The most radical environmentalists, those who want to reduce the population of the world by extreme measures within a decade or two, because they think the planet's ecology is in danger, are in some ways simpatico with the people who'd like to reduce the world's population drastically just because they feel there are too many black and brown people in it."

Paige said, "An organization of such extremes can't hold together for long."

"I agree," Clocker said. "But if they want power badly enough, total power, they might work together long enough to seize it. Then, when they're in control, they'll turn their guns on each other and catch the rest of us in the cross-fire."

"How big an organization are we talking about?" she asked.

After a hesitation, Clocker said, "Big."

Marty sucked on the straw, exceedingly grateful for the level of civilization that allowed for the sophisticated integration of farming, food-processing, packaging, marketing, and distribution of a product as self-indulgent as cool, sweet apple juice.

❋　　❋　　❋

"The Network directors feel modern technology embodies a threat to humanity," Clocker explained, switching the pounding windshield wipers to a slower speed, "but they aren't against employing the cutting edge of that technology in the pursuit of power."

The development of a completely controllable force of clones to serve as the singularly obedient police and soldiers of the next millennium was only one of a multitude of research programs intended to help bring on the new world, though it was one of the first to bear fruit. Alfie. The first individual of the first—or Alpha—generation of operable clones.

Because society was riddled with incorrect thinkers in positions of authority, the first clones were to be employed to assassinate leaders in business, government, media, and education who were too retrograde in their attitudes to be persuaded of the need for change. The clone was not a real person but more or less a machine made of flesh; therefore, it was an ideal assassin. It had no awareness of who had created and instructed it, so it couldn't betray its handlers or expose the conspiracy it served.

Clocker downshifted as the train of vehicles slowed on a particularly snowswept incline.

He said, "Because it isn't burdened by religion, philosophy, any system of beliefs, a family, or a past, there isn't much danger that a clone assassin will begin to doubt the morality of the atrocities it commits, develop a conscience, or show any trace of free will that might interfere with its performance of its assignments."

"But something sure went wrong with Alfie," Paige said.

"Yeah. And we'll never know exactly what."

Why did it look like me? Marty wanted to ask, but instead his head lolled onto Paige's shoulder and he lost consciousness.

❋   ❋   ❋

A hall of mirrors in a carnival funhouse. Frantically seeking a way out. Reflections gazing back at him with anger, envy, hatred, failing to mimic his own expressions and movements, stepping *out* of one looking-glass after another, pursuing him, an ever-growing army of Martin Stillwaters, so like him on the outside, so dark and cold on the inside. Now ahead of him as well, reaching out from the mirrors past which he runs and into which he blunders, grasping at him, all of them speaking in a single voice: *I need my life.*

The mirrors shattered as one, and he woke.

Lamplight.

Shadowy ceiling.

Lying in bed.

Cold and hot, shivering and sweating.

He tried to sit up. Couldn't.

"Honey?"

Barely enough strength to turn his head.

Paige. In a chair. Beside the bed.

Another bed beyond her. Shapes under blankets. The girls. Sleeping.

Drapes over the windows. Night at the edges of the drapes. She smiled.

"You with me, baby?"

He tried to lick his lips. They were cracked. His tongue was dry, furry.

She took a can of apple juice from a plastic ice bucket in which it was chilling, lifted his head off the pillow, and guided the straw between his lips.

After drinking, he managed to say, "Where?"

"A motel in Bishop."

"Far enough?"

"For now, it has to be," she said.

"Him?"

"Clocker? He'll be back."

He was dying of thirst. She gave him more juice.

"Worried," he whispered.

"Don't. Don't worry. It's okay now."

"Him."

"Clocker?" she asked.

He nodded.

"We can trust him," she said.

He hoped she was right.

Even drinking exhausted him. He lowered his head onto the pillow again.

Her face was like that of an angel. It faded away.

✾   ✾   ✾

Escaping from the hall of mirrors into a long black tunnel. Light at the far end, hurrying toward it, footsteps behind, a legion in pursuit of him, gaining on him, the men from out of the mirrors. The light is his salvation, an exit from the funhouse. He bursts out of the tunnel, into the brightness, which turns out to be the field of snow in front of the abandoned church, where he runs toward the front doors with Paige and the girls, The Other behind them, and a shot explodes, a lance of ice pierces his shoulder, the ice turns to fire, fire—

The pain was unbearable.

His vision was blurred with tears. He blinked, desperate to know where he was.

The same bed, the same room.

The blankets had been pulled aside.

He was naked to the waist. The bandage was gone.

Another explosion of pain in his shoulder wrung a scream from him.

But he was not strong enough to scream, and the cry issued as a soft, "Ahhhhhh."

He blinked away more tears.

The drapes were still closed over the windows. Daylight had replaced darkness at the edges.

Clocker loomed over him. Doing something to his shoulder.

At first, because the pain was excruciating, he thought Clocker was trying to kill him. Then he saw Paige with Clocker and knew that she would not let anything bad happen.

She tried to explain something to him, but he only caught a word here and there: "sulfur powder . . . antibiotic . . . penicillin . . ."

They bandaged his shoulder again.

Clocker gave him an injection in his good arm. He watched. With all of his other pains, he couldn't feel the prick of the needle.

For a while he was in a hall of mirrors again.

When he found himself in the motel bed once more, he turned his head and saw Charlotte and Emily sitting on the edge of the adjacent bed, watching over him. Emily was holding Peepers, the rock on which she had painted a pair of eyes, her pet.

Both girls looked terribly solemn.

He managed to smile at them.

Charlotte got off the bed, came to him, kissed his sweaty face.

Emily kissed him, too, and then she put Peepers in his good right hand. He managed to close his fingers around it.

Later, drifting up from dreamless sleep, he heard Clocker and Paige talking:

". . . don't think it's safe to move him," Paige said.

"You have to," Clocker said. "We're not far enough away from Mammoth Lakes, and there are only so many roads we could've taken."

"You don't know anyone's looking for us."

"You're right, I don't. But it's a safe bet. Sooner or later someone will be looking—and probably for the rest of our lives."

He drifted out and in, out and in, and when he saw Clocker at the bedside again, he said, "Why?"

"The eternal question," Clocker said, and smiled.

Refining the eternal question, Marty said, "Why you?"

Clocker nodded. "You'd wonder, of course. Well . . . I was never one of them. They made the serious mistake of thinking I was a true believer.

All my life I've wanted adventure, heroics, but it never seemed in the cards for me. Then this. Figured if I played along, the day would come when I'd have a chance to do serious damage to the Network if not vaporize it, pow, like a plasma-beam weapon."

"Thank you," Marty said, feeling consciousness slip away and wanting to express his gratitude while he still could.

"Hey, we're still not out of the woods yet," Clocker said.

*   *   *

When Marty regained consciousness, he wasn't sweating or shivering, but he still felt weak.

They were in a car, on a lonely highway at sunset. Paige was driving, and he was belted in the front passenger seat.

She said, "Are you okay?"

"Better," he said, and his voice was less shaky than it had been for a while. "Thirsty."

"There's some apple juice on the floor between your feet. I'll find a place to pull over."

"No. I can get it," he said, not really sure that he could.

As he bent forward, reaching to the floor with his right hand, he realized that his left arm was in a sling. He managed to get hold of a can and yank it loose of the six-pack to which it was connected. He braced it between his knees, pulled the ring-tab, and opened it.

The juice was barely chilled, but nothing ever tasted better—partly because he had managed to get it for himself without help. He finished the entire can in three long swallows.

When he turned his head, he saw Charlotte and Emily slumped in their seatbelts, snoozing in the back.

"They've hardly gotten any sleep for the last couple of nights," Paige said. "Bad dreams. And worried about you. But I guess being on the move makes them feel safer, and the motion of the car helps."

"Nights? Plural?" He knew they had fled Mammoth Lakes Tuesday night. He assumed it was Wednesday. "What sunset is that?"

"Friday's," she said.

He had been out of it for almost three days.

He looked around at the vast expanse of plains swiftly fading into the nightfall. "Where are we?"

"Nevada. Route Thirty-one south of Walker Lane. We'll pick up Highway Ninety-five and drive north to Fallon. We'll stay at a motel there tonight."

"Tomorrow?"

"Wyoming, if you're up to it."

"I'll be up to it. I guess there's a reason for Wyoming?"

"Karl knows a place we can stay there." When he asked her about the car, which he had never seen before, she said, "Karl again. Like the sulfur powder and the penicillin I've been treating you with. He seems to know where to get whatever he needs. He's some character."

"I don't even really know him," Marty said, reaching down for another can of apple juice, "but I love him like a brother."

He popped open the can and drank at least one-third of it. He said, "I like his hat too."

Paige laughed out of all proportion to the feeble humor of the remark, but Marty laughed with her.

"God," she said, driving north through gray, unpopulated land, "I love you, Marty. If you had died, I'd never have forgiven you."

❋　　❋　　❋

That night they took two rooms at the motel in Fallon, using a false name and paying cash in advance. They had a dinner of pizza and Pepsi in the motel. Marty was starved, but two pieces of pizza filled him.

While they ate, they played a game of Look Who's the Monkey Now, in which the purpose was to think of all the words for foods that began with the letter P. The girls weren't in their best playing form. In fact, they were so subdued that Marty worried about them.

Maybe they were just tired. After dinner, in spite of their nap in the car, Charlotte and Emily were asleep within seconds of putting heads to pillows.

They left the door open between the adjoining rooms. Karl Clocker had provided Paige with an Uzi submachine gun which had been illegally converted for full automatic fire. They kept it on the nightstand within easy reach.

Paige and Marty shared a bed. She stretched out to his right, so she could hold his good hand.

As they talked, he discovered that she had learned the answer to the question he'd never had a chance to ask Karl Clocker: *Why did it look like me?*

One of the most powerful men in the Network, primary owner of a media empire, had lost a four-year-old son to cancer. As the boy lay dying at Cedars-Sinai Hospital, five years ago, blood and bone-marrow samples had been taken from him because it was his father's emotional decision that the Alpha-series clones should be developed from his lost boy's genetic material. If functional clones could be made a reality, they would be a lasting monument to his son.

"Jesus, that's sick," Marty said. "What father would think a race of genetically engineered killers might be a suitable memorial? God Almighty."

"God had nothing to do with it," Paige said.

The Network representative assigned to obtain those blood and marrow samples from the lab had gotten confused and wound up with Marty's samples instead, which had been taken to determine whether he would be a suitable donor for Charlotte if she proved in need of a transplant.

"And they want to rule the world," Marty said, amazed. He was still far from recuperated and in need of more sleep, but he had to know one more thing before he drifted off. "If they only started engineering Alfie five years ago . . . how can he be a grown man?"

Paige said, "According to Clocker, they 'improved' on the basic human design in several ways."

They had given Alfie an unusual metabolism and tremendously accelerated healing power. They also engineered his phenomenally rapid maturation with human growth hormone and raised him from fetus to thirtyish adult with nonstop intravenous feeding and electrically stimulated muscle development over a period of less than two years.

"Like a damned hydroponic vegetable or something," she said.

"Dear Jesus," Marty said, and glanced at the nightstand to make sure the Uzi was there. "Didn't they have a few doubts when this clone didn't resemble the boy?"

"For one thing, the boy had been wasted by cancer between the ages of two and four. They didn't know what he might have looked like if he'd been healthy during those years. And besides, they'd edited the genetic material so extensively they couldn't be sure the Alpha generation would resemble the boy all that much anyway.

"He was taught language, mathematics, and other things largely by sophisticated subliminal input while he was asleep and growing."

She had more to tell him, but her voice faded gradually as he surrendered to a sleep filled with greenhouses in which human forms floated in tanks of viscous liquid . . .

. . . they are connected to tangles of plastic tubing and life-support machines, growing rapidly from fetuses to full adulthood, all doubles for him, and suddenly the eyes click open on a thousand of them at once, along rows and rows of tanks in building after building, and they speak as with a single voice: *I need my life.*

8.

The log cabin was on several acres of woodlands, a few miles from Jackson Hole, Wyoming, which had yet to enjoy its first snow of the season. Karl's directions were excellent, and they found the place with little difficulty, arriving late Saturday afternoon.

The cabin needed to be cleaned and aired-out, but the pantry was stocked with supplies. When the rust had been run out of the pipes, the water from the tap tasted clean and sweet.

On Monday, a Range Rover turned off the county road and drove to their front door. They watched it tensely from the front windows. Paige held the Uzi with the safety off, and she didn't relax until she saw that it was Karl who got out of the driver's door.

He had arrived in time to have lunch with them, which Marty had prepared with the girls' help. It consisted of reconstituted eggs, canned sausages, and biscuits from a tin.

As the five of them ate at the large pine table in the kitchen, Karl presented them with their new identities. Marty was surprised by the number of documents. Birth certificates for all four of them. A high school diploma for Paige from a school in Newark, New Jersey, and one for Marty from a school in Harrisburg, Pennsylvania. An honorable discharge from the United States Army for Marty, issued after three years of service. They had Wyoming driver's licenses, Social Security cards, and more.

Their new name was Gault. Ann and John Gault. Charlotte's birth certificate said her name was Rebecca Vanessa Gault, and Emily was now Suzie Lori Gault.

"We got to choose our own first and second names," Charlotte said with more animation than she'd shown in days. "I'm Rebecca like in the movie, a woman of beauty and mystery, haunting Manderley forever."

"We didn't *exactly* get to pick what names we wanted," Emily said. "We didn't get first choice, for sure."

Marty had been deep in wounded sleep back in Bishop, California, when the names had been selected. "What was your first choice?" he asked Emily.

"Bob," she said.

Marty laughed, and Charlotte giggled explosively.

"I like Bob," Emily said.

"Well, you have to admit it isn't really appropriate," Marty said.

"Suzie Lori is cute enough to puke over," Charlotte said.

"Well, if I can't be Bob," Emily said, "then I want to be Suzie Lori, and everyone has to always use both names, never just Suzie."

※　　※　　※

While the girls washed the dishes, Karl brought in a suitcase from the Range Rover, opened it on the table, and discussed the contents with Marty and Paige. There were scores of computer discs containing Network files, which Karl had secretly copied over the years, plus at least a hundred microcassette tapes of conversations that he had recorded, including one at the Ritz-Carlton Hotel in Dana Point that involved Oslett and a man named Peter Waxhill.

"That one," Karl said, "will explain the entire clone crisis in a nutshell." He began returning the items to the suitcase. "These are all copies, the discs and the cassettes. You've got two full sets. And I've got other duplicates besides."

Marty didn't understand. "Why do you want us to have these?"

"You're a good writer," Karl said. "I've read a couple of your books since Tuesday night. Take all this, write up an explanation of it, an explanation of what happened to you and your family. I'm going to leave you the name of the owner of a major newspaper and a man high in the FBI. I'm confident that neither of them is part of the Network—because both of them were on Alfie's list of future targets. Send your explanation and one set of discs and tapes to each of them. Mail it blind, of course, no return address, and from another state, not Wyoming."

"Shouldn't you do this?" Paige asked.

"I'll try again if you don't get the kind of reaction I expect you will. But it's better coming from you first. Your disappearance, the action in Mission Viejo, the murders of your parents, the bodies I've made sure they found in that bell tower near your folks' cabin—all of that has kept your story hot. The Network has made *sure* it's kept hot, 'cause they're desperate for someone to find you for them. Let's use your notoriety to make it all backfire on them if we can."

❊   ❊   ❊

The day was cool but not cold. The sky was a crystalline blue.

Marty and Karl went for a walk along the perimeter of the woods, always keeping the cabin in sight.

"This Alfie," Marty said.

"What about him?"

"Was he the only one?"

"The first and only operative clone. Others are being grown."

"We have to stop that."

"We will."

"Okay. Suppose we blow the Network apart," Marty wondered. "Their house of cards collapses. Afterward . . . can we ever go back home, resume our lives?"

Karl shook his head. "I don't intend to. Don't dare. Some of them will slip the noose. And these are people who hold a grudge from Sunday to Hell and back. Good haters. You ruin their lives or even just the lives of people in their families, and sooner or later they'll kill all of you."

"Then the Gault name isn't just temporary cover?"

"It's the best ID you can get. As good as real paper. I got it from sources the Network doesn't know about. No one will ever see through this ID . . . or track you down by it."

"My career, income from my books . . ."

"Forget it," Karl said. "You're on a new voyage of discovery, outward to worlds unknown."

"And you've got a new name too?"

"Yes."

"None of my business what it is, huh?"

"Exactly."

* * *

Karl left that same afternoon, an hour before dusk.

As they accompanied him to the Range Rover, he withdrew an envelope from an inside pocket of his tweed jacket and handed it to Paige, explaining that it was the grant deed to the cabin and the land on which it stood.

"I bought and prepared two getaway properties, one at each end of the country, so I'd be prepared for this day when it came. Owned them both under untraceable false names. I've transferred this one to Ann and John Gault, since I can only use one of them."

He seemed embarrassed when Paige hugged him.

"Karl," Marty said, "what would have happened to us without you? We owe you everything."

The big man was actually blushing. "You'd have done all right, somehow. You're survivors. Anything I've done for you, it's only what anyone would have."

"Not these days," Marty said.

"Even these days," Karl said, "there are more good people than not. I really believe that. I have to."

At the Range Rover, Charlotte and Emily kissed Karl goodbye because they all knew, without having to say it, that they would never see him again.

Emily gave him Peepers. "You need someone," she said. "You're all alone. Besides, he'll never get used to calling me Suzie Lori. He's your pet now."

"Thank you, Emily. I'll take good care of him."

When Karl got behind the wheel and closed the door, Marty leaned in the open window. "If we wreck the Network, you think they'll ever put it back together again?"

"It or something like it," Karl said without hesitation.

Unsettled, Marty said, "I guess we'll know if they do . . . when they cancel all elections."

"Oh, elections would never be canceled, at least not in any way that was ever apparent," Karl said as he started the Rover. "They'd go on just as usual, with competing political parties, conventions, debates, bitter campaigns, all the hoopla and shouting. But every one of the candidates would be selected from Network loyalists. If they ever *do* take over, John, only *they* will know."

Marty was suddenly as cold as he had ever been in the blizzard on Tuesday night.

Karl raised one hand in the split-finger greeting that Marty recognized from *Star Trek*. "Live long and prosper," he said, and left them.

Marty stood in the gravel driveway, watching the Rover until it reached the county road, turned left, and dwindled out of sight.

9.

That December and throughout the following year, when the headlines screamed of the Network scandal, treason, political conspiracy, assassination, and one world crisis after another, John and Ann Gault didn't pay as much attention to the newspapers and the television news as they had expected they would. They had new lives to build, which was not a simple undertaking.

Ann cut her blond hair short and dyed it brown. Before meeting any of their neighbors living in the scattered cabins and ranches of that rural area, John grew a beard; not to his surprise, it came in more than half gray, and a lot of gray began to show up on his head, as well.

A simple tint changed Rebecca's hair from blond to auburn, and Suzie Lori was sufficiently transformed with a new and much shorter style. Both girls were growing fast. Time would swiftly blur the resemblance between them and whoever they once might have been.

Remembering to use new names was easy compared to creating and committing to memory a simple but credible false past. They made a game of it, rather like Look Who's the Monkey Now.

The nightmares were persistent. Though the enemy they had known was as comfortable in daylight as not, they irrationally viewed each nightfall with an uneasiness that people had felt in ancient and more superstitious times. And sudden noises made everybody jump.

Christmas Eve had been the first time that John dared to hope they would really be able to imagine a new life and find happiness again. It was then that Suzie Lori inquired about the popcorn.

"What popcorn?" John asked.

"Santa's evil twin put ten pounds in the microwave," she said, "even though that much corn wouldn't fit. But even if it would fit, what happened when it started to pop?"

That night, story hour was held for the first time in more than three weeks. Thereafter, it became routine.

In late January, they felt safe enough to register Rebecca and Suzie Lori in the public school system.

By spring, there were new friends and a growing store of Gault-family memories that were not fabricated.

Because they had seventy thousand in cash and owned their humble house outright, they were under little pressure to find work. They also had four boxes full of the first editions of the early novels of Martin Stillwater. The cover of *Time* magazine had asked a question that would never be answered—*Where is Martin Stillwater?*—and first editions that had once been worth a couple of hundred dollars each on the collectors' market had begun selling, by spring, for five times that price; they would probably continue to appreciate faster than blue-chip investments in the years to come. Sold one or two at a time, in far cities, they would keep the family nest egg fat during lean years.

John presented himself to new neighbors and acquaintances as a former insurance salesman from New York City. He claimed to have come into a substantial though not enormous inheritance. He was indulging a life-long dream of living in a rural setting, struggling to be a poet. "If I don't start selling some poems in a few years, maybe I'll write a novel," he sometimes said, "and if that doesn't turn out right—*then* I'll start worrying."

Ann was content to be seen as a housewife; however, freed from the pressures of the past—troubled clients and freeway commuting—she rediscovered a talent for drawing that she had not tapped since high school. She began doing illustrations for the poems and stories in her husband's ring-bound notebook of original compositions, which he had been writing for years: *Stories for Rebecca and Suzie Lori.*

They had lived in Wyoming five years when *Santa's Evil Twin* by John Gault with illustrations by Ann Gault became a smash Christmas best-seller. They allowed no jacket photo of author and artist. They politely declined offers of promotional tours and interviews, preferring a quiet life and the chance to do more books for children.

The girls remained healthy, grew tall, and Rebecca began selectively dating boys, all of whom Suzie Lori found wanting in one way or another.

Sometimes John and Ann felt they lived too much in a fantasy, and they made an effort to keep up with current events, watching for signs and portents that they didn't even like to discuss with each other. But the world was endlessly troubled and tedious. Too few people seemed able to imagine life without the crushing hand of one government or another, one war or another, one form of hatred or another, so the Gaults always lost interest in the news and returned to the world they imagined for themselves.

One day a paperback novel arrived in the mail. The plain brown envelope bore no return address, and no note of any kind was included with the book. It was a science-fiction novel set in the far future, when humankind had conquered the stars but not all of its problems. The title was *The Clone Rebellion.* John and Ann read it. They found it to be admirably well-imagined, and they regretted that they would never have the opportunity to express their admiration to the author.